SATURN:

CLARE BAINBRIDGE

CAPITOL CRIMES

Book One in the Roma Capta Series

Copyright 2017 Clare Bainbridge

Also in the Roma Capta Series:
Unquiet Spirits

Dramatis Personae

The Great Ones: Three Men Controlling the State:
Marcus Antonius: a very experienced military man
Octavian: a very inexperienced military man
Lepidus: has a lot of legions, but no-one trusts him.

Everybody's Enemies:
Sextus Pompeius: son of Pompey the Great, in Sicily.
Lucius Domitius Ahenobarbus: has a navy, but whose side is he on?

The Torquatus Family:
Aulus Manlius Torquatus: friend of Octavian and head of his family
Manlia: his sister, married to Ahenobarbus
Vibia: Torquatus' mother, who finds him unsatisfactory and says so
Iunia: Torquatus' widowed sister-in-law, unlucky in love
Felix: a boy slave, and also Torquatus' half-brother
Iucundus: a new young slave from Gaul
Philip: an old body-servant of Torquatus' father
Stephanus: an old steward
Trofimus: a young steward
Demetrius: prince of secretaries
Becco and Pulex: Torquatus' bodyguards
Also Davus, Strato and Materna at the farm.

Octavian's Friends:
Marcus Vipsanius Agrippa: has military ambitions
Cilnius Maecenas: astute political thinker
Lucius Cornelius Balbus: brilliant older money-man and political insider
Cornelia: Balbus' daughter.

Some Senators:
Septimius: an unfortunate man, Flavia's husband
Old Annalis: even more unfortunate
Young Annalis: a man who makes his own fortune
Rebilus: a lover on the run
Volusius: Flavia's second husband

Some Roman Ladies:
Calvisia: Annalis' widow a friend of Manlia
Aemilia and **Postumia**, friends of Manlia
Flavia: very much less so.

Also featuring:
Philo: Antonius' freedman, with a murky past
Fortunatus and Modestus: two slaves

Also soldiers, caretakers, Treasury clerks, secretaries, security men, and priests.

Italy

Ravenna
Ariminum
Pisarum
Ancona
Trasimene
Perusia
Mevania
Fulginium
Nursia
ROME
Formiae Capua
Neapolis
Brundisium
Tarentum
Tempsa
Rhegium

Chapter 1

Torquatus woke in the stuffy darkness of his bedroom with a picture in his mind: small, fast mule carts, leaving Neapolis quietly, bringing the last (or so he hoped) of the deliveries. He imagined the carts swinging out by flickering torchlight through the great gateway of Balbus' house and onto the main road to Rome. He saw them hurrying up the via Appia, unnoticed among the swarms of lumbering ox-wagons, horsemen, laden baggage-mules, slave-borne litters and trudging pedestrians. He tried to put the thought aside, but it was impossible: he called for a slave and got up. Before dawn broke he had ridden out of the city through the Esquiline Gate, among the traffic hurrying to leave before the curfew on wheeled vehicles began at dawn. The road cleared once he was out, and he let Bucephalus lengthen his stride into an easy canter. A senator was always surrounded by a crowd of dependents, slaves, petitioners, friends, but now he was alone, and he was enjoying it.

The day was struggling into existence with a barely perceptible lightening of the sky in the east when Torquatus met the men just as they were leaving his farm. They were leading their mules, the empty carriages behind bouncing and rattling over the stony track. When they saw him they stood aside, as best they could in that narrow space, and he urged his horse forward into the lane, brushing past the overhanging branches and shivering as drips tipped down his back.

'You've brought the - the load?'

'Yes, lord. The last one.'

Torquatus felt light with relief. This was not going to happen again.

'You're sure of that?'

'Yes, lord. Dionysius - Balbus' slave - he told us, and he should know.' Short of getting the information from

Balbus himself, there could be no more reliable source, and men like these would never see Balbus in person.

'Good. And they looked after you, up at the farm?'

'A good breakfast, sir, as always.' The man was smiling tentatively and Torquatus smiled back.

'Then back off with you to Neapolis - and thank you.' Torquatus gave them each a coin that had them dipping their heads in thanks, before they hoisted themselves up onto the driving-seats of their carriages, and clattered off, the sound fading quickly in the murk. Torquatus watched them go, shivering, and rode on up the lane.

The farm was a simple, old-fashioned place, such as Torquatus' ancestors were supposed to have found sufficient for their needs. However that might have been, his family hadn't lived a such a house for many generations. They'd preferred to build themselves a sprawling pile on the Quirinal - a rather unfashionable place for a senator, but exclusive - and this little place, just outside the city, had been kept to provide eggs and chickens, fruit and vegetables for the great house. It sat as if becalmed in a sea of cabbages and leeks, the whole plot closed in with hazel-bushes and one or two ancient walnut-trees. It was orderly, everything in neat rows, not a weed in sight. Had it not been, Torquatus would have bought a new farm-manager. As he rode up the door opened and several figures appeared in the opening: Strato, the manager, looking anxious, Materna, his slave-wife, smiling, and Davus, the assistant Torquatus had recently bought them, holding back a large brown dog, then letting it go when he saw his master, and coming forward to take Bucephalus to the stable behind the house. Once they were all inside it felt unpleasantly crowded until Strato put away the bird-nets he'd been mending, and Materna went through to the kitchen, murmuring something about hot wine.

'I saw the drivers in the lane,' Torquatus said, rubbing his hands in front of the fire. 'The last load, they said, and thank all the gods for that.'

He didn't usually speak so plain. Strato had never been told why the cellar had been doubled in size a few months back, or what was in the wooden chests carried in from time to time and stacked down there among the onions and beetroot, but he'd have had to be a lot stupider than he looked not to have worked it out. Apart from anything else, the slaves had not been armed until recently. Torquatus sighed and sat back, relaxing, half-listening to Materna bustling about.

'And will the boxes be going on, like the others?' Strato asked.

'They will. I don't know when. The sooner the better, for me.'

The chests in the cellar were in fact filled with cash collected by Octavian the previous spring. Octavian and his great friends Agrippa, Maecenas and Torquatus had all been in Greece, officially studying philosophy, while also making friends among the army officers stationed there, and were all expecting to take part in Julius Caesar's war against the Parthian empire. Then the letter arrived which would shake up the pattern of their lives: Julius was murdered, and his great-nephew Octavian was his heir and adopted son. Please, Octavian's mother had ended, please don't accept this inheritance: Julius' enemies will never let you live. Octavian and his friends set out at once for Italy, landing near Brundisium and travelling incognito, unsure what the future held. They need not have worried. Offers of help and support flooded in, from veteran soldiers, furious at their general's death, from Julius' clients, and from those who simply saw Octavian as worth a bet.

Among these small sums, Octavian had also acquired much larger amounts of cash. One source was the war-chest Caesar had put together for his Parthian campaign, waiting in a well-guarded warehouse at Brundisium. Octavian publicly ordered it to be taken back to Rome: privately, messages were sent to the officers escorting the creaking ox-wagons, directing them instead to the vaults of

Balbus at Neapolis. Balbus, the great fixer and money-man who'd been an intimate of Caesar's, had come forward at once to offer Octavian the hand of friendship. The general view was that Octavian, at nineteen, could hardly be considered a serious player in the vicious game of Roman politics. Balbus disagreed.

Another vast sum which had gone to those same vaults in Neapolis had been sent there, not on Octavian's orders, but on those of the consul Marcus Antonius, and it consisted of a consignment of the taxes raised from the wealthy cities of Rome's eastern empire. This was a very different matter from the purloining of Caesar's war-chest, part of which had been raised by Caesar himself. The taxes were indisputably public money. Antonius was consul, and he had authorised both their deposit at Balbus' vaults, on the grounds of the city's instability, and the subsequent removal of substantial portions of them to Rome. That would have been that, except that in recent months Antonius had furiously denied that he had ever written any such letters: Octavian, he insisted to anyone who would listen, had stolen the money.

In the eighteen months since then, Antonius and Octavian had been enemies, led armies against each other, and finally agreed, along with Lepidus, the general in control of many of Rome's legions, to co-operate: three men to restore the state. That was what they said they were, anyway, though to many senators they were simply bandits. Money was what they desperately needed, so this quarrel over the cash in Balbus' vaults refused to die down, and, as acting Treasury Quaestor, in charge of State accounts, it concerned Torquatus personally. He had been drafted in after the previous incumbent had died in the usual summer epidemic last year. With typical sharpness, Octavian, campaigning in northern Italy, had sent his friend to claim the post as soon as he had heard of the death. Torquatus arrived when Octavian was already on the march to Rome: the Senate were becoming glumly aware that they'd underestimated his courage, tenacity and shrewdness. There was no-one, in other words, to stop Torquatus declaring himself acting Quaestor and getting on with the job. It was outrageous, of course. He was only twenty-one, nine years short of the minimum age for election to that post. But the outrageousness of his behaviour was soon forgotten when Octavian arrived and had himself made consul, for which post one must be forty-two. He was then just short of twenty years old.

Octavian's suggestion that some of his money might be stored at Torquatus' farm had filled him with horror, but it felt like a test of his loyalty, and he dared not refuse. He did suggest that Octavian's own house was much better guarded than his little farm, but Octavian brushed this aside. He'd already thought it through.

'I have money here, of course, but I don't want all of it in the city. And besides, my house is awkward for carriages to get to unnoticed,' he said, smiling that enigmatic smile of his. Well aware of Torquatus' reluctance, he was thoroughly enjoying himself. His blue eyes sparkled in the sunlight from the big window. 'Imagine if there were porters carrying boxes of bullion up and down the Ringmakers' Steps - everyone would see it.'

'And that would be a problem?'

'It would. There's Antonius for a start - how happy would he be to see quantities of cash being carted into my house? Remember what he was like last year, constantly carping on, telling anyone who'd listen that I'd stolen the taxes. But I have to work with him just now, and he's being quite co-operative - for him - so let's not stir him up. And if a riot broke out, which could happen for any number of reasons after all - the hunger caused by a bad harvest, for instance - my house might come under attack. No, it'll be safer outside the city.' They were in Octavian's study at the time, his backside half perched on a massive table with gilded legs: Torquatus wondered how in Hades that had been brought into the house. But Octavian was continuing, turning a pen over and over in his fingers as he spoke, as if thinking aloud. 'I don't want the money travelling in one big convoy either. You know the sort of thing: column of ox-wagons, soldiers swarming all over - no, I want it in dribs and drabs, unescorted, a couple of carriage-loads at a time, to sit quietly just outside Rome until wanted. No fuss, nothing obvious.'

Nothing obvious. The words might have summed Octavian up. And now Torquatus believed that it would soon be over. There had been several consignments recently, none of which had moved any further, and the cellar must be packed solid with wooden chests. It was December now, and in the spring Octavian and Antonius would probably be in Africa or Greece, at war with Julius' murderers. Before then the money would be transformed into ships, swords and shields, and the farm could resume its life, indistinguishable from thousands of others, albeit with an unusually capacious cellar, stronger locks on the door, and a set of good solid shutters over the windows. Torquatus' career was assured, because he had helped his friend get what he wanted. It was all going to be all right.

As Torquatus rode back through the dawn light he felt like singing with relief. When he got home his clients would be waiting to greet him in the reception hall, and he'd be late. He didn't care.

Chapter 2

The streets were busy, even before dawn, filled with people huddled into warm cloaks, their boots ringing on the cold ground. There was a group in rags among the pillars of a great building, their pleading hands outstretched: no-one but the boy seemed to see them. The December chill didn't encourage lingering, and anyway he was being hurried onwards by some nameless man from the slave-dealers. They began to climb, up into the fresh cold air. The crowds were left behind, but the streets weren't empty even here. A couple of pretty women came down the hill towards him, laughing together. Were they free, or slaves like him? he wondered. And just in front of them a little person so wrapped in a cloak that its sex was impossible to guess strutted along importantly. It was a big road, wide, the neat paving washed clean by last night's rain, with important-looking houses here and there. One of these seemed to be their destination: the man who had brought him here stopped him with a hand on his shoulder. The bustling little person had turned in to the same house, and the boy heard him ask for someone.

'It'll be Demetrius you want,' the doorkeeper was saying. 'He's busy with the master just now. You'd better come back later.' Behind him another face, pale and old, peered from the shadows of the doorkeeper's room.

The little man nodded, and pushed past the boy and his minder, heading back down the hill. The boy turned his attention to the house. To him it looked like a fortress. There were high stone walls, and in the centre two great studded doors, open, with a passage the size of a small road leading inside. On each side of the doorway a torch burned in an iron holder. People were hurrying in, brushing past them, nodding to the doorkeeper, and he stepped into the shadowed entrance passage, shivering. The draught in the corridor seemed to whistle through his clothes. The man behind gave him a push and he almost fell, his feet slipping

on the black and white tiles. Then they were inside: he
supposed it was inside, but there was a big oblong hole in
the roof, where a grey slice of sky could be seen, mirrored
below by an oblong pool, its steely surface brushed by the
fitful breeze. The place was full of men. Some of them,
wrapped in their togas, were standing as if waiting for
something, talking to each other or lost in their own
thoughts. Some were sitting on the benches that lined the
walls. Others were hurrying about with jugs of wine and
baskets filled with little warm bread rolls. They must be
slaves like him. The smell of the bread made him swallow:
he hadn't had any breakfast, and it was a cold walk from the
place where he'd been kept.

He looked around again. This was the biggest room
he'd ever seen. The ceiling was almost lost in the shadows,
but touches of gold glimmering in the darkness showed
where it was. There must be some stairs somewhere,
because high above his head there was a gallery, open at the
front between columns, running round three sides of the
great room. More gold glittered on the grille that ran
between these pillars, and in the shadows he thought he
could see doors opening off the gallery. Feeling dizzy from
so much looking up, he turned his eyes back onto the hall
below. At the back of it, folding doors or a screen of dark
wood had been pulled back to show another, smaller room
behind, with a big table in it. And behind that again he could
see through into a garden, where bare branches stood dark
against the lightening grey of the dawn. The place was
lighted by several tall bronze lamp stands, each one a mass of
tiny flames, but the great room seemed to consume the
flames because the walls too were made of dark stone in
different colours, dark red and yellow and green. He didn't
like it. Where he came from, stone wasn't for the insides of
houses, and no house, not even the king's, was so high and
so - he shivered - so cold. He dared not remember the
king's house.

The man who'd brought him was talking to one of

the young men with baskets. He watched them hopefully, longing for a bit of bread, but the basket-man shrugged and pointed off to one side and his minder disappeared into the crowd. He looked around again anxiously, trying not to think about his empty stomach. There was a clear space around the pool, into which knots of men tangled and unwound again. Beyond that, all down the other long wall, there must be more rooms. The door to the first one was shut, as he saw when one of the groups of men broke up,: the next was curtained off, but the curtain was looped back. And in the corner, on the far side of the main entrance-way, were some odd things: they seemed to be stands, each with a little house on the top, arranged in a careful semicircle The wooden tiles of their roofs gleamed with polish: they meant something. The two end ones were paler; perhaps they were newer. The wall behind these strange little houses had something drawn on it, little boxes, and writing, and swooping black lines darting this way and that between them. The whole place made his head ache, it was so strange.

He had moved up the room as he looked at it all, and now a man almost fell over him as he came through from the back of the house, and cursed him. It was in Latin, which he didn't speak very well, but he knew a curse when he heard one, and moved quickly out of the way. The newcomer swept past, a bulky white bundle in his toga but moving with quick decision, followed by two other men, one with a grumpy face, old, and walking with a stick, the other tall and thin and bald. The boy didn't think this big man in his toga was going to stand about like the others, and he didn't. At his entrance everyone turned towards him and for a moment the talk died down. He cast into the room a smile, a general greeting, and then a thin slave brought one of the waiting men to his notice, and they began to talk. He briefly touched the man's arm before speaking to the slave at his elbow; a word or two, a smile, and he moved on to the next. The two others who had come in with the master had gone, leaving with a nod to this man or that: their business

15

must have been important enough for privacy. The boy heard the master say something about being late: he had been called away urgently: no, no, just a problem at his little farm: he'd thought it better to go and see for himself.

So this must be his new master: a big man, very dark, and much younger than he'd expected, with a muscular body, long legs. He had a very Roman face, with smooth brown skin, large dark eyes, and finely arched brows almost meeting over a big nose. He was clean-shaven, and his black hair was cut very short. He carried himself like a soldier, which pleased the boy. If he had to be a slave this was a man one could serve without disgust. The boy watched him carefully, thinking that he had the bearing of a king or a great noble: he hadn't spent his life among the leading men of his people without learning to know their ways.

Just as he was thinking this, the man who had brought him here gripped his shoulder from behind. 'I've been looking for you,' he said. 'Come here.' He pushed the boy forward, in front of an old man: the same old man whose pale face had looked out from the doorkeeper's room. 'You're the steward, I believe? Well, this is the boy,' he said. 'I hope you find him satisfactory.'

'Yes, I'm Stephanus, but it's the master's secretary Demetrius you need to see,' the old man replied fretfully. The boy could see him shaking: the palsy of old age, perhaps. 'I know nothing about it.'

'Where is this Demetrius, then?' said the man. At that moment the thin slave who had been helping his master with the visitors appeared through the crowd. He walked past the old man as if he weren't there. This must be Demetrius, the boy supposed. 'This is the new slave, is it?' he said.

The slave-dealer's man smiled, with a touch of impatience. 'Indeed, sir, and a very good worker you'll find him.'

The boy wondered how he could say this, without even knowing his name. Demetrius sniffed and turned the

16

newcomer round with a sharp hand.

'Strong and healthy, I hope? Able to carry the master's armour, and look after his horses?'

He couldn't keep silent. 'Horses? Oh yes, I can care for horses. I love them.'

'H'm. The boy can speak too.' He fired some question out, but the boy blushed nervously, unable to understand. He said carefully, 'I have some Latin, sir, but I can't follow if you speak too fast.'

'Well, you'll learn.'

The boy swallowed hard, hoping that was true, and watched as Demetrius took the other man away to be paid. He was left alone again in the throng of people. He tucked himself out of sight behind a pillar, half wanting to hide himself away for ever, but the baskets of bread rolls, almost empty now, kept passing him by, and he was desperately hungry. The crowds of men were thinning out too, and everyone seemed to have forgotten him. At last he became bold enough to come out from behind the pillar and catch one of the basket-men. He gave the man's tunic a little twitch as he passed, and the slave turned with a courteous look as if about to apologise, but when he saw the boy his expression changed.

'What do you want?' he demanded.

'Could I have a bit of bread?'

'You, eat the clients' good white bread? I shouldn't think so. Who are you, anyway?'

The boy couldn't speak. Who was he? He knew who he had been. But now? The man shrugged. 'New slave, are you? You'd better come to the kitchens, and eat.'

But before they could go, Demetrius was back again, and this time his master was with him. They were a strange pair, the master so solid and assured in the bulk of his white toga, the slave wispy-thin with a narrow dark face and watchful eyes. 'Demetrius says you've just arrived, child.'

'Yes, lord.'

'Good. You're to be my body-slave, so you'll be working closely with me. Later, I'll show you my armour. You'd better keep it clean and the sword bright: there'll be fighting again soon.' He grinned, which made him look much younger. His teeth were quite white, the boy noticed, and none seemed to be missing.

'And the horses?' He was longing to see them.

The master nodded. 'Demetrius or someone will show you to the stables and you can start to learn from my head groom, Philip. He was out in Africa, but he's too old to go on campaign again. That's why I need you. And what's your name?'

'They - they said you'd want to give me a name yourselves,' the boy told him.

'Oh, did they? Really, slave dealers can't even be bothered to name their wares now,' said the master, laughing, and Demetrius laughed too.

'Didymus?' Demetrius suggested, but the master frowned.

'Does he look like a Greek?'

'Well, then, Fortunatus,' said Demetrius.

'Too much of a mouthful. Nice idea, though: Iucundus, that'll do.'

The master smiled, nodded and turned away, dismissing him. The boy heard him say to Demetrius: 'I want that letter taken to the Palatine at once: and when I come back from the Forum I'll look at the accounts from the Alban estate. I don't understand why they seem to have sold so little wine last year. Nothing wrong with the vintage, was there?' The two men walked off, and the boy's stomach made itself felt once again. He was relieved to see that the basket-man had waited for him.

By the end of the day Iucundus had discovered many things. The house was the size of a small town: the reception hall he'd seen in the morning had a great warren of rooms and courtyards around it. Would he ever be able to find his way about? This wasn't the lord's only house, either: even in Rome he had others, and gardens too, whatever that meant. None of the slaves he'd spoken to knew how many of them there were, though the old man Stephanus said he had known such things, once. They all seemed to have good clothes - clean warm tunics and boots. Since there were so many slaves, and only the master - no wife or children or parents - he wondered why the slaves didn't just kill him and run away. The thought of the long road back to northern Gaul made his heart ache with longing. But instead the slaves seemed proud that their master was Aulus Manlius Torquatus, the head of an old and important family. The stables contained only a few horses, but they were good ones, and there were one or two mules as well, as well as the donkey whose task was to turn the mill. More horses were kept outside the city, apparently. Next to the stables there was a locked store, where all the master's arms and weapons lived: one of his jobs would be to look after them.

In one corner of the stable court there was a store-room for a most odd contraption. It was a large box, or rather a platform with a rim round the edge and pillars at the corners, supporting a roof, all painted in red and gold, and with soft red leather curtains, and long poles that passed through brackets at the sides. And there was a mattress to go inside, and cushions, to make it comfortable. Like a carriage, he thought, except that it had no wheels. Philip, the groom, told him that it was for the master's family to ride in. The old master used it a lot. The ladies too, when they lived here, but the groom just made a long face when Iucundus asked him why they didn't live here now, and shook his head. The young master could ride in it, but he mostly preferred to walk, Philip said, which pleased Iucundus: it hardly seemed manly, to be carried about like a baby. Philip said there were four slaves, all black - black all over he insisted, though Iucundus didn't believe this till he saw them - whose job was just to carry the box.

Iucundus had discovered too that the cook had a

terrible temper: if you wanted something to eat it was better to ask the steward, the old man Stephanus he'd seen that morning, or one of the assistant cooks, Sosia, who could usually find you something. His speciality was making beautiful sweet things, apparently: wonderful cakes dripping with honey or full of nuts, little platters of pastry filled with fruit, sauces made with eggs and milk, and even something made with ice - ice! - which he couldn't understand.

All these people came in to eat once the master's dinner was served in his part of the house. Everyone sat wherever they could find a space in the kitchen, and Iucundus found that as a boy, and a new boy at that, he couldn't expect to be anywhere near the fire, or even on a bench, but must squeeze himself into whatever corner he could find. The men who served the master's food took it in, and stayed with him while he ate. Then the rest of the household could relax, Philip said, and enjoy their own food, knowing that for a while at any rate he wouldn't be calling for them.

Iucundus didn't find it relaxing. To be among all these people whom he didn't know made him feel lonelier than ever, though he noticed that one of the master's bodyguards looked like a Gaul. He was a huge man, with shaggy fair hair, a thick neck and little round eyes, but perhaps he'd be friendly, if Iucundus got to know him. He heard someone call the man Becco: definitely a Gaul, then. The other bodyguard was called Pulex: another mountain of a man with the meanest face Iucundus had ever seen, because quite expressionless, except that two cold black eyes looked out warily from the mask. Iucundus made an instant decision to avoid that one wherever possible.

He didn't notice the atmosphere at first, his hunger blunting his curiosity. There seemed to be knots of people who sat together without discussion, as if this was their habit: the groom Philip and the old steward Stephanus shared a comfortable bench by the fire; and the secretary Demetrius shared another with a pale prim man with very clean hands, under a row of heavy pots hanging from an iron bar. They were talking together very softly, more from contempt of the others, the boy thought, looking at their faces, than because they were afraid of being overheard. As he spooned up his beans and cabbage and his hunger began to be satisfied he became aware that there wasn't much talk, considering what a lot of them there were. Just as he was thinking this Demetrius said something to Stephanus. The old man looked shocked: Iucundus saw his hands shaking as he brushed some crumbs off his lap, but he said nothing. Philip glanced at Stephanus impatiently, then turned suddenly to Demetrius and answered him in a quiet, angry voice. They were speaking Greek, Iucundus thought, and he didn't understand what they were saying, but he could feel the current of dislike pass between them. No-one said anything more, and a kind of embarrassed silence lasted for the rest of the meal.

The master hadn't asked for him yet and he was allowed to curl up in the warm hayloft, with the sharp, familiar smell of the horses drifting up from below. As he was about to climb the ladder into the loft, he turned to Philip. 'Oh, Philip, you will know - what does Iucundus mean?'

Philip made a sour face. 'Happy. Joyful. That's what it means.'

Iucundus stared at him. 'Really? You're sure?'

'Sure I'm sure.'

'It's an odd name to give a slave, isn't it?' Iucundus said.

'Not at all: they like that sort of name, and we've got a few here. There's Felix, he's lucky. That's the boy who was serving the master's dinner tonight. Or there's the toga-slave, Victor, the winner. I'm called Philip: do I look like the king of Macedon? Or sometimes the names are a different kind of joke: that ugly great bodyguard - and you want to stay away from him, boy! - is Pulex, the Flea.' He shrugged. 'I wouldn't waste time trying to understand why they do it.'

Iucundus thought for a moment, then nodded and began to climb the ladder. He turned himself in the straw like a dog, and lay down with a sigh. This had been the longest day he'd ever lived through, and he was so tired. How would he ever manage here? He spoke some Latin, but the Latin he'd heard today - apart from Demetrius' and the master's - was rough, almost unrecognisable; and the slaves mostly spoke Greek among themselves, which he didn't know at all. His problems didn't weigh on his mind for long. In the slave-place, he had had to force himself not to think of the past when he lay down at the end of the day among the other slaves, but now without any effort he fell at once into a dreamless sleep.

And then he woke. Suddenly, in terror, his mouth dry, his heart pounding. The stable was silent, but he knew he had been woken by a scream. It started again. He knelt up in the straw, trying to remember where the ladder began. But while he was still feeling with shaking hands for the opening, he heard the old groom shuffling about. Philip's voice was gruff, and Iucundus couldn't catch what he said, but the sound was soothing, and a little reproachful. Only a bad dream, apparently. The sleeper - one of the slaves, presumably - grunted awake, spoke loud for a minute, too loud, then quietened down. The shuffling of feet began again, died away, and the man began to snore. Iucundus couldn't recapture his sleep: everything he wanted to forget had come rushing back. The burning of his father's house, the way the sparks poured up into the dark night like a fountain when the roof fell in, the screams of the horses trapped in the stables, the people running here and there like ants, the soldiers with their bright fierce blades and dark fierce faces, appearing so suddenly out of the night and then disappearing back into it. And, worst of all, his mother shoved against a wall without respect, so that she almost fell, the gathering of all the old men with the women and children in one of the barns, the terror as they thought they might be going to be burnt alive; his own shame at being counted one of the children and not a man. His mother, though, had regained her dignity, and spoke as a woman who was used to being listened to: they will make us all slaves, she had told them with a steady voice. The fighting men they will kill, but all those of us who have been saved have been saved only for that. The tears on her cheeks told of her shame, but from her voice you would never have guessed it. He didn't see her again after they were separated on the road to Rome. He turned his face into the sweet-smelling straw and wept.

Chapter 3

Next morning Iuncundus had to help Torquatus dress. The master's bedroom was one of a row of rooms overlooking the dead garden, warm and smelling of sleep, the figures on its painted walls seeming to shudder and sway in the uncertain lamplight. Since he himself had no idea what the master might need, Iucundus was relieved to find another slave already moving around the room quietly - the pale, prim man who'd sat with Demetrius at dinner last night. When Torquatus headed off to the reception hall, neatly togate, Iucundus tried to help, picking up the master's discarded tunic.

Victor took it out of his hands. 'I would advise you always to send for me when the master needs to change his clothes,' he said. 'His togas cost a fortune to clean. We wouldn't want one dropped on the dirty floor.' He shook out the tunic and folded it neatly. 'As for trying to arrange it on him, I wouldn't want you even to attempt it.'

Iucundus gave up trying to help. 'Where has he gone now?' he asked.

'Oh, just into the reception hall. He has his clients to see every day, of course. That's why it's so important for the master to look right. Luckily he's tall, and has good shoulders, so the toga looks just as it should on him,' Victor told him, stepping neatly round Iucundus so he could pick up and fold a blanket Torquatus had thrown onto a stool. 'If you're helping him and he wants a toga, you'd better send for me. You'll never manage it.' The man put the folded tunic and blanket away, releasing a waft of rosemary scent from the clothes-chest, before nodding dismissively and walking out.

Iucundus drifted back to the stables where he was put to work by the old groom. Philip brought out the master's horse, a fine chestnut Iucundus had seen him rubbing down yesterday, and ran gentle hands all over him, checking here and there for any swelling or discomfort. His hands were gnarled, the nails dirty and broken, but they knew what they were doing. Satisfied, he tied the horse to one of the iron rings in the yard wall

'You can muck out the stable,' the old man told Iucundus. 'I want to see it clean and sweet.' He nodded to a dark corner. 'Over there's the dung heap.'

Philip began to groom the horse with a brush and a wisp of hay, the creature leaning into his flowing movements with obvious pleasure.

'What's his name?'

'Bucephalus. And yours'll be mud if you don't get working.'

He took the hint. The stables were well built, with good drainage, stone gutters criss-crossing the brick floor of each stall. In the gloom he could just make out a net of sweet hay hanging on each end wall. He found a broom and began to clean out Bucephalus' bay. The old groom tramped in again and Iucundus heard him take out another of the horses, a little bright-eyed dapple grey. He stopped brushing and peered out into the yard. 'Oh, I like her.' The words burst out of him.

'Just as well. This is the one you'll be riding when you have to go with the master anywhere.' He looked at the mare with love and Iucundus understood that this was Philip's horse, the one he'd ridden in war and peace, going with his master, seeing all sorts of places, and now all that was over.

'I'll look after her, I promise,' was all he could think of to say. He was relieved when the door from the kitchens opened with a creak and a boy came through, a rough wooden platter in his hand. Iucundus had seen him yesterday, but he hadn't been in the kitchen at dinner last night: he'd been serving the master's dinner, Iucundus remembered. He was pleased that there was at least one other boy in this household. He was a sturdy child of about twelve, his black hair unbrushed and his tunic, a good one, so crumpled he might have slept in it, its hem rucked up at one side.

'Morning,' said the newcomer, ducking his head towards Iucundus. 'Hallo, Philip.'

The old groom made a tutting noise. 'If you want to help, all well and good', he said, 'but if you're supposed to be working somewhere else, just go, will you, or I'll be in trouble. And put your tunic straight.'

The boy tugged ineffectually for a moment at his tunic hem with his free hand. 'Nothing to do at the moment. But Sosia said this new one, Iucundus, might want something to eat. So I brought it.' He held out the platter, offering Iucundus a rather squashed hunk of coarse brown bread and a withered-looking apple. Iucundus had already had a bowl of barley porridge, but he was happy to share the bread and fruit with this dark, serious-looking boy.

'I'm Felix,' the newcomer told him, through a mouthful of crumbs. 'You're a Gaul, aren't you?'

Iucundus nodded.

'How old are you? Are you really going with the master when the war starts?'

'I'm fourteen. And yes, I believe I am.'

'Oh, it's not fair!' Felix burst out. 'I wanted to go. I begged the master to let me, but he wouldn't. And I'm only two years younger than you, too.'

'You're twelve?'

'Well, almost.'

'Perhaps he wants you to do some other work?' Iucundus suggested.

'Or any work at all,' Philip put in sourly.

'You can help me muck out,' Iucundus told him, 'if you've nothing better to do.'

Felix made a face, but when the old groom nodded his approval he followed Iucundus into the stable readily enough. The two boys worked their way through it, leaving it clean and sweet-smelling for the animals: there were two enormous Nabatean horses for the bodyguards to ride, and one or two others for general use. When they were all back in their stalls, Iucundus told Felix to stand aside while he piled the dung and straw onto the heap, fearing the boy would get into trouble if he got his good tunic dirty.

He was just finishing when Taurus, the slave who'd given him bread yesterday, came running in to tell Iucundus his master wanted him. He was to accompany Torquatus into the Forum, whatever that might be. It would be Iucundus' job to walk beside the master, clear a path where necessary, take any letters or papers anyone might want to give Torquatus, and to help defend him against attack. 'But you can't go looking like that,' Taurus said. 'Go and get changed - and wash your hands and face.'

'I haven't got anything to change into,' Iucundus said.

'Oh!' Taurus pursed his lips. 'Well, I don't know. Stephanus is the steward, so he ought to - but perhaps you should go and find Demetrius. He'll know what to do. Quick, now. The master won't expect to wait for you.'

Iucundus hurried off. As he went he could hear Felix demanding to go too, and the man telling him that guarding wasn't for boys. 'He's only two years older than me,' Iucundus heard Felix grumble.

Iucundus was quite surprised to see, when he hurried into the reception hall in a fresh tunic of soft dark green wool, his face and hands still damp and cold from washing, that Felix was there, joking with one of the other slaves and obviously prepared for an expedition. There was a crowd of them milling about: the bodyguards, of course, and a few of the household men, but Iucundus also noticed Stephanus hesitating in the background. The old steward looked unsure of himself, and Iucundus wondered whether he was going to go to this Forum too. Then the master came past, and Stephanus caught hold of a fold of his toga, and said something to him. Torquatus stopped, nodded, then patted the old man's arm with a kind of impatient affection before passing on. As he glanced away, Iucundus caught Demetrius' gaze fixed intently on the old man. Then his attention was distracted: one of the big men gave Iucundus a knife to carry and showed him how to tuck it securely into the top of his boot.

The party seemed to be complete. Demetrius went back inside. Stephanus hovered irresolutely for a moment or two, then followed him. Torquatus set off down the hill, not looking to see who might be with him. Iucundus stayed close to him but the big guys, Becco and Pulex, trotted ahead, and behind Torquatus a group of other men followed, slaves and morning visitors, looking around, talking among themselves, watching Torquatus. Glancing back, Iucundus thought they looked like a flock of sheep, eddying down the hill in their white togas. Felix was there too, chatting animatedly to one of the slaves.

This Forum was a big space, almost empty in the pale winter sun. There were lots of stony buildings and stony fountains, and some stony roads and stony steps. And Iucundus could see statues all over the place: on the tops of some of the buildings, and on columns and plinths and at the tops of steps, standing waving their arms in the air. There was even one of a man in a chariot, driving his team of horses straight over the edge of a stony arch. But where were the people? Around the edges there were a few booths and stalls, and he could see some women carrying baskets; that was all. When the master stopped to speak to another white-clad man, Iucundus seized the opportunity to question the big Gaulish bodyguard, Becco. 'Oh yes,' Becco nodded. 'The Forum's usually very busy, with the Senate, and the courts sitting, and sometimes assemblies. But these proscriptions have scared everyone away. I think they're all hoping that if they keep their heads down they'll be overlooked.'

None of this meant much to Iucundus. He picked on the most unfamiliar word. 'What are proscriptions?'

Becco gave him a dark look. 'You'll see.'

'People are afraid then? But not the master? He's not afraid to walk about?'

'He's got friends in high places, see?' was all Becco would say.

The far side of the Forum was a steep hillside, steeper than the one where Torquatus lived. Houses were piled up it, higher and higher, and in between them flights of steps twisted and turned, where the pale winter sun didn't penetrate. Up one of these the party climbed, up and up to a house at the very top, a house like Torquatus', though not quite as big. Torquatus went in alone and his followers drifted away chatting in groups, or hurried off separately, glancing to right and left. The slaves sat down on the steps to wait. Iucundus was thirsty: although it was winter the sun was quite warm. He heard the fountain at the end of the street before he saw it, and the gurgling of the water made him aware of his dry mouth. He decided to walk down to it and get a drink.

Iucundus almost fell, tripping on a fold of the toga caught under the dead man's legs. The man's feet were turned inwards, like a child asleep. He was lying face down - except that there was no face. There was no head. Iucundus found himself looking round as if it might have got mislaid somewhere, while at the same time shifting his feet carefully so as not to step into the blood. So much blood. He looked again, with appalled fascination. The man's head had been lopped off, roughly, the flesh of the neck torn, the bone shining white through the red mess of flesh. It must have been taken away, Iucundus thought, cold and calm, because there's no sign of it. And the body must have been lying here for a bit: a few flies were buzzing round that ghastly neck. Suddenly he retched and ran back to the others as if Ankou God of Death were after him.

'There's a man - ,' he began, breathless and shaking. Their faces stopped him. Becco nodded and said quietly, 'You wanted to know what proscriptions meant. That's what.'

Chapter 4

There was something wrong in his household, but it took Torquatus a while to register it consciously: unspoken words, glances between the slaves, a quietness that wasn't normal. Four days after the delivery he woke early again, listening to the silence. Perhaps he was imagining it. His sense of elation had faded, leaving him a prey to anxiety and fear. He could almost feel the weight of those money-chests on his shoulders, and longed to hurry over to the Palatine, to demand that they be taken away, somewhere, anywhere. This was folly: he shook himself and got up, calling for the new boy, Iucundus.

He had no visitors of any importance waiting to see him that day; no-one who couldn't be made to wait in the crowd, no-one who would expect to be brought through to his room, and asked to take a seat. He could hear from the shuffling of feet, the coughing and the murmur of voices that his clients had been let in and were collecting in the reception hall. Time to go and deal with them. The usual problems, no doubt: one man would be in debt; another would be looking for a husband for his daughter, and would be seeking advice, and perhaps some help with the dowry; a third would want Torquatus to speak for him in a court-case over a boundary dispute or a legacy. And then there would be plenty who, in exchange for a little money or a gift of food, would follow in his train as he went about the Forum. The usual, in fact.

Before Torquatus had even reached the reception hall, however, his secretary Demetrius intercepted him. Usually a quiet and careful man, Demetrius seemed quite flustered.

'Master, something's wrong.'

'Well, what?'

'It's Stephanus. He's not here.' Torquatus could see that this was unusual, though it hardly justified interrupting him at this important moment in his day.

'Shouldn't make much difference,' he said. 'It isn't as if he does much these days. I dare say he'll turn up.'

'He's never gone missing before,' Demetrius told him doubtfully.

'Oh well, go and look for him, then.'

Almost at once Torquatus realised that this was a mistake: he needed Demetrius to assist him, to keep a list of what money had been spent, promises made and so on. Iucundus had helped him dress, and on an impulse, Torquatus turned to him, saying, 'They tell me you can read and write?' He made it a question, and half-expected the boy to disclaim. He'd chosen Iucundus because he wanted someone bright and quick to learn, and the boy's alertness had stood out among the lacklustre slaves crowded into the dealer's yard; he'd wanted a Gaul because they were good with horses. If he'd wanted literacy he'd have gone for a Greek. But it was Demetrius who'd told him the boy was literate, and Demetrius was so reliable that he wasn't surprised when the boy nodded. 'Yes, lord.'

'Then you can assist me. I'll tell you what to do.'

The disappearance of Stephanus was soon forgotten in a new anxiety: the reception hall was only half full. He'd have to do something about that: it doesn't reflect well on a man to have a thin showing at the morning greeting. All the requests were as mundane as he'd expected, but at least the new boy seemed capable, flitting neatly to the household cash-box for money or to the library if Torquatus needed papers. His mind only returned to Stephanus' disappearance for a brief moment. A freedman of his father's, Momus, was droning on and on about his business plans, and Torquatus suddenly remembered how yesterday the old man had stopped him as he was about to go across to Octavian's house, saying he had something to tell his master. He'd told Stephanus to speak to him later, and had thought no more of it, except to remember that he ought to replace the steward, who was too doddery to hold such a responsible post. Stephanus hadn't spoken to him again. Probably it hadn't been anything important. He shrugged, and returned his attention to Momus.

One advantage of the half-empty hall was that the business didn't take long. Torquatus needed to go down to the Forum and canvass: he very much wanted to become a properly elected magistrate next year. But first he had better check that Stephanus had been found, and make it clear to the household that no-one had the right to leave the premises without his permission. He called Iucundus over, and told him to find Demetrius: he wanted to see all the slaves in the peristyle in a few moments.

Iucundus slipped off quietly, wondering where Demetrius was, and what a peristyle might be. He didn't have to search for long. As soon as he got near to the slave-quarters, he could hear raised voices, though he couldn't see much. That part of the house had plain dark walls and narrow corridors. He followed the sound and, just round the next corner, standing next to a doorway with an old faded curtain hanging over it he found the old groom, Philip, and Demetrius himself, staring at each other nose to nose like a pair of cats. Demetrius had a blanket in his hand, but Philip was tugging rather feebly at its outer edge. For a moment neither of them saw him.

'That's Stephanus' room, and his stuff, so who said you could wander in there and help yourself, you thieving Greek?' The old groom was trembling with rage; Iucundus could see it in the tense quivering surface of the blanket, and hear it in his tremulous voice.

'The master said so. That good enough for you?' Demetrius' voice dripped contempt. 'The old idiot's wandered off or something, and I've been ordered to find out where he's gone.'

'Wandered off?' said Philip. 'Not likely. Never been known to do such a thing. Might have been bumped off though.' He shot a malicious glance at Demetrius, who dropped the blanket so suddenly that the old man staggered slightly under its weight.

'How dare you say that?' Demetrius' voice was quite soft, but he was advancing on Philip with such purpose that Iucundus felt he should intervene.

'Demetrius?' he called out, as if he'd just arrived. 'Oh, here you are. The master wants all the slaves in the peristyle as soon as possible.'

Demetrius stepped back, the fury wiped from his face. 'Very well. You go to the kitchen, and tell them there. Philip, you can tell all the outdoor staff.'

As Iucundus and Philip approached the corner, the boy glanced back to see Demetrius pick up the blanket and duck in under the door-curtain.

It seemed that the peristyle was the big garden with colonnades all round the sides, the one you could see from the reception hall, and from the master's bedroom. It was rapidly filling up with slaves, all murmuring to each other. Everyone was milling about, with no-one to call them to order, but they all fell silent as the master swept in, obviously angry. He looked around impatiently, but before he could speak, the old door-keeper hobbled up to him.

'There's a man here, master. Says it's about Stephanus.'

More murmuring from the slaves. Iucundus could see Demetrius, white-faced in the shadow of the colonnade.

'Bring him here, then,' Torquatus told the doorkeeper, and at once a respectable-looking man in a freedman's cap came forward.

'I'm afraid I have bad news,' he said. He paused, and there was complete silence except for the soft crunch of gravel under someone's feet. 'When I went to open up the master's premises at dawn I noticed a little crowd of people at the bottom of the street, just above the entrance to the Forum. They were gathered around a body, arguing about who it was. Then we discovered it was Stephanus, your steward.'

There was a moment's shocked silence, then a babble of voices broke out. 'In the Forum? What was he doing there?' Whatever they had expected, it clearly wasn't this.

Torquatus raised a hand for quiet, and asked, 'Was it an accident?'

'Who knows?' The man shrugged. 'But he wasn't found in the Forum, exactly, lord. No. He was near the bottom of the Gemonian Steps, and from where he was lying, I'd say he'd fallen – or been pushed, of course – from the Tarpeian Rock.'

Torquatus gaped at him, bemused. How on earth did Stephanus come to be there, of all places? Was this some kind of sick humour? After all, traitors to the state are taken up to the Tarpeian Rock to be flung off; it isn't a death for slaves. 'What in Jupiter's name was he doing on the Capitol? I never gave him permission to go out.'

No-one was able to answer his question, and the slaves huddled together in the face of his anger. They were looking pinched and sick.

'How did you know it was Stephanus?' Torquatus asked.

'Oh, one of the men in the crowd was from your own bank, Eucolpus', which is next door to my master's, and he recognised your steward at once, lord.' The man seemed relieved to be asked a question he could answer. 'What would you like us to do with his body?'

'He must come back here, of course. Demetrius, see to it, will you? When he's been burnt, we'll put the ashes into our family tomb. That would be right and proper. Stephanus served my family well, for many years: we owe him that.' He looked round again, his eyes coldly scanning the slaves huddling in the chilly breeze. 'And if anyone knows anything at all about what Stephanus thought he was doing, you are to let me or Demetrius know. Is that understood?'

Torquatus didn't wait for an answer but turned and walked swiftly away. Iucundus hesitated, unsure whether he should follow, then decided to wait for an order. None came, so he got out a bridle that needed polishing, and the master's round cavalry shield, intending to check the straps inside it: he'd thought, yesterday, that the leather looked worn. He sat down on a bench out of the wind, where Felix soon joined him. As Iucundus worked oil into the shield-straps to soften them, he asked about this family tomb the master had mentioned, and Felix told him was a bit like a dovecot, with monuments to the family and little niches where they put the ashes of the family's slaves. Or some of them anyway. They couldn't have room for all of them. At first Iucundus thought this was nice, a way of including them, as if they mattered. Then he changed his mind: even when you died you had to do it the Roman way. Celts preferred burial, he told Felix, liking to imagine the body gently sinking back into earth, and plants sending their roots down into it, and flowers unfurling from it. But here the burning and the little stone jar and the little stony hole for the jar seemed to be what you got. And even that was only for favoured slaves, the ones the masters thought they knew. The rest got burial of a sort, Felix said, though it wasn't exactly respectful: they were chucked into common graves and covered over, just about well enough to stop dogs digging them up and eating them.

The usual household noises were subdued, and the scrunch of boots on the stone floors, the muttered instructions the men gave each other as they brought the body in seemed unpleasantly loud. The boys kept their voices low as they talked over their work. Then there was a different kind of stir in the house. A door banged in the distance; people looked up, and then quickly lowered their heads again, as if cleaning the floor or polishing the silver were the most important things in their lives. Felix was half-smiling.

'It's the mistress, the old mistress,' he told Iucundus, as voices approached the garden where the boys were sitting in the sun. 'The master's mother. And Iunia, who was married to his brother.' Two ladies appeared, walking briskly

35

along the colonnade. One was a lot older than the other, a plump elderly lady with a double chin and large eyes: too large, really; there was something frog-like about her. The other was younger and had a kind of faded prettiness, with light brown hair and grey eyes. She looked discontented, Iucundus thought, but he couldn't look for long, as the ladies were approaching. He laid the shield carefully on top of its leather case, and stood up. Felix put the bridle down and stood up too.

The older woman looked Iucundus over coolly, as if he were a dog or a donkey, which made him angry. 'Where's my son?'

'I believe he went down to the Forum, lady,' Felix told her.

'Well, then, I'll speak to that secretary of his, what's his name, Dionysius.'

Neither of them corrected her. Felix ran off to find Demetrius, and it occurred to Iucundus that it was unlike him not to be on hand when anything was happening. 'May I bring you some wine, lady?' he asked, coming to his senses.

She ignored this. 'You must be my son's new body-servant?'

'Yes, lady.'

She looked him over again. 'How old are you?'

'Fourteen, lady.'

'And where are you from?'

'Gaul, lady.'

She pursed her lips. 'I can see that for myself.' Her voice was tart. 'But where in Gaul?'

'The land of the Eburones, lady, the country of the Belgae.'

'Hm. Isn't that a wild, barbaric sort of place? I hope you don't carry a knife when you're around my son?'

'Only to guard him, lady,' Iucundus replied. Luckily, the lady seemed to have heard his words but not his tone. She nodded dismissively. 'Well, see that you give him good service. Though why he couldn't have got himself a slave from some civilised place -'

Felix was back, trotting along behind Demetrius, which was a relief. The horrible old lady's questioning had brought Iucundus close to tears, and he was glad she had swung the light of her attention elsewhere.

'What's all this I hear about Stephanus?' she demanded of Demetrius.

'Vibia, dear,' the younger lady murmured in a supplicating voice that seemed not to expect to be heard.

'Well, what, Iunia? Here's my old steward dead, and naturally I want to know why and how. I should have taken him with me when I left. I knew it at the time: I was a soft-hearted fool to leave him in this house.' She looked around with loathing, and Iucundus felt that if she had a soft heart she was hiding it very well.

'He was an old man, Vibia,' the younger lady insisted. 'Of course he must have died soon, whether you took him to our house or not.'

'He certainly wouldn't have been wandering about the city after dark if he'd been with me. At least, I understand that's what he was doing?' She looked accusingly at Demetrius, as if Stephanus' presence on the Capitol must have been his fault. 'Where is he now?'

'No-one knows why he went to the Capitol,' Demetrius told her. 'We brought him here: he's in his room.'

'Oh, he's not burned, yet?' Her pale little eyebrows rose. 'Don't tell me you've got him laid out as if he were someone important? Whatever next? Are you planning a procession to the Forum, ancestral masks, mimes, music? A eulogy praising his deeds?' The silence that greeted these remarks was awkward, but Demetrius smiled again after a long moment and said, 'We will take him to the burning-ground tomorrow. But his body had to be brought somewhere, couldn't be left lying in the street, so we put him in his old room while we arranged things.'

'Well, I'll take a look at him, since he's here. Maybe

I'll get a better idea of what happened to him. After all he cost me a lot of money, years ago.'

'I don't think you should see him, lady.' Demetrius was firm. 'He's not a pretty sight, I'm afraid.'

'I'll see him,' Vibia said with a decisive little bob of the head, and Demetrius bit his lip and turned away to lead her to Stephanus' room.

Iucundus tagged along behind Felix, wanting to be there when this Vibia saw the body. He was curious to know why a harmless old man had been killed, and he didn't think she would be fobbed off with a cursory glance. And just as he'd expected, she stepped straight up to the little old cot and twitched off the cloak that had been laid over the corpse with a brutal matter of factness which made Iucundus gasp. Demetrius made a sudden movement as if to stop her. Then Vibia, her face unmoved, was bending over the old man's body, waxy-pale, even smaller now than it had been in life, almost hairless, soft and vulnerable. Peering round her Iucundus could see how Stephanus had been marked by his fall. There were huge bruises all over him, and tears and scrapes in the skin on his arms and legs, the sort you'd expect if someone fell onto rocks, bumping and banging down a cliff on the way. The right side of the rib-cage no longer stood out, but was a pulpy-looking mess, and his right leg was twisted so far out of true it couldn't be straightened, and the foot stuck out at an odd angle. His face was bruised but still quite recognisable. Iucundus couldn't see the back of his head: there couldn't be much of it left. He moved round quietly till he could see the neck in a clear light, and thought he saw some marks shading it. They couldn't have happened in a fall, but they reminded him of the marks he'd seen once on the neck of one of his father's lords. The man had been detected in an act of treachery, and his father had grabbed him by the throat. Iucundus was back there again, seeing in his mind's eye the bulging eyes and rasping breath of the man as he strangled, his father's great hand squeezing and squeezing, hearing the boom of that furious voice.

Later that day, Iucundus remembered that the master's shield and the bridle Felix had been polishing were still in the garden, and hurried out to put them away before someone told him off for his carelessness.

Philip was in the stables, as usual. Iucundus put the shield into its leather bag and hung it up in the store where it lived among all the weapons the household had accumulated over generations, from ancient spears and a dusty bundle of arrows for which there didn't appear to be a bow to the long cavalry sword Torquatus would carry in battle. The short sword he would use if he fought on foot lived on the wall over the master's bed: he must remember to take it down and check its edge. He locked the store carefully, picked up the bridle again and went next door into the stable. As he walked in and hung the key on the nail where it lived he heard the old man calling out, 'Who's there?'

'It's only me, Iucundus.'

'Oh.'

'I just want to put Firefly's tack away.'

'Oh, very well.' The voice in the darkness wasn't exactly welcoming, but Iucundus walked in as if he hadn't noticed. The room where Philip lived was an entrance lobby to the stables, lined with rows of pegs for bridles, and heavy brackets for saddles. It smelt of horses and clean leather, and the grain which was stored there in great jars. There was a heavy old table against one wall, a little hearth, with a brazier on it, and a couple of stools. Philip was sitting beside the brazier on one of these.

'Felix and I left our things in the garden when the lady Vibia arrived,' he said. 'So I thought I'd better come and tidy up.'

'The mistress is here?'

'She was, yes. She and – and the other lady have gone now.'

'Iunia Aurunculeia,' Philip nodded. 'She was married to the old master's son Lucius, who died in Africa fighting for Pompey the Great. I was with him there.' He brooded for a moment. 'I wonder what they came for? They don't speak to the master much these days, not since he changed sides and went to fight for Caesar. Well, she won't have been pleased to hear about Stephanus,' he concluded with a kind of relish.

'She wasn't,' Iucundus agreed. 'That's why she came, because she'd heard that he was dead. She must have known him for years?'

'Oh, she did. He came here when old Lucius Torquatus married her. Stephanus was quite a young man then. So was I, for that matter. The master was consul that year, and the house was full to bursting, great dinners every night, all the senators visiting. Not the way things are now.' He shook his head sadly.

'How did it come about, that the master changed sides?'

'I wasn't here at the time, I was in Africa with Lucius Torquatus, this man's half-brother, but what I heard was that the master - this master, I mean - met Octavian, and they got to be friends. Old Lucius Torquatus, his father, wasn't happy about that and there was a terrible quarrel. He was a hot-tempered man, the old master, and rode his sons pretty hard. In those days you had to be on one side or the other, and our family was on Pompey the Great's side. Octavian was Caesar's family, so he couldn't be our friend.'

Iucundus peered at the old man through the half-light. 'So the master ran away to fight for Julius Caesar?'

'Ran away? No; he was thrown out. Like I say, there was a quarrel. Quite something, so I heard, the old master yelling and young Aulus refusing to listen. Imagine: daring to argue with his father, and him only seventeen.' He shook his head. 'Anyway, he left.'

Iucundus gazed at him. 'Go on. What happened next?'

'The young master went to Octavian, I believe. He fought with Caesar in Africa against Pompey's supporters after Pompey died, and in Spain too, against Pompey's sons.

Fighting against his own brother.' He spat into the straw at his feet.

'You don't like him, do you?' Iucundus asked slowly.

'Like him? What does it matter to him whether a slave likes him?'

Iucundus thought it did. Was this why the master wanted a new body-slave, because he didn't trust Philip? The man might be old but he was tough as a military boot, and Iucundus had wondered from the beginning why the master would choose to go into battle with an untried young slave rather than an experienced man.

'You must have got to know your master well. Young Lucius, I mean, I suppose you were together for a long time?'

Philip nodded. 'We were. Two years in the field together, and there's a closeness in that.' The old man sighed. 'I knew Lucius better than anyone except the old master himself. He was an arrogant man, I have to say, but honest, and better-tempered than his dad. I never remember them disagreeing in their politics, and in the end he died for what he believed in.' He shook his head, and seemed to be gazing back into those times. 'That was an awful campaign. Pompey's supporters were an dreadful bunch, argumentative, arrogant, insubordinate. My master was praetor that year. That's the highest you can be unless you get to be consul, as the old master did. He could have made a fuss and got a higher command if he'd been like the rest of them, but he didn't. And Caesar - I hated the man, but I have to say it - by all accounts Caesar would never have allowed his generals to behave like that. '

Iucundus pulled up the other stool and sat down quietly. 'What happened, then?' he asked.

'For a start, the master was put in charge of Oricum. No, you won't have heard of it: it's not a great city, but it was well placed to receive supplies and Pompey wanted to hold it. The master didn't have a big garrison, and when Caesar arrived the citizens just opened the gates and let him in. The soldiers changed sides. The master was furious, but there was nothing he could do. Caesar treated him very well, like a guest really, and wanted him to change sides too, but that wasn't the master's way.'

Philip fell silent, apparently deep in his reminiscent mood, twisting a plait of straw in his fingers.

'So what happened?' Iucundus prompted.

'Oh, we stayed there for about two months. Guests, supposedly, but the master couldn't leave the camp. Then Marcus Antonius landed his army further up the coast. Caesar had been waiting for Antonius, and broke the camp up at once, marching off to join him. In the confusion we got away.'

'We?'

'The master and me, and his secretary, Philo.'

'And your master died?' Iucundus asked.

'Oh, not then: that was getting on for two years later, after Caesar won against Pompey, and then won again against Pompey's supporters: those who were left. My master and the general, Scipio, were on board a ship, and they were caught. I was with him to the end, unlike some.'

Iucundus looked a question. 'His secretary, I mean. Stole the master's cash-box in all the confusion and ran off.' He spat into the straw at his feet. 'Didn't do him much good, though. We heard later that the box was found, smashed, by the side of the road, and his cloak too, slashed to ribbons. Bandits, no doubt: there were plenty of those just then.'

'What did you do then?'

'I came home, best way I could.'

'And all that time the master - this master, I mean - was on the other side? In the other army?'

Philip nodded. 'That's right. And then he went to Spain to fight against Pompey's sons as well, so he didn't come home till, oh, May of last year, it must have been. Him and that Demetrius. There were hardly any slaves here by then. Me and Stephanus and few others. And some of the women. But they don't count, not being interested in politics,' he said loftily, and Iucundus had to hide a smile. There seemed to him no reason why male and female slaves shouldn't be equally interested in politics, both being equally powerless.

'But the ladies - Vibia and Iunia, you said? - they were interested in politics, weren't they? That's why they don't like the master?'

'And they had reason. The old master died just a few weeks after young Aulus left. Of a broken heart, that's what I think.'

There was a long pause. Iucundus glanced at Philip and saw he had sunk into a mood of gentle melancholy.

'The mistress went to see Stephanus' body,' he said, and Philip seemed to rouse himself.

'Why did she do that?' he asked.

'She didn't say. But she took the cover off him, and had a look at his injuries.'

'Ah, well, I hope she'll tell the master what she saw, or persuade him to have a look too. They can say what they like about him falling; I don't believe a word of it.'

Iucundus didn't either. But he took the old groom's gnarled hand and said gently, 'I don't think you should say that.'

'Why not? If it's true?'

'Because if it's true there's someone around here who doesn't mind pushing people off cliffs.'

Philip sat quietly, apparently thinking this over. It seemed to take quite a while. Then he peered at Iucundus through the dying afternoon light. 'Can you read?' was his quite unexpected question.

'I can.'

'And write too?'

'Yes.'

'What, really write? Not just your name?'

'Yes. Do you want me to write something for you?'

The door swung open, making them both jump.

'Iucundus!' It was Demetrius, looking mean. 'Why are you never where you're wanted? The master is going out and wants you with him. Hurry now!'

He threw a spiteful look at old Philip, grabbed Iucundus by the arm and hustled him away.

Chapter 5

During the night the weather changed, and Rome was blanketed in fog: thick, yellowish-grey, acrid with the smoke of a thousand wood-fires. Torquatus tasted ash on his tongue and thought of the pyres up on the Esquiline where the dead were burned. Stephanus would be one of them today: he wondered uneasily what in Hercules' name the old boy had been doing up there on the Capitol, and who had sent him to his death. Was there a murderer in his household? Or could it possibly have been an accident? Under his feet the street was slick with greasy dirt, each cobble a slippery trap for the unwary. A senator ought not to be seen falling down in the street. He put consideration of Stephanus' death aside.

As his party descended from the Quirinal, the foggy air became thicker yet. The smell of the river, with its freight of excrement, animal guts from the meat market, yellowing cabbage leaves dumped by the vegetable sellers, dead fish and live ones, rose up in the Forum to meet the smoke coming down. The broad stairs at the bottom of the Argentarius were covered in wet, grey dirt. This was where Stephanus' broken body had been left to lie in the mud. What was going on in his house? His spine seemed to chill at the thought of slaves creeping about in the dark, their minds filled with hatred.

Perhaps it was only the desolate mood of the place infecting him. The Forum might be the heart of Rome, but it had once been a marsh, and in weather like this still felt like one. He shook himself and followed the slaves with their sputtering torches through the wide space where buildings loomed out of the fog, then sank back into the murk. Here a corner of a temple appeared, sharply familiar, there a colonnade ran regular and ghostly into invisibility. He was careful to walk as he had been taught by his father, upright, not deigning to look at the ground, however treacherous. Even when there was no-one to see.

The slaves cried out and jumped suddenly, their torches smoking darkly, and he himself felt the hairs on his arms rise. Out of the fog, looming down at them, a face had appeared. Its dead eyes stared. Beside its ears two hands seemed to waggle as if in a children's game. He knew that face, and swallowed hard. It would not do to be sick. Tears pricked his eyes. Cicero had taken far too many risks in these recent years, goading Antonius in speeches of great brilliance. Had the speeches been duller, they would have done less harm, but it had become a spectacle, each speech commanding a greater audience, the witty barbs flying out of the senate-house and into the Forum, to become the currency of every market trader or common citizen. He must have known what Antonius would do if ever he had the power. Well, now Antonius had the power, and here was Cicero's head to prove it: bruised, the sparse hair draggled and wet, the tongue stuck out, skewered by a hairpin. This must have been put up during the night, just in case anyone had doubted the Three's intentions.

And there beside Cicero, above Torquatus like gods on their ivory stools were the Three, the great men themselves. Octavian, a small, pale man, the sort you'd never remember in a crowd, Antonius, legs spread, his boxer's face grumpy, looking as if he wanted a drink, and Lepidus, sitting upright, coldly handsome. All three were very correctly dressed in togas and boots, and looked chilled to the bone. Torquatus knew they sometimes chose to come down in the morning to dispense justice, as they liked to call it, but he couldn't believe they'd stay there long on such a dark day. A number of heads on spears loomed out of the mist around them like a spectral bodyguard, though of course each man had a detail of soldiers to protect him too, standing at a not too discreet distance. Below them a pile of heads and bodies, of those not important enough to justify hoisting them onto the Rostra straight away, he supposed, lay in a jumbled heap, blood oozing down across the cobbles in a sluggish stream. The sharp iron smell of it was heavy in the foggy air. Torquatus took a deep breath and raised a hand in greeting. Lepidus returned the greeting ceremoniously, one senator to another. Well, Lepidus at least had no reason to wish Torquatus dead, as far as he knew. Antonius glowered, but nodded. Torquatus thought he probably wasn't important enough or rich enough to be on Antonius' hit-list – but who knew? Who knew? Octavian smiled, lifted a hand, greeted Torquatus quite warmly, for him. It seemed he was alive, for now.

They were not a natural team, Torquatus thought looking up at them, each being violently ambitious and ruthless. But they were formally bound by their ties to Julius Caesar: Octavian his adopted son and heir, Marcus Antonius a cousin and close colleague, Aemilius Lepidus one of his trusted generals, who had to be included because of the number of legions under his command. Informally they were forced together by fear of each other and awareness that no one of the Three was strong enough to fight the other two. And by their insatiable need for money. Looking up at them, Torquatus remembered the mild November day when they had marched into Rome to cheers and acclamations. Instead of fighting each other, these men promised to restore the state to health. The relief didn't last long, however: the very next morning a list was pinned up in the Forum of people whose property and lives were forfeit. Enemies of the state, they were called: anyone could kill them, even their own slaves (shocking in itself, of course) and claim a reward. The soldiers were there to help.

Some of the names of the proscribed were to be expected, Cicero's being the most obvious example. But everyone was shocked when the Three turned on their own families. It was as if they had signed a pact: each man to sacrifice someone close to him. That way none of them could claim that the others were worse than him. Not that that stopped them, of course: in later years such claims were made, and as time went on people even learned to listen to them with a straight face. But most of those proscribed were from the wealthy equestrian class: tax collectors in the provinces, import and export men, owners of large potteries and metalworks, suppliers to the army.

Torquatus called out to the slaves: 'Move on! What are you waiting for?' and was glad that his voice sounded cool, commanding. They walked on, murmuring among themselves, keeping close to him, almost as if it was he who was guarding them. Only the two ex-gladiators, Becco and Pulex, strolled in front unperturbed, wearing their muscles like armour, and behind them, walking as sedately as Torquatus himself, his new body-slave Iucundus, slim and graceful, apparently unmoved by the shambles around him. The flaring light from the torches caught a sudden spark from the knife tucked into his boot.

Torquatus walked once right through the Forum in the correct manner, neither hurrying nor moving with affected solemnity, his toga correctly arranged, sharply white in the grey fog, his arms held as his father had taught him, hands modestly covered by the folds of the toga, his boots the maroon colour appropriate to a patrician, clean and well-laced. The Forum wasn't busy: partly because of the weather, no doubt. The heads lolling on their spears drew furtive glances from the better-off, but a group of ragged children were jeering at them and pulling faces in mimicry of their dead stares. A senator stood by, clearly unsure whether to exercise his authority and drive them off, in the normal way, or whether to pretend he hadn't seen. Torquatus had already got his vote, so needed to do no more now than remind him that the elections were tomorrow and pass the time of day with him.

Some of the stallholders at the sides of the Forum were open for business. Torquatus caught an enticing whiff of onions and hot sausage as he passed a man with a small brazier, and a slave went by carrying a pie in careful fingers to his waiting master. Well-dressed women strolled in and out of the jewellers' shops at the far end of the Forum as if the times were quite normal. The fog had lightened and lifted somewhat. As he passed one of the main roads leading up into the teeming Subura, Torquatus stopped to greet another man he knew.

'Lucius Villius Annalis, can you be canvassing too?'

The man's toga was immaculate, his hair arranged in ordered waves and gleaming with oil. The young man with him was even smarter: his toga was whitened so that it shone brilliant even in the murky air. They seemed like a vision from a vanished world.

'Yes: this is my son, and he is standing for quaestor next year, like you.'

Torquatus had met the son and didn't rate him but he nodded politely.

'Excellent: it's a fine thing when fathers and sons can sit in the Senate together.' His tone sounded quite false in his own ears, but Annalis didn't seem to have noticed, saying, 'It's what we all want, isn't it? To take the consulship, to get to the top of the tree, when one's son is working his way up and can see everything one does.'

Not that Torquatus could imagine Annalis as consul.

'Have you enjoyed your time at the Treasury?' said the younger Annalis, a soft man with puffy eyes and a loose mouth. He looked, Torquatus thought, like a drinker.

'Enjoyed would perhaps be the wrong word. I've been privileged, I'm aware of that.'

The young man smiled perfunctorily, and gave his father an impatient glance. There was a slightly awkward silence, in which Torquatus was fully aware of their resentment. Fair enough. Young Annalis, who must be about thirty, was trying to get his first foothold in the Senate at the proper age, while he at twenty-one was already ahead. That was the advantage of being close to one of the Three. He could see there might be disadvantages too. 'I won't keep you from your work,' Torquatus said. 'Not that there seem to be many voters down here today.'

'No. Perhaps if this fog shifts people will at least come down to vote tomorrow?' young Annalis suggested.

Their eyes met, but no-one wanted to mention the pile of bodies, the heads rotting on their stands. 'I hope so, anyway,' he went on, with a slightly forced smile.

Torquatus turned away, putting them out of his mind. Annalis wasn't important, he thought; a backbencher, there to vote, not to speak. If he went off on campaign with Octavian next year it wouldn't matter that he didn't know men like Annalis: if he ended up back in charge of the Treasury he'd need to make alliances among the senators.

Torquatus strolled off. Several of his clients left him, quite correctly, once he had walked the length of the Forum. He turned back towards the Rostra, stopping to speak to one or two men as he went, and was just discussing the forthcoming elections with another senator when a sudden uproar made him jump. He swung round, to see the older Annalis heading off up into the Subura, his beautiful toga flying about him wildly and tangling his feet. The little crowd of slaves and friends who'd been with him were running in all directions. Torquatus looked around for the son: clearly Annalis senior had heard he was on the list. And there was young Annalis, with a group of soldiers, obviously intent on rescuing his father. Out of sheer curiosity Torquatus followed the son as he followed his father up the sloping street. Bystanders stood and cheered as if this were a game. Torquatus had lost sight of the older Annalis, but the son must have known where he'd gone, because he turned off down a side-street, closely followed by the soldiers. It was one of those narrow lanes that open onto all the main streets in the city, dark under the overhanging upper storeys of the buildings which lined it high on both sides. A minute later he was back, leading his father by the hand. The father, dazed-looking, still getting his breath, was smiling at this last-minute rescue. He probably never saw what was coming to him. He turned his head to say something to his son as the soldiers closed in behind him, swinging their swords, and a moment later, the son was holding his father's head aloft. Women screamed, and Torquatus heard someone retch behind him. The crowd melted away.

Torquatus followed Annalis at a distance as he marched back down into the Forum, his father's blood dripping down apparently unnoticed onto the beautiful white toga. Up to the tribunal he went, and held the head up as if in triumph. The Three nodded, lifted their hands in recognition. They spoke together for a moment in an undertone, then Antonius rose and stepped forward to speak. There was a little buzz in the crowd: everyone turned to watch, and Torquatus heard running footsteps behind – nothing to fear however, just the curious wanting to hear the speech.

'This man, our enemy, is dead,' Antonius announced, holding up the head so everyone could see. 'His son, Lucius Villius Annalis, who was standing for quaestor, has shown his devotion to the state and to ourselves by this act, and we declare that he is to inherit his father's lands and fortune.'

There was a murmur in the crowd. A few loudly expressed approval, but underneath there was a much quieter rumble of disgust.

Antonius' battered face was wreathed in smiles, and it soon became clear why. 'So great is our sense of obligation to this exemplary young man that we have decided to allow him to move at once to the next stage of his senatorial career. He will become not a mere quaestor, but an aedile, one of the two men responsible for good order in the city, and who provide the people with games worth watching. I am sure,' he continued with a pious look, 'so dutiful a young man will make a fine aedile, spending his money well.'

Young Annalis, white-faced, muttered out his thanks and hurried away. As Antonius sat down he made some remark to Octavian and the pair of them roared with laughter. Torquatus stood staring at them for a moment as they sat joking among the steaming human mess around them. Then a soldier tossed Annalis' head down onto the pile awaiting display, and he turned away, cold and sick to the stomach.

Chapter 6

The next morning, Torquatus woke with a sense of anticipation and excitement he hadn't felt since he was a boy. For the first time, he was officially standing for office. He remembered how, aged fifteen, the election of his half-brother Lucius as praetor had filled the house with people, well-wishers, campaign agents, freedmen of the family come to help, clients fulfilling their obligations, slaves running here and there with messages. Next stop: a consulship. But would today's election be a real one? The Three had simply chosen the men they wanted as consuls for the next three years. They hadn't named the junior men, the quaestors, so perhaps the choice would be as free as ever? He hoped it would. He wanted to win the way his father and brother had won.

When he was a boy the whole city had headed for the Campus Martius on election days. He looked forward to the noise as one approached, the crowds streaming in, the apparent impossibility of marshalling such a seething mass of individuals into anything like coherence, the silence that would fall so unexpectedly at the opening prayers, followed by more noisy pushing and shoving as the voters struggled to hear the names of all the candidates, who would be standing with the presiding magistrate, and looking dignified or embarrassed according to their dispositions. That chaos would intensify as people sorted themselves into their tribes, resolving itself almost miraculously into orderly lines of men, quietly waiting in the roped-off lanes, shuffling forward to cross the bridges into the voting area and make their choice.

It wasn't like that. The city seemed hardly aware that there was an election going on. His party walked down the Alta Semita as if they were going to the Forum, before swinging off to the right, leaving the city and passing the little temple of Semo Sancus, in its grove of pine trees, on their left. They crossed the Via Lata and entered the Campus itself. At that time Caesar's great voting hall was no more than a muddy field with some markers laying out where it was to go, in the middle of which the old wooden enclosure still stood, shabby and sad. It was being replaced because Caesar had thought it too small and too inconvenient. A bitter smile touched Torquatus' lips: would the splendid new building be only a monument to elections past?

At the tribunal at the north end of the enclosure, the presiding praetor, Lucius Cestius, stood in front of a small group of candidates, and Torquatus joined them, nodding greetings to the others, and wondering how many had the support of one or other of the triumvirs. Some did, for sure: an agent of Octavian's whom Torquatus happened to know was working the crowd, and no doubt there were others too. Torquatus was sure a tall man with a bald spot on the back of his head was one: his purposeful movements made him stand out from the milling voters. And there was little man with a staccato walk wrapped up in a thick cloak and scurrying about from one group to another: Torquatus thought he'd seen him before, but wasn't sure where. The agents weren't bribing, of course: if that had been necessary, it would have been done in the days before the election, not under the nose of the presiding magistrate. They were just showing by their presence that the Three would be aware of everything that went on.

It was time to start, but Cestius held off a little, obviously thinking that such a thin crowd was hardly adequate, and a trickle of men were still making their way in. A slight breeze had blown away most of yesterday's mists, revealing a hazy sun. Sad grey shadows lurked around the voting area, and the place seemed full of echoes. The trickle of citizens died away and the crowd, such as it was, became restless. Cestius pulled a fold of his toga over his head with an irritable shrug, muttered the prayers and declared that he had surveyed the heavens and that the omens were auspicious. He was a tall, thin man with a fussy manner, who looked as if he'd tried and failed to find bad omens.

54

The candidates were announced. By some oversight, the name of Lucius Villius Annalis was still on the list, and Cestius struck it out with a firm swipe of his stylus and a little cluck of annoyance. Each candidate stepped forward and made a speech, reminding the voters of any distinguished ancestors who had served the state. Torquatus could see people were impressed that a Manlius Torquatus was standing, even if a few heads were shaken over the impropriety of his doing so at only twenty-one. It was all very low-key, and the voters seemed unexcited. They swirled about getting into their lines, while the candidates chatted amongst themselves. They all knew each other more or less, of course: the pool from which Rome draws her leaders isn't large. Then the men came forward, dropped their voting tablets into the urns and moved off. Some of them didn't even stay for the declaration, but went straight out once they'd voted.

It was as they were waiting for the count, which wasn't going to take long, that Demetrius was summoned from Torquatus' side by an anxious-looking slave. Torquatus had noticed the man hurrying up through the voting-hall, and wondered what he was there for: anything in those days made men anxious and fearful. Torquatus pretended not to notice the troubled glances passing between his clients – and made his own face as placid as possible – till Demetrius returned.

'It's bad news, master. One of your properties has been attacked: the staff there have been killed, and the place ransacked.'

His guts turned to water. He didn't dare to ask which of his properties: he knew it was the farm. Torquatus could see the clients fidgeting. No doubt they were wondering whether it was safe to be seen with him. But at that moment Cestius hurried out from the back room where the counting had taken place and stepped up onto the tribunal, ready to make his announcement. He peered at the tablets in his hands, and began to read out in a dry voice the names of those successful, in order of the number of votes. Torquatus' wasn't the first name, or the second: obviously his youth was seen as a disadvantage. He forced his knees to stop shaking, and tried to act as if he was still interested. All he felt when heard his name called was relief. It would have been shameful not to have been elected, considering who he was. He knew he had to congratulate the other winners, and accept congratulations graciously himself, and somehow he got through it, noting with an odd detachment that he was managing to sound quite normal, quite unworried. Then, when the meeting had at last been dissolved and when Cestius had congratulated the winners and fussed off, Torquatus turned to his supporters, smiling and saying, 'Thank you all for attending me here: I shall expect to see you tomorrow.'

They looked a little reassured, and Torquatus hoped grimly that he was right and that he would be following his normal routine tomorrow. They couldn't have disappeared faster if a pack of wolves had been after them.

By noon Torquatus was riding out from the stable gate of his house, the election forgotten, without a toga but wrapped in a good warm cloak, to retrace the journey he'd made a few days before. Then he had ridden through a dark land, alone. Now, the fog had been blown away by a crisp cold wind, and plump white clouds chased each other across a blue sky. The horses were as fresh as the breeze, sidling and tossing their heads. Demetrius rode neatly but nervously, while the big men, Becco and Pulex, lumbered along on large and very expensive Nabataean mounts. They too looked as if they'd be happier when they felt the ground under their feet again. Unlike the others Iucundus sat his mare with the ease of long practice. He had been right to look for a Gaul to replace Philip, Torquatus thought. Iucundus had been sold to him as the son of a chieftain. Slave-dealers are artists when it comes to inventing interesting histories for their merchandise, of course, but he wondered whether in this instance it could be true. It was certainly exceptional for a Gaulish slave to be literate, and to know Latin.

Something about a rebellion: nothing too serious, a minor uprising in northern Gaul, and the Roman commander who'd put it down deciding that he needed to make an example. Torquatus didn't know much about the area, let alone the names of the tribes there. Since the end of Caesar's wonderful commentaries, no-one had paid much attention to northern Gaul, except the commanders sent to keep it under control, and he himself hadn't joined Caesar till after the dictator had left Gaul for good. Torquatus spent a few minutes trying to remember who was governing there now. Calenus, perhaps? It was a distraction, he knew: he'd much rather think about his new slave, and about the political situation in Gaul, than about what he would find at the farm.

The scene, when they got there, was one of devastation. For a moment Torquatus could scarcely take it in: the neatness and good order of a well-run farm had been overturned in a carnival of death and destruction. Every living creature seemed to have been killed. Davus and the dog lay side by side in the farmyard, incongruous in the sunshine. Davus was covered in sword-cuts, his tunic soaked with blood, now brown and stiff. The dog had been slashed open, its guts tumbled out in a heap. Even though it was December a few flies had appeared and buzzed lazily round the corpses. The house itself looked as if a violent storm had hit it. The shutters had been wrenched off and lay at strange angles, the door smashed down with such force that its frame was splintered and almost wrenched from the wall. A new lead pipe leading from the roof to a water-tank had been ripped away. Heavy boots had trampled the vegetable garden: the smell of crushed leeks gave an incongruously domestic flavour to the dreadful scene.

Torquatus went inside, his skin prickling with horror, and hesitating as the darkness robbed his eyes temporarily of sight. Gradually out of the darkness appeared a tumbled mound of fabric with an arm extending out from it across the floor: Strato's body. It lay in front of the trap-door to the cellar, which stood open, chained upright against the wall. He was not a fighting man, Strato, and although Torquatus had given him weapons to defend himself with, it seemed he hadn't been able to get to them, but had been cut down with ease. The poor man had evidently been trying to defend the cellar-door. Materna's body they found huddled in the corner of her own kitchen. She was curled up like a baby, but her back and arms had been slashed again and again. It was easy to see how they'd finished her off: her loosened hair had been yanked back so forcefully that a greyish hank of it lay on the floor beside her, stirring uncannily in the cold breeze. Her throat was slashed to the bone.

Torquatus could hear the two big men, Becco and Pulex, talking quietly outside, but the boy Iucundus had followed Torquatus in, as had Demetrius. The three of them moved quietly round the devastated room, saying little to each other. Torquatus was furious at the senseless violence of the attack. He had no one he could talk to here, no one to tell how angry he felt. No doubt the slaves had their own thoughts, probably not thoughts they'd want to share with him.

He sent the bodyguards to search the outbuildings, clinging desperately to the hope that the money, or some of it, might still be here. If it was all gone his prospects were truly terrifying. He told the secretary to get a fire going and Demetrius began delicately selecting some fragments from the pile of kindling. Torquatus himself went out and looked about the yard, Iucundus behind him. It was easy enough to see what had happened. Wheel-ruts and mules' hoof-prints criss-crossed the tracks of boots. There must have been quite a large group of men, with at least one mule-carriage. Torquatus wondered, with a cold stir at his heart, whether whoever did this had followed the last delivery. Perhaps when he'd ridden up the lane on his last visit, some spy had still been there, lurking in the bushes. If so, the watcher might have thought he knew just how many carts would be needed. He would have been wrong, of course: the deliveries had not been fully cleared as they came in: there had been a pile of boxes already before these last arrived. So perhaps they hadn't managed, after all, to empty the cellar? Torquatus knew he was putting off going to look, but told himself he was hunting for clues. He hardly knew what he was hoping to find. Whatever it was, he didn't find it. But just as he was about to go in again, Iucundus gave a sharp cry. 'Look, master! These feet are different, aren't they?'

Torquatus frowned. 'Different, how?'

'They haven't got the same - ,' Iucundus fumbled for the word, and Torquatus came across to look down at the ground. 'Studs,' he nodded. The boots that had been standing here had a distinctive pattern of nails on the soles, or rather the pattern was not unusual, but the studs themselves were star-shaped, not round.

'They're smaller than most of the others, too,' Torquatus pointed out.

'And look, master,' Iucundus went on. 'The man with star-feet seems to have been at the side of things, not carrying boxes, perhaps. He is here' – he went to the beginning of the hedge which marked the lane - 'and over here again.' He darted to the doorway where the prints appeared to one side of it. 'Do you think he was directing the others, master?'

'Well observed. Not that it helps us, unless I can get every man in Rome to show me the soles of his boots. But keep this to yourself: I wouldn't want anyone to throw away a pair of perfectly good boots unnecessarily.'

'No master, I won't tell anyone.' Iucundus' eyes were sparkling. He made Torquatus feel old. The boy had only just been sold into slavery, he had lost everything, and his life had been turned upside down, and yet he was – what? – fourteen, perhaps, and the sun was shining, he had a good horse to ride, there was something exciting happening, and how could he help responding?

He trudged back indoors. The muddy grit on the floor crunched under his boots: Materna would never have allowed so much dirt inside. But Materna was dead, and with her the household she'd managed. Now this was just a crime scene. He crossed to the solid wooden steps that went down into the darkness. Demetrius had found a lamp, miraculously unbroken among the chaos, and had lit it at his fire. The steps creaked as Torquatus went down, his heart thumping. None of the others had offered to come down with him.

The cellar wasn't empty, of course. In the old part of it, sacks of beetroot and turnips had been thrown aside, strings of onions ripped down from the beams. There was a small array of buckets and brushes tucked into a dark corner. But behind the sacks, in the new extension where the battered wooden chests would have been stacked, there was now nothing but empty space. Hardly surprising: but it was only as Torquatus stood there, alone in the close air of the cellar, staring into the flickering darkness, that he fully realised the enormity of what had happened. He was going to have to go to Octavian and tell him that the money had gone. What then? He didn't like to think. But he could hear the slaves shuffling their feet and talking quietly among themselves, and had to go back and face his fate. His legs like lead, Torquatus climbed back up into the light of day.

'Demetrius, you can arrange the funerals of these people. Becco and Pulex, clean up, and leave the place as tidy as you can. I'll send someone to repair the door and shutters. Not that it matters now. There's nothing left to steal.'

None of the slaves except Demetrius knew what had been stored here, but even the stupidest slave could work out that the door hadn't been smashed in for a sack of beetroot.

Becco cleared his throat. 'No, master. Was it

something very valuable you were keeping here, then?' His round eyes were solemn. Almost the stupidest slave, Torquatus corrected himself. He nodded, and Becco went on. 'We found the mule in the stable, master, and the chickens in their house. Shall we feed them?'

Common or garden thieves would have taken the animals. These had come only for the money, and they hadn't cared how they got it.

'Do so. I'll have to send someone over to take care of the place. Demetrius, Iucundus, you can come home with me.' The secretary wouldn't be a lot of help to the others as they cleaned up. Instead, he and Iucundus could escort Torquatus to Octavian's house on the Palatine.

The afternoon was drawing to a close when Torquatus left his house for the third time. The short winter day had darkened, heavy grey clouds scudding across the sky and a cold wind whipping dust about the streets. He was properly togate once again, every inch the respectable senator and, as such, one of the great ones of the earth. Or so he tried to persuade himself. The litter-men trotted off briskly, not expecting their master to stop for a chat with anyone at this time of day. The banks on the Argentarius were all closed. Of course the hours for business were coming to an end, but he wondered how many of the bankers were still in Rome. He averted his eyes from Cicero, but not fast enough to avoid seeing that the old man's face had begun to bloat in the morning's sunshine. Briefly he remembered Stephanus, another old, dead man. He pulled himself together and tried to think how he was going to find the money, and what Octavian would do if he failed, and then the litter-men had crossed the Forum and were climbing one of the sloping roads up to the Palatine and Octavian's house.

It was quite a small place, though an address anywhere on the Palatine is worth having. It was in fact the house Octavian had been born in, which had been on the market when he'd first come back to Rome after Julius Caesar's death. He'd liked the idea of living in the old house, though it had passed out of the family years ago, and he very much wanted not to go back to the house his mother shared with her second husband, the wealthy Philippus. Already people were saying he was of no account because of his age: to go back home to Mama would only encourage such talk. So he was here.

Torquatus walked straight in, half-hearing the doorman's invitation to the slaves to go and get warm in the slaves' quarters. He signed to Demetrius, whom he trusted and thought might be useful, to follow him. The room where Octavian worked was guarded by another slave. Before the man let him in he adjusted Torquatus' toga so that the fabric lay neatly pleated on his shoulder. 'The master's so particular, sir,' he murmured, then threw open the door: 'Aulus Manlius Torquatus.' Octavian, one of the overlords of Rome, was lounging in a battered old chair, his feet, wrapped in sheepskin, propped up on the table in the centre of the room. He seemed to be wearing several tunics, and his arms were covered to the wrist with some soft fabric too, so it was Torquatus who felt out of place. The room was very warm, and he felt sweat break out on his brow.

He glanced around the room. He had hoped to find Octavian alone, but Agrippa was hunched on a stool on the far side of a handsome tripod brazier, reading some document by the light of a many-branched lamp, in whose flickering light his heavy face looked grim. Agrippa at least wouldn't need the situation explained to him: he was Octavian's closest companion, and utterly discreet. Otherwise the big shabby room was empty. The huge table was covered with piles of documents, all meticulously arranged.

Octavian glanced up as Torquatus came in. 'You look as if you walked?'

'No. It's been a busy day. Quiet enough now, though: the streets are almost empty, the shops shut.

Rome's not looking its best. Perhaps the fog has its uses.'

Octavian smiled. 'Cicero's a vile sight,' he agreed. 'I'll get them to take him down in a day or two.'

'Everyone will have got the message by then, no doubt.'

'I certainly hope so.'

'Did you agree Cicero's death with Antonius?'

Octavian nodded Torquatus to a stool, and he sat, sliding it back unobtrusively from the brazier. 'Wasn't negotiable. Antonius had him at the top of his list. I had better things to do, believe me, than waste my energies trying to save the old fool.' He shrugged. 'Did you like him?'

Torquatus considered this. 'Not like exactly. But I'd known him all my life: when I was a boy, my father and he were close. They liked to dine and discuss philosophy. Cicero always seemed to like a good dinner, I noticed, tucked in like anything, for all his talk of a delicate stomach. And talked, of course. So yes, I suppose he was part of my childhood. Part of Rome.'

There was a silence, broken only by the click of wax tablets as Agrippa went on with whatever he was working at.

'I suppose you haven't come here to discuss Cicero – or philosophy.'

'No. It's not good news,' Torquatus admitted.

Octavian's eyes were alert, but he said nothing, and Torquatus had to go on. 'The money you left with me. It's gone.'

'What? How much?' Octavian swung his legs down off the table and sat up.

'Everything. The whole of the last delivery. And what was there already.'

'What happened?'

'I don't know. Seven days ago the last consignment arrived. It was just like the others, nothing unusual about it. Some time between then and today the farmhouse was attacked – '

'Weren't your people armed?'

'They were. But there were only three of them, and Strato and Materna were just ordinary slaves, farm workers. I gave them a strong companion, Davus, and a guard dog too. But it was clearly a large gang that did this.'

'They should have had more protection,' Octavian said briskly. He was sitting sideways, one arm along the table, his gaze intense. The clicking of the writing-tablets in the background had stopped.

'I thought the idea was to do all this very discreetly.' Torquatus made himself stop. It wouldn't do him any good to get angry. 'Davus died fighting, out in the farmyard. Strato died defending the steps to the cellar. Materna was killed in her kitchen.' He paused, moved again by the loneliness of those deaths. No other houses were within call. The attackers had been able to make all the noise they wanted. There was no-one to come.

'And did you get any idea where the money's gone?' Octavian hadn't moved, his eyes boring into Torquatus' face.

'None. I had my men search the farm thoroughly, of course, but it's clear from the bootprints and wheel-tracks that carts were used, as you'd expect. The tracks are clearly visible on the farm lane, but once they get out onto the paved road – ' Torquatus shrugged. 'It could be anywhere by now.' He got up and walked restlessly about the room. 'I think the attack must have happened a good while before we knew of it,' he added. 'The blood on the bodies was dry and hard and the fire was cold.'

Octavian looked away at last. Agrippa had put down whatever it was he'd been reading, and he got up and came round the brazier into the fading light from the window.

'I daresay your farm wasn't left in a good state?' he asked.

'It wasn't. But I can put that right easily enough.'

There was a moment's silence.

'You'll have to put the whole thing right.' Octavian's gaze was fixed on Torquatus again. This was exactly what he'd feared. And if he couldn't, what then? Agrippa shot Octavian a frowning look but said nothing. Torquatus didn't expect any help from that quarter: he knew well enough that once Agrippa had seen what Octavian intended, he'd never try and change his friend's mind.

'The first thing I need to know is how much was there,' Torquatus said.

He'd thought this a straightforward request, but Octavian's glance was chilly. 'You're Treasury Quaestor. Don't you keep accounts?'

'Of what's in the Treasury, yes. Of other people's money, no.' Again Torquatus had to pull himself up, take a deep breath.

'I can't tell you off the top of my head.' Octavian spoke slowly, as if he were thinking. Torquatus stared at him: he'd never supposed Octavian would be able to give him the figure himself. That's what slaves are for. But he made no move to call one. 'I'll let you know in a few days.'

Torquatus couldn't understand this at all. Why wasn't he able to get the information straight away? 'I reckon the last delivery alone must have been over six million sesterces?' he ventured. Octavian shot him a look, then got up and walked over to the shuttered window. He didn't reply. Torquatus badly wanted to pursue the matter, but there was a feeling of danger in the air. 'I've also lost the value of some good slaves, and whatever it costs to get the farmhouse repaired,' he pointed out. 'And three people who had done nothing wrong have met a dreadful death.'

Octavian turned back to him and looked an enquiry.

'The three slaves.'

'Oh.' He shrugged. 'Just farm slaves, so you'll easily replace them. As I see it, someone must have talked. No-one should have known about the money or its movements. So it's up to you to find it.' Octavian's smile was apologetic. 'I really hope you do. '

Torquatus dared not go further. He got up and walked over to join Octavian at the window, telling himself it was only the brazier that was making him sweat. 'Who do you think would have taken it?' he asked, and at this Octavian met his eyes again.

'Antonius, obviously.' Agrippa said what they were all thinking. 'He's always short of cash. He's always accusing you of stealing public money, so he probably thinks he's justified.' He sniffed. 'And beside, who else has a large gang of well-armed men? Him and his so-called bodyguard.'

'Gods, I hope it's not him, though I can't think who else,' Torquatus agreed, his heart sinking. If it was indeed Antonius who was behind this he had as much chance of getting the money back as of turning into the guardian goddess of his local fountain.

'I was having an argument with him the other day,' Octavian told them, wandering back to the table and straightening a pile of papers. 'Let's call it an argument. It would have been a quarrel if he'd had his way, but I'm not quarrelling with him just now. He wanted all the money spent on soldiers, armaments and supplies for the war we're going to have to fight against Brutus and Cassius in the East. I said we must spend a good bit of it on ships. Otherwise what are we going to do? Just sit here and wait for Brutus and Cassius to graciously condescend to come back to Italy – with their large armies? He thinks we can just force the Rhodians or someone to hand over all the ships we need.'

He clicked his tongue in annoyance and walked angrily about the room. 'Bloody fucking Senate, giving Sextus Pompey command of the seas. I'd kill the men who ordered that.'

'I think you mostly have.' The words slipped out: Torquatus could have bitten his tongue out. Octavian gave him a bleak look, but Agrippa laughed and said: 'And Sextus didn't waste any time, did he? Straight round all the sea-ports, collecting ships – and their crews, of course. So now there he sits, neat as you please in Sicily, while we can't find ships for our own armies. All on the orders of the Senate, which would do anything to stop you. Even now.'

'Surely they haven't got the leisure for that?' Torquatus couldn't believe that there was a single senator who wasn't more occupied with his own safety than the state's just now.

Octavian scowled. 'My spies tell me otherwise. Apparently there are some who think so highly of Sextus Pompey they'd like to bring him back to Rome. How well he'd get on with Brutus and Cassius, wouldn't he? Them with their army, and him with his navy: they could fight it out between them, over my body and Antonius'. Oh, and Lepidus' too, don't let's forget him. Apparently these fools think the three of them would just settle down, turn into good citizens, take turns being consul, just like the old days.'

There didn't seem to be anything to say to this, and another silence fell, broken by Octavian, who came back to the table and sat down with a sigh. Then his mood suddenly changed, and he turned to Torquatus, his eyes alive with laughter. 'On the first of January Caesar's cult will be established. His temple will be on the Forum, the altar in front of it exactly on the spot where his body was burned. And guess what? Antonius is going to be the first priest of the Divine Julius.'

Dire as his situation was, Torquatus couldn't help being amused. Antonius was Caesar's cousin, so it was quite suitable. Unless you were aware, of course, as everyone was, that he had known all about the conspiracy against Caesar's life. Although he had refused to join it, he hadn't warned Caesar either, so one might say he was morally responsible for Caesar's murder, even if he hadn't wielded a knife. He had also spent the few months after Caesar's death carefully removing everything the people had put up to honour the dictator - flowers, inscriptions, statues - and had resolutely pooh-poohed the very idea of Caesar's divinity. Not in public, of course: the common folk had loved Caesar, whatever the Best People thought. But at dinner with fellow-senators he had spoken frankly enough, and these senators had passed on the comments to their friends, who had kindly relayed them to Octavian.

'Antonius can't be the only suspect, surely?'
Torquatus said.

'Who else?' Octavian asked.

Torquatus had no idea.

'Anyway, I don't care who took it, I just know I
want it back, and I will have it, whether from you or from
wherever else.'

'I don't know where I could find a sum like that.'
Torquatus didn't even know yet what the sum was, just that
it was enormous.

Octavian raised his pale brows, surprised. 'That
place of yours near Neapolis would go for a good deal, even
in these times, and you have several more very nice villas, a
large one at Formiae and a smaller one at Cumae, as well as
the one near Ostia, I believe. And then there are the grain-
stores your father invested in at Puteoli; those must bring in
a handsome profit, surely? You've an estate in the Alban
hills, with a vineyard producing top-quality wine. Then there
are large estates in Tuscany, Picenum and Venetia, and
considerable shipping interests in Ancona, which will be
greatly increased when your mother dies. I believe your
father also owned substantial property in southern Gaul, and
a huge estate in Macedonia, too, which he bought when he
was governor. Do you still have that?'

'I do.' Torquatus' mouth was dry. He'd had no idea
Octavian was so hideously well-informed.

'Well then. I don't want to deprive you of anything.
On the contrary. I've known you for years and regard you as
a close and loyal friend. And as you know, I believe in
rewarding loyalty with loyalty. If you need help - soldiers,
say, you can have them. But I must have the money - and
before you take office.'

It was now the fourth day before the Ides of
December, and his office began on the first day of January:
twenty days to recover the cash. And seven of those days
would be taken up by Saturnalia: useless days, when

everyone would be drunk, hung-over, or away. Torquatus trailed home, trying to look like one of the great ones of the earth, and thanking all the gods that he'd had the sense to cancel the victory party.

Chapter 7

Torquatus generally found that a hot bath and a good massage were great stress-relievers. Not today. He tried to relax so that the masseur could get on with his job, but horrifying images flooded his mind uncontrollably: his house knocked down to some jumped-up freedman in front of a group of gloating soldiers; himself on the run, begging for food and shelter. Eventually he stopped pretending to relax, dismissed the masseur and just lay in the plunge pool letting his misery wash over him with the water. When he'd done that he tried what a large cupful of his father's old Falernian would do. It was generally saved for special occasions, but since he might not be living long enough to enjoy many more of those, Torquatus decided not to bother with thrift. Neither bath nor wine helped him to work out how to find the money and then get it back. If Antonius had taken it, where would he be keeping it? In his house? At the barracks of one of his legions? With one of his intimates? How in Hades would he ever find out?

As he wasn't entertaining, he told the slaves he'd eat at a table in his study rather than in a draughty dining room. A small room next to his bedroom, it was decorated with coloured panels containing delicately-drawn temples, their columns joined by swags of flowers. Torquatus' father had had the whole suite of rooms around the garden-court built not long before he died, and they were some of the most comfortable in the house. He was reclining on his reading-couch with another cupful, waiting for dinner and trying to read Cicero's On the Nature of the Gods – so important to give the household a strong moral example – when Demetrius came in, on soft feet as always, to say that a slave wished to speak to him. From the lady Manlia.

Torquatus sat up so sharply he banged his elbow painfully on the gilded horse-head which decorated the couch's head-rest, and swore. His mind flooded with anxiety again. He had thought his sister was safe, in spite of the fact

70

that her husband, Gnaeus Ahenobarbus, had been (wrongly) named one of Caesar's assassins, tried in his absence and found guilty. His property was forfeit; his life too, if he came within reach. Luckily, Ahenobarbus was safely at sea. Soldiers had arrived at his house shortly after the verdicts were announced, but Manlia, knowing what to expect, had already collected together as much portable wealth as she could, and had fled with her stepson Lucius, aged thirteen. As far as Torquatus knew she was still sheltering in the country with Lucius' grandmother, a sister of the famous Cato.

What the slave had come to tell Torquatus was that the lady Manlia had left Porcia's house, and was even now approaching Rome, where she wished to make her home with him. She had, of course, some slaves with her. No, she was not sure for how long she wished to stay.

'And the young Lucius Domitius, is he coming too?'

'No, lord. He remains with the lady Porcia for the time being.'

Torquatus informed the man that Manlia was naturally welcome here at any time, and when he'd gone he summoned Demetrius and told him that his sister would be arriving shortly, accompanied by an unknown number of slaves, to remain indefinitely. Demetrius received the news as calmly as if he'd been asked to take a note to a neighbour's, and padded off to make the arrangements necessary for Manlia's reception.

Restless and anxious, Torquatus couldn't even pretend to settle back to his reading. Having scanned several columns with his eyes without taking anything in, he threw the scroll aside and jumped up from the couch. He wandered around the room, picking up and putting down various objects. Perhaps philosophy might not be what he needed just now? He drifted off to the library in search of some lively traveller's tale of people whose heads grew beneath their shoulders, or who lived on fermented mares' milk, or built their houses out of huge leaves, to take his mind off his worries. Demetrius, though not there - no doubt he was in the kitchen, supervising the dinner arrangements - had left evidence of his activities; neat piles of wax tablets and small scrolls arranged in date order. He had asked Torquatus' permission to arrange the family's papers, and though Torquatus himself had seen little point in the enterprise he'd told Demetrius that as long as it didn't interfere with his real work he had no objection.

'There are so many letters,' Demetrius explained. You might want to publish some of them one day: the correspondence between your noble father and Cicero, for instance.'

Torquatus thought this very far-fetched. Cicero had liked to circulate letters among his friends, and look where that had got him.

'Your son, lord,' Demetrius had pointed out. 'He might want to know the history of his family, surely?'

His son! That was looking ahead, too far ahead for Torquatus. But of course it was true: every Manlius Torquatus would want and need to know what his family had said and been over the hundreds of years of its existence. So he had given the man leave to sort out the mess of documents. Torquatus wandered over and picked one up. His brother's well-known handwriting jumped out at him, neat and tight, the lines rising slightly at the end. He felt an all-too-familiar rush of guilty emotion, but read on.

The letter was addressed to their father, and dated from the February following Torquatus' own departure from the family home four years ago. It gave an account of the tensions between commanders in Pompey's camp, and expressed irritation with the general for not controlling his followers better. Lucius expressed a desire to meet his brother on the battlefield, where he would kill him like the rat he was. He closed with some perfunctory wishes for their father's continued good health. Torquatus reflected as he read it that their father, at the time these words were written, had already been dead for more than two months.

Lucius was dead too, now; but even if he had lived the two of them would have been sworn enemies. Manlia really was all he had left. He dropped the tablet back onto its pile, disconsolate, and padded back to his study. If he was going to worry about his sister, he might as well do it in the warm.

What could have brought her back to Rome at such a ghastly time, and in such a hurry that she couldn't even give him notice? Was her safety also threatened now? So far, the Three hadn't stooped to killing the wives and mothers of the proscribed. Torquatus sloshed a bit more wine into his cup, and wondered drearily what the future held for the pair of them. Ahenobarbus' was a great name, and as an independent he would surely be an attractive recruit for the Three, or for Brutus and Cassius; if he picked the right side he would have a chance to recoup his lost fortune. There was no denying though that the Ahenobarbi had always been an outrageously unappealing lot: bad-tempered, uncouth, with a taste for violence and low life. Manlia's husband was by far the best they'd produced as yet. Even her Gnaeus, though, could irritate an edgy warlord without really trying, and if the repair of his fortunes depended on his tact there wasn't too much to be hoped for.

To take his mind off his worries, Torquatus summoned Iucundus. He thought it might be amusing to hear the boy's story. Iucundus arrived looking nervous.

'Don't worry,' Torquatus told him. 'You haven't done anything wrong. But I wondered how you came to know Latin - quite well, too. That's pretty unusual for a young man from northern Gaul. Sit down and tell me about it.' He pointed to a stool beside him.

Iucundus sat, thinking quickly. What did the master want to hear? He didn't know this man yet, had no idea what would please him, what would make him angry. He shrugged mentally. 'I am the son of a king,' he said, and flushed and bit his lip as Torquatus smiled slightly. Iucundus turned his eyes to where a pattern of overlapping circles in black and red swirled across the mosaic floor. 'It's true,' he insisted. 'And as to the Latin, my father thought that it was necessary to know the Romans' language, so he had me taught.' Iucundus didn't say that his father had hated the Romans, and had made his son learn Latin only to make it easier to outwit them. Iucundus had been a quick learner, as he was with most things.   His heart throbbed as he remembered sitting with his tutor, stumbling through a conversation in Latin; then other memories flooded in, of things that had seemed so ordinary at the time. Hunting with his father's lords in the marshes of his home and complaining about his wet feet, learning to manage a difficult horse with his father critically watching, the feel of his first sword in his hand. Torquatus idly watched the boy's profile, outlined against the lamplight, with its straight nose and firm jaw, the long lashes lying against the cheeks as the boy seemed lost in thought.   Before he had time to question Iucundus any further, however, the noise of the lady Manlia's arrival drew the pair out into the entrance hall and Iucundus, seeing the master's attention distracted, slipped away.

It was just as well the house was a big one, because Manlia brought with her not only her own women, dressers, hairdressers, the cross-eyed one who looked after her jewels, and so on and so forth, but also her steward and a group of other older slaves.   These might have been her husband's property, but Torquatus doubted the soldiers would come here demanding them.   Boxes and bags and bundles were being carried in, along with a loom, baskets full of different kinds of wool, a small citrus-wood table, several silver mirrors of various sizes, and armfuls of book-rolls.

He cocked an eyebrow at his sister. She was being carefully unwrapped from a very becoming travelling cloak edged with fur, but twisted round to laugh at him. 'Yes - before you ask - I did have to bring what's left of my household with me. I didn't feel it was fair on poor Porcia to leave them there, eating her out of house and home.'

The women had finished now, and Manlia's maid went off with a group of Torquatus' slaves, the cloak over her arm, while Torquatus led Manlia away to the warmth of his study. A slave gave her wine and pulled up a chair for her, and she nodded thanks and sat, gracefully as she did everything, a small slender woman with a cloud of dark hair that wouldn't (she said) ever do what she wanted. Torquatus smiled down at her lovingly. 'To what do I owe the honour of this visit?'

Manlia gave a little choke of laughter. 'Boredom, mainly. I can only take so long in the depths of Lucania, I'm afraid. And much as I respect Porcia, she's not exactly companionable.'

Torquatus could see that. High principles and ascetic habits don't make for a comfortable household. 'I don't think you understand how violent Rome has become.'

'It may be dangerous here,' she replied, shrugging, 'but at least I shan't rust.'

'It is. Very. And might I ask why you couldn't have written to me before you started? I mean, what if I hadn't been here?'

'Octavian's here, so I knew you'd be here too. And anyway,' - she tucked a strand of hair behind her ear, and gave another little choke of laughter - 'I knew if I asked, you'd say, don't come, you won't be safe.'

'Yes. I would.'

Manlia sipped her wine thoughtfully, then looked at Torquatus enquiringly over the rim of her cup. 'What's troubling you? You haven't fallen out with Octavian, I trust?'

'No. I've just lost of a lot of his money.'

Torquatus sat down heavily. It was such a relief to tell Manlia, the only one who'd understand. Their brother Lucius had been born when their father was still a young man, and his public career had overlapped with his father's, so that the two had seemed inseparable to Aulus, twenty-two years Lucius' junior. Vibia, old Lucius' second wife, had been proud of her children, but she was not a warm woman, and her efforts had been directed mainly to establishing a place for herself among her husband's elite friends. Until Manlia had married at fifteen she and Torquatus had felt like a little family of their own.

'What in all the gods' name were you doing with Octavian's money?'

Torquatus explained, and Manlia pursed her lips. 'I've heard he was pretty devious. So now what does he expect you to do?'

'I don't think that's fair.' He poured more wine into his cup, but Manlia shook her head when he waved the jug towards her. 'He doesn't have much choice, not if he wants to survive. He's told me to find the money – or pay it myself.'

'And it amounts to how much?'

'Well, I've calculated as best I can, that it's about eighteen million.'

'Eighteen million? You can't be serious? That's eighteen million sesterces?'

'Yes.' It was almost a relief to get the figure out into the open. 'Mind you, that's just my estimate: I've never seen what's in the chests, obviously, but the cellar was packed solid right through the new extension.'

'But?' Manlia was looking quizzical.

'Yes, there is a but.' Torquatus smiled at her quick understanding: it had always been like that between them. 'It was Octavian. When I asked him for the total - because he must have had his staff counting the money in - he reacted as if I'd made a lewd remark about his sister. He didn't call for the figures, just said he'd let me know.'

'Do you think he really didn't know? Or did he just not want to say?'

'The way it looked to me,' Torquatus said slowly, recalling the scene in Octavian's study, 'he was doing some difficult calculation. You know, trying to work out what would be best to say? Least dangerous? Least misleading?'

They sat in silence for a few moments. Then he said, 'Or maybe most misleading?'

Manlia raised her eyebrows at this, but said nothing.

'Well, I have to pay it, whatever it is.'

'How could you do that?'

'Oh, Octavian had it all off pat. I never realised quite how ferociously good his memory is. He reeled off the names of my estates, probably could give a more accurate count of my slave-household than I can myself. He tells me that if I sell it all I could raise the money Though until I know how much was there I can't do much.' He shrugged, his guts churning again.

The strand of hair that Manlia had tucked behind her ear came loose again, and she pulled it across her lips and bit it thoughtfully. Torquatus couldn't help smiling, even at such a moment: how many times had he seen her do that, as a girl and a woman? She smiled back, reminding herself of the contours of his face. Such a Roman face, brown-skinned, with large dark eyes and finely-arched brows over an emphatic nose. She hadn't seen him for too long.

'Then we'd better find it,' she said, nodding decisively.

Torquatus couldn't help laughing, and once he'd started he couldn't stop. His eyes streamed, and the stress of the day seemed to leak out of him with his tears. And when he'd finished, and was choking his last sobbing guffaws into the sleeve of his tunic, and wiping his eyes with it, he felt ashamed of his loss of control, but also curiously relieved.

He was glad to have sobered up before the slaves came in with baskets of bread and more wine and water, and delicious-smelling covered dishes that made his mouth water. Late as it was, and disastrous as the day had been, he found himself able to eat, wondering idly why food shared with someone loved and trusted should be so much pleasanter than the same food eaten alone. When the slaves had gone he filled up the wine-cups again, though well-watered by now, and Manlia wandered over to the reading-couch, where she reclined gracefully.

'Can you find the money, do you think?' Her face

was troubled.

Terror stirred in his belly again: he forced it away. 'I'll manage,' Torquatus assured her. 'I must. If only to spite mother, who would gloat so horribly if I was ruined by Octavian whom she blames for everything.' He was trying hard to keep his tone light. 'I'll start with Balbus. The money came from his house in Neapolis, after all. Then, after that, I'll need to see Antonius – and Lepidus, I suppose, though I can't see what he would gain from this. Octavian and Agrippa seemed convinced Antonius must be behind it.'

Manlia looked sceptical. 'Do you think Antonius would bother himself for eighteen million? I mean it's a huge sum, but to him – '

'They - the Three - are simply desperate for money,' Torquatus told her. 'They are talking about a tax on women's wealth, on slaves, on the roof-tiles of city houses. And he wouldn't have to lift a finger, of course: he has people to do his dirty work for him.' Torquatus stretched, yawned, and refilled his cup. 'I hope by all the gods above and below that they are wrong, because I don't like the thought of trying to get the money back if Antonius has it. I shall see Balbus tomorrow, and try and sniff out some clues.'

'And your own household?'

'No-one knew anything about it except Demetrius, whom I trust.'

She nodded. 'And the bodyguards, I suppose, if they come with you to the farm? And the farm slaves themselves?'

'I don't generally go: on the one occasion when I did I went alone. I can't find out if the farm slaves talked, of course. But keeping secrets in a house like this has always been impossible, and you can't assume the loyalty of slaves any more. Not these days, when there's money to be made, and freedom to be gained, from turning the master in.'

Manlia digested all this, then asked curiously, 'What would you do if you were – ' She waved her hand airily, evidently not quite wanting to say ruined.

'Oh, well if that happened,' Torquatus told her in as light-hearted a voice as he could manage, 'I'd run off to join Sextus Pompey in Sicily. He's said to be gathering together a number of the proscribed. Do you think I'd be fit for a naval command? It's all he has to offer – so far as anyone knows. But you? You'd have to go to mother, I suppose.'

'We'd better find the money, then, so I won't have to,' she said very firmly, and they both laughed. They drank a little, in a comfortable, thoughtful silence.

Manlia said, 'My only comfort is that Gnaeus is still at sea, so they can't harm him. Porcia won't move from Lucania. Like all Cato's family, she could see off any number of violent unwanted callers, so she should be safe. If there is any such thing any more.' She slid down a bit further on the couch, stretching out her feet closer to the brazier. 'Don't tell Gnaeus I said that, will you? He's fond of her.'

There seemed little chance that Torquatus would be able to tell Gnaeus anything for the foreseeable future, but he didn't say so. Manlia sighed and lay back. 'I thought you were quite thick with Octavian?'

Torquatus grimaced. 'Not thick enough, evidently. I'm not sure that he doesn't distrust patricians like us, just instinctively.'

'Why should he?'

'Think about it: his closest friends are all outside the senatorial class: Agrippa, Maecenas, even Salvidienus. They're young, they're nobodies. They'll never be a threat – and they know it too.'

'But he has seemed to trust you?'

'I thought he did.' Torquatus thought back over the six years he'd known Octavian. 'Now I'm not so sure. Of course, if I can get the money back, then I'll really have proved my dedication to his cause.'

Manlia stretched out an arm for her cup again, and sipped a little, thoughtfully.

'I didn't approve of it at the time, but I can see now why you changed sides. At least with hindsight, Julius was always going to win. And now you have to support his son.'

His dark eyes were sombre. 'To know that I have your support is wonderful.' He drank. 'Your Gnaeus wouldn't agree with me, I know, but in my view the republic's dead. I don't know what will come next, but I can't see these Three gracefully co-operating for long. And when they don't - well, I'm for Octavian, and with a bit of luck I'll be able to save the family.'

'Is that what you're trying to do? Save the family?'

'Of course.' Torquatus stared at her, surprised by the question. 'What else? After so many generations, all those men striving to reach the top, a history that goes back into the mists of time, I simply have to do whatever needs to be done. But if I don't find the money then it's - ,' He didn't finish the sentence, but drew his finger across his neck. He felt as if there was a cold stone in his stomach.

Manlia sat up, briskly. 'Nonsense,' she said. 'We are going to find the money, and you are on the right side, I'm sure of it.'

Torquatus nodded, reassured in spite of himself. 'Octavian's a better man than Antonius, I'm sure of that. He's got lots of ideas for how to make things better. For Rome, I mean. Antonius just wants things to be better for Antonius.'

Just then, Demetrius came in, followed by a couple of slaves. The meal had seemed to be over, but Demetrius began to refill the wine and water jugs. He signed with an imperious gesture to the other slaves, and they brought a small table and placed it before Manlia, as if she were reclining at a formal dinner, Demetrius himself laying out dishes of nuts and plump raisins, one with some warm honey-cakes, and a platter neatly stacked with apples. Manlia looked up at Demetrius as he turned to go, and said rather sharply, 'Why are you doing this? Where's Stephanus?'

He looked a little put out, and Torquatus intervened. 'Stephanus is dead,' he told her. He had completely forgotten Stephanus.

80

'Really? Well, he was old, I suppose.'

'He was. But he didn't die of old age. His body was found at the bottom of the Gemonian Steps, at dawn a few days ago.'

Manlia stared at him. 'Whatever was he doing there?'

'Nobody knows.'

Torquatus waved Demetrius away irritably and the man left the room. 'I've had more important things to think of.'

'Well, you must replace him.'

Torquatus shrugged. 'Of course I will, sometime. I haven't really missed him. Demetrius just seems to do it all; he's so quick, and he thinks of everything.'

Manlia said no more, but lay with thin lips and a deep frown on her face. Then she turned to her brother. 'You shouldn't allow your secretary to go beyond his duties like that: it's not good for the household.'

He tried to turn it into a joke. 'Thus speaks the Roman matron.'

It didn't work: she gave him a very older-sister look. 'You don't like him?'

'I don't know him: how could I when you only brought him back with you from Greece last year, and I've been in Lucania most of the time since? And anyway my liking or disliking has nothing to do with it. The steward's the head of the slave household; the others take their orders from him, or should. What must they think when they see Demetrius putting himself forward like that? You should get a new steward, one the household will respect.'

Torquatus didn't want to get into an argument, especially as he knew she was quite right, so he said pacifically, 'I will get a new man. I'll send for some slave-dealers tomorrow – after I've seen Balbus though. But we were talking about Antonius.'

Manlia seemed happy enough to let the subject of Demetrius drop. She relaxed back onto the couch, a honey-cake in her hand. 'He's a great man, isn't he? And a good general, apparently.'

'He was. He didn't do so well last year, when he was forced to flee across the alps,' he reminded her. 'Whether he still is - well, that we shall find out.'

Torquatus didn't see the thoughtful look his sister gave him as he helped himself to a handful of almonds. She slid down a little further on her couch. 'And you'll need to get married for the family to have a future, anyway, ' she said in a neutral tone.

'Oh really, Manlia. Staying alive will be enough, till I get this money back. If I get it back. I can't think of anyone suitable, anyway. Can you?'

'It's just the kind of question I love.' Her long dark eyes gleamed at him. 'I promise to give it my best attention. You find the money; I'll find you a wife.'

Torquatus shrugged and smiled. 'It's a deal. But I know which of us has the harder job.'

'But before I can do that, there's so much I need to know about you. Do you realise what a long time it is since we saw much of each other? When I married and went away you were only fourteen. And those years were hard: Gnaeus was always away fighting somewhere. I had to hold things together for him. When I heard you'd gone to fight for Caesar I couldn't believe it. Was it only when you met Octavian that you changed?'

'Not really. Of course I admired Caesar - loved the idea of him. Remember how army-mad I was as a boy, how I used to talk my tutor into letting me stand by the senate-house doors whenever those Gallic War dispatches were being read. So self-regarding, I can see that now, but at the time they were just exciting, thrilling. I wanted to be there, in Gaul, not doing my lessons in boring old Rome. Even father admitted, though it nearly choked him, that they were beautifully written. And then Caesar came to call.'

'Caesar came here? I don't believe it.' She shivered.

'Are you cold? Shall I get the slaves to see to the

brazier?'

'Oh no. It was just thinking of Caesar. He was horrible, you know.'

'Horrible?' Torquatus stared at her. 'Whatever do you mean?'

Manlia was amused. 'No, you wouldn't know, would you? Except that you do know - you must - what a reputation he had. All those mistresses.'

'Oh, that. Well, yes, of course.'

'It's not very pleasant, having to share a dining-couch with a man like that. Especially when your husband's away: it can make you feel dreadfully vulnerable.' She looked down, rearranged some folds of her dress. Torquatus saw her swallow rather hard. Then he thought he must have been mistaken as she looked up again, her eyes full of laughter. 'Anyway it was nothing.'

Torquatus was horrified. 'I never thought - I didn't know - What did you do?'

'Oh, I just made myself look a bit prim. Very much the Roman matron, that kind of thing. He didn't persist, of course; he was far too experienced for that. But it put me off him. And I still can't believe Father could ever have invited him here.'

'Not here: the villa at Baiae. Do you remember how Caesar's soldiers mutinied and he galloped off down to Capua to get them back in line: no, perhaps you wouldn't They were marching to Rome, if I remember rightly, but hadn't got very far. He came to see us on the way back: I think Father asked him.'

'Father asked him? Oh, come on, Aulus, Father couldn't have done that. He loathed the man and everything he stood for, particularly because he wasn't some new man, some upstart with no manners from the provinces, but a son of one of Rome's oldest patrician families - well, you know what he thought. I've no doubt you could give the rest of the speech as well as I can.'

Torquatus was laughing. 'Even better, I should

think. You married and went away. I was left to listen to it, day after day. And I can see what you mean about him inviting Caesar: I can only suppose Father had some faint hope of saving Lucius. How terrible must it be, to see your adored eldest son heading for disaster?'

'But surely he was convinced the republican side would win?'

'I think not. Not once Pompey himself was dead. But anyway, perhaps it wasn't he who asked, but Caesar.' He shrugged. 'Equally unlikely, wouldn't you say?'

Manlia shook her head doubtfully. 'I didn't see any of this. I was just glad Gnaeus hadn't been killed. Too busy with my domestic duties, I suppose.' She brushed a few crumbs onto the floor and helped herself to another little honey cake, but shook her head when Torquatus held out the wine jug. 'So what happened?'

'Everyone was keyed up, waiting for Caesar,' he told her. 'Even mother had called a truce in her long war of attrition against father.'

'There was a war? I don't remember that.'

'No? I suppose it happened after you were married. He'd taken one of her weaving-women as a mistress. He never said, but I should think he regretted it pretty quickly. Mother was furious. He got the girl pregnant, too. And of course the child was just another vexation: every time Mother saw him she was offended all over again.'

'Oh, I do remember her making rather critical remarks about Papa, but she would never say what it was all about. But you know, although she and I were both in Rome for much of the time, I didn't see much of her. We didn't like each other much, I'm afraid. Father used to come round to my house, and I got on really well with him at that time, difficult as he could be: she didn't.'

Torquatus, thinking back, could see what she meant. With his sons, old Lucius had been stern, demanding, forcing them into the mould of the Roman gentleman. With Manlia, his only daughter, he was different. He remembered how as a small child he had seen Manlia kissed and hugged by their father. He felt again the sharp pang of jealousy. Then of course she had come running to him and had kissed him in his turn, and the hurt had gone away, or seemed to. Later, their father had been immensely proud of Manlia's marriage with the proud and wealthy Ahenobarbus, and had delighted in visiting her husband's house, so much more agreeable than his own.

'Go on,' she was saying.

'Oh, yes, Caesar. I must say I was disappointed at first. He was old, and not really at all heroic-looking. I don't know what I'd expected: Hercules with his lion-skin and club, or something. You know what boys are. But this was an ageing, harassed-looking man with a nasty comb-over. But I only saw him that way for a moment, before I felt his power. He walked in with a group of men, secretaries, I think, and one or two soldiers. Typical of him, now I come to think of it: he always made such a big thing of not having a bodyguard, but I don't remember ever seeing him without at least a soldier or two. He and Father went off to talk, once the greetings were over. And it was only then that I noticed the fair boy Caesar had brought with him. I couldn't place him at all, but he looked about my age, or maybe a bit younger, so I sat down to talk to him. He didn't seem very interested in the food and wine, but obviously shared my hero-worship of his Uncle Caesar.'

'Great-uncle, wasn't he?'

'Father, now, and he's called Caesar too, don't forget. He never does.'

'And he's turning out to be even more dangerous than his daddy.'

Torquatus couldn't help looking about: he thought he'd seen the curtain twitch, just a tiny bit, and got up to draw it back sharply. There was no-one, of course, the colonnade outside was empty, bleak and windy, long black pillar-shadows lying slantwise across it. Only the slave Iucundus was huddled against one of the pillars, waiting for orders. He came back into the warm room, sat down again, and mixed himself another cup.

'I never knew what they discussed. But before Caesar left Father gave him a slave-girl, the one he'd sent to him the evening before. What was her name? Oh, I don't know. It doesn't matter, anyway. Mother was particularly delighted as the girl was Father's fancy-piece. The whole mood suddenly lightened, just as Caesar was leaving, and I'd even begun to hope I might be allowed to serve under Caesar.'

'And then you and Father fell out?'

'Yes.' Torquatus still found it hard to talk about the dreadful scene that had torn the house apart. 'I was young, of course, didn't think to give Father time. So I just jumped straight in, told him I wanted to fight for Caesar.'

'And he was furious?'

'I'd never seen him in such a rage. Mother tried to calm him down, but he wasn't listening. He threw me out, said he would disinherit me. So there I was, with no slaves and nothing but what I stood up in, hitching a lift to Rome as a November night came on.' Torquatus was back in that awful time, cold and lonely - and furiously angry. He forced his knees to stop shaking.

'How did you get to Rome?'

'I slept in a barn the first night, and the next morning I was picked up by a farmer going to Rome with cheeses for the market, so I was lucky there. I had no money, but he was generous enough to take me anyway. I had thought I would come to you, but I had time to think, riding along in that cart, and I realised I didn't want to drag you into my quarrel. I decided to go to Octavian. His stepfather Philippus took me in and treated me with great kindness. You'd have thought I was just another friend of his stepson's, dropping in for a visit.'

Torquatus raised his cup to his lips again, remembering that time, when for all his unhappiness he'd basked in the warmth of Octavian's mother Atia and in the energy and bustle of that great house, at the heart of Roman political life in a way that Torquatus' own had ceased to be.

He emerged from his reverie to see that Demetrius had come in again and was clearing away the dishes. Torquatus signed to him to leave the wine. 'Octavian lent me money, Caesar gave me work preparing for his campaign. I never looked back. But I never heard from Father again; only Mother wrote to me, saying that Father had been taken ill shortly after I'd left, and that I should stay away, for fear of making him worse. I was just about to go off to Africa with Caesar, anyway. I don't believe he'd ever have seen me again, and I couldn't have gone to the funeral, even if I had been there.'

'But he didn't disinherit you?'

'No. Whether he didn't get round to it, or he changed his mind, I don't know.' Torquatus' laughter sounded harsh in his own ears. 'So here I am, in Father's place, ruling Father's house, the family reprobate.'

'But it was Father's heart that failed, wasn't it? And that could have happened at any moment. His doctor told me at the funeral, it had been irregular for some years. So you can't blame yourself for his death.'

'I know. But I do. And Lucius never forgave me either.'

'Aulus, you can't know that.'

'I think I do. When I got home finally, after the fighting was all over, I found a last letter from Lucius waiting for me; Philip had brought back what he could find of Lucius' papers. It was a long one, and I didn't read it. I didn't need to: when I asked Philip if he knew what it said, he squirmed, poor man.' Torquatus became aware of Demetrius, standing still right next to him. 'What do you want?' he asked, and the man seemed to give a little start, before saying, 'Shall I take the wine-jug, master?'

'No. I told you before, just leave it. Anyway, we'll be going to bed soon.'

When he'd gone Torquatus lay back with a sigh. 'So

you see - .'

'What I see is a beloved brother, a man of intelligence and ambition, a quaestor, high in Octavian's favour – .' She glanced at Torquatus, and stopped, but only for a moment. 'Tomorrow we will work out how to get the money back.' Her eyes were bright, her mouth resolute. 'And look – why are you sleeping in a room facing onto the garden colonnade? You'd be much safer in one of the rooms off the gallery upstairs. The slaves can easily make you a bed up there, and you could have one of them to sleep at your door? That boy you've just hired; that's what he's for, isn't it? Because you have an enemy, that's clear. And we can't be sure he isn't in this house.' She stopped, gulping back tears. Torquatus got up from his chair, and Manlia stood too, slowly, as if she was uncertain what her brother was going to do. She needn't have worried. All he wanted was to hug her close, breathe in her familiar scent, and thank the gods that there was at least one person in his life whom he could trust absolutely.

Chapter 8

The next morning Torquatus felt restless and impatient. If he could have told his clients not to bother him, he'd have done it: but where would an aristocratic Roman be without clients? At last their tiresome demands had all been met, and Torquatus was able to set off for the house of Balbus, from whose house in Neapolis the money had been brought. He took the litter this time, and as it jogged along he gloomily made a mental list of his problems. The money was the big one, the one he simply had to solve and was no nearer solving after a night's broken sleep and hideous dreams. Even the strange death of his steward seemed trivial by comparison. He reflected grimly that if he didn't find the money he wouldn't even have a household, and decided to concentrate on what he wanted from Balbus.

At that time Balbus lived on the Carinae. It's a convenient location for a senator, though the very best addresses are on the Palatine. On the Carinae, every house was overshadowed by Pompey's great palace on its crest, which at this point was the home of Antonius. Balbus' house, however, was far more modest: neither so old as to remind the observer that its current owner had no distinguished ancestors, no wax masks, no triumphal ornaments arranged outside his door or in his reception hall, nor so grand as to point to the tasteless extravagance of the arriviste. Instead it was the solid, comfortable residence of the wealthy eques, the status of knight being what Balbus had chosen. As one of Julius' intimate friends and his favourite fixer he could have had a senatorial career, but as a Spaniard he could never have got to the top. So he had preferred instead to stay outside politics, sitting at the centre of a complex web of money and connections, aware of every vibration.

The litter came to a halt, and was set down gently. The curtain was drawn back rattling on its rings and the black face of one of the litter-men appeared in the opening.

He offered a hand to his master, and Torquatus climbed out of the litter into the quiet street. Demetrius uncurled himself from the other seat and followed him. Two immaculate bay trees in splendid Greek pots flanked the black doors. The two or three shallow steps up to them were spotless. They were admitted by Balbus' doorman, leaving the litter-slaves to wait outside, and Torquatus was shown, by a beautiful and very supercilious young slave, into what was evidently Balbus' study. The walls were lined with pigeon-holes, each containing a scroll, a neat tag hanging from it for identification. Torquatus was just wondering what Balbus read when the man himself bustled in. 'A sad business, a sad business,' he said, shaking the visitor's hand.

The slave had pulled up a splendid ebony chair with bronze lion-heads on the arms. When Torquatus was seated Balbus glanced around, and for a moment Torquatus thought he intended to sit at the magnificent table that dominated the room. But after a moment's hesitation he signed to a slave to bring up another chair. A small table appeared at each man's side, and on it a silver jug of wine and a small crystal one of water were silently placed. Then the slaves stood back without a word.

'I shall be glad to offer you any help I can, though since the money was not taken from my house – ' Balbus began. 'Please tell me what happened. Octavian only told me that it had gone.'

Torquatus told the story, as far as anyone knew it. 'Of course,' he finished, 'what I need from you is any detail that might help me find the thief. How the money was stored and sent, for instance.'

Balbus frowned and put down his cup with a decisive little click. 'I can't see how those details can help you. As far as my staff were concerned, everything went as normal: the consignment was sent off two days before the Nones of December, and arrived, as I understand, the next day. Everything on time and as requested.'

'The drivers were your own?'

90

'They are. And the mules and carriages all belong to me. My staff didn't report anything unusual about this consignment at all.'

'And you would consider them reliable?'

Balbus raised his little dark eyebrows. 'They've been with me for years. Besides, as I say, the – the incident didn't occur while the money was under their care, did it?'

It was easy enough to see why he kept stressing this, of course, but Torquatus pressed on. 'Could you tell me how these consignments are sent off? Do you order it personally?'

Balbus sighed and leaned back a little into his chair, which creaked slightly in protest. 'I wouldn't generally bother with individual shipments like that. Certainly not. I meet my chief accountant regularly, to give him an overview of what's coming up. My chief secretary too. They then arrange all the necessary details. Of course there are systems in place for recording the receipt and dispatch of all monies. But as it happens I am kept informed of all transactions on Octavian's account. And as you can imagine, I employ none but the most discreet men.'

'What happens to – well, let's say, the less discreet,' Torquatus asked.

'They find themselves back at the slave market before they know it. And that would be for a careless error. If I were to find, for instance, that someone had informed anyone outside my house about any of my activities, they would die. I assure you of it.' He looked at Torquatus sombrely. 'Money is a serious business, believe me. Julius didn't reward me because of my pretty face' – and indeed his face was smooth and plump and not especially attractive – 'but because he knew that I was discreet and reliable. And honest.'

'All the same, I'd be glad if you would question your staff in case someone has, accidentally, of course, let information out.'

Balbus became very still, and his large, mournful

eyes seemed to observe Torquatus with melancholy interest. His visitor was content to wait, and sat quietly, savouring the wine, which was superb. It was a shame to water it as much as he had, but he needed a clear head.

'Very well. Not that I expect anything to come of it, you understand. And what happens if you don't find the money?'

Torquatus told him and he winced. 'So difficult to sell property just now,' he murmured. 'Many men who could afford to buy another house or an estate, men who would love to pick up some art works, are held back by fear. If they are rich enough to buy, they are rich enough to be proscribed. Some have even come asking for advice on taking money abroad. You'd be surprised how many people are looking for investment opportunities in Bithynia, or Massilia, or Rhodes. I should advise holding on, dear boy.'

Torquatus couldn't help smiling. 'I wish you would tell Octavian that.'

Balbus shot him a shrewd glance. 'But he trusts you, I'm sure.' There was the faintest question in his tone.

'Are you? One of his strengths, I'd say, is that he is slow to trust people, though I agree that when he does - think of Agrippa, for instance - he seems to do it fully.'

Balbus was turning his wine-cup round in his fat little hands, as if contemplating a purchase. 'You were with Octavian when he came back after Julius' death, weren't you: I remember meeting you in Neapolis, as you were on your way to Rome. And if I remember rightly you all stayed in a house of your family's when you landed in Brundisium?'

'We did. Octavian thought best to hold back till we could see which way the wind was blowing, and the place was ideal for that. My father bought it years ago, after he'd been governor of Macedonia and owned property there. Seemed to be always sailing off to Greece, he said, so he might as well have a house near the port, and avoid the noise and fleas of the local inns.'

'And I have heard from Octavian that you gave him

a great deal of help last summer?'

'I did what I could, yes. What any friend would do.'

Balbus' glance was shrewd, and Torquatus felt oddly embarrassed, as if he were a commodity the other man might buy.

'I think the help you gave to Octavian's mother and sister went a little further than that, didn't it? Atia and Octavia were in real danger from the Senate, and feared they might be held hostage?'

'They did, and I advised them to take refuge with the Vestal Virgins. That's all.'

'I heard that you gave them a military escort?'

'No. I had no soldiers under my command, but I walked from Atia's house with them, so that they had the protection of my slaves.'

'Thus clearly identifying yourself as Octavian's man.' Balbus leaned back, satisfied, but Torquatus sat very straight. 'I'm not anyone's man. I'm a Manlius Torquatus, I don't need to belong to anyone but myself.' The words came out sharper than he'd intended, and to cover his slight embarrassment he took another mouthful of the Falernian. 'This is splendid.' He sniffed the aroma appreciatively.

Balbus smiled, rather smugly. 'I liked the wine so much I bought the vineyard.' He took a delicate sip and regarded his visitor carefully over the rim of his wine-cup. 'I'd say what you did last summer makes you trustworthy.'

'I'd say so too. But it's not my opinion that counts here, or yours.'

'And you've been acting as quaestor in charge of the Treasury. Though there can't be much in the Treasury for you to supervise?' Balbus' large dark eyes were mournful again. Obviously the thought of empty money-chests was painful to him, even if they weren't his own.

'Very little indeed.'

They sat for a moment in silence. Torquatus still hadn't really got what he wanted from Balbus; he wasn't sure why. 'Could you give me the details, then, of exactly how this transport would have been organised?'

Balbus gave a plump shrug and sighed. 'It was, as I've said, just like all the other times.'

'You were there? In Neapolis? When were the orders given?'

'I must have been there, I think.' He turned to the slave behind his chair. 'Get that date, will you?' He turned back to Torquatus. 'I was down there until a few days ago. It wouldn't have made any difference, however. My men are perfectly accustomed to organising a job of this sort.' He was beginning to sound slightly irritated, Torquatus noted.

'So you gave the instructions to your secretary? In writing, or verbally?'

'Oh, verbally. He took notes, but anyway he knew what needed doing.' The slave had come back and spoke quietly in his master's ear. 'The orders for the transfer were given on the day before the Kalends of December.'

'Thank you. So on that day he will have gone and spoken to – whom?'

'The manager of the transport side of things, Dionysius. He controls the movements of the carriages and drivers, keeps everyone's hours, that sort of thing. Menodorus - that's my secretary - will have told him the day and time and the amount to be taken. And then he'll have passed the information to my chief accountant down there, to make sure the money was available when wanted.'

'And was it in coin or bullion? Sounds odd, perhaps, but I've never actually seen one of those chests opened.'

'Oh, mostly bullion. It's much easier to carry it that way, and it can be minted easily enough in Rome. Just how much money was stolen? I gather it was more than just the last delivery.'

'Unfortunately, yes. I think that in all it was about eighteen million.'

Balbus winced. 'Jupiter!'

'That's the best estimate I can make.' For a moment

Torquatus wondered whether to ask Balbus exactly how much money had been sitting under his farm: he couldn't believe the man wouldn't be able to conjure up the figure, to the last sestertius, with a snap of his fingers to a slave. But Octavian's hesitation had made him cautious. The two men sat in a wary silence, until Torquatus, deciding there was nothing more to be gained, roused himself. 'You say your manager would have done this or that. Have you checked whether that was the case?'

'No, but I can, of course.' He didn't sound enthusiastic.

'Thank you. It's possible that I might wish to interview them myself. Formally, as Treasury Quaestor, you understand.'

'The money didn't come from the Treasury, did it? It wasn't public funds.' Balbus got up suddenly, the slave stepping back quickly to make room for him. He walked over to the document-wall and tugged at a couple of the scroll tags to straighten them. He turned to face Torquatus again. 'I believe you saw the drivers yourself?'

'I did. I spoke to them just as they were leaving my place.'

'Do you generally do that? You must have had some slaves with you?'

'I've made a habit of riding over to the farm after each delivery, to check that the money is securely stored, but this is the first time I've seen the men leaving. And I didn't have any slaves with me.' Torquatus was annoyed at this attempt to put the blame onto his household.

Balbus didn't give up. 'It wasn't stored securely enough, it seems.'

Torquatus was on his feet too now and the two men stood watching each other warily. 'As well as it could be, in such a place,' Torquatus insisted. 'Octavian laid the blame on me. But I told him when he first hatched this scheme that the farm would be an easy target.'

'I told him too.' Balbus shook his head.

'Did you?'

'Yes. I thought it would be far safer to send the money all at once, well-guarded, and put it into the Treasury. He refused.'

The Treasury? That suggested Balbus thought the money was part of the public funds, rather than personal donations to Octavian.

'No, no, no!' Balbus reared back in alarm when Torquatus suggested this. He sat down again rather heavily, reached for his wine-cup and took a few hasty sips.

'Transparency was all I had in mind, dear boy; and then of course Octavian – Caesar, I mean – uses all his money for the state's benefit anyway, you know, so it really makes very little difference where it is kept.'

He gave Torquatus a look of limpid innocence. But that last statement was arguable to say the least; and when bankers start talking about transparency it's time to count the spoons. Torquatus decided to push a little harder.

'Can you clarify for me exactly where the money you held for Caesar had come from?' he asked.

The dark eyes were hooded now. 'You will have seen for yourself how many donations came in last spring.'

'Indeed. But that can't have been all? There were two major sources of funds, I believe? The war chest I know was sent to you. What about the revenues from Asia?'

'Ah, yes.' He paused, and took a careful sip at his wine, almost as if he feared it might be poisonous. 'The revenues amounted to 25,000 talents.'

'Great gods! Don't you think it odd that were they sent to you? Shouldn't they have simply gone to the Treasury?'

Torquatus wondered how much harder he dared push: Balbus was hugely powerful, after all. But the man was definitely looking a little uneasy. 'You'd need to ask Antonius that. The money was sent on his authority as consul.' I knew already that Antonius had authorised the transfer: I'd seen the letter myself. 'I am simply the holding agent, the banker, you understand. No doubt there are political motivations for a good deal of what happened last year.' His eyes were hooded and impossible to read.

'Well, yes.' That was a statement of the obvious, but Balbus sat back and took a larger slug of wine, as if feeling that he had acquitted himself quite creditably.

'Some of what came to my farm was from the war-chest?'

Balbus nodded. 'All that money Julius had collected together for supplies and pay in his war against the Parthians.' He shook his head sadly. 'A dreadful loss to Rome. No-one else could have contemplated such a campaign. Imagine all the wealth of Parthia, pouring into Rome's coffers.'

Torquatus refused to imagine it. 'And part of that war chest was sitting under my farm? It certainly didn't go back to the Treasury. And yet it must have come from there in the first place?'

'Some of it did.' Suddenly Balbus was all eagerness to explain. 'But most of it didn't. Julius had been building it up at his own house. He was convinced that it was safer that way, his house being so well-guarded.'

Torquatus nodded grimly. It was Julius who had set the precedent here: or rather, two precedents. First, that a man with an army could force Treasury officials to hand over state funds at the sword's point. Second, that state receipts could simply be diverted into his own coffers before the Treasury had even seen them. No wonder the bloody Treasury was empty!

'So you, presumably, are left with the revenues from Asia. Unless that's been shifted too?'

His face was bland. 'I still have some of it. Antonius has sent letters demanding portions of it. The last quite recently.'

Even Balbus' no doubt capacious vaults must have been overflowing, with not only the donations to Octavian's cause but also such an enormous quantity of the taxes from

Asia – some of the last to be sent to Italy, Torquatus
supposed, before they were diverted by Brutus and Cassius.
It was odd, come to think of it, that Antonius had sent it to
Balbus, who wasn't close to him, and even odder that he'd so
vehemently denied having done so, afterwards.

'Is Antonius still keeping his own accounts with
you?' he asked.

'I shouldn't really be talking to you about my
clients.'

Torquatus looked at him and waited.   Balbus
shrugged. 'Not any more. It was difficult, after Julius died.
Antonius expected that those of us who'd served Caesar
would support him in the same way, and had he been
Caesar's heir, as many of us were expecting, the situation
would have been straightforward. I had a difficult choice to
make: I knew Antonius well, but finally I reckoned that my
duty lay with Octavian.' Balbus got up again and paced over
to the window. 'I had a painful scene with Antonius when I
had to tell him that I wouldn't take his side against the young
Caesar, or back him when he wanted to come to an
agreement with Julius' murderers.'

'Why did Antonius send the tax revenues to you,
then, do you suppose?'

'I've no idea. Why don't you ask him? Without, it
goes without saying, mentioning this conversation.'

And that was all Torquatus could discover. It wasn't
much: Balbus' management sounded as competent as he'd
expected it to be, and it was highly unlikely that information
about the money had come from Neapolis. As he was
carried home Torquatus reflected that the next day's task
must be to interview Antonius. A far harder task.

That evening, sitting over their wine after dinner
once again, he told Manlia what he had learned from Balbus.

'Which is almost nothing,' she pointed out.

'Quite.' He couldn't help sounding a little sour. He
felt he needed support, not criticism. 'One or two things did

strike me, afterwards. Maybe I shouldn't give up hope of finding a leak from Neapolis: he was so very insistent on the subject of his own efficiency that that I wondered if he might be trying to reassure himself.'

Manlia considered this, helping herself to a handful of almonds as she did so. 'Possible, I suppose. What was the other thing?'

'Well, he became extremely cagy when I tried to pin him down on the source of all that money. But it was probably nothing more than his habitual caution.' Torquatus rolled his eyes. 'And tomorrow I have to tackle Antonius. Make offerings for me, will you?'

'I will.'

They sat for a few moments in silence.

'While you were trying to squeeze information out of Balbus,' Manlia said, sitting up and hugging her knees, 'I was picking up the threads with some of the senatorial ladies of my acquaintance, at Postumia's, just down the road.'

'She's Annalis' widow, isn't she?' Torquatus asked, picking out a handful of almonds from the bowl. 'And did you find out anything useful?' Torquatus didn't really expect the answer to be yes.

'I'm not sure. There are so many stories flying about at the moment. You know the kind of thing: tales of heroic wives saving their husbands from proscriptions, or even better, tales of heroic slaves offering their lives for their masters. Very reassuring. Then there are the tales of treachery, men betrayed by their families, that kind of thing. Hard to know what's true, and what isn't. They've all suffered, though. Aemilia, she was too ill to come. She's Ligarius' widow, and is starving herself to death. You know what happened to her?' Torquatus shook his head. 'She hid her husband when he was proscribed, telling no-one where he was except for one of her maids, and then only because she needed the woman's help in keeping him fed. The maid then informed on him, sold her master's life. After Ligarius was dragged from his hiding-place and murdered, Aemilia went down to the tribunal and begged the Three to kill her too, saying that since she'd hidden Ligarius she was subject to the same penalties. That's the rule, isn't it? Antonius, who was there, begged her to go away; so now, as I say, she's starving herself.

She took a deep breath. 'Flavia was at Postumia's: Septimius' widow, who married again the very day Septimius died, I heard. Postumia's not seen her since, not till today that is. I think Flavia must have had some very strong reason for going to Postumia's, because the others were pretty hostile towards her. I wondered what she wanted.'

'Why? What did they say?' Torquatus asked.

'Nothing. Nothing at all. They just cut her, really. Anyone else would have left, and I wondered why she didn't.'

Torquatus wasn't sure he even knew Septimius. He had a vague picture in his mind of a tall man, a bit overweight, red-faced; not a senator of any great significance.

'She was trying to be friendly, insisting that she would read a letter from her sister which would make them laugh, but when her freedman Celer gave it to her it was the wrong letter. She blushed and looked really awkward for a moment, before telling him he was a fool, and giving it back to him. As he put it back in his bag I saw the seal, and it was Antonius'. You know the one: Hercules with his club. He always uses it, doesn't he?'

'Are you sure? She had a letter from Antonius?'

'One that embarrassed her,' Manlia agreed. 'Oh, and Iunia came in.'

'Iunia? Lucius' widow? Really? What was she doing there?'

'Getting away from Mother, I expect. She's a friend of Postumia's, has been for years. She seemed very nervous, even more anxious than the others. She said Rebilus had been buying some ex-gladiators, and she would borrow some of them to guard her house.'

'Rebilus? Who's he?'

'Iunia's lover: didn't you know that?'

'No. No idea she had such a thing. Do they talk politics, these ladies?'

'They were today. Sextus Pompey was mentioned, and everyone looked at each other as if wondering whether to start a conversation.'

'And did anyone?'

No,' Manlia admitted. 'There was just an uncomfortable little silence. You know some people are saying that Sextus Pompey might be invited back to Rome once Octavian and Antonius are away dealing with Brutus and Cassius?'

'Yes, and the Age of Gold might return, when no-one needed to do any work because the earth simply poured out its bounty unasked. Only a complete idiot could believe a word of it. The gods know the Senate hasn't behaved very intelligently recently, but even they can hardly have failed to notice that Lepidus is staying in Rome. He's a perfectly competent general, is as ruthless as the other two, and will have quite sufficient troops to keep Rome quiet.'

'You don't think he could be involved in it too, do you?'

'In what?'

'Well, if people wanted to invite Sextus Pompey back to Rome, he'd have to be in any plot.'

'No.' On this Torquatus was quite clear. The mere idea of Lepidus' involvement was just ridiculous. He was at the apex of his career, and wasn't about to jeopardise it.

'Oh very well.' Manlia laughed, got up and stretched. 'I'm going to bed, and so should you. We have a busy day tomorrow.'

'I have an important interview,' he agreed, standing up too.

'And I'd really like to get that new steward in place. Do you mind if I look for one?'

'If there's anything left of me after Antonius has chewed me up and spat me out, I'll be available to interview staff.' Torquatus stretched. Gods! He'd completely forgotten about the murder of old Stephanus. In normal times, the household would have been convulsed by such a death.

Manlia looked a little guilty. 'I thought you'd say that.'

'So?' Torquatus prompted her.

'So I've told the best dealers to come here tomorrow with any likely candidates. You can see them once I've weeded out the rubbish.' Torquatus grinned, and didn't argue. One thing about having an older sister is that you get used, while still wearing a little boy's purple-bordered toga, to being bossed around. He put on a sententious face and quoted Cato at her: 'You remember: "We rule the world, and our wives rule us." He should have included sisters.' He gave her a kiss and turned to leave the room. But before he'd reached the door-curtain he looked back.

'You haven't seen my wax tablets, have you?'

'Wax tablets? I don't think so. What are they like?'

'They're good ones, that Father used to use. About the size of my hand, in an ivory case, with silver corners and a little silver chain to fasten them.'

'Oh, I remember those. No, I've not seen them. Did they have anything important in them?'

'No. Nothing at all, in fact, as I'd just had them rewaxed. No doubt they'll turn up somewhere.'

Chapter 9

Antonius' house at that time was a monstrous great palace. Pompey the Great had been a most dreadful show-off, and it was he who had built the thing, and filled it with all the gold, ivory and coloured marble his immense resources could command. Antonius, who never really had a lot of taste, added more of the same. So not only was Torquatus anxious about the reception his enquiries were likely to receive, he was dazzled by the sparkle of rock crystal and precious stones, and the duller gleam of gold attached to any suitable surface, and some unsuitable ones. He left the slaves outside, except for Demetrius, and trod up the wide shallow steps to a front door which would have done honour to a small town.

It didn't help that Torquatus was left to wait for the great man in what the slave had said was his study, but which, he thought, looked more like the kind of throne-room from which an eastern king might dispense justice. As he did so he could feel a speech coming on, about how our ancestors had lived frugally, content to eat the produce of their own simple farms etcetera etcetera etcetera. This did nothing at all to lift his mood.

But as he looked around he was forced to modify his views. True, if all this gaudy ornament had been auctioned off, the proceeds would have paid an army for a year or two. But there was also every sign that the owner was engaged in serious activities, and took them seriously. Leather-bound boxes stood along one wall, each filled with document-rolls and sets of wax tablets. Scrolls were arranged in rows of cubby-holes above the boxes. There was every appearance of system here. This might only mean that the man had competent secretaries, but as he waited Torquatus remembered a conversation he had had with Faberius, Caesar's freedman-secretary, who had been co-opted into Antonius' service after Caesar's death. Faberius had said that when Antonius took charge after the

103

assassination he had been very thorough indeed, for all his reputation as a hard-drinking, womanising waster. That might have meant no more than that he wanted to be sure not to miss anything that could be appropriated to his own advantage. But his actions since Julius' death had been by no means those of a stupid man. How was he going to feel about a mere quaestor asking him awkward questions?

His musings were interrupted as the great man came in. Antonius was a tall, heavily-built man, who really looked his best in armour, and who tended to put on weight in peacetime. His heavy body and slightly too-short legs made him look a little absurd in a toga. Which was no doubt one reason why he always wore armour whenever circumstances allowed, and sometimes when they didn't. Today he was in a toga, and his face was grim.

'Now then, you'd better tell me what all this is supposed to be about. I gather the Boy's lost some money, or you've lost it for him, and you want to blame me. That's an impertinence in itself. Your evidence?'

His eyes were hard, his shoulders set. Torquatus' worst fears were confirmed. How in Jupiter's name did he know all this? The polite note Torquatus had sent him yesterday simply requested a few minutes of his time at his earliest convenience. His information certainly wouldn't have come from Octavian. Well, that question could wait. Torquatus had never imagined that he'd get anything like an admission of guilt: if the man had set his heavies onto the farm, he certainly wouldn't be talking about it. The best Torquatus had hoped for was that Antonius' men had acted without authorisation, and that he might think maintaining his relationship with Octavian was worth more than the money. Now even that seemed optimistic.

'No-one knows where the money's gone, or who was responsible,' he began quietly.

Antonius, sitting at his desk as if he were interviewing a new clerk, was beginning to annoy him. Torquatus paused, forcing himself to at least look calm.

'May I ask how you knew what I wanted to see you about?'

'No.'

Gods!   This was going to be heavy going.
Torquatus decided to try surprise. 'I would be glad to know
what your relations with Balbus are these days.' He might as
well ask directly. Tact was clearly not going to work here.
But nor would openness, he feared, seeing Antonius' face
darken.

'I can't imagine what business that is of yours, or
anyone's, but I can assure you that Balbus and I are on
perfectly cordial terms.'

'I am asking because the missing money had come
up from Neapolis and I wondered whether anyone from
outside Balbus' own establishment might have become aware
of the planned movements.'

'Your implication being, I suppose, that I might
have been tempted to stage some sort of bandit raid to get
my hands on it. How much was it anyway?'

'Around eighteen million, I believe.'

'You believe?'   Antonius leant forward across the
table, pouncing on the slight uncertainty in Torquatus' voice.

Torquatus did not flinch, or cease to meet Antonius'
eyes. 'It was the whole of one delivery plus what was already
being stored.'

'How in Hades' name did it come to be at your
house at all?'

Torquatus chose to take the question literally. 'It
came in small quantities, each being transported in two or
three mule carriages. No guards.'

Antonius threw himself back in his chair. 'And you
are seriously implying that I might be tempted to criminal
activity to get my hands on a mere eighteen million?' He
seemed genuinely surprised.

'I'm not implying anything.' Torquatus was holding
his temper on a tight rein, speaking with calm deliberation,
and (he hoped) looking relaxed.   'If someone heard
something they shouldn't, they might have quite innocently

mentioned it to a third party.'

Antonius went on the attack again. 'Oh, so now my slaves and freedmen are corrupt and venal, and maybe not even working in my interest; or else they're too stupid to know when something should be kept secret. Is that it?'

'Not at all – ' Torquatus began, but he cut in, in a biting tone. 'When you find this stupid and talkative person, I'd be glad if you'll give me his name. I don't keep untrustworthy staff, believe me.'

'Do any of your staff visit Balbus' house in Neapolis?'

Antonius stared at Torquatus as if he were a cockroach that had unaccountably appeared on his dinner-table. 'At times they have done.'

'Could you tell me when?' Torquatus asked politely.

Antonius frowned, and for a moment Torquatus thought he would simply refuse, then clapped his hands and the slave who had let Torquatus in appeared at once. 'Send me Timotheus,' he demanded, and a man with the neat appearance of a secretary came into the room. Torquatus wondered if Antonius had always expected to have to produce him, and if so, why? Had he known already that the money had come from Balbus' house?

'When did we last do business with Balbus in Neapolis?' Antonius snapped.

'Not for some months, lord. If I remember correctly it was in August last year that you last had regular dealings with him.'

'Very well. You may go.' The man bowed and left. Torquatus watched Demetrius, uncomfortably perched on a stool at his feet, make a note of this, and reflected that by August of the previous year the antagonism between the Senate, Antonius and Octavian had become increasingly clear. It must have been then that Balbus had finally chosen to throw in his lot with Octavian. But if Antonius was no longer close to Balbus, how could he have heard about the movements of cash to Rome?

'Timotheus said "regular" dealings,' Torquatus pointed out. 'Does that mean there might have been other contacts?'

'There has been no business done with Balbus.' Antonius' voice was curt. Clearly Torquatus wasn't going to get anywhere on that subject. Torquatus decided to try another tack. 'One thing I'm not certain of is the origin of all the money that Balbus was holding - ,' he began.

'You're not alone.' Antonius' face suddenly flushed red, and his voice rose. 'Balbus was holding on to state money, money that should have gone to the Treasury. But when I tried to get him to give it up he pretended I'd sent it to him myself, oh, yes, and sent more letters ordering its release. Then he closed down on me: couldn't discuss state finances without Octavian's and Lepidus' agreement, he said. Balbus is no more than a criminal, but of course the Boy – ' he almost spat out his favourite epithet for Octavian – 'protects him, and Lepidus apparently owes him too, so I'm powerless to act.' His face became ugly. 'For the moment, at least. I hope there'll be a reckoning between me and Balbus one day.' He relapsed into a brooding silence, his flush subsiding. Then rousing himself, he clapped again.

'Why haven't you brought wine?' he demanded, and the slave hurried off.

'What was the money you thought should have come to Rome?' Torquatus asked. He knew what he thought the answer to that question was.

'The revenues from Asia, of course.' The flush mounting to his face again, Antonius leapt up from his chair, which almost toppled over before falling back onto its front feet with a thud. He kicked a box of scrolls out of the way, so he could stride up and down. 'I'm sick of hearing that I authorised the transfer of those funds to Balbus. I didn't. Whoever signed that letter, it wasn't me.' He rounded on Torquatus, as if he suspected that he was about to say that he'd seen the letter with his own eyes. 'Oh, and other letters too, ordering it to be moved, though where it went I don't know, as I didn't write those letters either.'

His brown eyes were hot with rage. 'And why would I send anything to fucking Balbus? Hadn't the man already turned his back on me? I was Caesar's trusted deputy, his right-hand man, Master of Horse, second only to himself as Dictator. His heir, as I believed. And when I say Caesar I mean Caesar, right, not fucking whey-faced Octavian. Faced with a choice between me and a callow little brat with no experience, Balbus chose the brat. So I wouldn't trust him with a single fucking denarius of my own money. Or Rome's. Believe me.'

Torquatus was relieved when the slave hurried back in, and for a few moments there was a welcome diversion as tables and wine-cups were arranged. The wine was excellent, as good as Balbus'. Torquatus again took his well-watered. Antonius did not. He allowed the slave to fill his cup – a large one – drained it, and held it out for more. From the boy's response, Torquatus gathered that this was his normal drinking style. He knew better than to think, however, that he might become indiscreet under the influence of the wine: Antonius was notoriously hard-headed.

'Do you yourself have any idea who might be behind this?' Torquatus asked, deciding to cut his losses.

Antonius shrugged. 'What was it? Eighteen million? Typical of the Boy to sneak his money around in small sums like that. He probably took it himself, just for the fun of blaming me. He's so bent you could fasten your cloak with him.'

He brooded, while Torquatus reflected that only one of the Three could think eighteen million a small sum. Antonius must have sensed the thought, for he glared at his visitor again. '200 million, that's what we need for this war. Yes, that makes you stare, doesn't it?' Antonius glugged down another half-cup. The wine seemed to be mellowing him. 'No, he won't blame me, of course, but you. It would be just like the little bastard, now I come to think of it,' he said, far more cheerfully, ' to set you up like that if he felt he'd get criticised for proscribing you. I bet he's told you to make the loss good?'

Torquatus' blood ran cold. He sat very still. Antonius' small brown eyes swivelled towards him. 'Thought so. So he'll end up with everything you've got, and will still be able to shed a few crocodile tears at your sad fate.'

Torquatus couldn't deny that Octavian's actions were quite open to that interpretation. He pulled himself together. 'Caesar' – it seemed important somehow to use the name Octavian preferred – 'has no reason at all to doubt my reliability.' He managed to sound quite convinced.

Antonius smiled sourly. 'When you find you're mistaken, come to me,' he said bluntly. 'I've seen you with soldiers, and I always have room for another military man who knows his arse from his elbow. From what I hear you've done well at the Treasury, too. Under – what shall we say? – not quite ideal conditions.'

There was real warmth in his voice now, and Torquatus suddenly understood why his men followed him with such devotion. What he offered was impossible, but Torquatus was grateful for the offer all the same. He opened his mouth to speak but Antonius held up his hand. 'No, I know you can't and won't. I know there aren't supposed to be sides, anyway. All one happy band of brothers, isn't it? I respect that. We all need loyal followers, more now than ever. But there might come a time when you need help, and then you may turn to me.'

Torquatus' gratitude ebbed away. There was reassurance in knowing that if it all fell apart he might retrieve his fortunes this way, but the word 'followers' grated on him, not to mention the man's lordly air. He smiled, thanked Antonius and turned the subject.

'My sister tells me that all the women are talking of a conspiracy to bring back Sextus Pompey to Rome.'

Antonius roared with laughter, his good humour now apparently restored. 'Wonderful, isn't it, what the women will dream up? I suppose they've nothing better to do over the honeyed wine and pastries.'

'I must say it seems impossible to me.'

He waved his hand dismissively. 'Don't let's waste time talking about it. When the Boy and I leave Rome, Lepidus stays behind. Lepidus isn't exactly charismatic, for which all the gods be thanked. I'm charismatic, believe me,' – he grinned, suddenly looking much younger – 'and even the Boy seems to have some sort of hold over stupid ignorant soldiers, though I can't see why. I mean, does he look like Caesar? No. Is he any kind of general? My arse.' He scowled, and drank again. 'But Lepidus is a good, solid conscientious man who knows there isn't any other side for him to be on. He'll have enough troops, and he knows how to use them. Believe me, Sextus Pompey knows better than to try such a thing. Whatever else he is, he's no fool.'

While Torquatus was inside the house, Iucundus suddenly found himself alone outside. Becco and Pulex had gone to a little wine-bar opposite: they hadn't invited him to join them. The litter-men were still there, a huddle of muscular glossy black arms and legs, their heads together, but he decided against joining them. They weren't exactly unfriendly, but the four of them were all Nubians, he'd been told, and spoke their own language together. Whether this cut them off from the rest of the slaves, or they simply preferred not to mix, Iucundus hadn't worked out.

He looked around. When he'd arrived at Torquatus' house he'd thought it was more like a town than a home, but it was small and shabby compared to Antonius' place. The steps up to it were as wide and grand as the ones at the big temples, and the courtyard between the two wings was big enough to exercise a troop of soldiers. And there was a troop of soldiers, too, though they weren't exercising. Some were playing with dice, using a board scratched in the dust: as he watched there was a burst of laughter, and one of the men threw up his hands laughing, and jumped to his feet, scuffing out the board with his heavy boot. He threw down a couple of coins, before reaching for his spear to draw a new board. Some of the other men were just lounging in the sun, bored; others were inspecting their sword-blades, heads together. Only the ones who were on sentry-duty were paying attention to the people going in and out continually, as if the house were a market. And jutting out from the wall facing the street were ranks of beams, phallus-shaped, with bronze sheaths. Whatever could they be?

There were a couple of soldiers close to him: their conversation came to an end and they separated. Iucundus took the opportunity to ask one of them, who grinned at his ignorance.

'They're the ramming-beaks from ships,' he said. 'And they were put there by a man called Pompey the Great. He killed all the pirates, or so they say, and these are from the pirate ships.'

Iucundus was impressed. There were so many of them, in rows placed neatly one above the other. 'These are just the commanders' ships though,' the man went on. 'There wouldn't have been room for them all.' He nodded briskly and walked in through the big doors. Iucundus watched idly as a couple of women slaves came out, blinking a little in the sun. He wandered over to another group of soldiers, feeling bolder now, and thinking too with a sore heart that he himself would have been a leader of soldiers if – but it was pointless to think of that. The men told him they were Antonius' bodyguard, soldiers from the legions who'd been offered this chance. They expected to make a lot more money working for Antonius himself, they said.

'Does he need so many of you?' Iucundus asked.

The men roared with laughter. 'Us? That's a good one. Believe me, son, when we're all drawn up together we look pretty much like a legion. And we fight like a legion, too. Or better. We're hand-picked, see, and Antonius knows a good soldier when he sees one.'

Another group came out of the house: slaves, well-fed and well-dressed. One, a little man with a big nose, even had a key-pattern woven into the border of his tunic. Iucundus, keeping his eyes on the door so he didn't miss his master, noticed that the little man stopped to speak to the doorman. He was clearly asking a question, and the doorman, after glancing about uncertainly, pointed in the direction of Torquatus' litter-bearers.

Iucundus watched the man stride across the courtyard before turning back to his companions. 'And what now?' he asked the soldiers, who shrugged.

'The proscriptions have given us something to do. But soon we'll be off to war again and things will be better.' So it's men like these, Iucundus thought, looking round the circle of laughing faces, who chase the senators through the streets and cut off their heads. He glanced over to the door again. There was a bigger group coming out now, and he looked carefully to see if his master was there. He wasn't.

Iucundus felt a tap on his shoulder, and he turned to see that the little man with the fancy tunic was behind him. 'You from the house of Aulus Manlius Torquatus?' he asked.

'That's right.'

'And he's in there now? Talking to the boss?'

Iucundus nodded, wondering what he could be wanting.

'Got his secretary with him, has he?'

'Yes, he has. Why do you want to know?'

'I want to talk to him, see,' the man said, with a conspiratorial wink, laying a hand on his arm and drawing him aside.

'Well, if you want to talk to my master, why don't you go to his house? It's in – '

'I know where it is. And it's not your master I want to see but Demetrius. You can take a message for me, can't you?'

Iucundus didn't like the man's clutch on his arm, or the way his eyes shifted, restlessly scanning the crowd. 'He'll be out in a minute, I should think. Why don't you just wait?'

'I haven't got time. And anyway, my business with

Demetrius is private.'

The way the little man lowered his voice on the word "private" made Iucundus even more uncomfortable. Anything to get him to go away. He nodded.

'Tell him that I'll come and see him this evening.'

'Just that?' Iucundus stared at him.

The little man smiled, which made his big nose look even larger. 'No. You can tell him I've been down in Neapolis. Had to do some business for Spurius at a goldsmith's. He'll understand.'

'And what name shall I say?'

The smile widened, showing a toothless mouth. 'Oh, he'll know who I am soon enough. Don't forget now - Spurius, at the goldsmith's, Neapolis.'

The man had been getting closer and closer, dropping his voice, though in fact no-one was listening, and Iucundus nodded quickly. 'All right, I'll tell him.'

To his relief the little man let go of his arm, nodded and hurried away. Iucundus stared after him: something about that scurrying back view was familiar. Of course! This was the person who'd been walking up the hill in front of him on the very first morning he'd arrived at the Torquatus house. He wondered why the man hadn't just waited for Demetrius, then became aware that behind him another group of soldiers were getting quarrelsome: he could hear oaths and loud exclamations, and the scuff of boots on the gravel. He swung round, his heart beating fast, knowing that the little knife in his boot would be useless against these heavily-armed men. Just as he was thinking this a hand grasped his shoulder, hard. Without thinking he twisted so that the man's thumb would be bent back, and wrenched himself free, grabbing at the knife as he did so. Then he stopped, crouching, knife in hand, his breath coming short and hard. It was only Demetrius. He lowered the knife and stammered an apology, but Demetrius looked at him as if the boy were something nasty he'd found stuck to his boot. The soldiers were laughing in a way which wasn't going to improve Demetrius' temper.

Without a word, Iucundus put the knife back in his boot. Demetrius said nothing, but jerked his head over his shoulder at where the litter-bearers stood waiting to set off. The secretary hurried off before Iucundus could speak, climbing into the litter with his master. The big men had come out of the bar wiping their mouths. The bearers set off at the trot, and Iucundus followed as closely as he could, wondering what it could be about Neapolis and goldsmiths that the little man wanted to discuss with Demetrius.

As Torquatus was carried home, two thoughts came to him. He wondered whether both he and Antonius were in danger of underestimating Rome's women. Ladies like his sister had known all the political players since their infancy, were married to them, were intimate friends with their mothers and sisters, and had a great deal of (unofficial) power. They knew what strings to pull, and usually were well aware of the very peccadilloes a man wouldn't want bruited abroad. He knew it, and Antonius must know it too since his own wife, Fulvia, was probably the most powerful of all. His second thought was that Antonius seemed to be surprisingly knowledgeable about Sextus Pompey. Not just about Sextus' movements, but his thoughts and feelings too. Could Antonius possibly be negotiating with him? If so, it was behind Octavian's back. One could see that there would be certain advantages to neutralising Sextus: it would be impossible to move troops across to Greece to fight Cassius and Brutus if he commanded the seas. Why not make an ally of him for now? The only reason was that this would be completely unacceptable to Octavian, whose plan was to knock Sextus out of action before tackling the assassins. What game was Antonius playing?

He was uncomfortable, too, about Antonius' insistence that he hadn't had the Asia revenues sent to Balbus. In Neapolis last year he'd been at Balbus' vaults in Neapolis, arranging for the war-chest to be stored there, when the letter authorising the transfer of those revenues had arrived. The news had been remarkable enough, the amount large enough even by Balbus' standards, that everyone in the vaults had downed tools and come running to look at the letter, signed and sealed by Antonius as sole surviving consul, the only man powerful enough to take such a step. It really wasn't possible that anyone would have dared to forge a letter from him, so why did he keep insisting that they had? What was the point of these repeated denials? Was he withdrawing the money for some secret purpose of his own?

It wasn't until the late afternoon, when the master had settled down to talk to his sister, that Iucundus gave Demetrius his message. The little man hadn't said it was secret, but his manner had been so odd that Iucundus waited to pass it on until he and Demetrius were alone together for a moment in the library. As he did so he wondered again what it meant. Demetrius received the message unemotionally, though he looked rather pale. Iucundus wondered if he was being over-imaginative when he got a strong feeling that it wasn't welcome. Whoever the little man was, he clearly was not a friend. The message was incomprehensible: surely Demetrius' job would never bring him into contact with a goldsmith?

While Demetrius was busy overseeing the master's meal, Iucundus escaped to the stables, taking some food for Philip, who hadn't turned up in the kitchen when the rest of the slaves went to eat. He couldn't have said why he didn't want to be seen slipping out, but he didn't. Philip was delighted to see Iucundus, and was so impatient to explain what he wanted that he could hardly be bothered to eat first. He picked at some bread, dipping it into his bowl of bean soup, but his heart wasn't in it, and he soon pushed the bowl aside.

'The other day,' he began, 'you told me you could read?'

Iucundus nodded.

'Then I've got something I want to show you,' Philip went on, with a sideways look at the boy. 'I can trust you, can't I?'

Iucundus nodded. 'You can. But what is it that's so secret?'

The old man hesitated, brushing crumbs off the table with one gnarled hand, and glancing at Iucundus. 'Perhaps it's too risky,' he muttered under his breath. 'But then – '

'What's too risky?' Iucundus' voice was sharp.

'I've got something I need to show you. But first you must promise me you'll say nothing.'

'You've already asked if you can trust me,' Iucundus pointed out. 'And I've said you can. But all the same, if it's something really dangerous – ' He pushed his stool back so that he could lean against the wall.

'That's just it. I don't know. Oh, if only I could read.'

The old man was in a lather of indecision, very unlike his usual taciturn self.

'Well, if I read whatever it is for you, and then I forget all about it, will that do?' he offered.

'That's what I want,' the groom nodded. Even then, however, he still didn't speak, but got up and fidgeted about, rearranging the measures on top of the feed bins, putting another log into the brazier as if placing it exactly were the most important task in the world. Iucundus watched him. At last Philip seemed to come to a decision, turned, and wandered off to the last of the row of feed bins, the largest and heaviest jar. Taking its lid off and laying it carefully down on the floor, the old man began fumbling around inside it. Iucundus could hear the grains hushing against the earthen sides as Philip pushed the corn aside, and then the old man's muttering to himself as he felt down further and further. Just when Iucundus began to think Philip would fall head-first into the jar, he gave a grunt of satisfaction and straightened up. As he turned around, Iucundus could see what he had in his hand, and he grabbed the sides of his stool as if to stop himself falling off. 'But that must be the master's,' he whispered, horrified. 'Where did you get it?'

'Master's, is it? I thought it must be. After all, who else would have something as good as this?' He held out for Iucundus' inspection a set of wax tablets. They were beautiful, the boy thought, and obviously very expensive, with an ivory case and silver bindings, and a fine silver chain now hanging loose and swinging slower and slower as Philip held it out. Iucundus jumped up off his stool and backed away, his hands behind him.

'Are you mad?' Iucundus' voice came out as a croak.

'Tell me what it says.' Philip's gaze was intent. The boy crossed the floor towards Philip slowly and took the tablets as if they might burn him. At once they fell open, the chain not being fastened. Inside, there was writing only on the first of the tablets. The message was simple, and he read it aloud: *You are to show this to a man you will meet at the sixth hour of night at Jupiter's on the Capitol. He will give you a letter. Tell no-one.* It was signed AMT, but it didn't need to be, since these were the master's tablets, written in his own hand.

Thoughts tumbled through Iucundus' head. Now he knew why Stephanus was wandering about the Capitol after dark. But who was this letter from and why did they have to send a letter to the master in that roundabout way? And how had it come into Philip's hands? 'Was this on his body?' he asked.

'No. But I was worried about him, the evening before he was found. He seemed restless and worried, and later I thought I heard someone moving around in the courtyard during the night, but couldn't see anything when I got up to look. And next morning the news came that he was dead.'

'And you tried to get into his room,' Iucundus nodded.

'I had to wait till that Demetrius had gone out,' Philip agreed. 'Then I went in and found them.'

'What, just lying there? Why hadn't he taken them with him, as he'd been told to? Iucundus wondered.

'I don't know.' Philip rubbed his chin, and the rasping sound was all that broke the silence. 'And they weren't exactly - But I was telling you what an odd mood he'd been in. Fey, you know. You're a Gaul, and they say Gauls sometimes know more than we do about - ,'

'About what?'

'Well, then, I'll tell you what Stephanus said to me, just as I was about to turn in for the night here. He took me by the arm, and he said, "Do you believe in ghosts, Philip?" Just that: do you believe in ghosts?'

'And do you?' Iucundus couldn't help asking.

'Of course I do. Silly question, isn't it? And then he said he'd seen someone he was sure was dead, someone who used to work here. A ghost? Well, perhaps. But maybe the man just wasn't dead. When I said that he started making all sorts of wild accusations against Demetrius. I don't like the man, but the idea that he would steal anything, let alone a gold ring, was just nonsense.'

'You still haven't told me how you found the tablets,' Iucundus pointed out, sitting down again.

Philip hesitated before admitting, 'We were old friends, you see, so I knew where to look.'

'He had a hiding-place?'

'That's right. Where he kept his money and things. The tablets were there, but I didn't find any gold rings.' Iucundus' head was spinning. He remembered Demetrius looking in Stephanus' room, on the morning the old man had been found dead. Had he been looking for these tablets? How would he have known about them? Who in the world could the master have sent Stephanus to meet? Why should he send a slave, an elderly indoor slave, to a meeting in a dark, secluded spot at such an hour?

'Why was the master sending Stephanus to the

118

Capitol?' Philip was asking plaintively as Iucundus sat up straight on his stool.

'It doesn't say. Has such a thing ever happened before?'

'Never. I can't make sense of it.' The old man shook his head mournfully.

'Well, the most important thing is to get rid of these. Wipe them. Clean the message. Then leave them lying somewhere so that they'll be found and returned to the master.'

'Oh, I can't do that.' Before Iucundus could stop him, Philip leant across and snatched the tablets out of the boy's hand and cradled them against his chest.

'Philip, you must. If the master finds out that you've taken them – ' Iucundus' voice was no more than a fearful whisper.

'You won't tell him? You promised!'

Yes, he thought, I did. Like a fool, I promised.

'I suppose I can't,' the boy agreed reluctantly. 'But we have to put them back. If he – if anyone – finds them here – '

Iucundus broke off, sweating, thinking of what might happen to Philip, and then to him too, once Philip had admitted Iucundus' complicity, as he no doubt would under the kinds of torture they'd apply. 'Look, it would be easy for me. I could wipe the page clean, with the little writing stick they use, and just put them among the master's things.' He sounded quite calm and reasonable, he thought, for someone contemplating a hideous death.

'No. They won't find them here,' Philip insisted. 'Who would look in a corn-jar for such a thing? But I still don't understand. Was it the master who had him killed, then?'

'We don't know that Stephanus was killed,' Iucundus pointed out. 'And why should the master go to all that trouble? If he wants to kill a slave, he can do it, he doesn't have to give a reason.'

Philip refused to give up the tablets, which he seemed to value almost as a talisman connecting him with his dead friend; in fact he wouldn't agree to any action at all. The two sat in angry silence for a few minutes.

'We have to put those tablets back.' Iucundus made his voice practical, calm, reasonable, but he could see to his fury that he was having no effect.

'I need to think about it,' Philip said. Over and over again he said it, until at last Iucundus was forced to give up, worried that Torquatus might be calling for him to help him to bed. He didn't want to be found here. His only comfort was that he saw the old man bury the tablets in the corn once again, and his only plan as he left him was to get Philip out of there on some pretext so that he could take the tablets and put them back where they belonged.

And he was just in time. As he pushed the stable door open to go back to the house he found Demetrius standing just outside. Demetrius was always pale, but this evening his face was like a ghost's. Iucundus feared that the secretary had found something for him to do, but he just nodded briefly at Iucundus, and ducked his head as he passed through the low doorway into Philip's room. Iucundus hurried off, the clatter of his boots loud in the cold night air.

Chapter 10

Torquatus never thought Lepidus would have anything useful to tell him: he'd decided to ask him for an interview solely to reassure Antonius that he wasn't being singled out. He came out of the house amused, in spite of his problems. For the second time in two days he'd been dazzled by a ludicrously extravagant house; he really ought to invest in marble workshops and experts in gold leaf, he thought - supposing he was ever in a position to invest in anything. This place had been built by Lepidus' father with money extorted from the hapless Sicilians when he was their governor, and further embellished by Lepidus himself with money extorted from the hapless Spaniards. And people wonder why our subject peoples rise up against us whenever we give them the chance, Torquatus reflected, dismissing the litter-bearers. He needed to think, and he could do that better walking. It was a beautiful winter afternoon, a golden light bathing the city. Well, it bathed the Palatine. As Torquatus began the descent into the Forum shadows fell across him and he felt a cold wind at his back.

The great man had been studiously vague, either as a matter of policy or because he really couldn't give a fart about Octavian's money. Still, Torquatus reflected sourly, things had improved as the interview went on: by the time he left Lepidus seemed to have grasped who he was. But what had he learned? That Lepidus knew no-one in Balbus' household and that his people never went there; that he hadn't known anything about the money or its movement; and that the deposits made with Balbus last year had been nothing to do with him. The last two statements Torquatus felt sure were true. Lepidus and Octavian had never been close. The first, however, he thought questionable: the Three had an insatiable appetite for money, and Balbus had lots. It would be very surprising if Lepidus really had no connection with the man at all. As to the money itself, he had made it quite clear, though rather less brutally than

Antonius, that he would regard the loss of a mere eighteen million sestertii in the way any other senator might view a denarius coin slipping down a drain.

Torquatus didn't have very long for these reflections before the path brought him round to where he could see down into the Forum and his attention was distracted. It seemed to be unusually full for such a late hour. And there was a buzz about the crowd, the sort of buzz you get when some great trial has finally come on, or when Cicero (as Torquatus remembered him from his boyhood) was due to speak, or when some contentious issue was about to be put to a public meeting. Men of all classes seemed to be hurrying to the speakers' platform. Ordinary men and senatorial gentlemen, affluent knights and what looked like tradesmen who had presumably run out into the street leaving their wives and slaves to mind the shop, as such people tend to do whenever there's anything going on. But there was an unusual number of women, too. Of course there are always women in the Forum as well as men, wandering into the affluent jewellers' shops, eyeing up the slaves offered for sale in the Vicus Tuscus, or just listening to the law-cases, or the orators addressing citizens' assemblies. Rome isn't Greece, and women are free to walk in the streets. But at least half this crowd were women, he reckoned, and that was unusual. He stared into the distance, where a speaker was standing on the platform, and others behind, in a little huddle as if wanting to give moral support but uncertain how to do so. That was strange too: men who speak from the rostra are trained for it from boyhood, and don't look nervous, even if they feel it.

Coming down into the Forum, the platform dropped from his view, and Torquatus told his slaves he was heading into the crowd to see what was going on. There was, as usual, a great deal of jostling as people tried to gain the best vantage points. Becco and Pulex pushed a way through for him: he was a senator, and not to be elbowed aside. Demetrius and Iucundus stayed close to him. The crowd grew denser the nearer they drew to the speaker, and Torquatus began to be able to hear what he was saying. Except: it wasn't he, but she. Torquatus stopped pressing forward, simply astonished: the speaking figure was as composed, her gestures as correct, as if she had been training for this all her life. A middle-aged woman, grey-haired, her figure swathed in a warm cloak, whether for modesty or warmth, she was perfectly well known to Torquatus and no doubt to many others present as the sister of one of Rome's greatest orators, now dead. He heard the name 'Hortensia' pass through the crowd in a respectful murmur.

The astonishment Torquatus felt at seeing a woman giving a speech from the rostra, however, was as nothing compared to the shock he received next. Scanning the huddle of aristocratic ladies backing Hortensia on the platform he recognised several very well-known faces, and among them, her face almost concealed under the fur-trimmed hood of her cloak, his sister. So great was his sense of outrage that for a few moments he stood staring, unable to listen. It was only when he was jostled by a man next to him, and realised that Becco and Pulex had been carried quite a long way in front of him when he stopped, that Torquatus came to his senses and began to concentrate.

'In the past, women have come to Rome's aid in her hour of need. We have offered our jewels, our valuables, everything we had, to save the city from disaster. In the dark days when Hannibal menaced the city, then we gave freely, without being coerced. For we love Rome as much as our brothers and fathers do!' Here the female half of the crowd cheered, while Torquatus also heard a kind of low growl from the men. 'Rome is ours too!' she declared, with a fine gesture towards her fellow-women. Again the women cheered and the men made that uncertain sound. 'But we will not be instructed to pay taxes! We will not! Men have the right to be heard, to deliberate, and they pay taxes as part of their responsibilities. But when did women ever get the chance to speak?' Hortensia was forced to break off here: a man in the crowd called out that women never did anything else. Some of the other men laughed at this, but the women shouted them down and an uncertain silence fell again. Looking round to gather the attention of the crowd - she certainly had studied her brother's technique - Hortensia went on. ' Who asked us to pay? Who explained to us what the money was needed for? But they don't need to explain: we know what it is for! It is to pay for a civil war! They want to take our money so that our sons and brothers and husbands and fathers can cut each other down on the battlefield. Why should we pay for that?'

There was a hush. Every eye was fixed on Hortensia, the women's full of tears, the men's thoughtful. 'Who asked if we agreed to the deaths of our sons and brothers and fathers and husbands? Wouldn't we rather have peace?'

The women roared their approval at this: a strange, high-pitched sound to Torquatus' ears, quite different from the usual masculine assent he was used to in that place.

'Wouldn't we prefer these three great men to work together? Don't we want to see our children grow up in peace, our old people die in peace?'

Again the cheers of agreement with a slight discordant masculine rumble below.

'So I say we won't pay this tax. Those of us who want to fund a military campaign can do it as Roman women have always done it, by private donation. But we don't have the vote. We can't go into the Senate and argue against this tax. We can't go to a citizens' assembly and argue against this tax. There is no-one to speak for us. We have asked Octavia to intercede with her brother for us. We have asked Julia to do the same with her son Antonius. And they have both agreed. But when we went to Antonius' house, his wife Fulvia spoke to us like a fishwife, called us names, and refused to speak to him: is she afraid he will beat her?' Here a great roar of laughter went up, from men and women alike: Fulvia's ferocity was well known. Hortensia waited a minute, smiling, for the laugh to die away, before coming to her conclusion.

'This I can promise we will do: we will come here, into the Forum, every day, until we gain our point. Treat us like women, respect our female nature, ask us to help make peace, but don't make us pay for our men to be killed!' She was going to say more but the roar of agreement at this point was so loud that she paused, striking a pose of forceful reasonableness that was definitely one of the orator's. The noise went on and on, and Torquatus had time to look again at the women standing behind Hortensia. Manlia was not the only one wearing a cloak or a hood, as if half-ashamed to be taking part in such an outrageous event. Some, however, were not. He hardly knew whether to be proud of Manlia for standing her ground or horrified at her taking part in such a public act.

It was clear that the women would have their way. Torquatus could see some of Antonius' bodyguard on the outskirts of the crowd. Octavian's agents would be there too, of course: they were to be found everywhere a few people gathered together. But in his estimate the mood of the meeting was too strong for intervention, unless the Three wanted a bloodbath. The heat and stench of the crowd were beginning to offend him, and he moved gradually back out of it again. Demetrius and Iucundus followed him, but Becco and Pulex seemed not have seen their master go and continued to stare as if mesmerised at Hortensia. He called them impatiently, but they were too far ahead by now to hear. As he made his way back, others were still pressing forward, as Hortensia had started to speak again. Torquatus began to move faster, impelled by a sudden urgent need to be free of this pushing, shoving, smelly mass of humanity. And at last he was out of it, and making his way between the scattered groups of citizens at the edges of the crowd. He caught snippets of heated argument as he pushed his way past, heading for Castor's temple, to wait for the slaves on its steps. He would get a good view from there, and be able to see how the meeting ended. He hoped the women wouldn't be mad enough to march on the Palatine: if they did the Three might feel they had to send troops into the Forum. Torquatus sent up silent prayers to every god he could think of and decided that he wouldn't leave the Forum until he had seen Manlia safe.

He saw Demetrius swallowed up again by the crowd: Iucundus wasn't visible. While he waited for them to find Becco and Pulex, Torquatus leaned against one of Castor's pillars, watching. After a few minutes he suddenly became aware of someone moving quietly behind him. Instinctively he stepped aside. A heavy weight crashed against his shoulder. He was thrown down, his mind exploding in a burst of light.

Torquatus regained consciousness to the sight of a ring of faces above him. Most were those of the kind of folk who would go anywhere and stand for hours for the pleasure of seeing a senator flat out on his back. He focussed painfully in on the only face he recognised: his secretary Demetrius, who was looking worried. When he saw Torquatus' eyes open he gave his master a tentative smile. 'I found you lying here, lord. Did you faint?'

'I did not.' Torquatus felt a fool, lying (as he remembered now) in the portico of Castor's. He forced himself to sit up, wincing at the pain in his shoulder, and then, gritting his teeth, to stand. His head was full of lightning-flashes, and he had to lean on Demetrius to conceal the shaking in his knees. 'I was hit on the head. No, the shoulder. It would have been my head if I hadn't moved, but' - he gently explored the lump on his head with his fingers - 'I must have hit the column as I went down.'

'Has anything been stolen?' Demetrius' question was reasonable, but Torquatus ignored it. He was looking around for Becco and Pulex. They were standing at the back of the little crowd, looking shamefaced and quite scared. Well, Torquatus would give them something to be scared about. Feeling a little stronger now, he let go of Demetrius' arm. 'What in Hades' name were you two oafs doing?' he called out to them furiously, and most of the heads in the crowd swung round to see who he was talking to.

'I didn't see you go while the lady was speaking,' Pulex admitted, and Becco nodded.

'Did anyone see the man who attacked me run off?' Torquatus asked, but it seemed the crowd had only gathered after Becco and Pulex started running and shouting.

'And where were you?' Torquatus asked Demetrius.

'I was just on my way back across the Forum, after telling Becco and Pulex to come back, lord. I saw - ,' he hesitated – 'someone bending over something on the ground, something white. It was just where you'd been standing, lord, so I ran as fast as I could. Has he stolen anything, lord?'

'I wasn't carrying any money. Why would I be?' If the man who attacked him was after money he was a fool. Torquatus' slaves would have been carrying anything he needed, obviously. Anyone would have known that much. Torquatus said no more, except to ask if Demetrius could identify him if he saw the man again.

'I don't know, lord. I wasn't very close to him, and he was rather ordinary-looking. Quite small. And of course I didn't see him hit you: he might have simply found you lying on the ground.' He shrugged, looking extraordinarily uncomfortable.

'Well, if he didn't hit me, someone else certainly did. And I wasn't there for more than a few moments. Was he togate, this mysterious person?'

'No, lord: his tunic was pale, and he wasn't wearing a toga. But – ' He stopped again.

Probably not a citizen, then. Torquatus sighed. 'But what?'

'It looked to me like Iucundus, lord,' he said, speaking reluctantly and slowly.

'Wasn't Iucundus with you?'

'No. I went after the bodyguards, and then realised

he wasn't following me. I turned, and saw - whoever it was. It looked like him, but I couldn't swear – '

'What could he have hit me with?' he demanded. He wasn't carrying anything but that little knife, was he?'

'No, lord.' Demetrius stooped, and the heads of the crowd followed his movements. When he stood up again he had a substantial piece of wood in his hand. 'One of the bars they put across the doors of the temple at night, lord. Or so one of the priests told me. Of course, anyone might have found it propped up behind the door.'

Torquatus' mind was in turmoil. 'Where is the boy anyway?' he demanded, suddenly feeling quite sick. He almost staggered, and leaned against the pillar once again.

'I don't know, lord. I haven't seen him since he ran away. Would the lord like a litter to be fetched?' Demetrius suggested, but Torquatus shook his head. 'Get me a cloak. I'll walk.' A litter would be comfortable, true, but he'd have to stand here and wait for it among the gawping citizens. And even when he was inside people would still look at it and ask whose slaves were those? Who was riding in the litter? What had happened would be passed from person to person till there was no-one who didn't know that Aulus Manlius Torquatus, quaestor, had been knocked down in the Forum.

'And what about the ladies on the rostra?' he asked. 'What happened to them?'

There was a moment of silent consternation as the crowd looked at each other. No-one had given any further thought to the speakers and their demands. Then a man at the back called out: 'Those women? They've gone. There's no-one down there now.' Torquatus' slaves had found him a cloak by the simple expedient of buying one for a silly price from a man in the crowd. He wrapped it round him, relieved, gave the sign to leave and the big men immediately set off in front of him, pushing anyone out of the way who might inconvenience their master. Torquatus followed them gladly.

It was a long walk home. He couldn't think just now, he was in too much pain, but things didn't look good for Iucundus. He held his head up high as he went, and didn't lean on the slaves, but by the time he had reached his own door he was sweating and his head felt as if it would burst.

As it happened, Torquatus and Manlia arrived at the house at the same moment. Through his headache he noted with relief that she had taken two of her slaves with her – one of her women and a strong man to guard her. He needed to talk to her, but as they passed through the entrance passage Torquatus became irritably aware that there were people – quite a lot of people from the sound of it – in the reception hall.

'Jupiter! Did we ask everyone to a party?'

Manlia had the grace to look a little abashed. 'I had expected to be back much earlier, Aulus,' she said. 'But what's happened? You look terrible.'

'Thanks: not as bad as I feel, I bet. I was hit on the head while I waited for you at Castor's. Yes, I was there in the Forum, and saw you making an exhibition of yourself on the rostra.' He knew he shouldn't be talking to Manlia like this, and took a deep breath. 'Demetrius saved my life; he came up before the attacker had the chance to finish me off. Iucundus has gone.'

They were in the great reception hall now, blinking in the light of a hundred lamps. A group of men was standing waiting for them. Manlia exclaimed, 'Gone where?' just as Demetrius said in his ear: 'Iucundus is here.' And there he was: white-faced and out of breath, he had just run in through the big doors. He pushed towards his master, oblivious of the people he was brushing past.

'Master! Master!'

'What were you doing attacking me?' Torquatus demanded.

Iucundus' face was whiter than ever. He caught his breath with difficulty. 'I didn't. I tried to catch the man who did, though. I don't know his name, but it was - ,'

'You say you didn't attack me?'

'Lord, I didn't! But I saw who did, and - ,'

Torquatus turned a cold face towards him. 'Your task is to guard me, not to go running off into the crowd. In fact, I can think of only one reason why you would run away like that.'

Iucundus' face became whiter still. 'No! I swear I didn't! I would never run away.'

Torquatus found this play-acting unendurable. 'Don't tell lies, Iucundus,' he said coldly. He turned to Demetrius. 'Find somewhere secure to keep him while I decide what to do with him.'

Demetrius took Iucundus' arm in an ungentle grip and hurried him away. Torquatus was swept by a moment of utter despair. Was his life under any greater threat than before? No. Had the political situation taken a turn for the worse? No. Simply, a slave of whom he'd had high hopes had turned out to be untrustworthy at the very least, he was aching with exhaustion, and his head felt as if someone had lit a fire in it. He heard himself give a great sigh, then pulled himself together. Manlia was looking at him with concern.

'And these people are - ?' he asked.

'Three of the best slave-dealers, and some men who might make good stewards. You remember, you gave me permission to arrange for them to come? But I can send them away, if you like.' Her eyes searched his face.

'No, but tell them they'll have to wait for a while longer. I can't deal with them like this.' He gestured at his crumpled, stained toga and scuffed boots. Since these men were here he might as well get rid of one of his problems – the least of them, admittedly. His mood lifted slightly at the thought of warm water, and he even smiled as he took in the presence of Victor, wringing his hands and almost weeping over the despoiled toga.

Clean clothes and a cup of good Falernian wine made a difference: when Torquatus went back into the reception hall he felt like a man in control. And it didn't, in the end, take very long. Manlia had gone to a lot of trouble, had found out a good deal about each man, and her choice was the same as her brother's: a tall, sturdy-looking Syrian, who'd been the steward of a large household already. His previous owner had been a wealthy knight. Torquatus didn't ask how the man had died. Whatever had happened, whether proscription or simply a sudden illness, Trofimus had ended up back on the market. Disappointing for him, of course: he might well have expected to be freed at his master's death. He seemed intelligent, experienced, and – at least as important to Torquatus – a calm, deliberate sort of man. He seemed to understand that his new master wanted a quiet household, where problems got dealt with before torturers needed to be called in. He smiled at that - even his smile was deliberate - and agreed that anything of the sort was most undesirable in a gentleman's residence. The man was expensive, but Torquatus could afford it, and he'd be worth every last sestertius if he could bring the house back into harmony.

'Thank you,' he said to Manlia, kissing her cheek as the new acquisition walked off to the back of the house to begin his work, and the other men clattered off chattering through the entrance-way. Silence fell so suddenly that he could hear the pigeons scratching about on the roof around the pool, and their fat soft cooing as they settled themselves for the night. He had never been so exhausted. He yawned, uncontrollably. 'I hope the baths are hot.'

A leisurely bath, another couple of cups of the Falernian, and his headache reduced itself to a niggle behind his eyes. Even after a massage, though, he wouldn't be engaging in any swordplay for a day or two. His shoulder had received a massive blow; had he not moved, he would probably have been dead.

Just as he was about to settle down to a rather belated dinner (again!), Demetrius came in and reverently laid before him a set of plain wax tablets, sealed shut.

Torquatus raised an eyebrow at him. 'From Balbus' house, lord. The list of those who knew about the movements of the lord Octavian's money. It's just arrived.'

Torquatus weighed the tablets in his hand for a moment, then laid them down with another yawn, before smiling across at Manlia.

'After dinner. After all, I don't suppose there'll be anything in them that he hasn't told me already.'

'No, lord.' Demetrius hesitated for a moment, before continuing. 'And Iucundus is being held in one of the store-rooms, lord, until you are ready to see him.'

'Tomorrow. He can have the night for reflection.'

'Very well, lord.'

'Oh, and, by the way, I suppose those tablets of mine haven't turned up? You know the ones I mean?' Torquatus asked him.

'Ivory, with silver corners and chain. Yes, lord, I do know. I haven't found them yet. But I wonder – '

'Well, what, man? Out with it.'

'I wonder, lord, whether it would be worthwhile to question Iucundus about them too.'

For some reason Torquatus disliked this idea. 'I'll think about it. I can't imagine why Iucundus should think of taking them: it's hard to see what use they could be to him, and – '

He broke off as the curtain was drawn aside, to reveal a couple of the slaves bearing big dishes from which most delicious smells were seeping, and behind them, watching with a shrewd paternal eye, his new steward, Trofimus.

Demetrius bowed, and turned politely away.

It wasn't long after dinner when Torquatus told Manlia he intended to go to bed.

'Is your head still aching?'

'It is. But I hope a good sleep will cure it. There's only one thing I still need to do.' He reached out to the side-table where Demetrius had laid the tablets from Balbus.

'This'll tell me no-one he's ever met could possibly have known about the money.' Impatiently he broke the wax seal and untied the thing. 'Oh. Jupiter, Juno and Minerva!'

'Goodness! Whatever is it?' Manlia exclaimed, sitting up and swinging her feet to the floor.

'Well, well. I couldn't have been more wrong,' said Torquatus slowly. 'Read that.'

He handed her the tablets and she peered at the tiny writing. 'Many apologies ... unfortunate lapse ... inexplicable ... ' Manlia murmured her way through the list of names that followed. She looked up, tucking the strand of hair behind her ear and smiling. 'Hercules! No wonder he's embarrassed. Here are six names, four of them from outside his household: a slave of Messalla Rufus, one from Maecenas, one from Rebilus, and, oh look, one of Antonius', too – Aulus, this surely gives us hope? Now we have a chance to find out what happened.'

'We do. And I think another talk with Balbus would be in order.'

He took the tablets back and looked over them again. 'Rebilus? I've heard something about him, haven't I? '

'Just yesterday - no, I mean the day before. I was telling you he's Iunia's lover,' Manlia nodded.

'And that he'd been buying gladiators.' He picked up his wine-cup and savoured the last mouthful. 'Interesting.'

Iucundus, meanwhile, was sitting in the dark, his thoughts in chaos. How had it come to this, that he was accused of attacking his master - or was it simply of not defending him? He, who had only lived in this place, if you could call it living, for less than a month. He, who only last spring was free, riding his horse across his father's lands carelessly, acknowledged by everyone he met as their future king. Why had his father risked everything, and lost it? Why could he not at least have taken his son into battle with him? Then he might have been spared the sight of his mother dishonoured; he would have been dead, not a slave called Iucundus.

He dared not think like this; he must concentrate on saving his life. When he tried to tell the master what he'd seen, Torquatus' face had been like one of those stony men's in the Forum, and his ears had been shut too. Demetrius had pulled him away, and shut him in this store-room where the air was dusty and cold. At some time, he'd be taken out and questioned again, and at the thought of what that questioning might involve panic bubbled up uncontrollably. The dark was intense, as if a thick black hood had been pulled over his head, and in his terror he saw once more the bright sparks flowing up from the burning roof, heard the screams in the black night. He forced himself to sit down on the floor, shaking, gripping his hands together, forcing himself not to scream.

In a little while his racing heart steadied and his eyes grew accustomed. He began to make out sacks of grain: he must be in the bakery store-room.

The hours passed. He was dreadfully thirsty, and aching, and cold.   Quite quickly the darkness outside seeped in through whatever little cracks and chinks there were, and returned his prison to dense blackness.   His courage seemed to ebb away with the light, until at last he was swept by a wave of despair. All his attempts to be reasonable, to look for practical solutions, were as pointless as the struggles of the fly in the spider's web. He lay on the floor and wept with real abandon for the first time since he'd come here. When he could weep no more he wiped his nose and eyes as best he could, and found a corner out of the way of the grain where he could piss. He heard something moving, a scuffle behind the sacks, and sat down on one of them, imagining rats with an inward shudder.

What was he going to say when he was questioned? He'd tried to tell the truth, but what was his word worth? What was he worth? In Lepidus' house he had seen the doorkeeper living like a kennelled dog, with a long chain shackled to his leg so that he could go no further than the door. The man had asked them into his room, which had a brazier, and was comfortable enough, but he had been shocked. Barbaric was the word that came to his mind. If the house caught fire, would the doorkeeper just count as another bit of property lost in the blaze? What if that happened to him, what if the master ordered him chained up like a fierce dog?

He drew a breath, steadied his mind, and forced himself to relive every detail of what had happened that afternoon. The master had come out of Lepidus' house and they had walked down to the Forum, which had been busier than usual for this time of day, and, as ever, speakers had been waving their arms on the platform up at the far end. The master started walking faster, and he went straight into the crowd, with Becco and Pulex using their own muscles and their master's authority to clear a way for him. He himself had stuck close to Torquatus. There were ladies speaking from the platform, but Iucundus had not paid much attention, finding the size and noise of the crowd hateful. Every now and then the whole mass of people shouted or cheered as if they were one large animal, making him feel horribly small. When the master began to work his way back out again Iucundus was relieved. The big guys had got carried forward with the crowd when the master stopped to listen, so it was just the master, Demetrius and himself who had squirmed and elbowed their way back out.

Then what? Once he'd got out of the crowd, the master said he would wait for them on the steps of one of the temples, the one called Castor's. He and Demetrius had to go back and find Becco and Pulex. And that was where it had all gone wrong. He was too tired and cold and hungry to think, but he knew he must.

He heard a sound. A light footstep, perhaps. Someone trying to move without being heard. The hairs on the back of his neck rose. He had no idea what the time might be. Was this someone coming to kill him? To remove an inconvenient, insubordinate slave? To carry him off to the torturers? His heart pounding, Iucundus eased himself down behind the grain sacks onto the floor, his fear of rats forgotten.

The door opened with a grating sound, and a thin shaft of lamplight fell through the narrow opening.

'Iucundus?' The voice was no more than a frightened whisper, and Iucundus scrambled to his feet.

'Felix?'

The beam of light broadened, then, as the door was pulled shut, seemed to flood the room. Iucundus, blinking, managed to smile at Felix. In one hand the boy was carrying a slopping jug of water, which he put down carefully before turning to pick up a plate of cheese and apples.

'I'm sorry I couldn't come before,' he whispered, 'but I had to wait until everyone had gone to sleep.' The little oil lamp was perched precariously on the edge of the plate, and Iucundus hurried to take it from him, and to shut the door again. The food and water did Iucundus good, but to be remembered warmed his heart. Felix didn't seem in any hurry to leave. 'What in the world happened this afternoon?' he demanded. 'I've never seen the master so angry.'

'I don't know what I did wrong,' Iucundus told him, pacing around the little room.

'Well, tell me everything that happened. Perhaps we can work it out. I mean, you're so new, perhaps you might not - anyway, tell me.'

So Iucundus told Felix how he and Demetrius had been sent back into the crowd to fetch Becco and Pulex. 'I stopped, you see, and looked back, and I saw this man, bending over something white on the ground which must have been the master - or his body, I thought. He ran away and I followed him, right into that part, the Subura, where I was the other day. I got into a horrible place, a little dirty alley: there were women there with dirty, thin babies, and some tough-looking men, and I couldn't understand their Latin. I panicked. I'd lost the man, after all.

'Back at the temple the master had gone, and the slaves too. I ran home as fast as I could. It was horrible. The crowds were breaking up, talking, arguing, laughing. It seemed to take ages to get through. And then the master wouldn't hear me. I don't know what to do.' He ended with a panic-stricken sob, and laid his head down on his knees.

'Well, I think you should tell the master tomorrow just what you've told me. He gets angry, but it doesn't last. He'll have calmed down tomorrow, you'll see.'

Iucundus looked up at him, his eyes red with weeping. 'Do you think so? Really?'

'Really. Sounds to me as if you did exactly what you should. And the others must have seen that man too, so they'll back you up.'

'I hope so. That's not all, though.' Iucundus peered at him through the gloom. 'Can I trust you? I mean, really trust you?'

Felix stared at him. 'Of course you can.'

'Well then. It's only a matter of time before the master finds he's lost some writing-tablets.' And Iucundus told Felix how Philip had shown them to him the previous evening. 'So you see', he finished. 'They simply have to be put back. What would the master do to someone who stole his things, do you think?'

'You didn't steal them, though,' Felix pointed out.

'No. But Philip did. Or, I suppose - ,' he stopped for a moment, thinking. 'Did anyone steal them? If the master sent the message - and it's in his writing - ,'

'But Philip took them from Stephanus' room, didn't he? Well, if I get the chance I'll get them from the stables and put them in the business-room.'

'No, Felix. You mustn't do that. It would be far too dangerous. Just think what would happen if you were caught. But if you could tell Philip that he has to put them back, that might help.' Iucundus sat slumped on his sack, overwhelmed by his situation.

To cheer Iucundus up, and take his mind off his

problems Felix told him about the arrival of the new steward, Trofimus. The excitement of Iucundus' imprisonment had been very quickly relegated to the background of people's minds by this unexpected event. The steward's was a powerful position, of course, and everyone's lives would be affected by how he behaved. 'He seems all right so far,' Felix said. 'Of course, Demetrius isn't very happy.'

'Isn't he?' Iucundus tried to sound interested.

'No. He'll have to keep to his own job now. Unless he manages to put Trofimus down the same way he did with Stephanus, but I don't think Trofimus will let that happen.'

'How do you know? He's only been here a few hours.'

Felix pushed back his untidy black curls. 'I'll tell you. Before dinner, while the master was at his bath, Trofimus decided that he wanted to see over the house, get to know people, find out what work was done and where. Demetrius, of course, immediately got up and said he'd show him, but Trofimus – oh, he was ever so polite, said not to trouble, and sent one of the slaves to ask the lady Manlia if she was free to do it. Demetrius was dumbstruck.'

Iucundus couldn't help being interested in this. 'Dumbstruck? That doesn't sound like him.'

Felix laughed. 'You're right there. Once he'd got his tongue back, he said it would be a shame to disturb the lady. Trofimus told him, very politely and calmly, that the lady Manlia had already offered to show him round. Demetrius tried to persuade him that he knew more of the details than she would, but as he's only been here for a few months – I admit it feels longer – and the lady Manlia grew up here, of course it didn't work.'

'Has Demetrius really only been here for such a short time? I can't imagine the house without him. I suppose he came back with the master last year?'

'I can, easily. He's quite new: the master bought him in Greece, I think. And then he's been away with the master a lot of the time. Anyway, Trofimus didn't bother to answer him, even. I really hope that things will get more comfortable now he's arrived: more like they used to be.'

Iucundus looked at him curiously. 'Was it better? More comfortable?'

'Yes, it used to be much better. Not this horrible atmosphere, as though everyone's watching everyone else.' He looked uncertain for a moment. 'Unless I was just too young to notice?'

'You were born here, weren't you?'

'Yes.' Felix sat in silence for a while. Iucundus had wanted to know the boy's story ever since he'd arrived, but he'd noticed that the slaves didn't talk much about their past. He was wondering whether to ask directly when Felix shrugged and gave a little laugh. 'I can feel how much you want to know,' he said. 'I'll tell my story if you'll tell yours. Fair dealing, isn't it?'

'It is. As long as you won't be missed? You'll get into trouble if you're found in here with me.'

'No. No-one knows I'm here, and anyway, they won't care.' His voice was bitter, and Iucundus looked up at him in some surprise. Felix shook his head. 'You go first.'

So Iucundus told how he came to be here in Rome, sitting in this prison, facing possible pain and death. Felix sat silent, apparently fascinated, his dark face barely visible in the soft light from the lamp.

'And now it's your turn, isn't it?' Iucundus said. 'I want to know what your position is: you're not like the rest of the slaves, I can see that.'

Felix reflected for a moment, his hands clasped round one knee. The light caught his dark eyes and for a moment they were full of life. Then his eyelids fell and the light was hidden. He sighed. 'Have I really got a story at all?' he asked at last. 'I've just always lived here.'

'Your mother was a slave?'

'Of course. She was one of the mistress' weaving-women. She was beautiful, and had the most wonderful hair:

thick, red-brown like a new chestnut. When I was little I used to pull out the hairpins and let it fall around me. It smelt warm, like honey. She laughed a lot – ' he stopped suddenly and pulled up his other knee, burying his head in his arms.

'Perhaps you don't want to tell?'

Felix raised his head. 'It's not that. But, you see, everyone here has always known who I was, so I felt safe. And now there's Demetrius, and you, and Trofimus too, so many new people. I don't feel safe any more. It's all different.'

'Perhaps. But perhaps it might be better, too?'

Felix ignored this. 'They can just get rid of you.'

This cold statement from someone Iucundus had regarded as a cheeky, confident boy shocked him. 'Why would the master want to do that? He hasn't wanted to before.'

Felix's eyes when they met Iucundus' were filled with a most unchildlike bleakness. 'What can I do, after all? I'm not specially good at anything. Some of them like boys my age. For sex,' he added impatiently, seeing that Iucundus hadn't understood. 'Did you really not know that? But the master doesn't seem interested in boys. So you see?'

Iucundus realised he had more to be grateful for than he had imagined. He swallowed hard. 'Well, what you need to do is to learn to do more things. There are lots of things slaves do: cooking, writing, reading, accounts. I haven't seen you with the schoolmaster much, have I?'

'He doesn't like me.'

Iucundus laughed, remembering something he'd overheard. 'You played up, didn't you? Wouldn't do the work and gave cheeky answers. Well, no wonder he doesn't care for you. Look, you've seen something really important, something a boy who was stupid wouldn't have grasped. You're a slave, and that means you need to be smart, or bad things can happen. So you've got to work hard, do as the teacher says, learn to be a really good reader, say, or quick with the abacus, and the master won't dream of getting rid of you. I promise you.'

Iucundus thought he sounded unbelievably bossy and probably wrong too, but Felix seemed to be encouraged. 'Well, I will.'

'And your mother?' Iucundus asked. 'Is she still in the house?'

'No.' Another silence. 'The master gave her away. Not this master: the old one, his father.'

'Gave her away?'

'Yes. It was a few years ago. Four, I think. There was a man called Caesar who came on a visit. There were lots of important visitors in those days. The old master had been consul - they're in charge of everything - and his son Lucius would have been consul too, I expect. There were big dinners every night then, and musicians and poets and philosophers – you know, people who talk a lot?' he added for Iucundus' benefit. 'The old master liked those kinds of people. It was a lot of fun, always something happening, you'd find people tuning up their instruments, or practising their recitation in every corner. And the dancers! They had lovely costumes, and there was one who danced with a snake, but my mother wouldn't let me see that. She was just a child when she came here with Vibia when the master married her – his second wife. Lucius' mother was somebody else, which is why he was much older than the lady Manlia or the lord Torquatus. Anyway – ' he took a deep breath, abandoning the complicated family history of the Torquati. 'Even for those days, when there were always visitors, this was a big fuss. We were down at the master's big villa near Baiae.

'The day Caesar came, my mother was called away. She was sitting at the loom, and she jumped up smiling and left the room, so quick and light always. I remember her feet as she walked out, how pretty they were in their light sandals, and how the hem of her blue dress had got turned up a little. I'd been sitting on the floor, playing with some loomweights, and as she went out of the room the shuttle fell from her loom and was left hanging, swinging on its thread.

'I don't remember much more about that day. There wasn't anything special about it, as far as I knew. Only – only – my mother came and kissed me as I was going to sleep, lying in her own bed. She'd had a bath, I think, and smelled of violets, her scent.' He stopped and knuckled his eyes. Looking away from Iucundus, he kicked at one of the grain sacks, muttering furiously, 'She never said goodbye.'

'Do you mean she didn't come back? What happened, Felix?'

'Oh, well, in the morning we all crowded into the reception hall. Everyone who could find an excuse, anyway, and who hadn't already seen this famous Caesar. I was only seven, so I could slip to the front easily enough. But I wouldn't have done if I'd known, I'd have run right out into the garden, and then perhaps it wouldn't have happened.'

He stopped, biting his lips, and Iucundus put an arm round his shoulders, but Felix didn't seem to notice. His eyes were looking at something far away. 'The master came in, and Caesar, with some of his slaves and soldiers, and I was looking at their armour. Looking at the young master, too, our lord, who was just a big boy then, almost a man, and at the boy who'd come with Caesar, who looked a bit younger. It was the lord Octavian, you've seen him. You could see he and our lord Torquatus had made friends. And then suddenly my mother was there, dressed in her lovely blue dress, her best one. The master said something, I didn't hear what. I suppose I wasn't really listening. Everyone smiled, even Vibia, though she was never much of a smiler. And then all of a sudden some of the weaving-women took me away. I don't remember where we went, only their skirts flapping in my face as they hurried me away down the corridor. I asked them where my mother was. They just looked at each other, and wouldn't say. I asked more and more as the day went on, and felt really frightened.

'In the evening, my mother's best friend among the women slaves, Thais, gave me some bread and milk and made me sleep in with her and the other women. I was crying and I shouted at her – ' His voice broke and came out as a husky whisper – 'where is she? Where's my mother?' And then she told me: gone. She'd been given to Caesar by the master. How can a person just give another person? How can they? And couldn't they have given me too? I wouldn't have been any trouble.'

Felix couldn't say any more. He sat with his head in his hands, and there was silence for a bit.

'I don't know where she is. I just don't know,' he said. 'How can I ever find her again?'

'I don't know, Felix,' Iucundus said, then asked: 'Do you want to tell me her name?'

'Nereis.' Felix's voice was so soft Iucundus could hardly catch the word. He sighed. 'And if I found her, what then?'

'You can deal with that once you've found her.' Iucundus was struggling to find anything helpful to say. What chance did Felix have of tracking down his mother? He had no idea. Another thought struck him. 'You didn't mention your father, Felix,' he said rather tentatively, thinking that a slave father might not be able to help him much. He was out of his depth, he knew.

To Iucundus' amazement Felix burst out laughing, then turned and said bitterly: 'Hadn't you realised? My father was the master, the old master. My mother was his favourite. Of course.'

Iucundus didn't have a chance to respond to this, because feet were sounding outside the door. Not stealthy feet these: boots crunched on stone, the door creaked open once again, and an unfamiliar face appeared in the gap.

'Trofimus,' Felix cried, and burst into tears.

Chapter 11

Just as Torquatus was leaving the house to walk down to the Forum next morning a slave arrived at the door. His clothes were probably more expensive than Torquatus' own, his manner very much haughtier. Octavian, his note said, wished to see him again. Torquatus thanked the man with what he hoped was the appropriate degree of grave courtesy and told him he would attend his master as soon as possible. Then he went down to the Forum, his head high, his heart in his boots.

What was he going to say to Octavian? No doubt he wanted to know what progress Torquatus had made, and what he had discovered. Well, that shouldn't take long. Had he actually made any progress towards reclaiming the stolen money? He had begun his search with no clear leads to follow, convinced that Antonius was behind the business, in which case the problem confronting him was simple – how in Hades to get it back? Balbus' little security lapse had thrown the field wide open, though one of the new names led straight back to Antonius. Torquatus admitted to himself that Antonius' most unsettling insinuation had been that Octavian might have stolen his own cash to give him a motive for disposing of a friend he no longer trusted.

He knew he wasn't at his best as he walked the length of the Forum, greeting and being greeted, bestowing his approval on this man, checking to see where he stood in relation to that, receiving congratulations on his election. Cicero's head had gone from the rostra, though there were plenty of others up there, bloated, jaws sagging open, their eyes pecked out by vultures, grinning blindly at the small crowd in the pale winter sunshine. Otherwise everything looked quite normal. Stalls had crowded around the edges of the Forum, selling Saturnalia gifts of precious glass phials of scent, wax candles and little pottery figurines, as well as every kind of luxury food, such as people can be persuaded to pay for at this time: jars of figs in honey, olives stuffed with herbs and garlic, specially-matured fish-sauce at premium prices. The sight of them gave Torquatus a jolt: could it really be Saturnalia so soon?

Men and women came and went, carrying baskets of bread or fish or cabbage, or prettily-wrapped gifts, or accompanied by slaves doing so. All quite normal: except that there was something subdued about the scene. Torquatus noticed a man cast a fearful glance towards the rostra, then quickly look away again as if hoping he hadn't been observed. That wasn't normal, for a free man. Women made their purchases at the stalls with less noisy haggling than usual, and fewer of them seemed to be standing around chatting; instead they were going quietly away once they'd finished their business. The whole place still smelt of death, though the killings had slowed to a steady trickle, now that many of the men who expected proscription had fled or been disposed of. The pile of bodies Torquatus had seen tossed down in a jumble of limbs and guts at the foot of the rostra had been cleared away: no doubt they'd been thrown into the Tiber and would eventually be washed out to sea. They certainly wouldn't have been given to the families for burial, since part of the punishment, the totality of the thing, was the refusal of memory, the very heart of the Roman family.

At the Ringmakers' Stairs he sent away any clients still with him, telling them he was going to visit Octavian. He could see they were impressed, which was why he'd said it: it was important for them to know that their patron was a friend of one of the Three. He only hoped it was true. He kept Becco and Pulex with him to guard him on his way home

This time, Octavian was alone, and he found the lack of Agrippa's reassuring presence ominous. Octavian wasn't looking well - a small, pale, sickly boy, no more - and Torquatus felt a stir of pity for him. If he didn't trust anyone, was that so surprising? Then he met those cold bright eyes and forgot about pity.

Octavian laid down the scroll he'd been reading and stood up. Since he was on his feet, Torquatus remained standing too. Octavian came straight to the point. 'What have you discovered?'

'I've seen to Balbus, Antonius and Lepidus, and -,'

'I asked what you'd discovered?' Octavian said gently.

Torquatus spoke carefully. 'I have reason to believe that one or more people may have learned of the movement of the money. There was a leak from Balbus' household.'

'Balbus. Ah.' Octavian was clearly turning this over in his mind. If Torquatus was wrong, and the security leak had had nothing to do with the business, he'd probably just made a powerful enemy of Balbus, for the rest of his life. Octavian looked at him for a long moment, then sat down. He didn't point Torquatus to a stool, and it seemed wiser not to take one unasked. 'I asked you to call on me today, partly because I wanted to hear if you'd made any progress, but also because I've received this.' He handed Torquatus the small scroll of papyrus he'd been looking at when Torquatus came in. 'Read it.'

The writing was that of someone who'd learned the art in youth but who had seldom needed to practise it. It was neat; it had clearly been thought out, sentence by sentence. Dictated, even, perhaps? It was, Torquatus thought, quite deadly.

Lord it began, without formal greetings or date, *Beware of Aulus Manlius Torquatus. His family have been bitter enemies of your divine father, and can the son really have changed? His father Lucius Manlius Torquatus was a supporter of Sulla, then of Cicero and Pompey, all men who opposed Caesar. His brother Lucius Manlius Torquatus the younger also died fighting against the divine Caesar, even after Caesar's generosity to him at Oricum. Generosity he rewarded by treachery. His sister is married to yet another of Caesar's sworn enemies, Gnaeus Domitius Ahenobarbus. She lives in her brother's house, and she is friendly with women whose husbands you have rightly declared enemies of the state: she visits the widows of proscribed senators every day. What do you suppose they talk about?*

He tells you your money was stolen. Do you believe that? What happens in Neapolis can happen elsewhere, and a man who commits forgery will hardly be scared of theft.

Perhaps you should ask this Torquatus, this friend of yours, what his brother knew.

Take heed of this warning, from one who loved and served the divine Caesar.

Torquatus dropped the letter. Or rather, it fell from his hands. Octavian was watching him as a snake watches a mouse.

'There are two - no, three - real accusations here.' Torquatus was relieved that he sounded as calm as if he'd been expounding some obscure point of law. 'The first is that I am disloyal, and indeed must be since my father and brother were Caesar's enemies. My answer to that is: look back. Look back to our first meeting at my father's villa, that day you came visiting with Julius. Remember how my father threw me out of his house because of my wish to serve Caesar, how I went to Africa as one of his aides, and fought even against my own brother for his sake. Remember how I came back to Italy with you after Caesar's death, how I took you to my father's house at Brundisium. How I have supported you ever since. Remember last summer, how I assisted your mother and sister when the Senate would have taken them hostage. If I were disloyal to you, wouldn't I have gone to Antonius? Or fled to Sextus Pompey in Sicily? This man – ' and he pointed a scornful finger at the letter where it lay on the floor between them – 'makes no specific accusations. He can accuse me of nothing I've actually done. He can't even find anything I've said that might throw doubt on my honesty.'

Torquatus paced over to the window, looked out blindly onto sunlit roofs where pigeons scrabbled and cooed. 'His accusations against my sister I regard as beneath contempt. Her husband's property was confiscated: she has nothing now but what came to her as dowry. What harm could she do, even if she wished to?' He looked seriously across the room at Octavian. 'You and I both know what it is to have a sister we love and trust: I would trust Manlia with my life. As to the final allegation - forgery - there I am in the dark. What does he mean? Forgery of what? When? By whom? If there has been wrong-doing within my household, be sure I will discover it. But all of this is to convince you that I might have stolen your money, which is nonsense. What possible motive could I have, that would be worth risking my life for?'

He stooped, picked up the letter, and laid it on the table. 'Neapolis' he said. 'What kind of forgery could have happened there, I wonder?'

Octavian laughed, and Torquatus glanced up at him, surprised. 'Oh, I shouldn't worry about that,' he said. 'That must be pure invention. Most of your household weren't even in Neapolis last year, and I'm sure those who were with you were far too busy to commit crimes.'

Torquatus stared at him, relieved and puzzled that he seemed not to take the accusation of forgery, to him the most dangerous, at all seriously. He himself was shaken to the core: a forger? a thief? In his own house? The accusation was so vague as to be meaningless: there was nothing he could get his teeth into. He passed his slaves under review. Which of them could have done such a thing, risking their lives? And for what? Profit? A cause? What kind of cause could make a slave put himself in danger? Or was it himself or Manlia who were accused?

Octavian's mind seemed to be moving in the same direction. He was sitting, his hands neatly folded, as Torquatus stood before him. 'And your sister? Are you so confident about all her friendships? Are there really none that might, well, bear investigation?'

'I think not. Her friends are ladies like herself, your own sister among them.'

'Ah, yes.' Octavian paused, thinking, half-smiling. 'Manlia was on the rostra, yesterday. Speaking against our plans to tax the wealthiest of the women?'

'She was there, certainly. I don't know whether she spoke or not. Unfortunately someone hit me on the head before I'd heard it all.'

'You were hit on the head?' He looked genuinely surprised, which surprised Torquatus. His agents were everywhere: witness the speed with which the soldiers had appeared in the Forum yesterday.

'Yes. I've no idea why. Robbery, perhaps. My secretary Demetrius scared the man off and he lost himself in the crowd.'

'Robbery? You had money on you?'

'Well, no. My slaves were carrying my purse.'

He nodded. 'Then something else perhaps?'

'I had nothing on me at all. And that being the case, I think murder was intended. Only luckily Demetrius came up before he had time to finish the job.'

'Luckily indeed.' Torquatus noted his look of mild incredulity.

'Or, of course, my assailant simply acted on the spur of the moment, without stopping to think how unlikely it was that I would have money about me.'

This drew an even more sceptical look.

'The other explanation, one I don't much like, is that someone doesn't want me investigating this theft. And having failed to knock my brains out, he or she has now turned to anonymous letters.' He didn't mention his fear that one of his own slaves had been bribed to make the attempt on his life: that was something he'd keep to himself for now.

'That's possible,' Octavian agreed, his face impassive. 'You say that the accusations are too general to have value. But the letter's comments on your sister aren't vague, are they? I am aware that she is friends with several of the widows of the proscribed: Annalis and Septimius, Ligarius. Most of those women are no threat to me or anyone. But Septimius at least was a potential traitor to the state. It was Antonius who proscribed him, for, well, let's say for personal reasons, but I also regarded him as an enemy. That's what my agents tell me. I'm still collecting information on the others.' His eyes, bright blue, were as cold as a winter sky. 'Warn your sister. I don't want to think the worst of you, or of her, but believe me, I'll see you both dead if I have to.' Looking at his face, Torquatus believed him. 'Then there's the question of your brother. What happened after Oricum? If I remember correctly, it was part of my father's supply-line in Macedonia. A useful little city, lying at the back of a deep bay, just right for supply-ships?'

'Yes, and the whole episode was typical of Caesar. No-one was expecting him to set out in January, because who sails then? So of course he did, and Pompey was caught on the hop. Lucius was in charge of Oricum, with a small force. When the citizens decided to open the gates Lucius was obliged to surrender. He stayed in the camp for several weeks, if I remember rightly.' Torquatus didn't add that he believed Lucius had taken the opportunity of the break-up of the camp to flee from what had in fact been a superior kind of imprisonment and return to his own side.

'No-one could call what he did treachery,' Torquatus went on. 'I didn't agree with him about what was best for Rome, but a traitor he wasn't. In fact he was a man of almost painful rectitude, so I don't know what that accusation means.'

Torquatus was deep in thought as he walked back to his house. It was Octavian's threats against Manlia that had shaken him, even more than the letter's rather wild accusations of treachery and forgery and theft. He needed to talk to his sister, to pass on Octavian's message, to try and find out what she knew about any of the women she visited, and to talk over the other accusations. But when he arrived at home, Manlia was in no mood for a quiet chat. Instead she pounced on him almost before he was in the house. But before she could speak, Trofimus somehow appeared between them.

'Your toga, lord. And perhaps you would care for a cup of wine? Something to eat?'

Torquatus wondered how Trofimus did it. He was a big man, to be sure, but he certainly didn't do anything as unseemly as pushing in between the master and his sister. Torquatus agreed with a sigh that a cup of wine would be very welcome, and Trofimus snapped his fingers for Victor to come forward and take the bundle of toga.

'And then, lord, there's the matter of Iucundus to attend to.'

Torquatus had forgotten all about the boy. With an odd pang he wondered what else Iucundus might be involved in? Nothing that happened in Neapolis last year could be put to his charge, of course: the boy had only just arrived. He put the thought aside, and said to Manlia, 'I need to talk to you,' but she shook her head.

'Once we've decided what to do with the boy,' she insisted.

As Torquatus opened his mouth to object, the boy Trofimus had sent for wine came back with a tray. Demetrius was hovering in the background.

'I'll send the boy in, shall I, lord?' Trofimus asked.

Manlia nodded. 'Yes, please.' Trofimus gestured to the boy to take the tray to the study and Torquatus resigned himself. He wished now that he hadn't taken his toga off, especially when he saw the captive. Iucundus looked dirty and dishevelled, having been locked up in the grain-store. A proper little barbarian.

Torquatus looked him over coldly. 'So,' he began. 'You saw your master attacked and you ran away. At least that's the most generous interpretation I can put on your actions.'

'No!' Iucundus said loudly, and Trofimus frowned. 'Lord, I didn't! I saw you lying on the ground, and a man standing beside you, bending over you,' he said, in a breathless, urgent voice. 'I ran towards you. He saw me coming and ran off. He went across the Forum and up that big road we went up the other day, when that old man got killed. He ran into one of those little side-streets, and I lost him. I was frightened of the people there, the way they crowded round, and I knew I couldn't hope to find him again. So I went back to the temple, but you'd gone, and I came back as fast as I could.'

Torquatus raised his eyebrows and turned to Demetrius. 'I want to hear what you have to say. And I want Becco and Pulex here as well.' Trofimus had them ready: he produced the bodyguards with a flourish, the huge men trying to make themselves as small as possible.

'You two. Did you see a man standing beside me as I lay on the ground?'

'No, lord,' Becco replied, with an apologetic glance towards Iucundus. 'But then, I wasn't looking that way. I was trying to check that Pulex was following me, you see.'

Torquatus' stern gaze was turned on Pulex. 'I didn't see him, lord. I think by the time I'd got free of the crowd he'd gone already. I did see Iucundus running, though: he was just at the bottom of the Argiletum,' he added as if this might help.

Torquatus turned to his secretary. 'Demetrius.'

'I saw no-one, lord. Except for Iucundus, running away.'

'I wasn't!' Iucundus burst out again. 'Demetrius, you must have seen him. It was the man I saw coming out of Antonius' house yesterday – was it yesterday? I don't know his name.'

'Well, I saw no-one, lord. Except Iucundus, of course. It looked as if he was running away, but of course if he says he wasn't – And I don't know who Iucundus may have seen at Antonius' house yesterday.' He shrugged.

Iucundus stared at Demetrius. 'But he came to see you, yesterday evening!'

'Another lie,' Demetrius said calmly. 'No-one came to see me yesterday evening.'

152

'He spoke to me outside Antonius' house, said he was coming to see you. I gave you the message.' Demetrius shook his head and shrugged, and Iucundus, despairing, turned and stretched out his hands towards Torquatus as if he would clutch at his tunic, but Torquatus ignored this mute appeal.

'Fetch the doorkeeper.' In fact the man didn't even need to be fetched, as he was standing at the back of the little crowd, half an eye on the doorway, half on the doings in the reception hall. He came forward. 'No, lord,' he said, avoiding Iucundus' eye. 'I can't say that anyone from Antonius' house was here last night. Demetrius went out, though. Just a for a little while, and I heard him speaking to someone in the street, I think.'

'I went down the road to Atticus' house, lord,' Demetrius put in quickly. 'You remember, you asked me to borrow a copy of Cornelius Nepos' new Life of Cato from Atticus. You wanted to read it.'

Torquatus nodded. He had indeed wanted to read it. He wondered if perhaps there was some insanity in the family: the very name of Cato, that stern upholder of the Republic, would bring the Three out in a collective rash. 'I asked you to do that a good two weeks ago,' he pointed out, and Demetrius looked a little uncomfortable. 'I am sorry, lord. We've been so busy - I admit it slipped my mind.'

Torquatus nodded again, accepting the explanation. 'Oh, very well.' Everyone was looking at him, silently waiting for his verdict.

'Becco and Pulex: I am not pleased that you allowed yourselves to become separated from me in the crowd. You weren't there to listen to the speeches, but to protect me. You've served me well so far, but if you forget your duty again you'll receive a severe whipping. Is that understood?'

The two men looked relieved, as well they might, and murmured protestations of constant vigilance from now on.

'Demetrius, I believe you saved my life. Thank you.'

Demetrius' narrow face relaxed.

'Iucundus: your story would be more impressive if any of the others had seen this mysterious attacker. I have to say I don't believe you. Nor do I believe you did this on your own. Who's behind this? Who has paid you?'

'Lord, I swear what I say is true.' All traces of panic and desperation seemed to have left Iucundus as he stood there, head up, looking at Torquatus almost with contempt, if such a thing were possible. Torquatus' fury flamed up at this insolence.

'I'll have you flogged, boy. Perhaps then you'll tell me who's bought you.'

Iucundus' face was very pale, but he continued to meet his master's eyes directly. 'Yes, lord. But I have told you the truth.'

There was an awkward silence for a second or two. Then Trofimus came forward. 'A flogging certainly seems to be called for, lord,' he agreed. 'But perhaps I might suggest an alternative punishment?'

Torquatus nodded and the steward put his hands together calmly over his rather solid belly. 'Inspecting the house, lord, I observed that the latrines appeared not to have been cleared out for some time. I was intending to set some of the garden-slaves onto it. But perhaps the boy could do it?'

Torquatus smiled. 'Oh yes, certainly.' He could imagine that it would be a most unpleasant job, which was no doubt why his stewardless household had left it undone. He hoped it would teach the lad a lesson, take him down a peg or two. He had spoken to Torquatus as if he were his equal, which was unforgiveable. 'And when he's done that he can go to the stables, or I may decide to send him to one of my estates. I don't want him working near me.'

He looked round the sea of horrified faces, carefully blank faces, faces in which excitement wasn't quite hidden. 'You may all go.'

The slaves hurried away, murmuring. As the hall

emptied, Torquatus called Demetrius back. When he was sure there was no-one within earshot, he asked quietly, 'Who was it you spoke to in the street last night?'

Demetrius' face was impossible to read. He paused a moment, then said, 'He's a freedman from Antonius' house, but he didn't come on Antonius' business.' Again he paused. 'I didn't tell you in front of everyone because it was a private matter. That man came to bring me a message about someone I knew, in Neapolis, who had died. That's all.'

'Really? Why didn't you invite him in, then?'

'I did offer, lord, but he was in a hurry.'

'I see. That seems reasonable. Who was the man who died?'

'He was called Spurius,' Demetrius said quietly. 'He did me a - a kindness once.'

The close-set black eyes seemed to scan Torquatus' face.

'I'm asking you because you can help me now. I badly need to know where this stolen money has gone, and I believe Antonius or one of his agents is behind the theft. I want you to make friends with this freedman. Take him out for a drink, get to know him, use all your ingenuity to discover the truth for me. I promise you your freedom if you succeed. And I remind you: I must get the money back by the end of this month. Use whatever you want of mine: money, slaves, anything. But get that man talking.'

Demetrius' face was expressionless in the gathering dusk, but Torquatus saw him nod. He turned away: at last he could go with Manlia to his study, where the long-awaited tray of wine stood on a side-table. Trofimus poured the wine himself, watered it to Torquatus' requirements, checked that there was a dish of tiny cinnamon pastries and a bowl of nuts at Manlia's elbow, and went off. The heavy curtain fell back over the doorway, shutting out the sounds of the slaves' feet and voices.

Torquatus took a good glug of wine and swirled it

round his mouth in appreciation. When he'd swallowed it he said again, 'We have to talk.'

'What's wrong, Aulus?' Her anxious eyes scanned his face.

'Manlia, Octavian told me that although he has no reason to regard you as an enemy at present, he will wipe you out without a second thought if necessary.'

'He what?'

'It's true. I was summoned to the Palatine today because he'd received an anonymous letter poisoning his mind against me. It pointed out our family's long history of enmity to Caesar, and drew attention to your friendships.'

Manlia stared at him. 'Jupiter! Did he name any particular friends of mine he doesn't like?'

'The wives and widows of his enemies: Annalis, Septimius, Ligarius, Rebilus were all mentioned.'

Manlia lay back. 'I know them all, of course. Some are friends. I told you about them yesterday. I'll need to warn Iunia if Rebilus is threatened.'

'Actually, I don't think he's been proscribed. Or he hadn't, this morning: I saw him walking about in the Forum. She'd better be careful."

'Yes, though I don't know what harm she could do. Did Octavian say what he suspects my friends of?'

'Some sort of conspiracy against him, I think. Or maybe just general hostility: you know, warning people when they are about to be proscribed.'

Manlia's smile flickered, and she shot him a sideways glance. 'From what I've heard, that's been going on since the proscriptions started, and is actually one of the few signs of normal human feeling in Rome just now.'

Torquatus couldn't help smiling back. 'Point taken. But please think carefully about this. Have any of them said anything to you suggesting political involvement?'

'Only what I've already told you.' She looked at her brother soberly, twisting a strand of her hair in her fingers, then turned on her side, reaching for her wine-cup. 'I don't want to get any of them into trouble. Haven't they had enough already? Besides, what woman of our class isn't interested in politics? They are – were – married to senators. Of course they knew what was in the air, what was being discussed in the Senate, what deals were being struck, who were friends and who were enemies. You know that as well as I do. And just now, when politics is – well, chaos, tyranny, pick your own word for it – of course everyone, men and women alike – is interested. What are women to do? Sit quietly at home weaving, I suppose.' Her eyes were bright with anger. She took a good glug of wine and lay back.

'Well, not weaving perhaps, not nowadays,' Torquatus agreed with a nod. 'But not the rostra either, please. I know I don't have power over you –'

'Well, I'm glad you know that anyway.' Manlia's eyes were still sparkling.

' – but you might remember that my own life's at stake here too. What Octavian actually said was that he would wipe us all out if necessary.'

Manlia was quiet for a moment, twisting that strand of hair over and over in her fingers. Then she said, 'I see. Well, as I told you some of my women friends are very jumpy, and I think that may be because they suspect there's a plot of some kind. I really don't believe any of the women themselves are involved, if there is one. With the possible exception of Flavia, Septimius' widow. She's got an eye for the main chance. But the others? No. Does he mean Aemilia? Antonius wasn't even decent enough to have her killed when she begged him to.'

Torquatus had no answer to give her. 'No doubt he was embarrassed,' he said at last. 'They want to believe in a world where people behave like decent Roman citizens, even when they aren't prepared to do so themselves.'

'I won't see my friends any more if it will compromise you,' Manlia told him. 'But you'd better come with me when I tell them. If you don't mind?'

'Of course not. We'll go down to Postumia's tomorrow.'

They sat in silence for some time. Finally, Manlia withdrew from her thoughts and asked, 'You said there was something else in this letter?'

'Oh yes. Two things. First, an accusation of forgery which was very vague, but I wonder -'

'Well, what?'

'Antonius was going on about the Asia revenues - again - when I saw him. And when you think of it, why should he have sent money to Balbus when he could have simply ordered it sent back to his own house in Rome?'

Manlia sat up, swinging her legs down off the reading-couch. 'It seems very far-fetched: who would be brave enough to swindle Antonius? But I can see you think it's possible, so what are you going to do about it?'

'I think it might be worth sending someone to Neapolis. Yes, it may be too late, but I think it would be worthwhile. Because perhaps there is a connection between this theft and something that happened last year.'

Manlia looked doubtful, but before she could speak Demetrius came in to ask if he should refill the wine-jug. Torquatus flapped him away, but he hesitated. 'Excuse me, master, if I've heard what I shouldn't, but as I came in I believe you mentioned sending someone to Neapolis as part of your investigations into this awful theft. I don't of course know what task you had in mind, but if it should be anything confidential - ?'

'As it is,' Torquatus agreed.

'Then perhaps you would care to send me, master? You know you can trust me.'

Torquatus did. But he'd also seen Demetrius on a horse.

'I'll bear it in mind,' he said without enthusiasm.

Manlia looked after the man as he left the room. 'How odd,' she said. 'I wonder why he wanted to go down there? And how long he'd been standing outside the door.'

Torquatus was impatient. 'Did he say he wanted to? Though it's odd that he should have offered just now: apparently it was a man from Antonius' household he was talking to last night. The man had brought him a message from Neapolis. Anyway, he's right that I could trust him. But I was telling you about this cursed letter. The final accusation was almost worst of all: that Lucius had done something underhand. That I don't believe: Lucius was stubborn, and he could be a prig, too, but he would never have done anything dishonest, for that very reason. But how in Hades do I prove it?'

'And there was no clue as to what?'

'Not really. Oricum was mentioned.'

'Caesar kept Lucius there for a couple of months, didn't he? Is the idea that Lucius did something wrong at that time?' Her frown deepened, 'It was ages ago: nearly seven years, isn't it? How could anything that happened then still matter?'

'I don't know. I really have no idea. But I'll tell you this: I'd swear the Lucius thing mattered a lot to Octavian. But the forgery didn't. He brushed it aside.' He shook himself, swallowed the last of his wine. 'Anyway, whatever Octavian thinks I'm going to take both matters seriously. Because I've a feeling these things are all connected in some way.'

'You don't think the writer of the letter - and who can he have been, I wonder? - was just lumping together any grievances he could think of? I suppose "he" is right?'

'No. It was quite short and to the point. No rambling. And I think it must have been a man: he signed himself "one who loved and served your divine father." A woman wouldn't have said that. One thing's clear, anyway: Octavian has been sold the idea that I may have stolen the cash myself.'

They both sat for a few moments in gloomy silence, then Manlia shook herself. 'Speaking of money,' she said, 'Balbus is coming to dinner. We really should be bathing and dressing now.'

'Balbus is coming to dinner?' Torquatus was surprised. He and Balbus had never been close, coming as they did from different generations. 'And who else? I suppose he isn't coming alone?'

'He isn't. It's a men's party, except for me.' And to Torquatus' surprise, she presented him with a most select list of the great and good of Rome, including Octavian's closest friends.

'Jupiter! You have been busy: this sounds like a serious dinner-party. But that means garlands, perfumes, special food, entertainment – are we prepared for this?'

Manlia laughed. 'It's all in hand, Aulus. Listen.' She held up one hand. Torquatus became aware of the voices of slaves, a clatter of silverware, the squeak of a couch-leg on the stone floor, a subdued laugh. Scents were drifting in, too, of flowers, incense, food.

'I can't keep up with you,' he complained.

'Well, don't waste time grizzling about it.' She was brisk. 'You've time for a bath if you're quick. I've bathed. And put on your best dining-gown.'

'Don't forget to tell me to wash behind my ears, will you?'

Manlia laughed. 'I was just about to.'

Afterwards, Torquatus remembered only two things about the banquet, the first being simply that it had happened. Nothing remarkable in that, one might say. But there had been little in the way of formal entertainment over the last few months, and Torquatus felt as though somehow he had announced his presence among the leaders of Rome, had declared himself not cowed by his troubles.

The second was that it was the first time he ever met Vergil, brought along by his patron Maecenas. The young poet, very shy, read to them from a series of eclogues he was writing. Torquatus liked to think, later, that he had instantly recognised the poet's genius, though in all honesty the only thing he knew for sure was that he had been delighted to have such a refined and cultured conclusion to his party. Later, Maecenas' extraordinary ear for verse, and his sophisticated understanding of how poets work, became proverbial. On this evening, Torquatus only felt as he listened that his hot dining room, in the centre of Rome, was transformed into the rich Italian countryside. Romans like to think of themselves as urban, sophisticated and smart, contemptuous of the heavy countryman's slow wits. And yet, they all have deep roots in that countryside, they all want farms, they want to think they are eating their own produce. The most urban of Romans had ancestors who lived on their own land, coming to Rome only when they must. Even Balbus, a man it was impossible to imagine supervising his own harvest, was moved by the poems.

At the end of the evening, Torquatus managed to get a private word with him. On the pretext of finding Atticus' Portraits, they wandered into the library. Torquatus was surprised to find Demetrius still there, working through the family papers. Piles of letters, leases, loan agreements, and so forth were spread about everywhere.

Torquatus found the book Balbus had been wanting, and they agreed an appointment for the next day, to discuss the implications of the apparent security leak.

And then suddenly everyone had gone. Torquatus could hear the slaves hurrying in and out of the dining room calling to each other, saw them scurry past the library door, first with stacks of plates and teetering piles of silverware, then with brushes, buckets and mops. Torquatus glanced idly at the documents Demetrius had been sorting: it seemed as if he was intending to read every scrap ever written by a Manlius Torquatus: there was his father's large, distinctive, script, there Lucius', similar but smaller and neater. Torquatus threw the letters back onto the table, yawned, and went upstairs to bed.

Chapter 12

Torquatus got his clients' business over with as soon as possible next morning, impatient to see Balbus without loss of time. His litter was waiting, and the bearers trotted off as soon as he was comfortably settled inside. As he was carried through the rain and murk of a foul December morning, Torquatus turned his mind to the investigation he wanted to carry out in Neapolis. Who could he send? The quickest way would be to send soldiers, who could command horses and anything else they needed, but he wasn't going to ask for Octavian's help till he was sure of his ground. The anonymous letter had been irritatingly vague: maybe the alleged forgery was nothing to do with Neapolis at all? Maybe he was simply being misled by Antonius' loud complaints? And then, with an audible gasp, Torquatus saw what a fool he was being. His spine tingling with this new terror, he thanked all the gods from his heart that he hadn't sent anyone to sniff around in Neapolis, because if Antonius was telling the truth any forgery committed last summer must have been for Octavian's benefit. Would even Octavian have dared to write letters in the consul's name? If he had, it would account for his insouciance about that particular allegation. And of course he'd have covered his back: he'd have made sure there was no proof. Jupiter! This whole affair was turning more dangerous by the hour.

Balbus was in his office, as he had been on Torquatus' last visit. When they each had a cup of wine and the slaves had stepped back, Balbus began by thanking him for last night's dinner. For a few moments they chatted agreeably enough, until Torquatus felt he could come to the point.

'And now. This list,' he began. 'It was longer than I'd expected.'

Balbus looked as close to embarrassment as Torquatus had ever seen him. 'It seems that one of my slaves made the mistake of discussing some details of the transport in a room where several visitors were waiting to see me,' he admitted.

'Details? Which details, exactly?'

He looked even more awkward. 'Well, how much, where it was going, how it would be transported.'

'Wonderful. He didn't happen to mention the date, I suppose?'

'He said not.' Balbus carefully moved a stylus from the right-hand side of a pair of writing-tablets to the left-hand side.

'But it wouldn't have been hard, would it, to find that out, if one hung around the stable-yard? One might work out that if a couple of fast mule-carriages had been ordered for somewhere just outside Rome, they might be worth intercepting?'

'No.'

Torquatus sat back, thinking. 'And this happened when?'

'On the fourth day before the Kalends of December.'

'Six days before the money was due to move. Ample time for the news to filter out.' Balbus said nothing. 'You say, "he said not." So do I assume he's not still with you?'

'Only in the sense that I am holding him here until I could be sure you didn't need to speak to him yourself. Then I'll get rid of him.'

Torquatus nodded. 'Thank you. I'll see him, just in case. But first, let's go through the list. Three members of your own household heard him?'

'Yes. One immediately told him to be quiet, and they all reported what had happened. They are long-standing members of staff. They say they were shocked at his carelessness, and certainly didn't pass on the information to anyone else. And indeed the way they reacted suggests to me that they understood the gravity of what had occurred.'

If they had passed anything on, they certainly

wouldn't have owned up. But Torquatus reckoned that Balbus' slaves and freedmen had far more to gain by behaving well than by doing wrong.

'Apart from the three members of your own household, then, there are these three other names. Marcus Antonius Philo, Fortunatus and Modestus. A freedman and two slaves, I assume.'

'Yes, that's right. Fortunatus belongs to Messalla Rufus, and Modestus to Maecenas.' Anyone from Maecenas' household could be ruled out: not even Agrippa was more loyal to Octavian than Maecenas. He'd speak to Messalla Rufus though. Torquatus scarcely knew the man: he was an elderly, distinguished writer - on augury, he thought - whom he seemed to remember as a friend of Cicero's and his father's. Hardly a likely plotter. 'And the other man?'

'A freedman of Antonius.'

'Obviously. Tell me more.' Torquatus finished his wine and laid the cup down on the table. Balbus signed to the slave, but Torquatus waved the man away.

'I don't know the man well myself. My staff tell me he's a sort of general fixer for his patron. He came here to get a loan for a metalworker.'

'A metalworker?' What in Hades could that be about?

Balbus nodded, and seemed to relax. 'Armour. He wanted a loan, to buy in the metal for a large stock of weapons. Knowing, of course, that the great battle against Caesar's murderers must take place soon, and seeing a business opportunity.'

'This armourer will supply Antonius, of course. And Octavian?'

'No doubt. Assuming he has the capacity.'

Balbus seemed to have cheered up, now that the conversation had turned to business. Torquatus nodded. Antonius' legions would come first, of course. And doubtless the man would also carry any information he'd gleaned at Balbus' house to his old master, too. Things were looking up.

They called in the stupid slave whose mistake had caused all this, a sad wisp of a man, hangdog and weedy. No doubt he'd had plenty of time to reflect on his future, or the lack of it. He knew nothing, anyway, corroborated everything Balbus had said, and they sent him away again, under the guard of two burly men who looked like retired gladiators.

Torquatus left the house deep in thought. Every clue seemed to point to Antonius, and the way into Antonius' household lay through Demetrius' contact there. Demetrius must be sent down there now, today.

Chapter 13

Manlia was waiting for Torquatus in the reception hall. Behind her, her maid stood waiting, the fur-trimmed cloak over her arm. Torquatus looked a question.

'We're going down to Postumia's, remember?' Seeing that her brother was about to protest, she gave him a chilly look. 'You promised you'd come with me.'

'I did. I'd forgotten, that's all. Do we need to go now?'

'They tend to get together in the mornings, so if we do it now, you'll meet them all.'

Walking down the slope of the Quirinal a few moments later, Manlia asked, 'Have you thought any more about how you can discover what happened in Neapolis? If anything did, of course.'

Torquatus checked that the slaves were far enough behind them to be out of earshot. 'I daren't,' he said simply, and waited for Manlia to work out what he meant. Her brow furrowed, she walked on in silence, then stopped and stared up at him. 'Gods! Only one man could have been behind it? That's what you're thinking?'

'That's what I'm thinking,' he agreed.

They walked on in silence. Torquatus said, 'You'd better explain who I'm going to meet.'

Manlia pulled herself out of her abstraction. 'Well, Iunia you know. And Postumia herself. Annalis' widow.'

'She's not the one who's starving herself to death?'

'You're thinking of Aemilia. I don't think Postumia is heartbroken, just shocked. Shattered. Hardly surprising: her son has had his father murdered, in the centre of Rome, at noon, and instead of the appalling death he should have faced as a parricide, he's promoted to aedile. No wonder she can't make head or tail of it.'

'Poor woman. Who else? You mentioned a Flavia?'

'Yes. I don't know if she'll be there, since no-one exactly made her welcome the other day. And there might be others.'

They'd arrived at Postumia's door, no longer standing open all day as a senator's door should. As soon as they stepped inside they could hear the sound of women's voices, and Manlia, nodding a greeting to the doorman, led the way to a comfortable room facing onto the garden. It was painted with mythological scenes, set into fanciful architectural features. The colours were discreet, with touches of a brilliant blue and a warm red. The mosaic floor was partially covered by rugs in reds and blues of the same shades. There were a few pieces of art: an exquisite little statue of Venus, naked but for her hair as usual, a couple of splendid bronze lamp-stands, and in the corner an easel-painting whose subject Torquatus couldn't make out. Chairs and a reading-couch had been arranged around a brazier, and the scent of spiced and honeyed wine was heavy in the air. Whoever had planned the décor, Torquatus thought, had perfectly understood senatorial taste: a display of wealth stopping - at least in the eyes of other senators - just short of ostentation.

The women looked surprised to see Torquatus, but made room for him and Manlia to join the group, passing him a cup of wine which he politely accepted, little as he liked it hot and sweet like this. He looked around as Manlia named her friends. There was Postumia herself, so crushed by her grief that Torquatus wouldn't have recognised her: even the shape of her face was different; Flavia, a bold-eyed redhead who lay back on the reading-couch in a way that showed off her splendid figure to advantage; and his sister-in-law Iunia, looking rather less subdued than she generally did.

'I brought Aulus with me today,' Manlia was saying, 'because we wanted to explain the difficult situation we're in. The fact is that Octavian has received an anonymous letter, warning him that people are plotting against him. Warning that my brother is doing so. The letter insinuates that my friendships with you all are compromising him.'

There was a murmur of indignation. 'Hasn't Octavian done us enough harm?' Postumia exclaimed. 'Him and Antonius both.' Iunia and Postumia both glanced at Flavia as Postumia said this, though Flavia pretended not to notice.

'And Lepidus?' Torquatus asked. The women nodded with a faint air of irritation. 'And him,' Postumia agreed.

'That may be so,' Manlia agreed. 'But as it is I daren't continue to visit here. For the time being, at least.'

'Who do you think wrote the letter?' Iunia asked curiously.

'No idea,' Manlia replied. 'But it's clear Aulus has an enemy. It's not just a war of words either. His little farm was attacked and the slaves killed some days ago.'

Torquatus looked towards her anxiously. She smiled reassuringly back at him. 'No-one knows why that happened,' she said. 'But you can see that someone is trying to harm him.'

Iunia's face was pale, even for her. 'Your farm was attacked? I didn't know.' She blushed a little. 'You had several slaves there, didn't you?'

Torquatus said, 'I did. But the place was attacked by a well-armed group. They didn't stand a chance.' Iunia stared at him, and he could see her hands shaking in her lap. Why had his news upset he so much?

'Can you tell me exactly which night this attack happened?' Postumia asked. She too looked pale and anxious, Torquatus thought.

'I believe it must have been on the night of the fifth or the sixth day before the Nones,' he told her, and saw her flinch.

'Funny thing,' said Flavia in a high, hard voice. 'Rebilus buys a bunch of gladiators, Torquatus' farm gets attacked, someone warns Octavian off his friend.'

'Rebilus has bought gladiators?' Iunia whispered the question, and Flavia stared at her.

'Surely you knew that, sweetheart? What do you and Rebilus talk about in bed at night?'

Torquatus stared at her. There was a poisonous silence for a moment. Then Postumia gathered herself together, and said with a dignity that surprised Torquatus: 'You're being thoroughly offensive, Flavia. I don't really know why you're here: you must have noticed that none of us welcome your company now. We've all lost our husbands, or fear we shall, while you seem to have dumped yours without a second thought. I think you'd better leave.'

Flavia sat up swiftly, her empty winecup clenched in her hand. For a moment Torquatus thought she was going to hurl it at Postumia, and instinctively he moved to protect her. The movement seemed to change Flavia's mind, and she burst out laughing, a harsh, mocking sound, before swinging off the couch, banging the cup down on a side table and snapping her fingers at her slave, who hurried forward with her cloak. With a last, contemptuous glance round the room she swept out, leaving an anti-climax behind her. For a moment the remaining ladies glanced at each other uncertainly. Then Manlia began to laugh, which set the others off too.

'What a dreadful woman. Thank you for getting rid of her,' Manlia said.

Postumia's smile was strained. 'Well, I can't stand her.' She glanced around as if afraid of being overheard. 'And besides, I wanted to show you something. Something I found. I wonder if you can help me understand it.'

Manlia stared at her. 'Of course we'll help you if we can. What is it?'

Postumia sat down with a sigh. 'I'd better explain. After my husband's death I was trying and trying to understand what made my son do such a dreadful thing. I just couldn't understand it. I've spent a lot of time in Annalis' study, looked through all his documents. I don't know what I was looking for, even.' Her smile was tight. 'I think I just wanted to be near him, and those papers of his

169

seemed to bring me closer, as if they still kept the touch of his hands. You know?' She glanced around and the other women nodded. 'I didn't find anything that helped me understand what had gone wrong between us and our son. But on the floor behind Annalis' work-table, just as if it had fallen off a pile of papers, I found this.' She turned away for a moment, picked up an object from a side-table, and put it into Torquatus' hand.

The weight of it told him at once that it was lead, the sort of little offcut you sometimes find lying about on building sites: the workmen usually pick up the larger pieces to melt down. Part of a sheet, it was about the size of his hand, creased along the middle as if it had been roughly folded over. He stared at it, wondering what it meant and how in the name of heaven it had come to be in a senator's study. Torquatus turned it this way and that, looking at its surface. At first he could see nothing remarkable about it at all; then as he moved his hand and the light fell across it he noticed that some of the scratches on it seemed deeper than others. Looking more closely he thought they were letters. Badly made, clumsy letters, but writing, nonetheless. He moved closer to the lamp, and let the flickering light of the tiny flames play across the surface, turning it this way and that.

Once he'd studied the little piece of metal thoroughly, he handed it silently to Manlia, who bent over it with Iunia.

'CATUS?' Manlia suggested, glancing up at him.

'No, Manlia, there's a U there, look: CAUTUS,' Iunia said.

'That's what I thought,' Torquatus agreed. 'And the only other word I could make out is SPES.'

'I think it's SPEM, don't you, Iunia?' Manlia said, and Iunia agreed.

'That's what it looks like to me.'

Torquatus shrugged. 'Same difference.' He took the metal back, weighing it in his hand, thinking. 'Careful about what? Hope for what?'

'I've no idea,' Postumia told him. 'But what could have made Lucius write on a piece of pipe like that?'

'Not your standard senatorial document, certainly. You could hardly identify his writing from this, though, and maybe he didn't write it, but received it from someone else. Do you have any idea where it came from? You haven't been having any building work done?'

'No. But I think he did write it. Because the day after my husband's death our son turned up at the house, rather the worse for drink, and rummaged about in his father's study for a while. He wouldn't tell me what he was looking for. I didn't want to argue with him,' she said, her eyes not meeting Torquatus'. 'I was afraid. But he must have dropped it. When the slaves cleaned that room the next morning they found it.' Postumia swallowed hard and clenched her hand on a fold of her gown of soft grey silk. 'I was desperate to read it. I was sure Annalis had written it: I still am. Annalis' last words.'

'And written to his son? I see. But why would he ever have needed to scribble on bits of drainpipe? Drainpipe? That reminds me -' He shook his head. 'No. I don't know what it reminds me of, but I'm sure there's something.'

He shook his head again, teased by the elusive memory. 'Thank you for showing it to us. I'm sorry we haven't been able to help explain it.'

As Torquatus and Manlia made their way back up the hill through a light, cold drizzle, he said, 'It really is an oddity. What on earth would make a man like Annalis send a message scratched on a piece of lead. An emergency, no doubt. But what kind of emergency would separate a man like him from his slaves, his writing-tablets?'

'Something underhand, something he wouldn't want the slaves to know about. A plot, perhaps.'

'Oh, this plot again.'

'No need to sound so sceptical, Aulus. There must be plenty of people around who'd love to see the back of the Three, surely?'

'No doubt.' They were back at their own house now, and hurried in through the cold, windy corridor. 'But so far the only conspiracies I've heard about involve Sextus Pompey, and seem pretty far-fetched.'

'They do,' Manlia agreed, shrugging off her cloak. 'And I have to say no one's mentioned Pompey to me, not even indirectly. Or a plot. On the other hand, you could see how edgy they were. Oh, isn't this hateful? When will it all end, Aulus?'

Torquatus put his arms round her and gave her a hug, wishing he could tell her. Characteristically, she returned his hug, then pulled away, wiping her eyes. 'By the way, have you remembered that it's almost Saturnalia?'

'Oh, gods, yes, it is. I can't say I've done much about it, though.'

'Much?' Manlia asked with a smile.

'Well, then, anything' he admitted. 'From what I've seen of Trofimus he'll have it in hand.'

'But it isn't only that, is it? You can't really get on with this until after Saturnalia.'

Torquatus smiled. 'I still have a few hours today, which I intend to make good use of. Before I went out this morning I requested the pleasure of Antonius' freedman Philo and of Septimius' freedman Celer for an interview at the Treasury offices. I'm going down there now and with luck I'll discover what Philo heard, and who he told. And also what that letter from Antonius was about. I'd bet it takes a good deal to make the noble Flavia blush.'

When Manlia had gone away to her own rooms, Torquatus dressed himself in his toga again, and set off for his interviews. He felt better for having arranged them: if he couldn't investigate in Neapolis he'd make himself felt in Rome at least. All this rushing round Rome waiting for the attention of Antonius or Octavian or even, by Hercules, Lepidus, hadn't been good for his feelings. Now he was acting as a magistrate should, exercising his authority. He wondered if the men would come alone: it was normal for a freedman in such a situation as this to ask his patron to support him, but he couldn't imagine that Antonius would be free to come with Philo. As to Celer, his position was an odd one, since his patron Septimius was dead. Septimius' widow, Flavia, couldn't act officially as a man's patron at all, so whatever she might do for Celer behind the scenes, she wouldn't appear in public.

It wasn't far to the Treasury, which was under the Temple of Saturn. Since Saturnalia was almost upon them, the temple itself was bustling. Outside, a skinny temple slave was washing down and polishing the bronze-work on the couches which would be arranged inside for the banquet in the god's honour. He looked frozen, and indeed the weather had turned much colder, with heavy clouds borne along by a strong north wind. Inside, priests directed groups of slaves who were washing the floor and the steps leading up to the great doors, and polishing the doors themselves. The cult statues were being cleaned, the incense-smoke wiped away so that the brightness of the paint and gilding shone through once again. Even the huge terracotta statue of Saturn himself was being carefully cleaned, ready for his ancient feet to be unbound and oiled as part of the ceremony. It wasn't, of course, this statue that reclined on a couch at the banquet, but a smaller one. Surrounded by his priests, his couch would be placed before the great statue of the god, and he would be honoured in the presence of whatever members of the public chose to attend. Quite a few might do so: the dinner would be formal and grand, though friends of Torquatus' who'd attended in previous years complained that the temple was draughty and the food not hot enough. Those poorer citizens who never got the chance themselves to dine in style enjoyed the theatre of a great festival dinner. There was always plenty to be handed out afterwards;

whether it was hot or cold it was welcome enough to those who couldn't afford to eat roast meat at home.

He made his way round the temple to the Treasury offices. The heavy, studded doors were standing open as usual, though with a soldier on guard at either side. Once, Romans were in awe of the gods, and no such guards were needed. Saturn's presence in the temple up above had been deemed sufficient. Not in Torquatus' lifetime, however. And yet, there was probably less now in the Treasury than there had ever been, since Julius, Antonius and Octavian had all felt entitled to help themselves to state funds on occasion. The soldiers recognised him, saluting smartly, and he went in, blinking in the sudden gloom.

Gloom or no, there was an unusual lightness about the place. Those offices are dark. For security reasons the only windows are small, high up and barred, so the clerks work by lamplight on all but the brightest days, but there seemed an unusual number of lamps today. A group of clerks stood by one of the big tables, laughing together. A wine-jug stood on another table, with a platter empty of everything except a few pastry-crumbs. Obviously the Saturnalia spirit had come early here. At the sight of Torquatus a hush fell. He hadn't been in the office for a while, and presumably they hadn't been expecting a visit so close to Saturnalia. Several men sat down quickly and began to look thoughtfully at documents: Torquatus suppressed a smile, wondering how many of them had sat down in their own places. He nodded to them and crossed the room to the little office where the senior clerk worked. Livius Strabo at least was behaving normally, hunched over his desk and writing industriously. He glanced up when Torquatus darkened his doorway, and got up. The two men shook hands. 'You seem very busy,' Torquatus said, glancing at the tablets on the table. 'Annual report?'

'That's it. I need to let you have it by the end of the month, and with all these days off – ' He shook his head sadly.

'Yes, I'd like to see it in time to check the figures before it's presented to the new consuls in January.'

'I don't think you'll find any amendments necessary.' Strabo's tone was slightly offended. Torquatus smiled. Normally, the new quaestors wouldn't be concerned, since the outgoing men would take responsibility for their year's work; but as Torquatus had been acting quaestor since the summer, he had an interest in at least part of this report. There's always a bit of tension at the Treasury, of course, between the elected magistrates – lazy, barely numerate aristocrats with a huge sense of entitlement, in the officials' view – and the permanent staff – lazy, venal and arrogant in the magistrates' eyes. So far Livius and he had got on pretty well, but it was Torquatus who'd have to run through the report in the Senate, and he wanted a reputation for efficiency, not one for making silly mistakes. Torquatus knew Octavian quite well enough by now to know that he at least would make himself master of the Treasury report down to the last detail.

'I'm expecting two men to visit me here.'

Strabo looked a question.

'A couple of freedmen. It's to do with a robbery from a house of mine: some money of Octavian's that I was storing for him.'

Strabo's expression said what he thought of people who kept large sums of public money on their own premises. Responding to this look, Torquatus pointed out, 'Julius Caesar did it.'

'Quite,' Strabo agreed in a voice so dry he decided not to pursue the point.

'I want somewhere private to talk to these men.'

'Shall I lend you my office?'

'No. I can see you're busy. You must have some empty store-rooms. '

'Too many,' Strabo agreed, with a pained look. 'I'll set one up for you. You'll want a clerk to take notes.'

'No, I've brought my secretary.'

Strabo's face fell into that look of critical disapproval again, but Torquatus didn't care what he thought. Strabo came to the door of his office and directed several of his staff, all of whom were now sitting, abacuses whirring, the very picture of public service, to get things ready for the interviews.

They'd hardly finished when the first man arrived: a bustling little person with a suspiciously direct gaze. He breezed in in a swirl of warm cloak, as if he thought that being an associate of Antonius put him beyond the reach of ordinary magistrates. Torquatus hoped he was wrong. When he let the cloak fall back, Torquatus saw that his tunic was of fine wool with a deep key-pattern border: he was obviously doing well. Torquatus had seated himself in the correct magisterial pose, Demetrius at his side with tablets ready, and Torquatus looked the visitor over for a moment without a smile.

'You are Marcus Antonius Philo?' Torquatus asked, even though the man who brought him in had said so.

'That's right.' The man was probably about forty, he thought: small, wiry, with an alert, rather cocky expression, as if he felt entitled to poke his big nose in wherever he wanted.

'Marcus Antonius' freedman?'

'Correct.' Torquatus stared at the little man. For a fleeting moment his expression had been one, surely, of dislike, even contempt. Then Torquatus decided he must have been wrong about that, since they had never met before. A trick of the light, no doubt.

'I am investigating a theft. A large sum of money belonging to Octavian Caesar.'

The little man looked indignant. 'I know nothing of that.'

'I haven't accused you. Yet. What I want from you is an account of a visit you paid to the house of Lucius Cornelius Balbus in Neapolis the day before the Kalends of this month.'

He was obviously surprised, looking suspiciously at Torquatus as if wondering what to say. 'What do you want to know about it?'

'Everything. Why you were there, exactly what happened during the visit, who you saw afterwards.'

The little man's eyes brightened. 'Balbus in trouble, is he?'

'He isn't. But you will be if you don't give me a clear answer.'

He had the grace to look a little abashed.

'Start at the beginning. When did you arrive in Neapolis?'

Philo hesitated. 'On the sixth before the Kalends.'

Torquatus glanced up. 'You saw Balbus on the fourth before, didn't you?'

'That's right.' The man hesitated again. 'I had some private affairs to settle in Neapolis, nothing to do with Antonius, and that's what I was busy with the day before. All right?'

Torquatus met his truculent gaze calmly. 'Certainly. And why were you seeing Balbus?'

'I'd gone to him on some business to do with the purchase and shipment of materials.'

'What materials?'

'Iron. Copper. Tin. For armaments, you know.'

'I see. But I didn't think Antonius banked with Balbus any more.'

'He doesn't.' Philo gave Torquatus a pitying look. 'But Balbus has ships and contacts with merchants all over. He's much more than a banker. Whatever we wanted, he'd be able to put me in touch with the right people.'

He was right, of course. You had to get up early in the morning to get past Balbus.

'And you saw Balbus?'

'In the end I did,' Philo agreed. 'Only after I'd had to wait for hours, though. You'd think, coming with a letter of recommendation from Antonius, I'd have been treated better, put at the head of the queue. But no.'

'There were lots of people there, were there? Anyone you knew?'

'Hordes.' The little man shrugged. 'And no, I'd never seen any of them before.'

'So you waited.'

'I bloody waited. And then, when I finally got to see the big man he wouldn't commit. I don't know why. Waste of my time. And when I got back to Rome and told Antonius I'd had to stay in Neapolis overnight he just gave me a couple of coins, hardly enough to cover the costs.'

Antonius was short of cash, to be sure. But short-changing clients is never a good policy, Torquatus thought: you never know when you'll need them. Unless, of course, he wasn't pleased with Philo, didn't think the man had done a good job? He said, 'Frustrating for you. And all that waiting must have been dull.'

'It was.'

This was like drawing teeth. Either nothing had happened at all, or the little man hadn't remembered, or he didn't want to tell. Torquatus looked him thoughtfully, deciding that his obvious resentment against Balbus might be worth exploring. 'And yet I've heard,' he said, 'that security there isn't all it should be. Something about one of his slaves speaking out of turn?'

'Oh, that? How did you come to know about that?' Torquatus sat in unresponsive silence: it wasn't for Philo to ask questions. Philo seemed to realise this, and blushed and shuffled his feet. 'Well, it certainly livened things up a bit, for a little while anyway. Yes, this fellow wandered in and started asking the slave in charge of the waiting-room – quite a senior man from the look of him – about how to organise the job he'd been told to do.'

'What did he say? Exactly, mind.'

The man shot Torquatus a look: he seemed to have picked up the eagerness Torquatus was trying to hide. 'Well, he came in, and looked around, obviously wanting to find someone. Then he went straight over to the overseer-man, once he'd spotted him, and said, as near as I can remember, that he'd been told to order some mule-carriages to go to Rome. He said they were to carry bullion. "Where do I get them?" he said.'

'Do you remember where the money was going?'

Philo shuffled a bit, and for the first time failed to meet Torquatus' eyes. 'I think I heard your house mentioned.'

'My house?'

'"The Torquatus place", if you want the actual words.'

Torquatus sat back . 'Anything else?'

'He said it was to arrive on the day before the Nones —'

'Ah.' Torquatus couldn't help the sudden expulsion of breath. Now he was getting to the heart of the matter. The man stopped, looking an enquiry.

'Not so fast, if you please,' Torquatus told him, as calmly as he could. 'My secretary can't keep up.' And Demetrius was in fact writing away industriously. 'What happened then?'

'Oh.' The little man's attention had been turned to Demetrius too, but the slave didn't look up. Philo looked back at Torquatus. 'The overseer-man took him by the arm and led him out of the room really quickly. He looked as if he was about to do a bloody murder. Then there were quite loud voices outside the room, a bit of shouting, you know? After that everything went quiet again. Not much excitement.' He shrugged. 'But it helped to pass the time.'

Wonderful. So even if that roomful of people hadn't initially been listening, the fuss would surely have caught their attention.

'And who else was there in the room with you?'

'I've no idea. There weren't many left by that time: just a couple of slaves, if I remember. I don't know whose. They all went in before me, that's all I know, so they must

179

have had very important patrons indeed. Jupiter, perhaps, or Mars.' He smiled sourly, pleased with the joke.

'You're clearly an observant person, and you say they went in before you, so I think you must have heard their names.'

'I wasn't listening.' Torquatus sat and waited, his hands folded, as if he had all the time in the world. At last Philo said, 'Well, one of them came from that Etruscan pal of Octavian's, Maecenas: I noticed him specially because he only looked about twelve. Fancy having to wait for some kid to get his request in. Doesn't seem right. The other one belonged to Valerius Messalla Rufus, whoever he is.'

'You left Neapolis that day?'

'No, it was too late. I started the next morning and was back in Rome by dinner-time the following day.'

'And when you got back to Rome, what then?'

'Then nothing. I haven't done anything in particular since then.'

'And have you told anyone what you heard?'

'No.' He looked at Torquatus very directly. 'I'd forgotten about it till you asked.'

'Not even Antonius?'

Philo pursed his lips. 'I don't bother Antonius with gossip,' he said. Then, more quietly, 'I don't see Antonius every day. He's a busy man, perhaps you've noticed.'

Philo might not see Antonius every day, but a freedman is under an obligation to get useful information to his patron. Of course he'd have passed this useful titbit on double-quick.

Torquatus got up, and the freedman followed him cautiously. 'You may go now,' Torquatus told him. 'But I may need you to sign a record of this conversation, in case it is needed in court.'

Philo looked a little less cocky at this. He agreed to sign anything he was asked to. Not that he had a choice in the matter, as he was no doubt well aware. He struck Torquatus as the kind of man who always knows his rights.

Torquatus sent him away. As he left, Torquatus saw Livius Strabo in the corridor with what he couldn't help thinking of as his second witness. The two men passed in the passageway, and then Strabo came in, leading an insignificant-looking fellow, medium height, mousy hair, neat: the sort of man you'd see a hundred times and still be quite unable to describe him.

Torquatus looked him over, than told him he could sit down. Behind him he heard a click as Demetrius turned to a fresh page in his tablets.

'You are Septimius Celer?'

'I am.'

'Freedman of the senator Septimius. And your patron now?'

'Septimius' widow, Flavia, introduced me to Lucius Volusius, and – '

There was a sudden stir in the doorway, and the little lamp flames all leant to one side as a gentleman swept in. Behind him, Livius looked distressed. 'And this is Lucius Volusius,' Celer exclaimed.

Torquatus sent Livius away again, and looked over the new arrival, thinking that he had never, in a life spent among the aristocracy of Rome, come across a man so exquisitely arrayed as this one. His toga seemed made of superfine cloth, and draped immaculately. His hair, arranged in ordered waves, glistened with scented oil. It could have been cast in bronze. His plump fingers were laden with rings. His boots, neither patrician nor senatorial, were made of such soft leather one could see the edges of his toenails. Even had he been on his way to a dinner party, he would have looked over-dressed. In the Treasury offices the effect was laughable. A harassed-looking slave had followed him in and was watching him warily, obviously under orders to effect any tiny adjustments that might be needed to keep his master's appearance perfect.

'Now, what's all this?' Volusius fussed, in a high, reedy voice that came oddly from such a plump body. 'I just got home to learn that Celer had been summoned to talk to you. But I don't understand how he could possibly help you: he's a most honest person, I assure you.'

'I invited Celer to come in today as I believe he may be able to help me to track down some stolen goods. As Treasury Quaestor I am responsible for the public funds.'

Volusius blinked at him rather rapidly, as if he'd never heard such an idea expressed before, then his little red mouth pouted. 'I fail to understand what you think Celer might know about such things. He's perfectly respectable.'

'You are welcome to stay and listen to the questions I shall put to Celer,' Torquatus replied. He wasn't, actually, but there was no point in trying to choke him off. 'Antonius is aware of my investigations, which are on behalf of Octavian Caesar, and is doing all he can to assist.' Placing the most generous interpretation possible on Antonius' words to him, Torquatus thought that was almost true.

Volusius looked a little shaken by this. 'Oh, very well.' He snapped his fingers at his slave, who immediately came forward to ensure that the precious toga fell into the most graceful folds as his master sat. Torquatus ignored him, and turned back to Celer.

'So you were the freedman of Septimius? How did that come about?'

Celer looked away from Volusius and shrugged. 'I'd been doing his accounts for him for years. Then he decided that he might as well free me and set me up in business. I could go on working for him, while he could steer a lot more work my way. His clients, friends, and so on. He took a cut, of course.'

'Naturally. So when Septimius died you had to find another patron. I gather that the lady Flavia acted on your behalf in the meantime?'

'She did. She didn't want me to suffer through Septimius' death, so she very kindly advised his clients that they should continue to use my services, and even found me some more customers. People, you understand, who had not previously been wealthy enough to need an accountant but who now found themselves in possession of estates, slave households, and so forth.'

In these days of proscription it wasn't hard to imagine the kind of people he meant.

'And I'm assuming Lucius Volusius is your patron now?'

'That's right.' Celer was looking very relaxed, Torquatus thought. If this man knew anything, he wasn't anywhere close to it. 'Septimius left no sons, and all his wealth, except his daughter's dowry, was forfeit, so I needed to look elsewhere for protection.'

'The lady Flavia introduced you?'

The two men's eyes met. 'You could say so,' Celer agreed cautiously.

Torquatus looked a question.

'When I married Flavia – ' Volusius began, but Torquatus stopped him. His voice when he spoke was very dry. 'I understand you. You inherited Flavia's responsibilities along with her dowry.'

Volusius smiled, nodded, and gave a little flourishing wave of one hand. Torquatus considered him carefully. So this was the man his sister had spoken of, who had married his mistress on the very day of her husband's death. The effeminate popinjay looked quite pleased with himself, drawing himself up a little, with one hand resting on his knee, in the pose of a magistrate giving judgment.

Torquatus turned back to Celer. 'My main area of concern is a letter that I understand you carried to the lady Flavia from Antonius.'

He looked surprised, then slightly sulky. 'What if I did?'

'Do you know what was in it?'

'It was sealed,' the man said quickly.

'I'm sure it was. But you might have got an idea of the contents from the person who gave it to you.'

'I didn't.' The man had the typical look of a slave

accused of an error, round-shouldered, hunched, defensive. Torquatus gave him a cold look. 'I think you should take my questions a little more seriously.'

Celer glanced towards his patron, but Volusius didn't respond and he turned back to Torquatus looking scared.

'What do you want to know, then?'

'How did you come to be taking a letter from Antonius? What connections do you have with his household?'

'A man from Antonius' household asked me to take it, as a favour.'

'And this man's name?'

'Couldn't tell you, I'm afraid. I was there on some other business, and this man - he must have overheard me saying where I was from, I suppose – asked me if I would take it to the lady Flavia. Which is what I did'

'And when was this?'

He screwed his eyes up as if trying to remember. 'The Nones. Yes, I'm sure that's right.'

'And the man who gave it to you, did he give you any kind of hint as to what was in it?'

'I've already said he didn't. I didn't get the impression it was all that urgent: there were slaves flying around in all directions, so I think if it had been important, he would have found one of Antonius' own men to go.'

'And just what was the business that took you to Antonius' house that day?'

The man hesitated, and Volusius cut in. 'He was taking a letter to Antonius for me. Antonius is a friend of mine.' He swelled slightly, and Torquatus couldn't help smiling. His opinion of Antonius wasn't all that high, but the idea of him hob-nobbing with this little creep wasn't one that he could entertain. 'Very well. I am going to send you home now, to fetch me the letter that Antonius wrote to the lady Flavia.'

Torquatus had no idea whether the letter still

existed, but it was worth a try. For some reason neither of these men seemed to want to come out into the open, and Torquatus' suspicion of them was growing fast.

'I'll go along with Celer,' said Volusius, rising to his feet and standing stock-still while the slave arranged his draperies perfectly around him. 'My house is on the Palatine: it won't take long.'

'Thank you,' Torquatus said. 'And of course I'll send two of the clerks here with you.'

Volusius pouted, but if Celer felt any annoyance he kept it well hidden. Years of practice, no doubt. 'How pleasant it is to see a patron giving his client such support. Quite like the old days.'

Torquatus hoped his unctuous tone grated on Volusius, and from the man's expression he thought it did. Just as they were leaving the room he said, 'Oh, by the way, Celer,' and the freedman turned to him again. 'Was it Marcus Antonius Philo who gave you that letter?'

For a moment Torquatus thought the man was going to faint. The cold, clammy air of the room seemed very still. Then Celer seemed to pull himself together. 'I don't know anyone of that name,' he said, and ducked out under the low archway.

Torquatus had some time to wait while they went for the letter, time to reflect on what he'd learned, little though it was. Thinking back to the first interview, there had been one or two unexpected details in Philo's account of his visit to Neapolis, which he would follow up. But the second interview had been even more surprising: why should there have been so much coming and going between Septimius' house and Antonius? He couldn't see any obvious connection between them. And there was something in the back of his mind, too; something about the little piece of lead Postumia had found in her husband's study. Again he wondered why Annalis should have written – scrawled – a note to the son he saw every day , and on a piece of lead pipe? Only in some emergency, they'd agreed. But what emergency? Antonius was in his mind, and he wondered whether there was some connection between Annalis and Antonius, just as there had been with Septimius. And between Antonius and the cash. Had Antonius proscribed both of them, he wondered? It came into his mind, as he stood there in the flickering dark of a Treasury store-room, that Antonius - well, any one of the Three, actually - might make use of a man and then ensure his silence by listing him. Or, of course, either Octavian or Lepidus might have marked him down if they'd seen Antonius using him for some underhand scheme. But this was all speculation, and got him nowhere. He had been walking about impatiently: now he forced himself to sit and think.

The thing he'd forgotten had to do with the fragment of lead, he was sure. The words on it had said something about being careful and about hope. It had been found in Annalis' study, and Postumia had thought her son had dropped it. Suddenly, two thoughts came together. In an emergency, a man might well send to his son to tell him to come somewhere. But where? A temple, of course: people pass in and out all day long, and the priests are so used to the sight of small groups of men chatting in the portico that they don't bother to check names and faces.

What kind of emergency would make a senator scribble a note on a bit of drainpipe? An highly unusual one, if there was no slave to send with a message. As soon as he thought this, he saw in his mind's eye the raid on his farm, the carts coming and going in the flickering torchlight, the bodies of the murdered slaves, the smashed shutters. And he saw the broken drainpipe hanging from the wall. Torquatus almost jumped out of his chair. How could he have missed something so obvious? He started towards the doorway, Demetrius close behind, and almost bumped into Livius Strabo coming in. The clerk was closely followed by Celer and his patron. Torquatus stood back to let them

enter, told the visitors he'd be back in a minute, and led
Livius and Demetrius a few paces down the corridor.

'Demetrius,' he said, 'I want you to write a letter to
Octavian. I need a detail of troops: not many, a dozen men
or so will be enough. They can meet me here as soon as
possible. It's in connection with the missing money. Take it
at once, please.' Demetrius settled down on a stool in the
corner to write the note, and Torquatus went back to his
visitors.   Antonius' letter had not been destroyed; Celer
handed it over.   But it was disappointing.   It simply
confirmed, in the neat handwriting of some anonymous
clerk, that Septimius' name was added to the proscription
lists.   Antonius' Hercules seal was still partly visible,
imprinted on the broken wax.   If Celer was involved with
anything shady for Antonius, this wasn't it.   That was
Torquatus' first thought.   Then he read the letter a second
time, and the full enormity of what he was reading dawned
on him.   Flavia had not just profited from her husband's
death, she had requested it.   Antonius was granting a
request. For a moment he felt almost unable to breathe, so
close and cold was the air. What man would marry a woman
capable of that?   Volusius looked unworried: did he never
wonder whether Flavia might decide she'd had enough of
him, too?   Once she'd spent his splendid fortune, perhaps?
He took one hand off the little scroll and it rolled up with a
snap.

'Thank you. That's all I need for now. You might
be requested to come in and sign a statement confirming
what you've said today.   And in the mean time, if you
remember anything, however insignificant, that might have a
bearing on the theft of Octavian's money, I want to hear of
it. Is that clear?'

The two men agreed, without any apparent sense of
urgency, that they'd tell Torquatus anything they discovered,
and left.   Torquatus made his way back down the dim
corridor to the smoky warmth of the main office, where
Livius Strabo was waiting for him.   'Will you be needing

anything else?' the clerk asked in a neutral tone.

'No. I'm hoping – ' Torquatus bit back the words. Best not to say what he was hoping till he was sure he was right.

Strabo looked at him curiously for a moment, then said, turning to move a lamp which was dangerously close to Torquatus' arm, 'They knew each other, those two.'

'What, Celer and Volusius? Of course,' he replied, then stopped short, feeling stupid.

'No. Celer and the first man you saw: Antonius Philo, wasn't he? It struck me as odd. You meet a man you don't know, you glance at him and pass on; you meet a man you know, you give a greeting. But those two, their eyes met, but they didn't say a word. Odd. From what you said before, I couldn't work out any link between them.'

'I actually asked him whether he knew Philo. He denied it.'

'You believed him?'

'Given that I thought for a moment I might be having to revive him, no. I'd say he's a man whose job has never involved lying, and that he needs practice.'

Strabo sniffed. 'Some people, once they start lying, they find they like it.'

'I'll bear it in mind. Thank you.' Torquatus heard the regular crunch of military boots outside, and smiled. 'I must go.'

He walked out without another word. 'The temple of Hope,' he called out to the centurion, and they marched off. It's not far from the Treasury to the temple of Hope. Three little temples, to Hope, to Juno and to Janus, huddle together in a row on the edge of the great dusty space which Caesar had ordered cleared for his new theatre. At that time Rome's temples were in a wretched state: blackened with smoke, crumbling from want of maintenance, left filthy and untended by priests who, often enough, were away fighting, or who had died and never been replaced. The little party marched briskly down towards the river in the teeth of a rising wind. The Vicus Iugarius was almost deserted, and became even more so as people spotted the soldiers' approach. They swung to the right past the sanctuary of Mater Matuta, and strode across the top of the Vegetable Market, kicking aside the rubbish that the vegetable sellers always leave behind them: yellowing cabbage-leaves, broken baskets, apples so rotten not even the poorest will buy them. The market was closing, the stall-holders clearing away any left-over produce, a muddle of mules and handcarts brought in for loading, slaves and farmers running backwards and forwards with baskets and boxes, or stamping their feet to get them warm.

The temple of Hope was the furthest of the three, a shabby little building with heavy Doric columns. Its doors were shut. The steps up to them were cracked. Weeds poked out from between the stones, and from the edge of the roof a small shrub of some kind poked up its twigs to the darkening sky. The soldiers, their faces expressionless, waited by the steps while one of them, at Torquatus' command, ran up and knocked vigorously on the doors. The only reply he got was a thudding echo from the buildings round about. Torquatus directed the centurion round to the back, and there, as he had suspected they would, they found a solid little door. It took several attempts to get the priest to open up, and when he did his pale, frightened face looked more like a ghost's than a living man's in the gloom. He couldn't refuse to let them in, however, and the men were soon trotting about the temple, peering into corners, and lifting curtains with the points of their spears. The cult image was a mediocre copy of some Greek original, soft-faced and vacuous. Torquatus supposed sourly that it had been a while since anyone had put any money into renovating a temple to this particular goddess.

The men knew they were looking for money-chests. Torquatus had already almost lost hope, however: where in this small and rather impoverished temple could one hide them? But there would be vaults below, he knew, and that's where he'd have put the money. They made the priest take them into those vaults, which smelled dank and weedy. They had been made into two large store-rooms, as well as the room at the front where the priest lived. The store at the back, closest to the river, lay a little lower than the other, and the stones of its floors were green, slippery and stinking. It was prone to flooding, the priest told them unnecessarily, and nothing was kept there. The other contained only an old scarred table, on which lay a clutter of vessels: the shallow dishes in which offerings were made, jugs for pouring libations, and a couple of lamps, one with a gladiator motif, the other depicting a satyr doing something unspeakable to a nymph. No money-chests.

Torquatus raised his lamp, shining the dim light into every corner, unwilling to admit that the room was innocent, that his quest had failed. At least there was still the priest's own room, the one furthest from the river, and into that Torquatus pushed, in the face of the man's noisy objections. It wasn't a large room, but it had been comfortably furnished, with some good Greek rugs and a bed piled high with soft blankets. And there, by the flickering light of his lamp, Torquatus saw a couple of boxes sitting in the darkest corner of the room. They were bigger, much bigger than the standard-issue army money chests he was expecting, but perhaps at least some of the cash had been transferred into these commonplace storage boxes? If so, means could be found to induce the priest to say who'd brought it. His spirits soared. His heart beating fast, Torquatus told the soldiers to open them, and as many of them could get into the little room crowded round, ignoring the priest's protests. The first lid creaked open, and they saw folded fabric inside. The priest pulled out two togas, one quite new, both clean and neatly folded. There was also a heavy cloak with a hood, and a rather battered hat, such as travellers wear. Under those was a pile of blankets. In the second were some clean but well-worn tunics in various colours, and a single large blanket with a handsome geometrical pattern in orange and brown at bottom and top, such as one might throw over a reading-couch. And underneath this, on the very floor of the box, lay a large key wrapped in a clean cloth. Torquatus pounced on it and held it up triumphantly..

'It's a spare key for the main temple door,' the priest told him, trying to pick up his tumbled clothes and bedlinen from the floor. Maybe it was just the stooping to pick them up that had made his face red. 'I'll show you if you want. You'll see it fits.'

It fitted.

Chapter 14

Things couldn't get any worse. Surely? Waking the next morning, Torquatus found himself blushing at the recollection of yesterday's abortive search. The centurion had kept his face straight, his thoughts to himself, but as the group marched smartly off, Torquatus had heard two of the soldiers sniggering to each other. Well, that was yesterday. Today he must follow up the other leads he had. Young Annalis, for instance, who must surely have been the recipient of that deceitful little piece of lead. But the more Torquatus considered the whole business, the more convinced he became that Antonius was behind the theft. Or if not Antonius himself, someone working on his behalf, with or without his knowledge. Someone like Philo? Or someone like Annalis or Septimius?

He got up and dressed, and was on the point of taking himself down to the reception hall to greet his clients when sudden footsteps pounded along the gallery outside his room. He swung round to see what was happening, nearly knocking Victor flying, just as Demetrius rushed into the room, with Trofimus close behind him, the boy Felix bringing up the rear. For a moment his stomach knotted, then Demetrius skidded to a halt and Torquatus saw that his hands were empty. He was suddenly furious, his brows snapping together, his dark eyes as hard and bright as obsidian.

'What's the meaning of this?' he demanded, but Demetrius didn't seem to be listening.

'Master!' he gasped. Torquatus' heart sank. Now what?

Trofimus spoke before Demetrius could get his breath back. 'It's the old groom, lord,' he gasped out. 'He's dead.'

Torquatus glared at the two of them. Philip was an old man, so his death hardly seemed to justify all this rushing about. Torquatus said as much. As he did so he was half aware of Felix trotting quietly away down the gallery

'His throat's cut.' Trofimus' broad face was quite pale.

'His throat's cut? You mean he's killed himself? Why should he do that?'

Demetrius shook his head. 'I don't know, lord. His behaviour had been very odd. I wondered if he was up to something. But I don't know what could make him do this.' He shook his head again, as if to dislodge some persistent memory.

Torquatus could see Trofimus frowning, and turned to him. 'I haven't been here long enough to judge his behaviour, lord,' the steward said slowly. 'What could he have been up to?' he asked, turning to Demetrius. 'Was it something to do with Stephanus' death?'

'Oh, no, that was just an accident, I'm sure. No, but one thing I do know: Philip stole your tablets, lord: the ones you've been asking for.'

'Philip stole my tablets? Come on man, I doubt whether Philip can read. Whyever should he do such a thing?'

'I think it was Stephanus who had them. I can't say for certain how Philip got hold of them: it's my belief he found them among Stephanus' things. But however he got them, I know for a fact he had them. I overheard Philip and Iucundus discussing what to do with them.'

Torquatus was suddenly sickened by this whole business. Was his household riddled with spies, thieves, traitors? 'Why should they be doing anything at all with them? What's going on here?' he asked sharply.

Trofimus answered this, rather slowly. 'Even during the short time since I arrived, lord, I have been aware of Philip's resentment against the new slaves. He was still intensely loyal to your honoured father's memory, you understand. And to your half-brother's as well. And from what I've heard, Stephanus felt the same.' Trofimus was picking his words carefully, and Torquatus didn't blame him.

'What business of my slaves are my politics?'

Neither man answered him, but simply stood with lowered eyes. For the slave the household is his country: how many times had he heard that old saw? Was there no end to the damage Rome's civil wars were causing? Slaves could sell you to your murderers, and now they could disagree with your politics, apparently.

At last Trofimus said, 'I gather that Philip was with your father and your brother on the battlefield, and no doubt that creates a rather special bond.' Torquatus cursed under his breath and swung round to Demetrius again, and the secretary stepped back in alarm.

'If you knew what was going on, it was your duty to report it to me, as you very well know. And you've been pretending to me you didn't know where the tablets were, haven't you?'

Demetrius' face was white: his eyes seemed closer together than ever. He clasped his hands together till the knuckles whitened. 'But I didn't know where that stupid old man had put them! I still don't. I wanted to find them for you, lord, so I could tell you the whole story. That was all.'

Torquatus turned back to Trofimus. All the time he could hear the buzz of voices in the reception hall, and knew he must not stay. 'You say you doubt Philip killed himself?'

'I don't know, lord,' Trofimus told him. 'Though I think not.' His expression indicated that his experience hitherto had not equipped him to speculate on causes of death, and that he was unwilling to do so now.

'Who found him?'

'It was Iucundus, lord.' This was Demetrius again. 'The boy was sleeping in the hayloft, it seems. He says he heard nothing but came down the ladder in the morning to find the old man dead.'

Torquatus cursed. 'I will see the place. And I will see Iucundus,' he decided. 'My clients will have to wait. Trofimus, make them comfortable. Demetrius, you can come with me.'

194

The two men walked in silence to the place where Philip had lived and died. The body still lay where it must have fallen, the legs half under the old table, a cumbersome rustic affair which looked as if it hadn't been moved in years. There was no other furniture except for a couple of small stools. Torquatus glanced at Philip's face, then quickly looked away: the great gaping wound in the throat, almost severing the head from the body, wasn't a pleasant sight. Nor was the blood which had spurted everywhere. Philip was still wearing the coarse, homespun tunic of an outdoor slave. He'd have been better-dressed when he'd accompanied Torquatus' father and then his brother onto the battlefield. His feet were bare and dirty, the ankles swollen. Beside the cold brazier was a stool, where presumably he'd sat warming himself the evening before. Torquatus looked around, but there was no sign of a knife.

After a moment or two, Torquatus forced himself to look again at the dead man's body, lying on its back. The grey hair, which the old man had worn shoulder-length, had fallen backwards from the face: it was impossible, he thought, to say whether it had been pulled back. But one thing he thought he could say was that a man who cut his own throat could never make a deep wound like this, a slash from ear to ear, right through to the spine. That and the absence of the knife seemed to settle the question.

Torquatus had just turned away, wiping his hands on a cloth, although he had touched nothing, when a pale face suddenly emerged from the shadows. His skin crawled. It was a moment or two before he recognised Iucundus. The boy's hair was matted, still not quite clean from the foul job he'd been set to. As he moved Torquatus caught a sweet, sickly whiff of the latrines. For a brief moment he remembered the boy he'd seen at the slave-dealers, graceful, his silky brown hair long, in the Gaulish way, his eyes bright and curious.

'Come here.' Iucundus came, light on his feet, shy as a deer surprised in the forest. But his eyes were those of a beast caught in a trap, Torquatus thought, one who expects his death. 'Demetrius tells me you knew that Philip stole my tablets?' Behind him, Torquatus heard Trofimus' heavy step pacing across the stable yard.

Iucundus' face seemed to shrink. 'Yes, lord.'

'Why didn't you tell me?'

'I promised him. He wanted me to read what they said, and he made me promise.' Iucundus' voice was hardly more than a whisper.

Torquatus stared at him. 'Perhaps you don't yet understand what a slave's life is? No promise you might make to another slave can ever override your duty to me. Ever.'

'No, lord.' Those despairing eyes, looking out from the fringe of dirty hair, still refused to submit.

'So, just as a matter of interest, what did the tablets say, that could have been of such overmastering importance to Philip, and to you – oh, and to Stephanus too, I understand? And how did he come to have them?'

Now Iucundus looked puzzled for the first time, uncertain of himself.

'Philip found them in Stephanus' room,' he said slowly.

'That can't be true, lord,' Demetrius broke in. 'I myself sorted through Stephanus' belongings after his death, and they weren't there then. I found his spare tunics and boots, a blanket or two, a knife, a lucky coin he had, with a hole through it. That was all. There wasn't any money, and I assumed he must have asked you to keep it for him. But Philip certainly tried to get into the room while I was clearing it. Twice, he tried. He was up to something.'

Iucundus nodded reluctantly. 'I saw him try to get past Demetrius and go into the room. Philip believed that the tablets were there, because Stephanus had told him about them, but they weren't on his body when it was found.'

'And what then?'

'Demetrius turned him away, as he said,' Iucundus

196

agreed. 'But Philip told me Stephanus had had a secret hiding place, in the straw of his mattress. He knew of it because they had been such close friends. And he told me he was afraid the mattress would be burned, and the tablets destroyed. He went and found them during the night, after Demetrius had finished. That's what he told me.'

'And where are they now?'

Iucundus shrugged, his shoulders sagging wearily. 'In the corn bin over there, as far as I know.'

Demetrius and Trofimus went across to the great jar, and started digging down into it with their hands.

'You'll have to dig down deep,' Iucundus told them. 'It was as far down as Philip could reach, close to the side of the jar.'

Torquatus told Demetrius to let Trofimus do it. There wasn't room for two, and Trofimus was taller and had longer arms. He dug and dug, looking more and more heated, but eventually he gave up. It was clear the tablets weren't there. Most of the grain was on the floor around his feet. Torquatus turned to Iucundus again. 'What do you have to say now?'

'That was where they were, three, no four nights ago. I can't say any more than that.'

'Well, at least you can tell me what they said, boy.'

Again he gave Torquatus that odd, puzzled look. Then he drew nearer and spoke very softly. 'Lord, you must know.'

Torquatus was suddenly furious. 'How dare you speak to me like that? Take him away, Trofimus, and keep him away from me. He can work outside: make sure he's under observation all day, and that he sleeps among others. I must go: my clients are waiting.'

Trofimus took the boy by the arm, but Iucundus shook him off and walked out proudly, the steward close behind. Torquatus was in despair. Another unexplained death among his slaves, and not a natural one. Where was the knife that had slashed Philip's throat? What on earth could Iucundus be up to? And how could he have misjudged the boy so badly? He'd wanted him to be a kind of noble savage, he thought angrily, but the boy was just a corrupt and vicious slave. Halfway back across the peristyle gardens, so beautiful in summer but at present rattling with dead leaves, dry and dark as the underworld itself, he turned to Demetrius, who was following close on his heels. 'What did you make of all that?'

The secretary looked rather surprised, then pursed his lips and shook his head. 'I can't make Iucundus out,' he said. 'When he first arrived he seemed an innocent sort of boy. But I'm sure, master, that he attacked you in the Forum, though why I don't know. It hardly seems the sort of risk he'd run on his own account, does it?'

Torquatus nodded. 'There must be someone behind him, you think?'

'How else can one make sense of it? He's new to Rome, and I think someone who means you harm has bought him.'

The two men crunched heavily across the gravel around the pool with its dolphin fountain, now silent.

'He'd just come here straight from Gaul, hadn't he?' Torquatus asked.

'That's what the dealer said, yes.' Torquatus noticed how Demetrius had worded his reply, then pushed the whole affair out of his mind. He had a crowd of men to deal with. And tomorrow, oh gods, tomorrow was Saturnalia. Seven days of sacrifices, gift-giving, feasting, drunkenness. Pursuing his enquiries would be impossible: sensible people would be keeping their heads down while their slaves drank their best wines and ate their way through the store-cupboard; stupid ones would pretend to enjoy being ruled by their own slaves, currying favour by trying to be one of the boys. And when that was all over there'd be only a few jaded days left before New Year, on one of which, he remembered with a kind of disgust, they'd all been ordered to go out in the streets and cheer for Lepidus as he triumphed. The New Year saw in the freshly elected consuls, who'd in fact been selected by the Three in November. And then Octavian would want to see his money back, by whatever means. How in Hades was he going to do it?

While he dealt with the clients, Torquatus sent Demetrius off to write to Antonius, asking him to send Philo for a second interview, and wished once again that Iucundus hadn't proved untrustworthy. The boy had been quick and clever in Demetrius' absence, finding documents he needed, remembering the names of some of the regular visitors. It was no use to think like that: better to remember that he'd also attacked his master for no reason, had refused point blank to tell the truth, had been thoroughly untrustworthy. Torquatus put all thoughts of him aside, and summoned the boy Felix to assist him instead.

His visit to the Forum that morning was as short as he could possibly make it. Luckily, many other people seemed to feel the same. The place was busy enough, but with a different crowd; not making speeches or arguing about politics, but buying and selling Saturnalia gifts. Torquatus dismissed his clients with relief, and joined in. He knew Trofimus was buying things he could give to anyone: candles, good wine, those clay figurines that are special to Saturnalia, amphorae of fish sauce at specially inflated prices for the festival, nicely wrapped baskets of nuts and raisins, scent in glass bottles and so on, but he had his own personal gifts to see to. He went into one of the jewellers' shops, where he hesitated for a while over a fine set of turquoises – a heavy necklace, bracelets and earrings all mounted in silver – and a splendid rope of pearls. He decided finally on the pearls, and tried to beat the man down, but the jeweller knew at Saturnalia he could get the full price and he refused to negotiate. Torquatus didn't really care: Manlia deserved a handsome gift, and against her warm skin the pearls would look wonderful. Now he only had to get something for his mother and Iunia. He bought them each a pair of bracelets, graceful, elegant things: not half as expensive as Manlia's pearls. He headed home. He reckoned he still had time to see Antonius Philo again, to find out how he knew Celer, and see if he could penetrate the web of obligation, friendship and money that might be covering something altogether more sinister. This was probably the best part of the holiday, he reflected as he walked through the crowded streets. He didn't expect to enjoy tomorrow much. Saturnalia was always the same: family quarrels that had rumbled on perfectly decently all year would at the festival be forced into the open for the world to see.

Everyone knows what it's like in the house the day before Saturnalia. There's a mood of gathering anticipation. You hear the slaves laughing and joking among themselves as they decorate the reception hall with greenery, a constant succession of cooking smells wafts out from the kitchen quarters, people give each other smiling, secret glances. Not this year, not in Torquatus' house. He noticed that it was very quiet, as if everyone was remembering the deaths, and the farm still locked up with only a single caretaker in residence, and the slave-boy degraded and under surveillance. On this thought, Demetrius came through from the back of the house, with a letter in his hand. 'From the house of Messalla Rufus, lord. The slave is waiting to carry back any reply.'

Torquatus held out a hand for it, saying, 'Have you managed to get anything from your contact at Antonius' house yet?'

'No, lord, but I hope to have a drink with him in a couple of days' time.' Seeing Torquatus' expression, he went on, 'I can't alarm him by being too insistent.'

Torquatus nodded, suppressing the impatient words that rose to his lips, and opened the letter, a courteously worded, formal little note, informing Torquatus that the master was absent, at his daughter's house in the Alban Hills for the holiday, and that he would no doubt be happy to help Torquatus in any way he could on his return. Torquatus hadn't ever supposed that Rufus himself would be involved in anything shady. He was elderly, a distinguished writer who he seemed to remember spent most of his time at his country estates since being pardoned by Caesar. If he really needed to he could send out someone to see Rufus straight after Saturnalia: by the time the old man came back to Rome it might be too late.

Torquatus waved Victor away: he'd stay in his toga for the rest of the day. He still had a lot to do. Just as he was handing back the letter to Demetrius with a message for the slave, a bustle behind him announced the arrival of a visitor. Antonius Philo came in, wrapped in his warm cloak and stamping his boots. Torquatus took him to his study: the reception hall was too cold to sit in at this time of year.

He got straight to the point. 'Why didn't you tell me yesterday that you'd passed on to Antonius the news that the cash was being sent to Rome?' Torquatus didn't know for certain that he had, but his guess was right. Philo looked surprised for a moment, then said calmly: 'I didn't know how Antonius would feel about your knowing.'

'And now you know he doesn't mind?'

'Now I know he doesn't mind.'

Torquatus threw himself back in his chair, exasperated with the man. 'This is an official enquiry. These questions are being put to you by a serving magistrate. If you don't give honest answers I can have you punished.'

Philo considered this, his head on one side. 'Antonius is my patron,' said at last, in the tone of one reasoning with a child. "I don't deny you're an elected quaestor – coming into office in January – but what I'm not sure is that you can do anything worse to me than Antonius can. I know he would, too, whereas I don't know whether you would or not. Do you follow me?'

Torquatus did, of course. Philo gave him an odd, intense look. 'And then it was Antonius who freed me. I owe him.' This was a statement of the obvious.

'And you didn't tell me you knew Celer, either.'

'You never asked,' he shot back.

'Well, I'm asking now.'

He shrugged. 'I know him, yes.' He stopped. Torquatus waited. 'We have a drink together from time to time.'

'So, four days before the Kalends of December you saw Balbus and heard about the movement of the money. You were back in Rome on the Kalends. Then what?'

Philo looked a question.

'Where did you go? Whom did you see? What did you talk about?'

'Oh, I see. That night I dined with Antonius.'

'Did you? I thought you said you didn't see him often.'

'I live in the house, so I see him, of course. But that doesn't mean he sits chatting to me for hours at a time.' He glanced at Torquatus. 'I went there to try and get some money to cover my costs, and he asked me to stay to dinner. I wasn't anywhere near him, of course, I was given a place on a couch in one of the secondary dining rooms.'

Philo seemed to have dried up again. 'And who did you see while you were there?' Torquatus asked.

'Lots of people. I was alongside some men from Spain. Engaged in shipping olive oil and wine, mostly, from what they said. Not the really huge players, obviously, or they'd have been placed closer to the big man, but the next tier down. You know what I mean: men who grow on quite a large scale and sell their crop to the big buyers; men with ships the buyers sometimes use when they haven't enough capacity themselves.'

'And Antonius?'

'Yes, I saw him, before dinner. Like I said before, he wasn't very generous, seemed to think that an invitation to dine compensated me for a long expensive journey.'

Torquatus gave him a hard look. 'And yet yesterday you were telling me that you didn't see him?'

Philo didn't reply. No doubt the answer would have been the same as the one he'd given earlier: Antonius had to be cleared first.

'And you told him?'

'Yes. I told him what I'd overheard, just the same as I told you yesterday.'

'I see. Well, it's good to get that straight. And since we're being honest, let's have a little more, shall we? Who else did you talk to? Think carefully now.' Torquatus smiled, but not in a friendly way. 'You said that Antonius could do worse things to you than I can. As a matter of simple fact, either of us could have you killed: the only difference would be that I would be doing it openly and legally, and I don't suppose that's a difference that would concern you. So who else did you see before or after you lay down to dine?'

'Antonius' steward, of course. And Celer, he was there.'

'And did you tell the steward what had happened in Neapolis?'

'I don't remember. I may have done. Anyway, he'd have heard me telling Antonius, because he was in the room when I was explaining to Antonius how much time and money I'd wasted. Several other slaves were there too, of course.'

Of course they were. In houses like Antonius', or his own, there would be slaves everywhere. They are like part of the furniture; but it does make keeping secrets difficult.

'And Celer? Did he stay for dinner?'

'Yes, Celer was there with Septimius and Flavia - sitting on the end of their couch with the other freedmen. They shared a table with Annalis and Postumia.'

At last, some real information, linking Annalis and Septimius solidly to Antonius. 'This has been very helpful. Are you sure there's nothing else you should tell me?'

Philo looked as if he was considering this, then said, 'No.'

Torquatus was sure he'd penetrated to the heart of

the mystery. But knowing that Antonius had taken the money was one thing. Getting it back was quite another.

Chapter 15

When Torquatus' clients arrived at dawn the next day, he was ready for them, seated on his ivory chair in the reception hall, among all the signs of his family's distinction: the masks of his ancestors in their freshly-polished houses, the hearth-fire burning brightly, the shrine clean and decorated with a vase of leaves and berries, bunches of greenery hanging in the corners and on the house-doors, the office behind him tidy, the bronze hasps of the family money-chest gleaming in the lamplight, the Saturnalia gifts ready and waiting. A house at peace with itself, secure and confident.

The slaves were too quiet, though. Even Felix, normally a boy much given to gossiping, wasn't chattering in his usual way. Torquatus only had a few moments for these thoughts before the doors swung open and the crowd streamed in. The humble men went straight to the benches to wait their turn, while the more important ones came to greet him and exchange gifts. For a while there was a pleasant bustle of gift-giving: Torquatus' visitors seemed well-satisfied with theirs, and he himself was pleased with his. His friends and clients clearly didn't see him as a man on his way out. Last Saturnalia he had been skirmishing around Italy with Octavian's army against Antonius, and there had been no Saturnalia celebrations in his house, and for a first Saturnalia as master in his own house, this was very satisfactory.

Once he'd done his public duty at home, he walked down to Saturn's temple with his sister and some of the slaves. The crowds were immense, as usual at Saturnalia. Becco and Pulex pushed a way through for them so that they watched the sacrifice in reasonable comfort. Torquatus wondered what the population of Rome might be. He knew it was a question that interested Octavian: perhaps he would find out one day. Whatever it was, it felt as though every single member of that population was there, their breath steaming in the cold air. The last weeks had been dreadful. Perhaps next year would be better? He offered up a prayer of his own, his arm round Manlia, as Lepidus, his head bare in the Greek way of sacrificing, said the words of offering, and the slaughterman raised the sacred axe and swung it down hard and true on the bull's neck.

While Torquatus and Manlia were out, Iucundus had managed at last to see Felix. Ever since that night when the boy had come to him in his prison, he'd kept away. Felix nodded when Iucundus asked if Trofimus had told him not to talk to the new boy, but said, 'It doesn't matter today. Everyone will be busy, and if we keep out of sight we can talk.' Iucundus felt himself actually smile when Felix said this. He had so much he needed to share with someone, and Felix was the only one who would listen.

'I think you're right,' Iucundus agreed, glancing around the stables. The two men who normally watched him had gone. 'They must expect a holiday on Saturnalia too,' he said, almost cheerfully. 'We can sit in here safely enough. Are you sure you won't be missed, though? I don't want to get you into trouble too.'

'No,' Felix said, settling himself down on the other stool. 'They think I went with the master to the temple to see the sacrifice, so they won't be looking for me.' He looked across at Iucundus curiously. 'It must have been horrible, cleaning out that latrine,' he said.

Iucundus shuddered. 'Two whole days it took me. It must have been years since it was last emptied, years of everyone's piss and shit flowing into it. I thought the smell would make me faint at first. Then when I thought I'd finished they told me to load it onto a cart. Would you believe the farmers buy it to spread on their fields? I didn't think I'd ever get the smell off me. But let's not talk about that. Felix, I need to see the master, but Trofimus won't let me.'

Felix's face was serious. 'I know. But it's not

Trofimus, it's the master. They all - everyone - believes you have done something terrible, either attacked the master yourself or helped someone else to do it.'

Iucundus looked at him in silence. Then he got up, and searched out another log from the little pile by the door. When he'd placed his log carefully in the brazier he sat down again on his stool. 'And you? Do you believe that too?'

'I don't know. They all seem so sure - ,'

'I see.'

'But I can't believe it,' Felix burst out. 'It doesn't seem possible. You're just not that kind of person.'

'Well, I'm glad of that,' Iucundus said with a sad smile. 'Because I did see that man next to the master, that day in the Forum. I know no-one believes me, but that's what I saw. I've been over and over it in my own mind, and I know it was him, the man who spoke to me outside Antonius' house. He gave me a message for Demetrius.'

'I wasn't there, that day,' Felix said, almost apologetically.

'No.' Iucundus' voice was bitter. 'And no-one who was there seems to have seen him.' He pushed his dirty hair aside with hands that shook. 'I don't know what I can do, how to persuade the master that I'm telling the truth. And now Philip's dead, the only man who believed me. Will it be me next?'

'Well, I think,' Felix began, then swung round on his stool, staring at the door. Footsteps were approaching across the yard. Before either of them could move, the door swung open and Demetrius' face appeared in the opening. The two boys looked at him guiltily.

'I thought you'd gone with the master,' Felix gasped out.

'I didn't,' Demetrius told him. 'I know you have this liking for criminals, so I thought you'd probably sneak off when no-one was watching. You can come with me.'

Felix got up at once but said indignantly, 'You know very well I'd never harm the master.'

Demetrius ignored him, looking at Iucundus with distaste. 'And as for you, I'll make sure the two men supposed to be in charge of you come back here and do their job, Saturnalia or no Saturnalia.'

Once back home again, Manlia and Torquatus shut themselves up in the study, ignoring the shouts and laughter from the slaves, who were preparing their own feast, to be held in the dining room. For once they would recline like citizens, eating the sorts of fine food they didn't normally taste – roast meats, figs in honey – then dice for money over their wine. Torquatus was relieved to think they had recovered their spirits enough to enjoy their treat. When he judged they must be coming to the end of their meal, he went into the dining room and handed out presents, which seemed to please them. They had voted one of the garden-slaves King of the Feast: he reclined on the top couch, his wine-cup slopping perilously, looking in truth rather flushed, uncomfortable and hot. Trofimus, Torquatus was glad to see, appeared quite sober, although he had a large wine-cup in his hand. Not all the slaves could recline, of course, and Torquatus was amused to note how closely the household followed its master in protocol. The garden-slave was the only humble person reclining: Demetrius, Trofimus, Victor the toga-slave and Manlia's own maid were among the fortunate ones. Iucundus ought to have been there as his master's body-slave.

At Torquatus' own banquets, clients and slaves of the guests sat on the ends of the couches or huddled on benches around the walls, waiting for a share of the food: here the humbler members of the household did so. They couldn't all be here even so, he thought, and from the sound of it, some had simply taken portions of food away to eat in small groups elsewhere. For a moment he thought how odd it was that he didn't know how many of them there were. He left them to their pleasures, hoping that it wouldn't be too long before Trofimus called them to order and they got on with cooking a meal for the master's family. They always ate late at Saturnalia.

When he returned to the study, Torquatus found his mother and Iunia sitting talking to Manlia, with expressions on their faces of determined goodwill. Saturnalia is a day for family. Torquatus tried, with the aid of a rather good Caecuban his father had laid down some years before, to get himself into the appropriate frame of mind. Manlia added her gifts to the ones he'd bought yesterday: Mother and Iunia were polite about their bracelets, while casting envious eyes over Manlia's pearls. Torquatus was unmoved: let them support him as Manlia had, and he'd buy them all the pearls they wanted. It wasn't even support he wanted from them, he thought sadly, it was love, and that he'd never get. They all smiled sweetly at each other, and even managed to find topics of conversation that wouldn't drag them onto contested ground: politics, of course; the decay of modern morals; and, generally leading on seamlessly from that, Torquatus' supposed failings as a son and a citizen. When the dinner was finally announced, Felix served at the table, and did it very neatly. Torquatus wondered whether to take the boy as his new body-slave. At least Felix, being a home-bred slave, would know the rules. On the other hand, he was really too young.

While Felix was serving the master's dinner Iucundus was back in the stables, his guards, slightly drunk and not in the best of tempers, sitting gambling by the door. He had a great deal to think about.

Saturnalia was supposed to be fun, apparently. It definitely hadn't been fun for him. After Felix's visit this morning, he'd been expecting more punishment, but instead, Trofimus had ordered that he and his minders could come to the feast. The other slaves were still avoiding him, perhaps because he still smelt from cleaning the latrines, even though he had washed and washed. He felt abandoned and afraid, but most of all he felt angry.

But Iucundus, turning over and over in his bed of

straw, had a lot more than his anger to keep him awake, having seen something today that he would never forget. Trofimus was kind: kinder than he could ever have guessed. He went back over the scene in his mind. He had come in out of the cold with his minders, fearful of his welcome. No-one turned him out, and his guards apparently felt free to leave him to his own devices while they crowded into the master's dining-room. Once Iucundus had got a plate heaped with food he took it back down the corridor to the kitchen. The last thing he wanted was to draw attention to himself by trying to find a place on one of the benches in the dining room, let alone trying to eat lying down, which didn't appeal to him. He was comfortable enough in a corner by the big bread-oven, and pleased that Demetrius and the other important slaves were all absent. Emboldened by his meal, he decided that he would try some of the dried figs and dates that made up the last course, and wandered off to the dining room in search of them. The meal was evidently coming to an end: the diners were returning to the kitchen, and when he got back with his fruit he found a lot of the others settling down to games. Allowed to gamble at Saturnalia, they were intent on the fall of the dice. Even some of those not playing were crowding around, watching the game and commenting on the fortunes of the players.

Suddenly he saw that Trofimus too had returned. He and Iucundus were the only two not involved, apart from a group of the lady Manlia's women, who had their heads together in a far corner of the big room, and Demetrius, pouring wine into one of the master's best silver cups for Iunia's maid. Iucundus watched Trofimus, who caught his eye and smiled. Encouraged, Iucundus smiled back and moved closer to him.

'Please, Trofimus,' he said softly, 'do tell me why I can't talk to Felix. I won't do him any harm. If you're thinking I was discouraging him from studying, you're wrong. In fact, I told him that he should be learning everything he can.'

'Did you? When was that?'

'The night after the master was attacked in the Forum. I was shut in the grain-store, remember, and Felix came to me, brought me food. I can't ever forget that. And then you came and took him away. I've scarcely seen him since.'

Trofimus' dark face seemed to be almost wavering in the fitful lamplight. He sighed. 'Felix's position is an odd one,' he said abruptly.

'He told me: he's the old master's child.'

Trofimus nodded. 'It's a common enough situation. I've worked in houses where the master has quite a few natural children among the slaves. But he's the only one here.'

'And that makes a difference?'

'It does.' Trofimus laughed, something he didn't often do. 'It means he's been very spoiled. Allowed to get out of doing any regular work. Allowed to avoid the schoolmaster. That's something an attractive child can get away with. A spotty youth can't. He has to be given a chance to learn something useful.'

Iucundus nodded and leant forward eagerly. 'That's why I told him he should pay attention to the teacher. He was afraid – ' he broke off, remembering that Felix had shared his fears in confidence.

'He's right to be afraid. This is a decent house – if one sets aside the rather high death-rate,' Trofimus added in a dry tone, 'but there are plenty where pretty boys are seen as desirable playthings. If the master were to decide that he's a useless mouth – well, I don't want that to happen.' His dark eyes were serious.

'So where is he now?'

'Serving at the master's dinner-table.' He paused for a moment, then added, 'I think the master may be thinking of training him to be his body-slave.'

Iucundus' heart sank. 'Oh. He'd be doing what I came here to do?'

211

'Yes.'

For some reason Iucundus was horrified at this. It felt as if he was almost ceasing to exist. He hated this city, this house, with a passion, so why did it matter who waited on the master who had judged him so harshly? But it did matter. Iucundus swallowed hard and looked away. 'I suppose since I'm not trusted – ' he began, but Trofimus stopped him with a severe look.

'You need to think carefully. I want to help you. But how could you have been such a fool as to suppose that a promise made to another slave could mean anything to the master? Of course he just saw it as another example of your inability to fit in, to understand your position. And when he added that to your running away, what else could he think?'

'I didn't run away.' Iucundus' voice was so loud even some of the noisy crowd round the gambling table heard him and turned their heads curiously. After a moment, seeing the two of them sitting quietly by the embers of the fire, they went back to their game.

Trofimus was shaking his head. 'Look, we all sometimes do something we shouldn't out of fear. You're young, and new to all this,' and he nodded briefly towards the room with its gambling men and chattering women.

'Even you don't believe me.'

'How can I, Iucundus? No-one else saw this mystery attacker, after all. It would be better if you told the truth: no-one can believe you attacked the master without being directed by someone else.'

'I suppose I should be grateful for that.'

Trofimus sighed. 'You still don't seem to understand how dangerous your situation is.'

'Oh, I do. The master could have me killed and no-one would blame him, if you all believe I attacked him. But I don't care. I'm not going to tell a lie, not even to get out of this situation. Haven't I been humiliated enough? I would rather have been whipped than set to that job, with everyone sniggering at me, up to my knees in shit.' Iucundus had to

212

stop, choking back tears. 'Why did you do that to me? I could have shown some courage under the lash; turning out the latrine was shame from beginning to end.'

Trofimus' normally benign face was closed and dark, and Iucundus feared he had gone too far. His anger dying away, he watched the silent steward anxiously. Trofimus, after glancing around to see that no-one was looking, got up and walked out of the room, gesturing to the boy to follow him. Puzzled, Iucundus trotted out behind him, into the garden where a melancholy wind whipped round the deserted walks. Then Iucundus gasped as, in one swift movement, Trofimus turned his back and pulled up his tunic. Iucundus' hand flew to his mouth, whether to stop himself speaking or being sick he didn't know. The steward's back was destroyed. From side to side, and right down to his buttocks, it was ridged like a field, with bars and lumps of hard scar tissue. In between it was red and shiny, the skin smooth in places and puckered in others.

'Does it hurt?' he asked in a whisper.

'Not too much now, no, as long as I don't take a knock. It took a long time to heal, though, and it was painful enough until it did.' His face was serious in the gloom as he pulled his tunic back down and straightened it tidily. 'I wanted to spare you that. Believe me, a beating like that is a total humiliation. You don't show courage: you shit yourself, you scream and beg for mercy, you lose consciousness. What you had to do out there will be forgotten, and whatever scar it leaves on you is for you to deal with yourself. In years to come, if you are lucky enough to be freed, no-one will see you at the baths and know you were a slave.'

Iucundus stared at him, sick and horrified. 'What had you done?'

'Oh, nothing. I was about your age. My old master died, and his son, my new lord, was a drinker. He came back one night, drunk already, and calling for more wine. I didn't bring it fast enough and he ordered me flogged, still with the wine he'd vomited staining the front of his tunic. He laughed as he watched. He was a cruel man, who enjoyed seeing the blood flow.'

Iucundus stood silent, his belly cold.

'So make sure you never forget, Iucundus. They can kill us, sell us. You need to tell the truth and trust to the master's mercy. I don't think, from what I've seen of him, you'll ask in vain. And of course,' he added, on a lighter note, 'the masters don't want to lose the value of their purchase – at least, the more rational ones don't – so he will probably give you another chance, if you let him. And now let's go in again, shall we?'

The day felt interminable to Torquatus, struggling with his strained family party. Only one thing happened of any interest. The conversation had turned to weaving, an interest of Vibia's as well as Manlia's, and the pair of them went off to the weaving-room to examine Manlia's work. When they had gone, leaving Torquatus alone with his sister-in-law, he poured them each another drink, wondering rather desperately what they could find to talk about. He was sure that Annalis and Septimius had been concerned in some way on the attack on his farm, and perhaps Rebilus might have given Iunia a hint of the conspirators' motivation. 'Rebilus has gone abroad, hasn't he?' he began.

Iunia shivered. 'Yes. He should be with Sextus Pompey soon. If - that is - if he's managed to hide his identity.'

'That must be hard for you?'

She met his eyes with a kind of mild defiance. 'It is. I'll have to stay with Mama now, and we had hoped - Rebilus and I - that we could marry and settle down, somewhere away from Rome. He's not a senator, doesn't have to stay in the city.'

'Perhaps he'll be able to come back. After all this is over.'

'Perhaps.' She didn't meet his eyes and Torquatus

knew she was thinking, as he was, that unless it was Sextus Pompey who won, all those who'd gone over to his side were doomed. 'I - I hadn't realised just how terrifying it would be without him. Mama and I aren't sure whether to stay in the city. Whether we dare.'

Torquatus stared at her. For the first time, he realised how frightening the lives of women like his mother and sister-in-law might be. Manlia had always been exceptional in his eyes: now he saw just how extraordinary her courage and refusal to be beaten really were. He didn't want to talk about this to Iunia, and, trying to think of something, anything they might have in common and could discuss without coming to blows, he jokingly asked why Rebilus hadn't left them some of his gladiators. It was a stupid thing to do, and as the words left his lips he'd have given anything to have recalled them. He knew she would have every right to be offended, but to his surprise she flushed scarlet, then looked as if she might burst into tears. Horrified and embarrassed, he started to apologise, but she cut him off. 'No. He shouldn't have bought them - and if I'd known what he meant to do - believe me, Aulus - I'd have stopped it.'

Torquatus stared at her, almost stunned by what she seemed to be suggesting. She rushed on, twisting her cup in her hands till he thought the wine would spill on her dress. 'When he told me - it's all my fault, you see. He wasn't in it the first time, but when he asked me about that little farm of yours, I told him, because how would I know what he meant to do, and it seems he told the others where it was.'

And then Manlia and Vibia came back in. Manlia could see at once that something had been going on, and she made an excuse to get her mother out of the way again, a little later. Torquatus took the opportunity to offer Iunia - and his mother, too, of course - the shelter of his house.

'You could come and stay here,' he offered with a sinking heart.

She gave him a shrewd look. 'That would be

wonderful, wouldn't it? Mama trying to run the place, countering your orders and constantly carping at you for a traitor. Manlia sidelined and put down. Your slaves resenting hers.' She buried her nose in her wine-cup.

Torquatus hadn't been able to argue convincingly against her.

After that Iunia had gone monosyllabic, and stayed that way till the end of the evening. Torquatus, too, was hardly the liveliest of Saturnalia hosts. He had much to think about: tomorrow he would talk it all over with Manlia, but he thought he knew now what Rebilus had done with his gladiators. While the women talked in a desultory way, he found himself considering a really interesting new question: what had happened the first time?

At last it was all over. The slaves tidied away, looking rather tired and a bit bilious. Torquatus went to bed, and spent some hours awake with the kind of indigestion to be expected when one eats late and in disagreeable company. A normal Saturnalia, then.

Chapter 16

No humble visitors this morning: even Saturnalia had its good side.

Holiday or no holiday, Torquatus needed to press on. That odd little piece of lead with its scribbled words seemed to lie at the heart of the mystery. It had been dropped, as Postumia supposed, by young Annalis in his search through his father's papers, and to Annalis he would go for an explanation. Should he request the young man to pay him a visit? No: he was a quaestor, true, but Annalis had the higher rank of aedile-elect. Besides, there might be something interesting to be learned from his place itself, or from its staff. According to Manlia he had moved out of the family home into a very pleasant apartment on the Aventine some years previously. The litter-men carried him there through cold wet streets.

The Aventine was historically the heart of plebeian Rome, but in recent years, there had been some quality development there, and Annalis' street was very pleasant and quiet, close to the temple of Luna. A good area, and not cheap. Demetrius had to knock several times. The doorman, when he finally appeared, was staggering slightly. Torquatus' nose wrinkled fastidiously as he stepped inside: the whole place smelled of stale wine and stale food. In the dining-room he could see through a draped curtain the Saturnalia feasting had not yet been cleared away. Couches were still spread with crumpled blankets; crumbs and fragments of bone and shell littered the floor; and on the serving table against the wall, the bones of several different kinds of roast fowl lay jumbled together in congealed fat on a large dish, while a striped cat licked at a trail of meat-juice that had run down one handsome table-leg. As he crossed the hall to wait for the master, he shuddered as something squashed under his foot: only a grape. The slave didn't bother to offer him a seat, but Demetrius found him an upturned stool which appeared sound, and he sat down on it cautiously. And waited. In the distance he could hear slaves chattering, a petulant, whining voice, laughter, the glugging of some liquid being poured. Not more wine, surely?

At last young Annalis appeared. His eyes were bloodshot, his lids puffy. His greasy hair looked as if it hadn't seen a brush for days. Torquatus didn't want to go near enough to smell his breath: luckily there was no particular friendship in the case, so he didn't need to kiss the man. It was a holiday, so Torquatus had left his toga at home, but compared to Annalis he might have been about to defend an important client in court. The young man's tunic looked as if he'd slept in it, after being sick on it. He peered about, looking for something to sit on – where were his slaves? – then finally unearthed another stool from over by the hearth-fire (out) and the shrine to the household gods (untended). Having sat down, he seemed to feel that there was something missing, clapped his hands – twice – and, when a slave finally appeared, called for wine.

The wine was cheap, rough stuff, and Torquatus wasn't sorry to water it well, once the slave had been summoned back again with a jug of water. Annalis didn't. He knocked back a cupful while they were making polite conversation, and was well into his second, his face already flushed, by the time Torquatus got round to the interesting questions. He told Annalis about the attack on his farm, and Annalis nodded. Torquatus hadn't expected it to be news to him.

'I'd forgotten about it. A lot's happened recently,' Annalis said vaguely, suppressing a belch.

It had indeed. He'd been having his own father murdered, for one thing. 'And you are preparing to become aedile. A big job, and you'll be planning the games you'll be giving already, no doubt.'

He looked a bit wary at that. 'I hope so certainly. But things are so uncertain, and it'll cost a lot of money.'

'You must have inherited a handsome fortune,

surely? After all, the Three didn't in the end take any of your father's estate, did they?'

Annalis seemed to remember that Torquatus had been there on the day of his father's death, and to think better of any further complaints.

'Well, yes. And now the period of mourning's over I'll be able to take my affairs in hand. Of course I haven't been able to think of anything else until now.'

The little rat actually tried to put on a pious expression. Torquatus took a swig at his drink, hoping it would wash down his nausea.

'Did your father bank with Balbus, by any chance?' Torquatus asked him. If he'd hoped to catch Annalis out, he failed.

'Oh no, he didn't care for Balbus at all,' Annalis told him, refilling his wine-cup yet again. 'He believed all the stories. You know: that Balbus wasn't really a citizen, and that he'd come by his wealth dishonestly, and that he was sitting on a lot of money Octavian had stolen. But my father was a devious sort of man. I didn't always know what he was up to, and he seems to have spread his money around a bit. Why did you want to know?'

Torquatus ignored this question, and waved away the wine-jug. 'So you don't know who your father's banker was?'

'Oh, I don't say that. I've found receipts from a number of bankers already.' Annalis told him.

So much for the sacred period of mourning. 'But you suspect there are more?'

Annalis passed a slightly shaky hand over that lank hair, and shot him a suspicious glance.

'Fathers!' Torquatus said quickly. 'We Romans are supposed to revere them, and yet they can make our lives impossible. Mine clung so tight to Pompey I'm lucky to be alive now.' Torquatus felt bad, sacrificing his father in this way, but he was dead, and no-one else could hear him. Anyway, it was in a good cause. Anyway, it worked.

Annalis smiled and relaxed. 'You're so right.' He reached for the wine jug – the slave had disappeared again – tipping it up to see how much was left. 'I just know the old boy had a load of money stacked away somewhere. He'd been boasting for a while that he'd see me praetor, and consul too, if he lived long enough. He'd be able to grease the wheels for me, no-one would stand in our way. He scared the wits out of me, I don't mind saying. Those Three, they're not safe to mess with, and I'm almost certain this money had something to do with them.'

'Horrible for you, ' Torquatus ventured sympathetically.

'It was. I couldn't get an answer out of the old fool.' Having looked in vain for the slave, Annalis poured the rather sludgy remains of the wine into his cup. 'Jupiter knows, I tried. He was up to something'

'A plot? He was acting with others, then?'

Torquatus knew he'd misjudged the tone, in his eagerness to get to the kernel of the matter, and Annalis gave him a hazy, suspicious look. He hastened to cover up. 'Bit of a risk for you, if other people knew what he was doing?'

'Oh, I think I'm safe enough.' The man really couldn't helping boasting. 'I believe the other man's dead too. If it's who I think it was.' Jupiter! Torquatus was ashamed to remember how he'd been scoffing at Manlia's conspiracy theories. Annalis belched again, this time without trying to conceal it. Torquatus looked an enquiry, but Annalis shook his head and giggled, before raising the cup to his lips again. Torquatus thought that if he had much more he'd either fall asleep or throw up, but the jug was empty now, and the slave certainly wasn't rushing in with refills. He needed to get whatever he could out of Annalis before he became incapable. He remembered who Manlia's friends were again, and took a risk.

'Septimius in it too, was he?' Torquatus said, smiling, and to his relief Annalis laughed. 'Don't know how you worked that out, but you're right.'

'And Rebilus?'

'Dunno. If you say so.'

Torquatus thought of what Iunia had accidentally told him. 'And all this came to a head on the night of the sixth or seventh day before the Ides, didn't it?'

'What makes you say that?'

Torquatus had been guessing again, but it seemed he'd put the clues together right. Annalis was eyeing him muzzily, swaying slightly on his stool. Torquatus reckoned he only had so long before the confidences came to an end and went for the direct approach. 'Something went wrong, didn't it? Your father sent you a note, on a bit of scrap lead, asking you to help.'

Annalis' face was white now. 'How in Hades did you know that?'

'Ah well.' Torquatus shook his head mysteriously. 'I know more than you think. You may as well tell me the rest. Help me, and I'll see that you aren't implicated.'

Annalis suddenly looked as if he might burst into tears. 'I never did anything.'

'But would a court believe that?'

Drunk Annalis might be, but he knew what Torquatus meant. There weren't any courts sitting around that time: the Three meted out their own justice. He shrugged, and the effort nearly tipped him on the floor. Clutching the sides of his stool, he muttered, 'Anyway, I didn't do anything when I got the note, so I'm in the clear. It was such a dreadful scrawl, see, that I couldn't make it out.'

Torquatus briefly requested the gods to ensure that, if he ever took part in a conspiracy, no-one like Annalis was in it too. The young man was hurrying on, keen to explain himself now: 'And my slaves couldn't wake me up at first. I'm a heavy sleeper. When they did wake me, like I said I couldn't make sense of it. I couldn't get back to sleep after all the fuss, so in the end I got up and went round to his house. I met him just as he was coming in. So you see I didn't –'

'What time was that?'

'Oh, just about dawn. His morning visitors were waiting for him, and I heard the steward tell someone in the crowd that the master had been out to visit a dying friend.'

Torquatus tried to keep his voice calm and neutral. 'So where did your father say he'd been?'

'Damn him, he wouldn't say.' Annalis was scowling like an angry child. 'He was upset because I hadn't come to him. In a foul temper. He hardly spoke to me. He went straight to the clients and friends who were waiting, once he'd changed his clothes, and then he sent me home to do the same. He wanted me looking my best so we could go and canvass. And then, of course, he was killed.'

'You mean, you arranged to have him killed.'

Moral indignation was wasted on him.

'Sure, but if I'd realised they would come straight away I would have held off a little. As it was, all I ever got out of him was that our money worries were over. Then he clammed up.'

Annalis sadly held the jug upside down over his cup. Before he could think to call the slaves back, Torquatus asked, 'So you didn't go with your father wherever it was he went that night? And you never knew any more about it?'

'That's right. He just said he didn't trust me. Said I drank too much.' Annalis' eyes filled with tears. 'What kind of a way is that to treat your son?'

Looking at this crumpled, smelly young man, Torquatus could hardly blame the older Annalis. 'He may have just been trying to protect you. Because your father was at my farm that night, wasn't he?'

Annalis looked even more confused. 'Why should he have been there?'

'He went there to steal the money stored at the farm. The fragment of lead your father used for his note had been torn off the new drainpipe I'd recently had installed. And I think that wasn't the first attempt your father had made on the money, was it?'

He had his hands over his mouth, and his eyes, wide and appalled, stared at Torquatus without meaning. Torquatus got up, and made his farewells. He had to clap his hands twice for the slave to come and open the door. As he was about to leave, he saw something lying discarded in a corner, something that brought back vividly to his mind how alert and interested Iucundus had been at his farm that morning.

'Those boots,' he said, pointing into the corner of the room. 'An interesting design. They yours?'

Annalis stared at him suspiciously, and slowly lowered his hands from his face.

'They were my father's,' he said at last. 'I'll need senator's boots now, of course, and I'm having some more made, but my feet are the same size as my father's, and so I thought I might as well use his up.'

It might have been true. In which case the account he'd given Torquatus of his movements on the night of the raid was probably true too.

Torquatus sank back into his litter with plenty to think about. He thought he knew now how the money had been stolen, could almost see the mule-carts in the flickering torchlight, with Annalis directing the slaves. What was terrifying was that he still had no idea where it had gone: Annalis hadn't taken it to his house, that was clear from his son's account of his arrival, alone, at dawn. Septimius had been dead before the raid even began. It didn't seem as if Rebilus had been a major player. Could there have been others involved, others he didn't yet know of? Even if he discovered the name of every plotter, and found out every detail of how the raid had been carried out, that knowledge was worth nothing if Antonius managed to keep the cash hidden for just a few more days now. Torquatus left the leather litter-curtains open, looking out sightlessly across an almost empty city. They crossed the desolate spaces of the Forum Boarium, but just as they turned up the Vicus

Iugarius Torquatus snapped out of his reverie at the sight of a group of soldiers marching smartly towards them. The litter-men had seen them too, and immediately moved to the side of the road.

As they came nearer, Torquatus could see they were Antonius' men. He'd had the fancy to equip each member of his bodyguard with a breastplate bearing his family emblem of Hercules. The effect was slightly spoiled, however, by the presence at the very head of the troop, leading the whole party, centurion and all, of a little man with a big nose, whom Torquatus immediately identified as Antonius' freedman Philo, stomping along looking comically like a child playing at generals. He told his bearers to wait while they passed, wanting to see where Philo was off to in such a hurry. The soldiers marched into the vegetable market, just as Torquatus had done himself two days ago. As he watched, his head stuck out of the litter, they halted smartly at the temple of Hope. Thoughtfully, he waved the bearers on.

His own house seemed a haven of calm and order after Annalis' dump. Trofimus told Torquatus that Manlia was at her weaving, and he went and found her at her loom. From the doorway, he said, 'Cato would have been proud of you.'

She glanced over her shoulder at him, laughing. 'He would. But even that thought isn't enough to stop me weaving when I'm in the mood for it.'

Torquatus crossed the room, and picked up the end of the cloth she was working on. The wool must have cost a fortune. It was so fine it looked as if it must break on the loom, and so soft his hands felt coarse and rough handling it. The colour was wonderful, a rich, reddish gold.

'It's for you?'

She nodded.

'Lovely colour. It'll suit you. Is it Baetican?'

'It is. Hard to believe, isn't it, that this colour is quite natural? Pity it's so hideously expensive.' Manlia put the shuttle down carefully. 'How did you know about Baetican wool? And what did Annalis have to tell you?'

'I know all sorts of things, lady. And if you can tear yourself away from your housewifely pursuits, I'll tell you what I've learned.'

Together they made their way to the study they'd used as their regular sitting room in recent days. Torquatus told a slave to bring wine, but it wasn't necessary: Trofimus had evidently decided that his owners needed refreshment, and jugs of wine and water, the latter beaded with condensation, stood ready on the side-table, along with bowls of nuts and dried fruit.

'So. Annalis,' Manlia began, stretching herself on the reading-couch and waving away the wine-jug.

'Indeed. Annalis told me a good deal more than he intended to. His father and Septimius were involved in some plot, as you suspected, so I owe you an apology. I don't know what it was, but perhaps something in aid of Sextus Pompey, as you suggested. If the father was anything like the son, I shouldn't think it had much chance of success. But what I do know is that it was those two who planned the raid on the farm.'

'Annalis and Septimius? However did you find that out? He didn't just tell you, did he?' Manlia swung her legs down again, and sat up very straight, staring.

'Oh no. But he didn't deny it. I owe you an apology. If it hadn't been for what you told me, I wouldn't have guessed. But there must have been someone else, mustn't there, because I still don't know where the money is.'

'No. Rebilus?'

'I don't think so. If he had he'd have used the knowledge to get himself off the list.'

Manlia considered this, twisting a lock of her hair. 'And did Annalis tell you anything else?'

'He told me he'd received the note from old Annalis in the small hours of the sixth before the Ides but couldn't read it.'

'Well, that makes three of us, then.'

'Quite. In the end, he went to Annalis' house, arriving at dawn, where his dad was furious with him and refused to tell him anything except to repeat that their money worries were over. He told me that he wouldn't have had Annalis killed quite so quickly if he'd realised the old man wasn't going to spill the beans.'

'Oh Aulus, he couldn't have said that! I mean, I know he's a ghastly man, but surely – '

'He said just that. Believe me.'

She stopped laughing and shivered a little. 'Well, if you say so. He seems to have told you a lot.'

'He was drunk. He wouldn't have told me otherwise, I'm sure. He told me himself that his father refused to confide in him.'

'Because he was a drunk?'

'Indeed. He also told me that he met his father coming back into his house at dawn that morning, old Annalis' absence being explained by the steward as due to visiting a dying friend. Annalis tried to explain that he hadn't been able to make out the note because he was – '

'Drunk?'

'A heavy sleeper,' Torquatus amended. 'So now we know that Septimius and Annalis planned the theft. He admitted Septimius was in it too, but didn't seem to know about Rebilus. The plot obviously went wrong: we need to know how. And who else was involved: someone from Antonius' household, I'll bet.' Torquatus got up and prowled restlessly round the room, feeling as if precious time was being wasted while he fumbled for answers.

'Could we really prove any of this?' Manlia asked.

'Depends what you mean: we aren't likely to be taking anyone to court, exactly. But I'll tell you something: Annalis had some boots with a design of star-shaped studs. The only time I've seen a pattern like that before was at the farmhouse.'

'But I thought young Annalis wasn't at the farm.' Manlia bit at the lock of hair.

'He wasn't. The boots were his father's. They have the same size feet apparently, and now that he is going to be a senator, he needs appropriate footwear.'

Manlia made a face and pushed the hair back behind her ear. 'He could afford to buy his own, you'd think.'

'It's very Roman to be frugal, isn't it?' Torquatus replied, coming back to his chair. For a moment or two they sat in silence, then Manlia said, 'You haven't told me what Iunia was telling you yesterday.'

'I haven't. I hadn't really understood it until I had a chance to think it all over last night. She told me four things, all rather jumbled up: that Rebilus shouldn't have bought the gladiators, and that if she'd known what he was going to do with them she'd have done something; that Rebilus wasn't in it the first time; that she'd told him about "the little farm"; and that he'd told the others. She was very upset.'

Manlia lay back thinking. 'So it was Rebilus told Septimius and Annalis about your farm. I can understand that. But what's the "first time" mean?'

'I think the successful attack was the second attempt, and that Rebilus only asked about my houses when the first attempt had failed.'

'I can see why Iunia was upset,' Manlia said grimly. 'She's caused you a huge amount of damage, and who knows if we'll manage to put it right?'

'True. But she certainly didn't intend to harm me. Anyway, we aren't as far on as you'd think,' Torquatus pointed out. 'We still don't know where the money is, which is the one thing we must find out. Presumably it went to the house of one of the conspirators. And I'm sure Antonius is involved somehow or other.' He paced about impatiently. 'I'm missing something, I'm sure of it.'

'You are. Because if the money was taken by Septimius, Annalis and Rebilus, it was going to be used against Antonius and Octavian, wasn't it? So why would he have known anything about it?'

'I've no idea. But there he is, sending soldiers here, there and everywhere, giving a very good impression of a person really trying quite hard to find something. What if there were two lots of people trying to take this cash: one on behalf of Antonius, one for these stupid conspirators, now dead.'

Torquatus got up and walked about again, fidgeting with the door-curtain and the wine-jug until Manlia told him to stop. He sat down again and sighed. 'Oh, I desperately need to find this money, and two of the men who could tell me where it is are dead and the other one's vanished.'

'Septimius' death must have been one reason why it didn't go as planned. When did he die, anyway?' Manlia asked.

'The sixth before the Ides, I think. I'm not sure.'

'Just before the raid. There must be someone in his house who would know?'

'I think all his slaves have gone, and I've already talked to Celer. I didn't get the impression – but I'll see him again.'

Manlia sat up. 'And in the meantime, I have some news for you.'

'What's happened now?' Torquatus didn't like the expression on her face.

'This morning, after you'd gone out, Trofimus and Demetrius came to me. I could see at once that something serious had happened.'

Torquatus heart sank. 'Well, what was it?'

'Those tablets. The ones you'd lost, the ones Demetrius accused Iucundus of taking.'

'Well, what about them?'

'Demetrius has found them. He said he'd decided to look in the hayloft where Iucundus was sleeping, and they were there.' She looked sceptical.

'I know you don't like Demetrius,' Torquatus began.

'I don't. But I don't think he's at fault here. It just seems too pat, yet I can't see how. He did find the tablets where the boy had been sleeping; one of the grooms was with him.'

So much for Iucundus protesting his innocence. 'So what did they say? Iucundus wouldn't tell me, remember.'

'Why, nothing. That's odder than anything, isn't it? I mean, Iucundus must have cleaned them himself. No-one else has had them. But if he did that, why not put them back where they belonged?'

'I'll speak to Demetrius,' Torquatus decided.

'He's in the library, working on your papers.'

'What, again? He seems to live in there.'

Demetrius was so deep in his work that he never heard the door open, and for a moment they stood watching him. He was surrounded by scrolls and sets of wax tablets, which he seemed to be arranging into piles as he read them. After a moment he became aware of being watched, and looked up, colouring slightly. 'Lord! I'm sorry, I didn't hear you come in.'

Torquatus wandered over to the table, and picked up a small scroll.

'Ah, yet another letter from Lucius.' He let it roll up and dropped it back on the table.

'Yes, lord. I am trying to arrange the family archive so that all the letters are in date order, grouped according to the person who wrote them. I think it's better to divide them that way. But if you prefer, I could arrange them all in one chronological sequence, so that you could see, for instance - ,'

'Oh, just do whatever you think best. I can't imagine I'd ever want to read them again anyway.'

'It would be good to complete the sequence,' Demetrius insisted. 'But I can't find the last letters your brother wrote from Africa. There must have been some, mustn't there?'

'Yes,' Torquatus agreed. 'There was a whole

collection that Philip brought back after Lucius died. I found them waiting for me when I came home myself.'

'Did you, lord? I haven't found them here,' Demetrius said cautiously.

'Well, never mind that now. My sister tells me that you've found my missing tablets?'

Torquatus thought the man looked annoyed: his smile, when it came, seemed forced. 'Yes, lord, they were among Iucundus' bedding.'

'And? What was this mysterious message that Iucundus wouldn't tell me?'

'Nothing, lord. They were clean, had nothing written in them at all. I've put them on the table in your business room.'

'I wonder why he kept them?' Torquatus asked. 'Nothing could be more dangerous, after all.' He thought back to when he'd last seen the boy, before Saturnalia. He'd hardly thought of him since. 'Hasn't he been under guard? That's what I ordered, as far as I remember.'

'Well, that wasn't what Trofimus thought,' said Manlia. 'And actually, I don't think you did: you just said he was to be kept away from you, which he's done. Trofimus set him to work in the stables and the gardens, with a couple of other slaves with him at all times. He swears the boy hasn't been left alone. And at night Becco and Pulex and some of the other men have been up on the roof guarding the house.'

Torquatus looked surprised, and Manlia went on: 'Trofimus and I were worried that there might be another attack on you, and decided that you - I mean, the house - needed protection. Anyone wandering around in the dark, let alone trying to get near you, would have ended up with a spear through him. If Iucundus knew that, perhaps he was simply waiting for an opportunity to put the tablets back?'

Torquatus sighed. Every time he thought his problems were coming to an end, something else would crop up. 'I'll have to have the truth out of him. Even if it means calling the torturers in.'

'Yes. I'm afraid it will come to that,' Manlia agreed. 'I don't like it, but if all this drags on, the consequences – ' She shrugged. She didn't need to spell them out: they were keeping her brother awake too. She said: 'It upsets the other slaves, though. Do you think there's any chance of getting the truth from him yourself?'

'You weren't there when I spoke to him last, were you? I almost doubted whether the boy was sane. He looked at me so strangely, insisted I must know what was written on the tablets. And remember what that anonymous letter said, that there was a forger in the house. I must admit I thought it was just nonsense at first, but now I'm wondering. There's someone here who takes tablets, puts writing on them, takes it away again. It's like living in a mirror. I have to get to the bottom of it. If I don't, I'll never be able to trust my own slaves again.'

Torquatus stood irresolute for a moment, then made up his mind. 'Demetrius, get Victor, will you. I want my toga. And then go and find Iucundus. I'll see him now. And bring the tablets.'

The man padded off. Manlia, her fingers automatically straightening the little piles of documents, said over her shoulder, 'I hope he sees sense. I can't bear the thought of hurting him.' She turned and smiled at Torquatus. 'But if it's what you have to do, we'll get through it, you know.'

Victor came hurrying in, the toga neatly folded over one arm. It was almost like a dance, Manlia thought, as the two men moved expertly round one another until the heavy garment swathed her brother just as it should. Victor adjusted the folds on his master's left shoulder, than went quietly out as Demetrius came back, one hand on Iucundus' shoulder. He pushed the boy roughly in front of Torquatus. Iucundus looked puzzled, but, as always, met Torquatus' gaze directly. Demetrius silently handed over the tablets, and Torquatus held them up in front of the boy. 'These have been found in your bedding. How do you account for that?'

'I didn't put them there, lord.' He still held Torquatus' eyes, but his expression, Torquatus thought, was one of despair. 'I haven't seen them since the night that Philip showed them to me.'

'You refused to tell me what was written on the tablets. You'll tell me now.' Torquatus' face and voice were soft but menacing. Iucundus shrugged. 'Very well, lord. The message was that Stephanus was to go to the Capitol that night. The writing was your own.'

Manlia gasped, and Torquatus stared at him through narrowed eyes. 'Have you learned nothing? I'd have preferred silence to insolence like that.'

'You asked me to tell you the truth, lord, and that's the truth.'

'Take him away, and this time you can lock him up,' Torquatus told Demetrius.

As the two pairs of footsteps faded away Torquatus said curtly: 'It'll have to be the torturers.'

Manlia's face was taut and pale in the fading light.

Seeing her expression, Torquatus said, 'I'll ask them to start gently. And perhaps he'll break quite easily, so they don't have to take extreme measures.'

And if he did, told who was paying him, what he had done, what then? She tried to smile. Torquatus took her hand in a reassuring clasp. 'And when all this is over, perhaps the shadow will go from the house, and we can be normal again.'

'I really don't think I know what normal means, any more.'

Torquatus went off to bathe, by which time Trofimus was ready to serve dinner: a quiet one again. They were both glad of it: neither seemed to have much appetite. Torquatus was lost in his own thoughts. It is the Roman way, to see every slave as a potential enemy, except when sentimentalising the pretty slave-children, or lusting after the gorgeous boy who poured the wine. Torquatus remembered

232

his father saying that a household where torture is practised is a household where discipline has failed. He wanted to agree, but wondered uneasily whether all his father had meant was that it was more comfortable for their owners when slaves appeared contented.

'Make the most of your quiet evening. We're dining at Balbus' tomorrow,' Manlia said as she crumbled bread on her plate.

Torquatus snapped out of his reflections. 'Are we?'

'Yes. He's going to Neapolis the day after, so this is a kind of leaving party. It's going to be very grand: I hear Octavian's going.'

'Octavian! Gods!' A grand party indeed. Octavian had no taste for banquets, ate very lightly, and only attended parties where he knew he would cause offence by staying away. 'I suppose we're invited because we invited him: Balbus never does anything without a purpose.' He drank, considering the matter. They were still sitting over their nuts and wine, Torquatus remaining at the table while Manlia had drifted, as was her custom in the evening, to her brother's reading-couch, and now lay along it, her gown elegantly draped, a little table to hand with her wine-cup and a bowl of nuts where she could reach them.

'I went to see mother and Iunia today,' she said, picking out a handful of pistachios. 'Goodness, it was hard work. They'd had a quarrel, I imagine, so I could talk to one or other of them, but not both at the same time.'

'Do they quarrel a lot?' Torquatus wasn't very interested, but could see Manlia needed to talk.

'More than they used to, I think. Mother doesn't like Rebilus.'

'Doesn't much matter now he's gone, does it? She's a bit faded, anyway. I wonder why he fancied her?'

'Oh, be fair, Aulus.' Manlia sounded unusually impatient. 'The poor woman's had, what, eleven years of marriage. About half of that time, her husband's been away. Even when he was in Rome, he was no doubt increasingly busy with his career, getting as far as praetor. No children. When he went off to join Pompey six years ago, what was she supposed to do to pass the time? For the last three years she's been a widow, and without any family of her own still alive that's left her with little choice except to stay with Mama. If she's a bit crabby, who can wonder?'

Torquatus glanced across at her, surprised at her vehemence. Then he thought that the story she'd just told could almost as easily have been applied to her. True, she wasn't a widow, but there was every chance she'd never see Ahenobarbus again. He shivered at the thought. 'She can do what she likes, for me.'

Manlia smiled, but before she could speak, the curtain was pushed aside, and Trofimus came in. 'Excuse me for interrupting you, lord, but two slaves from the household of the senator Septimius - the late senator Septimius, I should say — have arrived and have asked to speak to you. They won't tell me what their message is, but they seem distressed, and convinced it's urgent.'

Torquatus sat up straight. 'Send them in, please.'

Manlia began to get up, but Torquatus waved her back to the couch. 'If it's about the theft, you know as much as I do. Don't go.'

The two men who were shown in were senior slaves, neatly-dressed, well-fed, polite. They were also, as Trofimus had noted, quite clearly distressed.

'We are sorry to disturb you, lord,' the older of the two began. 'But you remember, perhaps, speaking to Celer at the Treasury the other day?'

Torquatus nodded. 'Your names?' he demanded.

'I'm Conon, lord, and this is Leo.'

Torquatus nodded, and Conon went on. 'After he'd seen you, he came to the house. You'll understand, lord, that no-one's living there at present. We aren't sure who owns it now, whether it has been sold, or not.' He paused, and gave Torquatus an apologetic look. 'Anyway, the house and all the master's property went to Antonius after the master's death. The mistress, Flavia, has married Volusius, as you know, and now lives at his house. She took her own slaves with her, but the rest of us have stayed in the house, waiting for instructions.'

Torquatus nodded rather impatiently, and Conon took a breath and hurried on. 'Celer told us to notify you if anything important happened.'

'So has something important happened?'

'Tonight, lord, just as darkness was falling, some soldiers of Antonius' came to the house. They searched it from top to bottom, and made a terrible mess. No; they wouldn't tell us what they were looking for. Whatever it was, they didn't find it, and they went away at last, their hands as empty as when they'd arrived. So we talked it over, Leo and I, and decided you should know of it.'

Torquatus and Manlia stared at each other. 'Thank you. You were quite right,' Torquatus said. 'Tell me, did they search among Septimius' papers, or were they looking in store-rooms? What sort of thing might they have been hunting for, do you think?'

Leo seemed the brighter of the two, for while the older man puzzled over Torquatus' question, he answered straight away. 'Oh, not documents, lord, I think. They were looking through every room, and inside some of the big storage-jars and so on. But there aren't many documents left, anyway. The lady Flavia took a good lot with her, saying they related to her own property, and she had everything else burned. Her maids did it, in the courtyard, before following their mistress to her new home. No, it was bigger stuff they were after, but we can't imagine what.'

Torquatus sat back, his heart beating fast. Antonius too was after the money. He wasn't sure what that meant, except that it seemed to confirm Manlia's insistence that he hadn't been behind the raid.

'You were right to tell me. Thank you. And while you're here there are one or two other things I need to know. No need to look like that. Just tell me the truth and there'll be no trouble. I would like you to tell me whether anything happened on the night of the sixth day before the Ides.'

'The sixth before the Ides?,' Conon replied. 'That was the day the master died, lord, so we were all in confusion. But there wasn't anything particular, I don't think.'

'Nothing happened that night? No-one went out?'

'There wasn't anyone left, that night. The mistress got married in the afternoon, as I've said. Not that it was a big wedding.' Torquatus was glad to know Flavia and Volusius had shown that much good taste, at least. 'It wasn't late when she and her slaves went away, not by the standards of the household, but we were tired, so we cleared up and went to bed. We were all feeling quite shaken, and anxious too, not knowing what would become of us.'

Leo had been nodding in agreement with his colleague's account, but a slight frown now drew his rather heavy brows together. 'Didymus did go out.'

The two slaves stared at each other in silence for a minute. 'He did, didn't he?' Conon agreed. I'd forgotten that. That's the master's secretary, lord. I don't know when he came back home, but he was certainly there next morning. Said he'd remembered something his master had intended to do, but he never said what it was. Well, we didn't really care. It was too late for the master anyway, wasn't it?'

'Didymus would be close to your master?'

'Closer than anyone, barring perhaps the master's own body-slave, who helped him dress and went everywhere with him. And he was dead too by then, killed trying to defend his master.'

'Do you know what time Didymus went out?'

'Oh, it was very late. I'd never have known he'd gone if I hadn't had to get up to piss in the night.'

'Had he ever done anything like that before?'

Leo and Conon looked at each other. 'No, but - '

'Well, what?'

It was Leo who went on. 'Didymus and the master went off one day together. I don't know what they were doing, but it must have been something unusual.' He turned to his companion. 'You remember? It was very early in the morning, when the master would generally be seeing his clients. He was fretting to be gone, and Didymus looked really anxious?'

'Oh yes,' Conon agreed. 'And wasn't the master in a temper when he came back in? I'm sorry, lord, it doesn't sound much, put like that, but it was odd.'

'No,' he said. 'I'm glad you've told me. And that would have happened on the day before the Nones, I'm guessing?'

Manlia and Conon looked equally astonished, while Leo was obviously silently counting. 'Yes, lord, it was.'

'And nothing else has happened since?'

'The house has been as quiet as a grave, lord,' Conon said seriously.

Leo made a quick little movement: perhaps, like Torquatus, he was stifling a smile. Torquatus made his face straight and asked another question.

'Going back to the night of the sixth, just after your master had been killed: I suppose Celer knew Didymus was out?'

'Celer? Well, he certainly saw Didymus come back,' said Leo. 'He was in the reception hall when the man came in next morning. Now I come to think of it, didn't he take the man off with him, tired as he was, saying he needed to know what was going on?'

'You're right. I'd forgotten that.'

The last piece of the puzzle, Torquatus thought: except for where the money had gone, the one piece of information without which the rest was useless. He thanked the men, told them to send Didymus over in the morning and heard them go off, with Trofimus offering them refreshment before they returned home.

'Antonius obviously wants this money as much as Octavian does,' Torquatus said. 'I wonder why he thought it might be at Septimius' house?'

'Well, he was in it, wasn't he? And anyway they might have been searching for something else.'

'They might. But I saw the soldiers going to the temple of Hope, too, which suggests that they've got the same clues, somehow. Philo must have got that from Celer, I suppose. Yes, that fits: Volusius is close to Antonius, so Celer will no doubt be sent there more frequently. No doubt Philo's been tasked with getting to the money before I do.' Torquatus felt exhausted but febrile. He wanted to hurry off somewhere, anywhere, to bring this nightmare to an end. He had an unpleasant image in his mind, an image of Antonius' soldiers running round Rome in the dark, hunting for hidden treasure.

Manlia gave him a very sisterly look. 'Now you need to explain. What was all that about Septimius rushing around in the early morning?'

'Ah, well, that was the first attempt. I've been thinking about our conspiratorial friends, and their attempts to steal the money. Iunia made it clear that the second, successful attempt was the raid on the farm. So what was the first attempt?'

'I've no idea,' Manlia said.

'Philo told me that he'd heard the money was being sent to Torquatus in Rome. So he would naturally assume that meant it was coming here, wouldn't he?'

'To this house? Oh, of course.'

Torquatus nodded. 'Now, if you were going to try and carry off a whole heap of money, would you choose to attack it while it was still packed neatly into carriages hitched to frisky mules and dispatched without armed guards, or would you wait until it was stashed away in a locked store under careful surveillance?'

Manlia opened her mouth and closed it again.

Torquatus went on: 'I think they went out with as

many heavy men as they thought they needed and hung around, perhaps among the tombs along the Appian Way - plenty of places to hide, there. But of course the money didn't come that way. It turned off well before it got to Rome and took the Via Labicana, heading for my farm. And I think it was only after that first attempt failed that Rebilus questioned Iunia about my other properties, and not until after the second attempt that she realised what Rebilus' gladiators were for.'

'No wonder she was upset. These precious conspirators couldn't have acted without her information.'

'No. And I went and warned her that Rebilus looked as if he might end up listed. I really am my own worst enemy sometimes. Naturally the man cleared off.'

'Of course he did. And you couldn't have known you needed to talk to him.'

Torquatus grunted. 'Trouble is, a suspicious person might suspect collusion on my part, don't you think? In the morning I'm going to call on Postumia again. Because her house will be next.'

Chapter 17

Torquatus called in the torturers. It was the only way he was going to get to the truth. The household went very quiet.

For a few more days, while the festival lasted, there would be no morning visitors, and since neither Torquatus nor Manlia had slept well dawn was only just breaking as they sat over the brazier in his study, going over all the evidence.

'You said yourself,' Manlia began, 'that if Antonius had stolen the money he'd hardly be running all over the town looking for it, would he?'

'Probably not. Although it's clear something went badly wrong. Perhaps only Septimius' death. Until we find out whether that was all, we'd better not rule him out entirely.'

'Oh come on, Aulus, you're just determined for him to be the villain.'

'I don't say he took it,' Torquatus insisted. 'But suppose he knew about the conspiracy. He might well decide to let the plotters have their heads - sorry, that's a joke in bad taste, isn't it? - well, then, he might think he'd let them get the money, then proscribe them, and clean up. And they all ended up proscribed. I rest my case.'

Manlia's tone was dry. 'Careless of him, then, to proscribe them before he'd found out where the money was?'

'If only we knew what it was that went wrong!'

'Whatever it was, it's inconceivable that someone wouldn't have told Antonius, surely? If he knew about it.'

'If they were alive they would,' Torquatus agreed rather sourly. He meant it as a joke, but Manlia sat up straighter.

'We should have thought about that,' Torquatus went on. 'We've been assuming that whoever attacked the farm is sitting on the money. But perhaps they aren't?'

'What do you mean?'

'Well, Annalis was involved: he died the next day.' Torquatus ticked the known conspirators off on his fingers. 'Septimius was involved: he was dead even before the raid. Annalis' son wasn't there: we know Annalis was in some sort of difficulty, and summoned him, but unfortunately seems not to have told his son where the money was. Rebilus was probably there, but as he's run away, it seems he hasn't got some useful secret he could buy his life with. The raid must have been a real muddle. I suppose they didn't even know Septimius was dead until this Didymus went to tell them. What if he's the only one left alive who knew where the money was hidden?'

'Why should it have been hidden anywhere?' Manlia objected. 'Wouldn't the thieves simply take it to where they wanted it? Or – wait – of course! What if they couldn't bring the money into Rome as they'd intended?'

They stared at each other. 'The curfew!' Manlia exclaimed. 'Of course. All wheeled traffic must be out of Rome by dawn. So they were stuck with the stuff and had to hide it somewhere.'

'Hope!' Torquatus had jumped out of his chair with excitement. Manlia was staring at him. 'This will teach me not to overlook the finer points of grammar. Remember when we were deciphering the little piece of lead? I read 'spes' but you thought it was 'spem.' Of course. Not the temple of Spes, but the old shrine -'

'Ad Spem Veterem. Aulus, of course. How could we have overlooked that? So close to the farm, too.'

'Trofimus! Demetrius!' Torquatus shouted, and the two came running, almost knocking into each other in the doorway. 'A message to Octavian,' he said briskly. 'Ask him for a detail of soldiers. A large one. At once. And we'll also need several mule-carriages; nine or ten if - please Jupiter! - it's all there. The soldiers can meet us at the old shrine of Hope: Ad Spem Veterem.'

Demetrius hurried off.

'I'll go down and warn Postumia, shall I?'

'Please. I shan't even bother with this Didymus. I'm going straight to the shrine. Becco and Pulex can come too, and several more of the strongest slaves, as many as we have horses for. Arm them, please, Trofimus.' Torquatus smiled, his spirits soaring.

Trofimus took this spate of orders with his usual calmness, and moved off to see to everything.

Slaves were running everywhere. That awful sense of foreboding seemed to lift. The big men were already by the door. Victor was helping Torquatus into his boots. Torquatus was about to hurry out when a thought struck him. Suddenly serious, he went across the reception hall to the household altar and laid his hand on it in front of them all. Silence fell. Manlia and the slaves watched curiously. Torquatus glanced round, caught their eyes. 'I promise this to the three great gods of Rome, Jupiter, Juno and Minerva: the sacrifice of a fine bull in thanks, if what I have lost is found. And I swear this: I shall rebuild Hope's temple to honour her.' He turned away, reaching for his cloak, and as he did so a metallic clanking told them that the torturers had just arrived, bringing their fearful instruments. Torquatus only had time to impress on Trofimus that they were to use the minimum force necessary before hurrying off. As Trofimus led the men to the back of the house he almost fell over Felix, who was running in.

'No,' the boy cried out. 'No! I must see the master.'

'Not now,' said the steward, and Torquatus saw his big strong hands clamp down on the boy's shoulders as he steered him away. Then he went out to where his horse was waiting, and the troubles of the household fell away from him.

It was a fair way to the ancient shrine, but the six of them (all there were horses for in the stables) galloped along the dusty roads in the cold wind as if a host of demons were after them. Being a holiday, even the road which crossed the top end of the Subura was quite quiet. They left the city at a trot through the Porta Esquilina, once the party of hard-faced soldiers guarding it had scrutinised them, then cantered gently along the grass verge which marks the beginning of that area of farms and gardens. The Via Labicana cuts straight through this part of Rome, forking only where one must choose between the roads to Praeneste and to Labici. And at this very spot, less than a mile from Torquatus' farm, there were the ruins of a shrine or temple – hard to tell which from what was left - to Hope. One reason why he'd never considered it when searching the temple of Hope in the city was that he had known it all his life. Another, of course, was that it was hardly the sort of secure storage you'd need for chests full of cash. But if his guess was right, no-one had ever intended the money to stay there for so long.

Like all crossroads, the place had acquired a certain seedy character of its own. Run-down shops and stalls clustered round the junction. The largest was a dirty bar, with the adjoining shop incorporated as an eating-house. The smell of fried onions bore testimony to the industry of the shopkeeper. Holiday or no holiday, people would still need to eat. Next to this, a tumbledown building had an old-clothes shop on its ground floor, with a rail outside on which a collection of dirty, ragged tunics swayed in the cold wind. Two aqueducts, one on each side, marched the road to Labici firmly to the distant horizon. The bigger road, to Praeneste, had a few travellers, but otherwise they had the place to themselves. Or they would have had, except for the presence of a group sprawled about on the remains of the shrine buildings.

Torquatus brought Bucephalus to a halt and looked around, hearing his party reining in behind him. A fringe of dusty trees marked out the limits of the precinct of what must once have been an important shrine. Now, however, what lay within their enclosing arms was little more than heaps of rubble scattered over the broken paving. Columns poked through it here and there, with ivy twining round them, and in one corner a section of the roof was still intact, some of its tiles hanging off in a perilous manner. Brambles had poked up through the rubble, and still held a few withered brown leaves and some hard, blackened berries. The whole place looked and smelled dirty and unwholesome. Torquatus hadn't expected it to be quite empty: in any empty space near Rome one can find groups of those whose roots barely cling in the soil of the city, beggars, pickpockets, men and women who live in tombs or under the arches of aqueducts, or offer by the side of the road a few vegetables, a stolen tunic, or their own sex. What he didn't expect was to find a party in full swing. It was a fine, bright day, but cold.

Wood had been collected to make a good-sized fire in the space between the heaps of rubble and the road. Around this fire the revellers sat or reclined among broken pots, bits of old rag, scorched paving suggesting previous fires, and, from the smell, a good deal of human waste. The group, of perhaps twenty or thirty people, adults, skinny children and even skinnier dogs, had paid little attention to Torquatus' party as it approached. No doubt they assumed the horsemen intended simply to pass by. Why should a rich man, accompanied by his slaves, pay any attention to such as them?

After a few moments, they began to realise Torquatus had stopped, and the sober ones among them lowered their wine-skins and stared at him suspiciously. They were the sort who don't live long, who don't come down into the city except to prey on the citizens, almost unseen by people like Torquatus as they move between their comfortable houses and the Forum. They were dressed in ragged tunics whose colours had washed out long since. Some of them had a few more scraps of rag, stiff with dirt, wrapped around their feet. Their hair and beards were matted and filthy. Torquatus and the beggars looked at each other as if they had come from different worlds. He beckoned to one of them, a young man with wild black hair and a bushy unkempt beard, and he came over at once, limping badly, and took Bucephalus' rein. Torquatus slid down from the saddle. The men, and one or two of the women, the lowest and most desperate of whores from the look of them, got to their feet and stared at him open-mouthed.

'Sorry to spoil your party,' he told them, 'but I'm going to search this building.'

One of the women cackled, showing black teeth. 'A building is it? Buildings have roofs, darling, and we'd love a roof. Give us a roof, do.'

'Looking for some old stones, are you? There's nothing else here. If there was, you'd have taken it long ago,' another one joined in, and they all cackled a bit more, took another pull at the wine.

Torquatus struggled to understand their rough Latin. He himself spoke briskly, in a commanding tone. 'I'm on government business, and I intend to search this place.'

The beggars seemed to understand him well enough. 'Come on tribune, give us a break. Saturnalia, isn't it?' one of the women asked.

'I shan't do you any harm as long as you don't get in my way.' And Torquatus beckoned to Becco and Pulex to come forward. At the sight of the big men, the beggars reluctantly began to move. They shuffled across the dusty ground and huddled together under the trees. One of the mangy dogs dared to bark at Torquatus from a safe distance, but finding it got no response it slunk after the beggars.

Torquatus and his party walked right round the mounds of stone, looking for any sign of disturbance. There were none. The temple area was quite small, typical of these ancient holy places. All Torquatus' life it had been like this, a ruin, a hangout for the destitute. His spirits sank. This was going to be the temple of Hope all over again. In the distance he could see a cloud of dust approaching down the road: Octavian's men, no doubt. He only prayed it wouldn't be the same group of soldiers as he'd taken to the temple. They'd walked almost all the way round, poking and prodding at the rubble, when Torquatus suddenly burst out laughing. He was a fool. The hairy man holding his horse looked a little alarmed when Torquatus strode over to him, still laughing a little.

'Where did you get the money for that?' he asked, pointing to the wineskin hanging at the man's waist.

'It's just an old skin a guy gave me.'

'No, not the skin, the wine. How did you afford it?'

'Well we beg, see, and at Saturnalia we put all we've got in together, and get as much as we can.' The man's voice died away.

Torquatus said loudly: 'You've found the money that was stored here, haven't you?' He called Pulex over, and told him to get his knife out. At the sight of that bright blade, the man shrugged and mumbled something about not needing to threaten him, before he handed the horse's rein to one of his fellows and led Torquatus away. He began to walk away from the mounds, back towards the trees and the one standing corner of the old building, to where a bramble bush grew raggedly through the paving. Torquatus followed him. Behind the bush, almost hidden under the thorny shoots that had been drawn over it, steps went down to a half-blocked doorway. Calling to the others he went down, leaving his guide to wait.

It must always have been partially underground; now the entrance was almost blocked. Some of the stone surfaces looked fresh and new, as if they hadn't been exposed to the weather for very long. It was a hard job to squeeze himself through the little gap between the lintel of the door and the jumble of masonry which lay beneath it. And of course when he did get through he couldn't see a thing. His heart was pounding so hard he could scarcely breathe. He could feel that he was in a small space - surely too small to make a useful store. His affronted nose told him it had been used as a latrine for a long, long time. At last his eyes cleared.

He could see at once why the chamber had felt so small. The whole of what must once have been a large store-room was packed almost solid. All he could see at first was more rubble: piles of stones lying wherever they had slid in the building's collapse. But behind and beside the jumbled stones, under a solid angle of masonry, there was a more regular space. And in it he saw other regular shapes: piles of boxes. Torquatus was just moving cautiously towards them across the broken stones when a shout came from outside and Pulex's head blocked out what little light came through the doorway.

'Master! Soldiers!'

'Yes. I ordered soldiers,' Torquatus reminded him calmly.

'But these aren't the right ones, lord.'

Gods! These must be Antonius' men. Torquatus came out of that stinking place in a scrambling hurry that left him breathless and bruised, just in time to see the men wheeling neatly onto the dusty forecourt of the old shrine. Pulex was correct: they bore Antonius' Hercules on their breastplates. They looked as if they meant business.

Torquatus swallowed hard and turned to the centurion with a casual nod. He was a big man with a face like a brick. "Good morning. I'm afraid you're too late.'

'Too late?' He stared at Torquatus suspiciously.

'Yes. I presume you've come from Antonius, and are searching for the money, stolen from my farm during the night six days before the Ides. I thought so. I am Aulus Manlius Torquatus, by the way. Treasury Quaestor.' Torquatus spoke pleasantly enough, but the centurion understood him well enough. Still, he wasn't giving up without a fight.

'I was sent to find that money, stolen from Antonius last year. And I'm not going till I've searched this place.'

'Search all you like.' Torquatus' voice was calm and pleasant. 'You won't find anything. The money – my money, stolen from my property, I remind you – has been sent into Rome for safe keeping.'

Torquatus was mentally offering up prayers to any

247

god who would listen that Octavian's soldiers, and the mule-carriages they were bringing with them, would stay away till he'd got rid of this fellow. Another idea struck him. 'The money's now on its way to the Treasury. I'm surprised you didn't see the slaves taking it away.'

'It is, is it?' The centurion was eyeing him suspiciously. Torquatus hoped desperately that he wouldn't ask why his own money, as he'd just claimed it was, should be sent to the Treasury.

'That's right.' His expression was, he hoped, convincingly bland and confident. For a few agonising moments the centurion stared at him, then he swung round, jerking his head at his men. He led them off. Torquatus watched anxiously as they went, just he'd hoped they would, down the Via Labicana. Then after no more than fifty yards they swung off, to the right again, on to the Via Caelimontana. Torquatus could feel the sweat running down his body.

'Won't they meet Octavian's soldiers coming up?' one of the slaves asked anxiously.

'No. You saw them take the right fork, which is the quickest way to the Treasury. Octavian's men will be coming up the left-hand road. Or they should.'

The story had been pretty thin, but Torquatus didn't really think that Antonius' soldiers would get into a fight with Octavian's, especially if they were clearly empty-handed. What they wanted was the money, supposedly dispatched under no more than a guard of slaves. All he needed to do now was to get the money out and away before they found they'd been misled.

And here, at last, were the mule-carriages with their mounted guards, and the troop of marching soldiers, small in the distance, but growing larger and clearer by the minute. Torquatus ordered his own men to clear the doorway and then begin emptying the store-room. For no consideration on earth was he going back in there himself. It took some time to get the boxes out. Torquatus could only imagine

248

how it had been for the men who'd brought them there, struggling to hide them away in the growing dawn, angry, confused, frustrated at the partial failure of their plan. Even in the broad daylight, the boxes caught on the doorframe and weighed far too much to be easily manhandled. You could tell which ones held coin, since it shifted and unbalanced the load as the men tilted the boxes to manoeuvre them through the narrow opening. The ones holding silver bars were a lot easier. And then Octavian's men were there, marching onto the precinct, as Antonius' had before, and their centurions set them to join the slaves in getting out one box after another and stacking them neatly in the carriages while the mules stood quietly, shaking their heads and whisking their tails at imaginary flies. Torquatus found himself shaking with exhaustion and relief. The boxes were all unbroken, their hasps intact. All except two. One, as the younger of the two centurions pointed out, was split and cracked along one edge, but had not been opened. The other had been stove in at one corner, a task which must have taken a considerable time and an immense amount of sweat. These were official money-chests, carefully designed to be secure in a world full of the light-fingered. But this was a place where large chunks of rock abounded, and – Torquatus glanced over at the disconsolate little group still huddling under the trees – people with an infinite amount of time on their hands. He summoned them over.

'These boxes,' he said. 'All complete except these two. What do you know about that?'

They glanced at each other and shifted uneasily. Those with wineskins made a move to slide them behind their backs. The man with the bushy beard said angrily, 'You've got more there than a man can carry away. Much more. Yes, and a horse to ride on, and slaves and soldiers to command. We never took no gold, only a bit of silver to buy wine with. Can you not leave us to enjoy a little Saturnalia of our own, man?'

The others muttered their approval. One of the

women let out a hoarse laugh, then shouted, 'We've drunk it all anyway. If you want it back, it's in our bellies, so come and get it.'

There was a shout of laughter.

Torquatus felt they had a point. These people could have squirreled away considerable sums, but they hadn't: all they'd taken was enough for a little bad wine. He relaxed, and smiled at them. His nightmare was over and he could afford to be generous.

'I'm sorry I've spoiled your party,' he said, and summoned Becco to bring his purse, which he emptied into the bushy man's hand, taking Bucephalus' reins in exchange. But before he left them to their Saturnalia, he still had one question to ask.

'Why did you stop trying to open the other box?'

The bushy man stared at him. 'Gold's no use to us, lord,' he said carefully, as if instructing a child.

'Gold?' Torquatus' world swung round him again, and his mouth was dry.

The man waved his wineskin towards the other box with a grave and gracious gesture, inviting Torquatus to inspect it. It had only been cracked at one side, but the split was wide enough to see through, and the centurion silently pointed to the glint coming from the contents. Torquatus dropped the horse's rein and knelt down, willing himself to see something else, but it was still unchanged: the warm gleam of gold.

'They'll be the new coins, the ones Caesar introduced,' the centurion said thoughtfully, and for a moment his voice seemed to float down from very far away. Torquatus heard the man answer him: 'Ah, that'll be for the soldiers. They get paid in gold, they do.'

The centurion laughed. 'They wish.'

Torquatus' head was spinning. How many others of these boxes held gold? Why had Octavian never told him that the cash wasn't all silver? What was this hoard really worth? He stood up again, brushing the dust from his hands, and turned back to his horse, standing patiently. He mounted, and forced himself to smile, falling in behind the soldiers as they marched off.

Torquatus thanked all the gods that the ride back into the city gave him time to think. He decided that the wisest thing to do would be to ask no questions as yet, so he saw the money safely carried into Octavian's house, and told the centurions not to dismiss their men. He sent in a message to request an interview with Octavian next day, intending before he made his report to search Annalis' house, in the hope of finding real evidence of the conspiracy which he'd doubted for so long. The house was just down the road from his own home: with luck he could conduct his search before Antonius' men arrived, and then perhaps he would be able to give Octavian a full account of what had happened.

Annalis' house was a fine place, but already it had that sad look houses get once they've been abandoned. This one hadn't been though; not quite. Postumia, widow of the older Annalis and mother of his murderer, still lived here. One of the soldiers knocked on the door, a great booming sound that echoed in the quiet street. Not a head appeared anywhere, to see what was going on. That was Rome, now: if you heard a noise in the road, you pretended you hadn't. At last, after a second bout of knocking, the door creaked open, and an old slave's head poked out, like a turtle's out of its shell. He seemed surprised that Torquatus wanted to come in, but (seeing the soldiers) made no objection.

Postumia looked even smaller and older than she had on Torquatus' last visit. She must have a been a pretty woman once, but now looked as if she neither ate nor slept very much. 'Of course your men must search if they need to,' she told him. 'But please ask them to be respectful.' A glimmer of a smile touched her mouth. 'The place has suffered enough, one way and another. So please leave me some furniture fit to use. And don't hurt the slaves.'

Torquatus told the men to be careful. They knew

what they were looking for, and it wasn't going to be hidden in Postumia's jewel-box. Then he went back and sat with her while they got on with it.

'I'm glad to have the chance to thank you for explaining what a difficult situation you were in,' she told him. 'People just seem to drop each other these days when there's trouble. It's because everyone's so frightened, of course, but Manlia was wonderful after Annalis died. I miss her.' She looked vaguely around the room.

'I'm glad she's been able to help you. I'm sure she'll continue to do so.'

'But I thought she wouldn't - ,' Postumia began, in some confusion.

'That's over now.' He smiled reassuringly. 'The money that was stolen has been recovered and returned to Octavian.'

Torquatus had hoped he might have got some kind of reaction to this news, but Postumia just smiled back and said she was so glad to hear it. She could be a brilliant actress of course, but he thought she wasn't: sweet and pretty, but not very intelligent or at all interested in public life, he guessed. Well-satisfied with her rather mediocre husband and son, she looked like someone who, having everything she wanted, would have little practice in lying.

'Your husband and Septimius were friends?'

'Yes, that's right. Only latterly, though: I don't remember hearing his name much until about, oh a year ago, maybe a little more.' She gave him an embarrassed look. 'I didn't care for Septimius myself. I used to go out of the room when he came. There was something rather crude and unpleasant about him to my way of thinking. A domineering sort of man.'

'Do you think he led your husband astray?'

'I didn't say that.' She picked up some little piece of sewing and fiddled with it. 'I didn't know what was going on.' She said that softly, but with a kind of despair that was chilling.

'You think it was something bad, though?'

'I did think so. And now I know it.' She stopped and the sewing fell from her fingers. 'I don't – I can't – ,'

'If you're worried about your son – ,'

'Who murdered his own father!' she burst out in a harsh, bitter voice. 'And yet – how can I say anything that might lead to his death? Wouldn't I be as bad as him?'

'I'm not interested in anything your son's done. In fact, I don't believe he knew anything about this conspiracy – if that's what it was. He told me himself his father didn't trust him. But I do need to know what Septimius and your husband were planning.'

She sat silent, pleating and pleating the fabric of her dress.

'I'll tell you what I know,' he prompted, when she still didn't speak. 'I know that Annalis, Rebilus and Septimius planned and Annalis at least carried out the attack on my farm.'

She cried out, and covered her mouth with her hand. 'I wasn't sure. I feared it but I hoped I might be wrong. I'm so sorry.'

'It's a fact, I'm afraid. He was there, left his boot-prints on the ground.'

'But why should he do that?' She sounded genuinely puzzled.

'He didn't seem to you to be short of money?'

'Well, he sometimes used to complain he hadn't enough, but only the way we all do, you know. We were very comfortable.' She gestured vaguely with one hand around the opulent room, now gathering shadows in its corners. 'Besides, he had art works he could have sold – he loved Greek statuary, had some wonderful pieces.'

Torquatus thought he might as well run Manlia's theory past her. 'Did he ever mention Sextus Pompey to you?'

He quite expected her to shake her head – "oh, I know nothing about politics, I'm afraid!" – but she said at once, 'Well, of course he did. He hated all those Three, said there was nothing to choose between them, that they'd killed the Republic, or what was left of it after Caesar. He said to me that a Rome that had no room for a man of Sextus Pompey's calibre and breeding was a Rome he didn't want to live in.'

All the while there'd been the noise of the soldiers in the background, their boots ringing on the floors, their hard voices. But now, suddenly, a shout went up. Torquatus got up and looked through into the colonnaded garden. He could see a soldier gesturing to the others to come, and others running across the garden and pounding down the colonnades. Torquatus excused himself and went to join them. The group of men had gathered in a handsome exedra, a semi-circular bay let into the garden-wall at its corner. From it there was a wonderful view across the Campus Martius. His eye was drawn out along the long line of the Via Flaminia. It was the sort of spot that spoke of an owner who liked to sit in the sun with philosophically minded friends, and discuss the meaning of life, while enjoying the fine prospect. It wasn't the view the soldiers were interested in, however: they were leaning over the low wall, calling down to one of their number who had discovered in the supporting wall below them a door, solid and well-maintained. The old slave who had let them in was hobbling towards this man, escorted by a couple of other soldiers, a large key in his hand. The men all dashed out of the exedra, and Torquatus followed them more leisurely. You'd never have guessed the house had all this extra land below the formal gardens he'd seen from inside the house. It was approached down some stone steps, and had been planted with fruit trees of all kinds.

As Torquatus approached the store-room – an apple-store from the smell of it, with a good number of garden-tools hung up neatly on one wall – the men started to come out with what they'd found. Bundles of spears, their tips bright and new. Boxes of short swords. Helmets. More spears. Shields. Still more spears and swords. The store-room must have gone much further back into the hill than one would have supposed from the small outer door. The men stood back respectfully for Torquatus to go in, ducking his head. The whole space, including a half-storey of solid wooden planking above, had been filled to capacity with weapons. Torquatus thought there would have been enough space in the storeroom for the money, too, had Annalis not been killed when he was. So perhaps the initial plan had not been to ambush the carriages outside the city: had those carriages been bound for his house as the plotters supposed, they'd have had to pass this one. What could have been easier than to overpower the drivers in the darkness and divert the carriages? Torquatus heard a gasp behind him and turned to see that Postumia had followed him down.

'You didn't know about this, then?'

'Not a thing.' He believed her: her white face was evidence enough.

'There must be an entrance on this level?'

'Yes. The house is on a steep slope, which is why we could make this orchard down here. There's an entrance onto the lane behind the house.'

'Not onto the road?'

'Oh no, it's just a quiet lane.'

It was, very quiet. And a gate wide enough to take a cart. Very convenient for the gardeners - and for anyone who had anything to hide. So Manlia had been right. The talk of conspiracy wasn't just women's chatter: these men had been planning for an uprising behind the back of Antonius and Octavian. Torquatus wondered what they'd planned to do about Lepidus, who was to be left in charge of Rome. It was on the tip of his tongue to ask Postumia whether his name had come up too; then he thought better of it. If Lepidus was involved it was no affair of his. The less he knew about it the better, in fact. And she would probably have enough sense to keep her mouth shut too. Antonius and Octavian could look after themselves.

'Who had a key to this place?'

'Only my husband.'

'Really? Wouldn't your steward have had to keep one too?'

'Oh no.' She shook her head vigorously. 'Annalis was very angry with our steward, said he'd made some mistake, and took all his keys away. He made the poor man ask for a key every time he needed one.'

'Did he indeed? And when was this?'

'About two months ago, I suppose. I kept thinking he'd forgive poor Urbanus and give the keys back, but he didn't.'

No doubt it suited Annalis not to have the steward poking his nose into that underground store. How it was all falling into place!

'I'm going to leave a guard here,' Torquatus told her, 'and send the rest of the soldiers back to get transport, so we can take all this to safety.'

The men had become very serious. Whatever soldiers are ignorant of, they do know about weapons. Torquatus took Postumia back indoors.

'You needn't worry about this,' he told her. 'Thank you. You've helped me a lot. And I don't think you've made your son's position any more dangerous.' That was true enough. Annalis' son was already in about as difficult a situation as a man might be. 'I can't promise to save him, but I won't do anything to harm him.'

'No. I can see you can't help him. Do I even want you to, after what he's done? I don't know. He's all I've got, you see.' And she choked back some sound which might have been a sob or a laugh.

If Torquatus was going to fulfil his promise to Postumia there was one thing still to do. Torquatus left one of the centurions organising the guarding and transport of the weapons, and set off on foot to the Aventine, to young Annalis' place, taking only the younger centurion and Becco with him. As soon as they got there, it was clear that something had happened. The front door stood open. They went in, treading cautiously and looking around as they went. Inside, the smell of wine was even more overpowering than it had been yesterday. A handsome bronze lamp-stand lay on the floor, its lamps scattered, and the curtain draped in the dining-room entrance had been pulled down so hard its rod hung drunkenly at an angle to the floor. The bottom of the curtain was heavy with wine soaked up from an overturned amphora. Torquatus shouted for a slave, but no-one came. The place echoed with emptiness.

They went into the main room its long windows into the courtyard now letting in the last glimmers of winter sunlight. On his reading-couch, his back turned to the room, lay young Annalis. Spilled wine had run down and stained the floor, soaking a pair of soft leather slippers, as well as a gaming-board and some dice. But there was far too much of it to have come from a wine-cup. And it was surely thicker and stickier than wine? His spine prickling, Torquatus took a second look and saw that those wine-lees were mixed with blood. Blood had soaked the rumpled tunic which had been pulled up around Annalis' hips, had spurted onto the fine blanket which covered the couch, and was still hanging in congealed drips from the lower edge of its frame. Torquatus walked across, trying to avoid stepping in the sticky mess, and signed to Becco to turn him over. Both men gasped: there was very little left of Annalis' face. Smashed to a pulp, with fragments of bone jutting through the mess, one eye stared madly out. His throat had also been cut. Becco dropped him back onto the couch and stepped gingerly away.

In the slaves' quarters, there was every sign of a hasty departure. Food was scattered about, but the bread-bins were empty, and a covered cheese-dish contained nothing but a few rinds. The slaves, it seemed safe to say, had murdered their master and made a run for it.

'Will you set up a search for them?' the centurion asked.

Torquatus hardly needed to consider. 'I think not. The man had killed his own father. I believe he was the last of his family. His mother will need to be told: I'll help her clear up this mess. Let the slaves go.'

Becco nodded, but the centurion threw him a rather contemptuous look. He said nothing, and Torquatus dismissed him, since there was nothing now for him to do. He himself wandered round for a little while, wondering at this strangest development. How would Postumia take the news? He would ask Manlia to take on the task of telling her. He wondered if she had slaves enough to clear up here, prepare her son for his funeral pyre. The thought of that ageing woman left alone with only a few old slaves in that rich, lifeless house disturbed him: perhaps Manlia could persuade her to live with them for a while, till the big house was sold. What a unpredictable city this had become: a place where the bizarre and the terrifying were everyday occurrences, and yet the markets would open after Saturnalia had finally run its course, meals would be cooked, letters would be written, people would take baths, make assignations, drink together, sleep.

Torquatus knew he was wasting time. He was putting off the one thing he still had to do before he left. There were aspects of Annalis' life here that he didn't want Postumia to hear about, and at last he made himself go back into the wrecked room, and look again at Annalis' wine-soaked, blood-soaked body. There was a disagreeable picture in his mind of the drunken young man enjoying the climax of his Saturnalia by making his slaves give him sex. He and Becco struggled to complete the task: the corpse wanted to fall off the couch, and for some reason Torquatus thought it shouldn't. They were sweating and bloody by the time they'd finished, but Annalis' tunic was now arranged around his legs in the proper way. His mother didn't need to know he'd made the slaves suck him off: in Torquatus' view a considerable mitigation of their fault in running away. Many of his friends, most perhaps, would have disagreed: a

258

slave must do as his master bids, whatever that may be. Logically Torquatus couldn't fault it. But his heart wouldn't follow his head in this. As for Becco, he said nothing, but Torquatus hadn't needed to explain what needed to be done; and that perhaps told its own tale.

He secured the place, as best he could, and the three men made their way home. Torquatus was dog-tired, ravenous, but absolutely triumphant. He knew the whole story now: there could be no more ghastly surprises. The discovery of the gold came into his mind like a cold, uncanny draught: there were implications in that he didn't want to consider as yet. But his future was secure.

Chapter 18

The house was very quiet. Trofimus looked smaller than usual. Taking a second glance at him, Torquatus could have sworn he'd been crying. He didn't seem the sort of man to weep easily. In fact every one of the slaves looked pale and downcast. Manlia, too, looked older, and not at all like a young woman about to go out to dine at the house of one of Rome's most powerful men. It seemed they'd all just been waiting for Torquatus' return. His mood of elation leaked away. Manlia stepped forward.

'Aulus, I'm very sorry. Iucundus is dead.'

They offered to show him the body. His gorge rose slightly at the thought, but he knew he must. The boy had been Torquatus' property, and his responsibility. The thought flashed into his mind that perhaps he was not as different from the despised Annalis as he'd wanted to think. They'd laid him out, they said, crowding round in their eagerness to explain, in the little room that had once been Stephanus'. Torquatus walked to it with leaden legs, surrounded by a silent group: far too many of them crowded into the close, stuffy space. Torquatus was vaguely aware that in the background to his thoughts people were telling him what had happened. The boy's eyes had been closed, and he looked, as he had when Torquatus first saw him, like a young prince, graceful, proud, sure of himself. The uncertain lamplight flickered on his face, and for a moment Torquatus thought he saw him smile. As one would expect, the torturers hadn't touched it, so as not to reduce his value too much. Gently, he pulled the blanket back from the body. There were burn-marks on his arms, his buttocks, his genitals. The boy had been dishonest, a liar, a traitor, a thief, perhaps a forger too. He deserved to die. And yet, looking at that young body, its vulnerabilities and immaturities exposed, Torquatus' heart was opened and he wept.

The torturers were still there, waiting to explain themselves. Trofimus had refused to pay them until

Torquatus came in, and they were huddled, hostile and resentful, on a bench in the business room.

'How could we have guessed?' their leader asked. 'We'd only just started when he fainted. Well, they often do. We didn't think anything of it, but anyway we laid off. No point in going on when they can't feel it. So we waited. And after a bit, when he didn't come round, we took a look at him, and then we realised he'd gone. Must have had a weak heart or something; you get that sometimes. Not our fault anyway. We were doing just what you said, nice and gentle, see.'

Torquatus despised himself for asking; but asked anyway. 'Did he say anything?'

'Literally not a word, lord. He just looked at us as if we were muck, wouldn't even say his own name when we asked him to confirm it. Nothing.'

Torquatus was disappointed, and also unaccountably proud: something in him was glad not to have to think of Iucundus cringing, whining, begging for mercy. So you still want to believe in a noble savage, do you? he asked himself contemptuously. He pulled himself together, paid the men and sent them off, together with their box of chains and tools, which they carried between them, trusting their little slave-boy with a coil of rope almost as big as himself.

Whatever secrets Iucundus had, he'd taken them into death with him. Torquatus thought uneasily that perhaps he'd never know the truth about what had gone so terribly wrong in his household. He bathed and dressed in no very jovial mood, telling himself that he should be triumphant. He had achieved the task he'd been set. He'd saved his life, guaranteed his future. But all he could feel was grief and guilt. And anger: anger against himself for doing something unworthy. He called himself a fool, demanded to know what else he could have done with an untrustworthy slave? Even Felix, who helped to dress him, was silent and sullen-faced, not a bit like his usual irrepressible self. Torquatus remembered that he had been close friends with Iucundus.

'This has been hard on you,' he said, kindly, he thought.

Felix scowled at him. 'Iucundus was my friend. He was good. He never did anything wrong.' His eyes filled with tears, and he turned away, pretending to look for his master's dinner-napkin, which had been laid out ready on the toga-chest.

Torquatus hesitated. He would have liked to be angry with the boy. Instead, annoyingly, he heard a note of self-justification in his voice. 'No, Felix. He told me lies. He attacked me. No slave can do that and hope to live.'

'He didn't. ' The boy's eyes were burning in his flushed face. 'He didn't. I was trying to tell you this morning, so you wouldn't torture him, but you wouldn't listen.'

Torquatus remembered how the boy had come running into the reception hall, how Trofimus had pushed him out. 'I couldn't have listened to you then. And anyway, what could you have said that would have saved him?'

'I'll tell you. But it's too late now.'

'What can you possibly tell me that would have made a difference?' Torquatus was humouring Felix, and he sensed it, stiffening and giving his master a hard look, unlike his usual boyish grin.

'If you've got something to tell me you can do it tomorrow: I don't have time now.'

Torquatus worried about what Felix had said for a few minutes. He knew he was right, though, and he put his pain and grief aside, to remember that he was a successful man with powerful friends. And as the evening wore on he did begin to enjoy it. Balbus was a superb host, and he'd seldom been at a party where the conversation had been so pleasing, the food and wine so delicious, the company so well-chosen. It was a much larger dinner than his own had been. If the purpose of his had been to say that the Manlius Torquatus family was back, then Balbus might well have been pointing out that he had never been away from the centre of power. The number of guests required three dining-rooms: Torquatus and Manlia were in the best one, where Balbus dined himself. Torquatus supposed he was talking and smiling like the rest: it all felt like a rather pleasant dream.

The guest of honour was Octavian himself. There he lay, a neat little man, not eating much, listening more than he talked. He smiled when he saw Torquatus. 'Thank you for the delivery this afternoon,' he said. 'A fine Saturnalia gift.'

As lightly, Torquatus replied, 'I thought it would be what you'd like. I'm only sorry it's a little late.'

'Oh, I never mind waiting for what I want.'

Balbus said something to him just then, and he turned back to his host.

Octavian left quite early. People were getting up and moving about before the serious drinking began, as they do, and Torquatus was able (on the grounds that he needed the privy) to catch him as he left. His slaves were wrapping him in the thickest possible cloak, tucking it high under his chin as if he were a little boy. Torquatus wondered, fascinated, whether the attentions of his over-protective mother had left him with a liking for being cosseted. He caught Torquatus' eye.

'I shall see you tomorrow,' Octavian nodded. 'Or rather, will you make it the day after? I think that would suit me better. Come and tell me all about it.'

'I shall. I have a good deal of information for you,' Torquatus told him quietly.

'Indeed? I shall be glad to hear it. The threat is at an end?'

'I'm sure of that.'

Octavian smiled that catlike smile of his. 'Until the next time, no doubt.'

Torquatus couldn't think how to answer this, but at that moment Balbus came bustling up to bid the distinguished guest farewell, and Torquatus stepped back, and returned to the hot and smoky dining-room, where the wine was just being served, and dancers were ready to entertain them. Torquatus resigned himself: he didn't greatly care for watching dancers, but he knew they must stay for a while. He lay there, wine-cup in hand wondering how soon Manlia and he could leave without being rude.

Next morning, Felix appeared in Torquatus' bedroom before he'd even got out of bed.

'What is it, Felix?' said Torquatus, sitting up anxiously, fearing that some other unforeseen complication had arisen to blight his life.

'You said I could tell you about Iucundus,' the boy reminded him.

'Well, you could at least have waited till I was dressed,' Torquatus complained. Seeing the boy's anxious face and heavy eyes, he relented, swung his legs out of bed and wrapped a warm cloak around himself, over the tunic he'd slept in. 'Go on, then. Convince me.'

'Well, you know when he saw you being attacked in the Forum?'

'He said he did, yes.'

'He told me all about it, and there wasn't any reason why he should lie to me. He said the man was the one he saw outside Antonius' house, and gave him a message for Demetrius.'

'I know all this, Felix' Torquatus' voice was as gentle as he could make it. 'Iucundus told me the same thing.'

'But it was true!' Felix was gazing at him in despair. 'Because the message was to say that he - the man Iucundus saw - was coming to visit Demetrius that evening, and he did.'

'Demetrius denied it, and the doorman backed him up. There were no visitors that evening.'

'I know. But I'll tell you what I saw. Demetrius said

he'd gone out to borrow a book you wanted. But I saw him go, and he didn't look like someone who was just going on an errand. He came into the reception hall, looking around to see if there was anyone watching.'

'Why didn't he see you, then?'

'Because I was upstairs, on the gallery, and I saw him through the grille. He didn't see me because I was wearing quite a dark tunic that day, my blue one, and there isn't much light up there in the evening.'

'Why were you there, Felix?'

The boy sat down on the end of the bed. He looked as if he was carrying an almost unbearable burden of sadness, and Torquatus turned his eyes away. At last Felix looked up and said: 'I like being on my own sometimes. And I was unhappy - about Iucundus, you know. I was thinking whether I could take him some food: he had been shut in the grain-store.' He met Torquatus' eyes directly. 'And I did. You perhaps think I shouldn't have?'

Torquatus said slowly, 'Well we needn't talk about that now. I think I like your being so thoughtful towards your friend. Go on. You were on the gallery, thinking.'

'Yes, and Demetrius came into the hall below, and seemed really furtive, like I said, glancing around. He didn't see me, I could tell. Then he went out, and I heard him say that he was going to get your book. I came down and followed him out, and he was talking to someone.'

'I know about that. Did you hear anything, see any more?'

Felix looked annoyed. 'No. The doorkeeper called out to me from inside, that I was to come back in again: Trofimus wanted me.'

'Well, that doesn't really tell me anything, Felix. I already knew Demetrius had spoken to that man. There wasn't anything furtive about it. And what about those tablets of mine? No-one but Iucundus could have written anything in them - supposing there ever was anything written at all, which I sometimes doubt.'

265

'But why should he?' Felix asked. 'I mean, he hadn't even been in the house for more than a week or so.'

'It only takes a few moments to suborn a slave,' Torquatus pointed out. 'A new slave, with no allegiance to me; probably with a great deal of hatred in his heart in fact. He might think he would have nothing left to lose. No, Felix. Don't say any more. The evidence against Iucundus is just too strong: I only wish we could have known the whole of it, so that you could see it straight. You'll forget him, in time.'

The boy jumped up, his eyes bright with tears. 'No! I'll never do that. It was just wrong, killing him, and I shan't forgive it. And anyway, you haven't heard all of it. I haven't finished telling about the tablets. They did say what Iucundus said: I saw them and there was writing on them, your writing. And I put them back in your business room, but then someone must have taken them again, and cleaned them, and put them in Iucundus' blanket.'

'What do you mean, you saw them?'

'On the morning when Philip was found dead: I ran over to the stables before you could get there. Iucundus had told me about the tablets: he was worried that Philip would get into trouble. Iucundus was being watched so carefully, I hadn't been able to get into the stables, but I knew while they were telling you what had happened might be my only opportunity, so I went in, and I found them, and I put them back in the business room later, after your clients had gone. And they did say what Iucundus said they did. I read them, and I know.'

Torquatus stared at him. 'You're telling me that someone else cleaned the message off? And then moved the tablets again?' He shook his head. 'I can't believe all that, Felix.'

'Well it's the truth! And it's true that Iucundus saw the man who attacked you in the Forum. And now Iucundus is dead.' And with that Felix turned and ran out of the room, almost colliding with Victor in the doorway.

Torquatus pondered over what Felix had said about the tablets. He couldn't make any sense of it, and came to the conclusion that the boy had had misconstrued some scratches in the wax into words, or had seen what he wanted to see, or was perhaps even telling a lie in an attempt to vindicate his friend. He was depressed at the thought of any of these. He really couldn't get rid of Felix, but how was he to live with the boy?

Nothing else of any great importance happened that day. Manlia went to see Postumia, to try to persuade her to come and live with them for a while, but she preferred to stay where she was. Manlia was silent and downcast: the news from Postumia was that their friend Aemilia had finally succumbed to her self-induced starvation. Another funeral in prospect.

Even the weather seemed to be conspiring against them. Colder still, the clouds were heavy with rain that refused to fall. Persistent cold draughts slunk through the house, penetrating even to the warmth of the study. He pretended to read, but it was impossible. Manlia, when he went to look for her, was in her bedroom, talking to Felix: or rather, Felix was weeping wildly, while Manlia held him, murmuring softly to him and patting his hair.

Torquatus gave up and went to bed early.

Chapter 19

At last the day had come when Torquatus could vindicate himself. He'd be basking in glory, for a while at any rate, and then his life could return to normal. He lay in his bed, warm and comfortable, listening to the slaves beginning their day's work. Feet moved quietly along the gallery outside his room, careful not to disturb his rest. Voices were lowered. Soon he would get up, but there was no hurry.

His mood of self-congratulation ebbed away. Trofimus had told him of resentment and anger among the slaves, and two of them had been murdered. He had to assume that they'd been killed by their fellow-slaves; so he had a murderer in his house. He didn't relish spending the rest of his life looking over his shoulder, fearing the silent dagger or noose or poisoned cup: a life full of such distrust wouldn't be worth living. He was the master, and if he wanted to he could sell the lot of them and start afresh. Perhaps that would be the best thing to do? In the old days, he'd have called a council of all the older men in the family. The women would have known about this, of course, and would have advised their men beforehand. That was the proper Roman way of doing things. Now he and Manlia were all that was left of the family, and they'd have to rely on their own good sense.

Selling the slaves, he recognised, wouldn't help him overcome that lingering sense of shame and dishonour – however inappropriate such sentiments might be – that had filled his mind since Iucundus' death. He pushed away the thought that had kept trying to intrude yesterday: that perhaps he'd been wrong about Iucundus. He didn't see how Iucundus could have been the forger - if there was such a person. But as to the attack in the Forum, he was sure of Iucundus' guilt there. Surely he couldn't have two criminals among the slaves?

This was no use: impatiently he flung off the

blankets and swung his feet out of bed, calling for the slaves, and his toga. Holiday or no holiday, he would be making, in effect, an official report, and he'd better dress appropriately. The day was unusually cold and grey; it felt as if snow might fall. Lepidus' triumph would take place tomorrow: weather like this would keep the crowds small. He wondered whether that was why Antonius and Octavian had planned it for now, or whether it was simply impossible to hold it later, since the Three would all be busy elsewhere as soon as the weather improved. How easy it was to look for the sly and the cunning in everything these days!

On an impulse, he sent for Felix again. The boy came, heavy-eyed and sullen. 'I was so surprised by what you told me yesterday,' Torquatus began, 'that I didn't ask you whether you saw enough of the man Demetrius was speaking to describe him to me.'

'Of course I did. He was a little man, with a big nose, and a big cloak.' Torquatus gasped, and Felix stopped, looking up at him suspiciously.

For a moment Torquatus couldn't speak. Why, why hadn't he asked that question before? Nothing was as it seemed. What was it Demetrius had said? That Philo - as it must have been - had come to tell him that a man he'd known in Neapolis was dead. A man who'd done Demetrius a favour.

'Thank you, Felix. Thank you very much,' Torquatus said, and walked out, his head in a whirl. He had been going to take Demetrius with him, but he certainly wouldn't do that now.

His litter-bearers were waiting outside the front doors, looking chilled to the bone. A quick run to the Palatine would warm them up. All the way over to Octavian's house, he turned over and over the hideous new suspicion: was it Demetrius, not Iucundus, who'd been corrupted by Antonius' people? Well, he couldn't think about that now. As he descended from the litter Torquatus felt the first prickle of ice on his lips: snow. He hurried into the warm house. Frugal in so many things, in that provincial way of his, Octavian clearly never minded what was spent on fuel. The boys crowded in behind him, and he heard them clattering off to the slaves' quarters for refreshment as he himself was shown into the study, where two soldiers stood on guard outside the double doors. Last time he'd come, a single slave had sufficed: was Octavian under some new threat?

As the door closed quietly behind him, the noise of the household dropped to a murmur. The master himself was seated at that immense marble table, immersed in documents, rolls arranged neatly before him in separate groups. Before he looked up, Torquatus had time to think that of all the situations he'd seen him in since they'd been boys together, this was surely the most characteristic: the little frown of concentration, the fair head resting on one hand, pen poised in the other, ready to pounce on inaccuracy or inconsistency. Octavian raised his head, put the pen into its holder, and smiled. 'Torquatus, I'm sorry. I didn't hear you come in. Come and sit down. You look cold.'

'It's just beginning to snow,' Torquatus told him, glad for once of his friend's devotion to braziers. 'I hope it isn't going to spoil Lepidus' triumph.'

Octavian smiled rather sourly. 'His choice to have it now. Both Antonius and I asked what the hurry was. He could always have waited until we could have triumphed together: Caesar didn't triumph until he could hold a single big one to show how he'd defeated all his enemies, after all.' His eyes narrowed in amusement. 'Could it be that he thought his celebration of successful negotiations with Sextus Pompeius might be overshadowed by the real military triumph Antonius and I will be able to hold?'

Torquatus hardly knew how to answer this. Octavian and Antonius, if they succeeded, would be celebrating the deaths of Brutus and Cassius, although Romans were not expected to rejoice in the defeat of other Romans: even Caesar, always a law unto himself, had tried -

though not very hard - to dress up his defeat of Cato and the republican rump as the conquest of Africans. Luckily Octavian didn't seem to need an answer. Pushing back his chair he stretched his arms over his head and sighed with satisfaction. 'Still, that's not what you're here to discuss. The money is all safe here in my house – all but twenty sesterces – for which I thank you, and congratulate you too.' Octavian paused there, almost as if he were expecting Torquatus to pull out a purse and hand over the missing twenty.

'Thank you. I have also sent to your soldiers' barracks a large supply of weapons, all new. No doubt they've reported this already.'

He nodded. 'They have. It seems certain senators were planning an uprising of some kind?'

'Yes. The old Sextus Pompey scenario. The fools seem to have imagined that when Brutus and Cassius had defeated you they and Sextus would all work together in the good old republican way.'

Octavian couldn't repress a smile.

'They found out about the movement of the money from some loose talk in Balbus' place,' Torquatus continued, keen to remind Octavian that the leak had been no fault of his. Octavian nodded.

'How did you come to suspect these men?'

'My sister told me that some of her friends, the wives of these senators, feared that something was afoot. She got them to talk to her. Not that they knew very much, but she picked up some evidence.' He was glad to be able to point to Manlia as his informant.

Octavian's eyes were hard now. 'I want names, Torquatus. Not just of those you know were involved, but of others who might have been on the fringes of this plot.'

'Of course. Annalis and Septimius were the planners, and they were both proscribed. In fact, it was Septimius' death that led to the partial failure of the raid on my farm. They took the money, killed the slaves, left my farm in ruins, as they'd planned. But then things went wrong: there was far more money than they'd anticipated, because the cellar wasn't empty when the last consignment arrived. Loading it all slowed them down, and when Septimius failed to appear, the operation became delayed even further, with the result that they couldn't bring the money into the city without falling foul of the curfew on wheeled traffic. So they hid it.'

'Hid it? Wherever could they find that would be secure enough to hide chests like that?' Octavian was staring at him, fascinated.

'In the ruins of the old shrine of Hope, out beyond the Esquiline gate, and only a short distance from my farm. I've vowed to rebuild it, as soon as peace returns.'

'Gods! I know the place. Just stashed among the old stones, eh? Well, well. Extraordinary that no-one found it there.' He got up and walked over to the window, shuttered now against the cold. 'I'm glad you are going to rebuild the shrine. It troubles me that so many of Rome's holy places are in such a derelict state. Even Jupiter Best and Greatest. How can a city that doesn't honour its gods expect their protection?' He had sounded almost as if he were speaking to himself, but now he turned back to Torquatus. 'Never mind that now. Those aren't the only names, are they? I suspect Rebilus was in this too.'

Torquatus nodded, though he'd have liked to be able to deny it, for Iunia's sake. 'He's fled, or so I've been told.'

'And when you found the money, some was missing?'

'Just the twenty sesterces. Some beggars, derelicts, had found the chests and broken into two of them. It's extraordinary that they took so little, isn't it? It shows just how poor those people are. If they'd hidden enough money for a lifetime without want, who could have blamed them? But instead they just took enough for – well, twenty sesterces would buy about eighty pints of wine. That would give them one triumph of a party.'

'Can one really buy eighty pints of wine for twenty sesterces?'

'One can. If one isn't too fussy.'

'I'd no idea.' Octavian shuddered, and Torquatus smiled to himself. How would he have known, brought up as he had been in one of the wealthiest houses in Rome? Probably even Philippus' slaves drank better wine than that. But had Octavian never noticed how the ordinary soldiers enjoyed themselves?

'And the other chest that was opened,' Torquatus went on, after a steadying breath, 'contained gold. Gold coin.'

'That's right,' Octavian said easily. 'But none of the gold was missing, I believe?'

'No. They hadn't finished opening that box. What use would gold be to them?' Torquatus paused, wondering if Octavian was going to say anything about the value of what had been stored at the farm. He had been unable to help speculating as to the proportions of gold to silver, or asking himself what the full value of the haul had been. Octavian said nothing, and Torquatus let the question go. He didn't really need to know. He went on: 'I was interested to see that Antonius suddenly began to take an interest in this money.'

'Did he, indeed?' Octavian sat down again, carefully aligning a pile of documents.

'Oh yes. In the last few days it's been a race between us. I saw his men marching down to search the temple of Hope, just as I had done myself. He must have had the same clue as I did, through Septimius' freedman Celer, and drawn the same conclusions from it.'

'And what clue was that?'

'Oh, Annalis had written a note to his son, demanding his help, when things began to go wrong. It was an awful scrawl on a scrap of lead, but there was something in it about Hope. I realised it might refer to the temple, and so, obviously, did Antonius. Like him, I got the wrong one at first. Luckily, I realised my mistake just in time.'

'Antonius' men came up to Old Hope as well, then?'

'They did. I bluffed, and told them I'd already sent the money, under escort, to the Treasury. They marched off at top speed.'

'Neat. So from what you've told me, young Annalis must have been involved?'

'He was, though not fully. His father didn't trust him enough to give him the details.'

'We'll question him, though. And there must have been others. Who were they?'

One thing one could never say about Octavian was that he wasn't thorough, Torquatus reflected. 'Young Annalis is dead.'

'Dead? How's that? He wasn't proscribed.'

'I think his slaves killed him: I found his body when I went to question him.'

'And the widow: can you be sure she wasn't involved?'

There was something avid in Octavian's determination to discover every detail that suddenly sickened Torquatus. 'I'm very sure she wasn't,' he said, almost too emphatically, he thought. 'She was worried sick herself; told me that she feared Septimius had led Annalis into something he couldn't handle. She was right, I think.'

Octavian gave him a quizzical glance. Torquatus could sense him thinking that he might be protecting Postumia, his sister's friend. He wondered whether Octavian was even wondering if he had stolen the money himself, and then pretended to find it once he'd realised he couldn't get away with the theft. Then Octavian's mood seemed to change. He sighed and relaxed. 'And Annalis' slaves? They'd run off, no doubt?'

'There was every sign of a hasty departure, yes. And the place stank of booze: they'd been gambling and drinking with Annalis.'

Octavian shook his head. 'I'm a gambling man myself, but masters and slaves shouldn't play together. That kind of social mixing is dangerous. As we see.'

'True. Though I think all Sextus Pompey will gain will be a few slaves with bad hangovers and worse consciences.'

The questioning seemed to be over. Torquatus relaxed, and Octavian sat back, thinking.

'May the gods send me only enemies like these! How could they suppose such a plot would work? What can the fools have been thinking of?'

Torquatus hardly liked to answer this, so sat in silence. Octavian shot him a sharp, irritable glance. 'Oh, I can see well enough what you're thinking. But you're wrong, you know. Lepidus has been warned off any dealings with Sextus Pompey. Believe me.'

So Lepidus had already come under suspicion. Interesting.

'Antonius is to visit me soon', Octavian said, getting up from his chair and stretching.

'Antonius?' Somehow, Torquatus didn't think they met very often, for all that they were meant to be working together.

'Yes. We met yesterday, to discuss strategy.' His mouth set, hard and mean. 'We couldn't find agreement, so decided to break off, take a pause for reflection, and meet again today.'

Torquatus wasn't particularly surprised they'd found it hard to agree. Both men were astute and ambitious. It was becoming clearer by the day that they were competing for the same ground. Power, to a greater extent than anyone wished to acknowledge, lay in the hands of the legions, so each of them wanted to be seen as the avenger of the soldiers' hero, Julius Caesar. Antonius had ground to make up, having negotiated quite happily with the murderers, for excellent pragmatic reasons, no doubt. But on the other hand, he had a good history as a general, and a military swagger which the men loved. Octavian, astuter in many ways, had presented himself from the beginning as Caesar's heir and Caesar's avenger. As Antonius quipped, Caesar's name was all he had, but he had used its power to the full, with the result that this untried and frankly uncharismatic young man was still in competition. But in the spring they would face a hard military campaign. Antonius would easily take all the glory. Octavian had almost no military experience and no obvious talent for war, so he would be dependent on Antonius' military skills. No wonder they couldn't agree. 'Then I won't keep you,' he began. But Octavian interrupted him.

'You mustn't go yet. We haven't spoken about your marriage.'

'I'm not getting married, as far as I know.'

'Oh, I think you'll find you are.' Octavian's face was full of sly amusement. 'You'll agree that you ought to: the last of an ancient patrician family, you owe it to Rome.'

Torquatus stared at him. 'Well, it's true that Manlia has promised to look around for me.'

'Oh, we needn't trouble your sister.' Octavian was rubbing his hands together: whatever surprise he had in store for Torquatus was filling him with glee. Torquatus' heart sank. What was he getting into?

Octavian met Torquatus' troubled eyes and laughed outright. 'Don't look so horrified. The idea occurred to me the other evening, at dinner. Such an excellent dinner, it put me into a match-making frame of mind, and I suggested to Balbus that you might marry his daughter. I thought it would be some reward for all you've been through.'

He sat back, obviously awaiting expressions of delight. Torquatus wet his lips. 'I'm - I mean - I don't think I knew Balbus had a daughter.' His head was spinning. The match would be a superb one, of course: the girl would be immensely rich, a huge catch, but he'd never even seen her. An image came into his mind: a female Balbus, short, fat, shrewd, managing. He hardly knew what he thought, but there didn't seem to be any way out, if he even wanted one, and he forced a smile to his lips, saying, 'That's wonderful. And Balbus was happy with your choice?'

For a moment Octavian frowned. 'Well, no, initially he didn't seem keen, but I wrote to him yesterday to urge him to agree. Our old patrician families need renewal. And this morning I had a letter, saying he was willing to do as I asked. I daresay you'll find a message from him yourself, when you get home.'

Torquatus was winded. He pulled himself together, hardly knowing what he felt, and feeling foolish. On the one hand, Octavian had oiled the wheels for him, had helped him to a most advantageous position. On the other, the thought that he would owe Balbus' consent to the actions of his – the word patron was the one that sprang to his mind - appalled him. He felt a momentary desire to spurn the proposed marriage. Impossible, of course. He must have stiffened, because Octavian put out a hand towards him, saying 'I hope – ' but whatever it was he hoped was lost in the sounds coming from outside the door.

Boots ground on the stone floor, commanding voices echoed in the entrance hall. The doors were flung open, and Antonius himself stalked into the room, still wrapped in his warm cloak, a gaggle of his followers behind him. He seemed to take up an exceptional amount of space. He greeted Octavian with a patronising smile, and Torquatus with obvious impatience. Torquatus glanced at Octavian, expecting that he would sign to him to leave, but then, as Antonius crossed the room, and his retinue spread out a little, he noticed Iucundus' little man with the big nose, and decided to stay.

'Antonius Philo,' he said. 'How nice to meet you again.'

Philo smiled back, but his eyes slid anxiously towards Antonius, who was now surrounded by assiduous slaves, taking his cloak, showing him to a seat, and who didn't appear to see him. Suddenly several pieces of

277

information clicked together in Torquatus' head. He turned to Antonius politely. 'Before I leave you, Antonius, I'd like your permission to put one or two questions to your freedman here.'

Antonius looked surprised and none too pleased. 'Of course, if you wish. You realise, however, that Octavian and I have important matters to discuss.'

'My questions won't take long.' He swung round on Philo so suddenly that the man took a step backwards. 'What was it made you attack me in the Forum?' His heart was beating fast: if he was wrong he was going to look quite exceptionally stupid.

Antonius leapt to his feet, a commanding presence. 'What nonsense is this?'

Philo said quietly, 'I didn't. Of course not.'

'I have a witness,' Torquatus told him.

'And who might that be?' The man's tone was cocky; he seemed to have decided that Antonius would support him.

'My slave, Iucundus. He was with me on that day, and saw you hit me and then bend over my body. He described you, very accurately.'

Antonius looked Philo over contemptuously. 'This something else you've been up to? I begin to think I've made a mistake to trust you – even as far as I have. Tell the truth now, or it'll be the worse for you.'

Philo hesitated. Torquatus could see how close to panic the man was and piled on a bit more pressure. 'You heard your patron.'

Philo crumbled visibly, and turned desperately towards Antonius. 'It was to help you, lord,' he began.

Antonius rounded on him. 'To help me? You hit senators over the head and think you are helping me?'

'You said – you said the proscriptions hadn't caught every man who deserved to die. Just after you'd been speaking to Torquatus. You must remember. And you said you thought he might be going to meet with an unpleasant

278

accident.'

Antonius scowled. 'I didn't suggest you go and kill him, did I?'

'No, lord.' Philo was wringing his hands together. 'But I thought Torquatus had all that money in his house.'

Torquatus pounced on this. 'Money? In my house?'

'Well, yes, lord. From what I heard at Balbus' and - and then from what the lord Antonius said, I got the impression — I must have been wrong, of course - and very stupid — I somehow thought you'd stolen the lord Octavian's money, and —'

'I'd stolen it?' Torquatus burst out. 'Why in the name of all the gods should I have done that?' So Antonius too had suspected him of taking the money for himself. He forced himself to be calm. 'Believe me, I'm neither as venal nor as stupid as that.'

'I don't know,' Philo stumbled on, 'but many men, even great men, find themselves short of money.'

'Men worth anything don't make good their cash flow problems through theft and violence.' Torquatus was too furious to mind what he said, but at once realised that he'd described the Three pretty accurately, and hurried on. 'It seems to me you can hardly think at all,' he told Philo. 'You'd better tell the whole story.'

The man glanced towards Antonius, who nodded briefly, his face like thunder. The freedman looked like a deflated bladder. 'Well, you see, lord, when I came back from Neapolis — like I told you the other day — I told one or two other people about the money Balbus was sending to Rome. I wish I'd never mentioned it to anyone now.' His voice was bitter. 'I'd found out something in Neapolis.'

'The day before you went to see Balbus, I suppose. That's why you went early, to sniff around and see if you could make a scandal.'

'Well, lord, if you or - or anyone had been forging documents, Antonius would want to know about it.'

'So who was it you saw in Neapolis?'

For a moment, Torquatus thought Octavian was going to halt the questioning, but he fell silent again.

Philo hurried into speech once more. 'I didn't, lord, that's just it. The man I wanted to see, a goldsmith, was dead, had died last summer, in fact, not long after you and your household had passed through the city on your way to Rome.' He smiled rather smugly. 'I thought Spurius' death might be of interest to my patron.'

Torquatus was still trying to puzzle this out when Octavian stepped forward.

'Why?' he asked, in a voice as dry as a winter leaf. 'What business was it of yours or his?'

That was always one of Octavian's most disagreeable habits: he could make himself almost invisible when he wanted to hear what people thought. He'd done that now, and Philo had obviously forgotten his presence. He started, and blushed again. Octavian went on. 'Torquatus, I'm not sure your questioning is going anywhere. If it is, perhaps you could hurry up.'

In the background, a rumble from Antonius seemed to suggest agreement.

Torquatus could sense how little Octavian wanted any of the last summer's events discussed, though he had no idea why. He hurried to head Philo off. 'So you thought you'd take the money, in Antonius' interests? But you failed, because it wasn't going to my house but my farm.'

'I know nothing about that, lord, truly.' Philo was sweating heavily. 'Celer must have passed the information on, I think. I only heard about it later. But it was Antonius' money, that's what he said, stolen from him by a forger's trick.'

'It was you who wrote that anonymous letter,' Torquatus said. 'And it was you who attacked me in the Forum.'

'I was just trying to put things right,' Philo said miserably. He looked despairingly towards an unresponsive Antonius.

'You felt, perhaps, that you needed to do something to retrieve yourself in your patron's eyes?' Torquatus made his voice sympathetic, and Philo turned to him with obvious relief.

'Yes, lord. I thought that if I could get the money back Antonius would be grateful. I'm very sorry about what I did – it was on the spur of the moment, you understand.'

'Oh, I don't think it was. On the contrary: I think you've hated my family for years.' Philo, white-faced, stared at him, and he went on. 'You see, just a few moments ago I suddenly remembered the name of my brother Lucius' secretary, the man who abandoned him just before the final battle between Caesar and his enemies in Africa, four years ago. That name was Philo.' The freedman's face was drawn, the nose standing out sharply from the white face. 'Something happened, didn't it? Something that turned you against my family. I think I can guess what that was. My brother had half-promised to free you, I suppose?'

'No. He absolutely promised, in front of witnesses, and then he didn't do it.' The man was furious now, and his words came tumbling out. 'He was going to fight his last battle - his last stupid battle - and he told me he wouldn't free me because I'd made a mistake, picked up some papers, apparently, something of Caesar's. I don't even know what.'

Behind him, Torquatus felt Octavian go very still.

'Just because of some stupid papers, he was going to leave me in slavery.'

'So you took his cash-box and ran?'

'I did. Didn't get very far, though. I fell in with some fellows, said they could help me get home - home to Ephesus, I mean, where I come from. We drank together, and then I don't know what happened, whether I drank too much or they'd put something in my drink. Anyway, I woke up in the back of a cart, my arms and legs tied up, on my way to the slave market. They'd taken my money and handed me over for sale. I was taken to Italy, and sold as a farm slave, to work on one of Antonius' estates. Do I look like a farm slave?' He shrugged and sighed. 'I made it my business to tell the farm manager - and keep on telling him, too - that I could do a whole lot more than dig onions. In the end, I was taken to Rome and given work in Antonius' household.'

'I'm sure this is all very fascinating,' Antonius burst in. 'But I came here for a meeting, not to hear my freedman's life history.'

'Of course,' Octavian agreed. He glanced to one of the slaves. 'Get wine, will you?' He smiled at Antonius. 'I'm sure this won't take long.'

Antonius grunted and subsided, helping himself to the wine when it came, and sitting in the biggest of the chairs.

'And you contacted my slave, Demetrius.' Torquatus knew, now, that he'd been wrong about almost everything.

'How did you know about that?' The little man's eyes were starting out of his head. 'I never came into your house.'

'You wouldn't have dared, would you? What if some of my old slaves, Stephanus or Philip, for example, had seen you? They'd recognise you, for sure. What did you want with Demetrius?'

Philo wasn't even looking to Antonius for approval now, but spilling out his story. 'Oh, I hoped he might tell me where the money was, where it was stored, for instance. I assumed it was in your house.'

'Why should he have told you anything? You were blackmailing him in some way, I suppose,' Torquatus guessed.

'Why would I bother? I'd heard he didn't much love you, either.'

'Didn't he?' Torquatus was beginning to wonder whether selling all his slaves and starting again might not be the best thing to do, after all. 'Never mind that. What did you intend to do once you'd killed me?'

'I thought your household would be all over the

place, and that if I struck in quickly with a demand for the return of the money, in my master's name, there wouldn't be much resistance. I understood – forgive me, lord – that there was only your sister in charge, and that quite a few of your slaves were old, and some others hadn't been with you long, so you see – I'm sure I'm very sorry, lord.'

Even at this moment, Torquatus couldn't help smiling. 'I must introduce you to my sister some time. But here I am, you see, quite alive, though no thanks to you.'

Antonius banged his empty cup down on the table and stood up, waves of anger sweeping from him. He turned on Philo.

'You stupid man. You deserve to die for what you've done. You and your tales of letters and rings!'

The little man, who had been growing more confident, seemed to shrink again. 'I know, lord. I am so sorry – '

'Sorry!' Antonius was sweeping up and down the room now as if his anger needed more space to express itself, kicking a wooden stool out of his way. Torquatus found himself mechanically watching as it skittered across the floor and shuddered to a halt. 'I'll come back tomorrow,' he threw at Octavian. 'Perhaps then we can discuss matters of state without interruption.'

'Very well,' Octavian agreed, in such a placid tone that Torquatus shot him a quick, enquiring glance.

As Antonius turned to go, one of the guards stepped in through the open door. 'Excuse me, lord. There is a lady –'

And there was. Manlia swept in, her eyes flashing, her cheeks flushed with the cold air. She blinked at the crowded room, before looking round for her brother, then Octavian and Antonius. For a moment she stood still, as if gauging her welcome. Then she turned to Octavian. 'I do beg your pardon,' she said quietly, her eyes modestly lowered. 'I won't interrupt you when I can see you are very busy.'

'Not at all,' Octavian replied, politely offering her his hand. 'Is that - ,' and he pointed to the strange black object her slave-woman was carrying, 'something you wanted to show me?'

'I brought it for my brother, but I think perhaps it should be given to you. It was thrown into the river by my brother's secretary, Demetrius.' Torquatus caught the odd look she gave Octavian, one he couldn't interpret. What could Demetrius be doing, throwing things into the river? And how did Manlia know about it?

Octavian turned to Antonius. 'As you said, it does seem to be one of those days, doesn't it,' he said easily. 'I promise you that tomorrow I shall tell my household I am at home to no-one.'

Antonius made a grumbling sound in his throat. 'I should hope so. And since I can't imagine what the activities of Torquatus' slaves have to do with me, or anyone else, for that matter, I shall leave you.'

But before he could go there was yet another intrusion. The guard appeared once more, looking profoundly embarrassed. He shut the door carefully behind him. 'There is a man here, insisting on seeing you, lord.'

'You hadn't thought of telling him I was busy, I suppose?' Octavian's voice was frosty.

'Of course, lord. But he is from Torquatus' house, and as the lord Torquatus - and the lady Manlia – are with you, I thought it might be important.'

Octavian looked at Torquatus. He stared back, unable to imagine what domestic disaster could make Trofimus send to him here. 'Who is the man?'

'Says his name's Demetrius.'

'Oh, he does, does he? Send him in straight away.' Whatever Demetrius was doing, Torquatus wanted to know about it.

Antonius hesitated, curious, no doubt, like the rest. Torquatus stepped back a little, Manlia at his side. They hardly needed to have taken the precaution, however.

Demetrius rushed in so fast that he never saw either of them, and indeed the guards ran in after him, fearing he might mean some harm. He brushed past Antonius and threw himself at Octavian's feet.

'Oh, get up, man,' Octavian said. 'And tell me what you've come for.'

Torquatus' jaw dropped: he was speaking to Demetrius as if he knew him well.

'It's my master.' Demetrius looked up at him from his kneeling position.

'What about him?'

'I think he's found out about -' and suddenly he seemed to sense that he wasn't alone with Octavian. He gazed wildly about him, caught sight first of Manlia, then of Torquatus, and finally of Antonius. He looked as if he might faint, then seemed to pull himself together. He got to his feet.

'What might your master have found out about,' Antonius asked, suspicion in his face and voice.

'Oh, simply something I did for the lord Octavian last year, lord. Only I didn't get my lord's permission, you see, so I am afraid he will be very angry with me.'

'When last year would this have been?'

Demetrius took a deep breath. He glanced about him like a hunted animal: first towards Octavian, who also seemed pale in the weak lamplight, then towards his master. 'Whatever it is you've done, you'll tell us, or have it whipped out of you,' Torquatus told him.

'It was during the time when the lord Octavian was marching towards Rome, last August. You remember, lord, how you helped Octavian's mother and sister, escorted them to the protection of the Vestal Virgins?'

'Of course I remember. What of it?'

'Well, you see, the lady Atia gave me a present of money, later, for carrying her message to the lord Octavian, and I never told you. The money was meant for you, you see.'

285

'And you kept it for yourself. I see. How could you have kept it hidden, among all the other slaves?' Torquatus asked.

'I have a bank account.' His voice was surly.

Antonius stepped forwards. 'I am sure this is all very fascinating. But I have the state to run, wars to plan for – that sort of thing. Perhaps you'd come to my house tomorrow?' he said to Octavian. 'I can at least guarantee that we shan't be disturbed by slaves who want to tell you about their banking arrangements.'

Octavian looked regretful. 'I'm so sorry. The afternoon certainly hasn't gone as I planned it. I will be quite at your disposal tomorrow.'

Antonius swept out, his retinue falling in behind. Philo, as he passed Torquatus, gave him a most unloving look. The boots stamped and ground again over the stone floor outside, the outer doors closed with a thump. For a moment they all stood silent, fixed in their places. Then Octavian stumbled to a stool and sat there with his head in his hands. For a moment Torquatus thought he was ill. Then he realised that the sound he could hear was of suppressed laughter. Manlia, Demetrius and Torquatus looked at each other, uncertain what to do. At last Octavian stood up and wiped his eyes. He walked across to the maid and took the object Manlia had brought, a little leather bag, black and slimy, oozing with river-mud. 'How did you come by this?' he asked.

'This morning, our slaves were searching for Demetrius along the quays, when suddenly they saw him. He saw them too, and threw this into the water before running off. They let him get away, unfortunately, but managed to get this back. It took them some time but they found someone in the end who was prepared to dive for it.'

'Do you recognize it?' Octavian asked Torquatus, who came to with a start. Why had his household been searching for Demetrius?

'No. But then I never saw Demetrius with any kind

286

of purse. Except mine, of course.'

Octavian laid it down on the table.

Torquatus was just about to ask what it was when he caught sight of Octavian's face. It was always a hard face to read, but at that moment it was a study in anger, embarrassment and – Torquatus was sure – fear. He was suddenly furious with all of them, Demetrius, Manlia, Octavian. He would have the truth, whatever it cost. 'Start at the beginning,' he told Demetrius. 'Why did you throw this in the river?'

Demetrius looked at Octavian, but, getting no response, his shoulders sagged. He sighed. 'I didn't dare take it with me,' he said. 'I've been to every gate leading out of the city, but could see you had men watching them. So I threw it in the river. I thought no-one had seen me. Then they started shouting and running, so I took off, lost myself in the back streets.'

'You shouldn't have kept it,' Octavian said quietly.

There was silence for a moment.

'I understand it now, I suppose.' Torquatus spoke slowly, still feeling his way. 'Antonius has always denied, after all, that he authorised the transfer of a vast amount of money – a substantial part of the tax revenues from Asia Province – to Balbus at Nice.'

'Antonius is very good at denying things,' Octavian put in. 'Whenever it suits him, in fact.'

'And I've always assumed that was just what he was doing. After all, I'd actually seen the letter. But perhaps I didn't see a letter from Antonius after all. Perhaps it was a forgery, sealed with a copy of his ring. A copy that is in that purse. But what I don't understand is how you came to do it, Demetrius. What could you have gained that would make a risk like this worth running?'

The man's hands were shaking, and he gripped them together. He fixed his eyes on his master. 'I couldn't help it, didn't seem to have a choice. I don't know if you remember the lord Octavian saying to you one day, when we were in

287

Brundisium, that he didn't know where he was to find enough money to avenge his father? You and the lord Agrippa had been talking the day before about the ship full of tax money that was lying in the harbour under guard, waiting for instructions from Rome. I didn't say anything, but perhaps my face gave me away? However it was, that evening, a slave of the lord Maecenas came to me. I don't know how he found out, or whether he'd just guessed the truth, but he bought me a lot of wine and I - I suppose I got drunk, and I told him I'd been sold by my master after forging a letter.' Demetrius was shaking all over now. 'I agreed to do what the lord Maecenas wanted, but I said I'd need a seal. I got it made: maybe you remember that I went on business for you into the town one day, and you told me off when I came back, for taking such a long time?'

Torquatus shook his head. 'I don't remember that. When I bought you, I wasn't told that you were a criminal. That's illegal.'

Demetrius shrugged. 'My old master sold me for far less than I was worth, because of it. I suppose he thought I'd go to the mines or the fields. But the dealer sold me on to another dealer, who put my price up, lost my history, and sold me on again for a good profit to a specialist slave-merchant in Rome: the man you dealt with, who sells readers and accountants, copyists, architectural draughtsmen. It happens all the time.'

He waited for Torquatus to reply, then went on. 'The money went to the lord Balbus. The letter wasn't questioned, except by Antonius. The lord Maecenas suggested that I keep the ring, in case it was needed again, which it was, when the money had to be withdrawn from Balbus' vaults. I wrote two letters ordering that. But we were back in Rome by then, and that's when my troubles started. Stephanus hated me. And you. Unworthy slave of a treacherous master, he called me, and said I was just like Lucius' secretary who had run off with his master's money-box after that final battle.'

'Philo, you mean. The man who was here a moment ago.'

Demetrius' face was blank with shock, and Torquatus realised he'd been in such a panic, he hadn't taken in who was in the room.

'Philo was blackmailing you, wasn't he?'

Demetrius looked from one to the other of them, as if searching for an ally. 'Yes. Yes, he came to me, and told me he'd been to Neapolis, knew about the ring. He guessed I'd killed Spurius. And in the meantime, Stephanus resented me, and all the new slaves. But particularly me. He must have searched my room: the ring disappeared.'

'You should never have kept it once we'd returned to Rome,' Octavian put in sharply.

Vaguely, Torquatus heard Demetrius remind him that he'd needed it to authorise the money's removal to Rome. To his farm. He was almost dizzy at the implications of all this.

'When the ring was stolen I was terrified, and I knew who must have taken it.' Demetrius turned his eyes desperately to each of them in turn. 'What if Stephanus showed it to you, lord? I had to get it back. I tried several times to get into his room, but when I did I still couldn't find it. The cunning old bastard was keeping it on him, I reckoned. Then one day I saw him talking to you, lord, looking very serious. I was in a panic: what if he was telling you what he knew? I was convinced he must be carrying the ring around with him, and decided there and then that I'd have to get it from him by force, but I knew I couldn't do that in the house.' He gave a painful little smile and spread his hands. 'Once you've found out how easy forgery is, you can always do it again. People don't look, you see. If the thing makes sense, and it's signed by the right person, who looks any further? And your handwriting, lord' – he turned to Torquatus with a dreadful attempt at an ingratiating smile – 'is very neat. Much easier to copy than Antonius'.'

'So it was you who summoned Stephanus to the

Capitol. Did you really have to kill him? He was an old man, after all.'

'I didn't mean to. It was the perfect night, cold and foggy. The place was empty. I was trying to get him to give me the ring or tell me where it was, but he wouldn't. There was a scuffle. My foot slipped on the wet ground, and I lost my footing. I ended up falling against the parapet. But he – he went over – and there was just a thin, old man's scream. Then a silence.' He shivered. 'I ran down the steps so fast I nearly fell myself. He was dead, of course, and the ring was on him, on a string round his neck. I was frightened the tablets would have been smashed in his fall, and I wondered how I'd ever explain that. But when I searched his body - it seemed to take for ever, and I was terrified someone would come along at any moment - he hadn't brought them with him, as I'd told him to. And although I searched again and again I couldn't find them.' He drew a trembling breath.

'Go on. You killed Philip too, no doubt?' Torquatus asked. Octavian had walked over to the window and twitched the heavy curtains over the shutters, as if this tale of revenge and death among Torquatus' slaves was nothing to do with him.

'I had no choice. He accused me of writing the message on the tablets. 'I listened to Iucundus and Philip when they were talking, because it was clear that if he told anyone what he knew it would have been that boy, but I couldn't make out where the tablets were.'

'I hold you at least partially responsible for Iucundus' death,' Torquatus told him. 'You made up that story about seeing him attack me in the Forum.'

'Well, I did see a person, someone small.'

'I know very well who that person was. He's confessed. And you must have seen Iucundus, chasing him. As you should have been doing.'

Demetrius shuffled, and wouldn't meet his eyes. Torquatus fell silent, feeling stunned. His household had been engaged in its own civil war, apparently, and he hadn't seen the half of it. Octavian, forgotten by the window, turned at last.

'It's for you to decide what to do with him, Torquatus. What do you think?'

Torquatus didn't have to think. 'He's a traitor, a thief, a forger, a murderer. He dies.'

'I see.' Octavian walked over to where master and slave still held their positions, as if in a tableau, his face thoughtful.

'What would you suggest?' Torquatus looked down at him sharply. 'For months this man's been pretending to be my loyal slave, committed to my interests. In reality he's killed two old men, men faithful to my father and to my brother, and his lies have led me to have another slave tortured to death. For no consideration whatever would I keep the creature in my house for so much as another night. Nor would I sell him to another man. If I told the truth no-one would buy him. If I lied, he'd poison another household.'

'But what could I do, lord?' Demetrius burst out. 'I didn't dare say no to the lord Maecenas.'

Manlia got up. She'd been sitting silent by the brazier for some time. Like Octavian, she was very good at listening. She crossed the room to her brother and took his hands in her own. 'The man has a point. I've never liked or trusted Demetrius, as you know, but it is hard for a slave to resist the powerful. What did you plan to do? Send him to the games, for the lions to eat? Kill him yourself? Or just send him to the mines? Slaves don't last long there.'

Octavian smiled. 'I'll make you an offer, Torquatus, which I hope you'll find acceptable.'

'You? But why?'

'The man has done wrong, but I think he has some - shall we say? - useful qualities. So what do you say to 40,000? A very good price for a slave, I'm sure you'll agree.'

40,000 sesterces would be an absurd price, even for a slave as beautiful as Narcissus, as musical as Apollo and as smart as Ulysses. Torquatus goggled at him. 'You aren't short of secretaries, are you?'

'I'm not, although I could always use more. But no. I have something different in mind for Demetrius. Information: the key to everything.' He was smiling more broadly now: relaxed, comfortable, a man having his little joke.

'Have him, then. But I'm surprised you'd trust such a creature about you.'

'Demetrius isn't going to be about me. He's run away, hasn't he?' With his eyes half shut Torquatus thought he looked as if he might break into a purr at any moment. 'You, Torquatus, are going to go home and call your men off the search for Demetrius. And tomorrow Demetrius is going to set out for Sicily. I really have to know a lot more about what Sextus Pompey is up to. This conspiracy, for instance: to what extent was he behind it, or were those fools simply acting alone? He's just what Sextus Pompey needs. A runaway: clever, unscrupulous, and a man who can make up a good enough story at need – though I was surprised that Antonius could have believed my mother would have offered money to Torquatus. She'd never have done anything so crude.'

Manlia was holding her brother's hands tight. Warm and strong, they brought him back to a sense of where he was. He didn't find anything he wanted to say. 'We've taken up too much of your time,' Manlia was apologising to Octavian. 'And I'm afraid we've forced you to postpone your strategic discussions with Antonius.'

Octavian grinned suddenly. 'Yes. Thank you for that. He insisted on coming today, but Agrippa isn't here, and I feel far more comfortable discussing military matters when I have his support. He'll be back tomorrow.' He clapped his hands and the guard appeared. 'I want 40,000 sesterces in cash, and a contract for the purchase of a slave.' He smiled at the surprise on Manlia's face. 'I've told my staff always to have draft contracts ready for any kind of transaction: it saves so much time.'

While they waited, Octavian turned to Torquatus with a purposeful air that made him quake again. 'There's one other thing I need to ask you. Have you by any chance found any documents among your brother's papers which - well, which weren't written by him?'

'There are many, of course: his secretary wrote most of them. Do you mean someone different again? Demetrius would be the man to ask.'

'I haven't seen them.' Demetrius' voice was sullen. An odd look passed between him and Octavian. Torquatus stared, on the point of speaking. Philo's words came into his mind: Lucius had refused to free him because of some mistake he'd made. Papers of Caesar's, which had appeared among Lucius' own, and which presumably had been taken when they left Oricum. Were these what Demetrius had been looking for while 'arranging' the Manlius Torquatus archives? At Octavian's direction? He took a deep breath, his blood freezing in his veins.

'I think the papers you have in mind - presumably the ones Philo mentioned earlier? - will have been in the bag that Lucius sent home from Africa by Philip, just before he died.'

Demetrius nodded. 'I knew there must have been at least one more letter. The lord Torquatus even mentioned it one evening, but didn't say where it was.'

'And where are these papers?' Octavian spoke calmly, but Torquatus could feel the man's excitement as if it were heat.

'In my family tomb.'

'In a tomb?'

'Why not?' Torquatus was quite unable to keep the anger out of his voice. 'I knew what kind of letter Lucius would have written me. I'd heard it all from my mother, hadn't I?' Torquatus turned away and carefully straightened one of the innumerable piles of documents. His voice was quiet. 'Over and over again I'd heard it. Traitor to the family's history and values, turncoat, enemy. Why would I want to read it? And as to his other papers, what use would they be to anyone? When Philip gave them to me, I'd just come back to Rome with Caesar, after that dreadful battle at Munda against what seemed at the time his last enemies: if you remember, Caesar said himself it was the only time he'd had to fight for his life rather than just for victory. He won and the world changed: Lucius and his concerns were in the past. We had no body, no ashes, since what was left of him was in the sea somewhere off Mytilene, so why not put his last words in his tomb instead? I never even opened the bag, just had the whole lot sealed up behind his memorial tablet.'

Torquatus stopped, unsure whether it was safe to say what was in his heart, but he found he no longer cared. 'I didn't know there was anything of Caesar's with them, and I would have given you the whole lot straight away, if I'd known you wanted them.'

'I believe you would.' Octavian smiled, and sighed with pleasure. 'Too late to get them today. Tomorrow we'll go together and do it. No. Tomorrow we have to triumph, don't we? The day after, then.'

There seemed nothing more to say. It might have been awkward, standing there, each with his own thoughts, but Octavian's staff worked fast, and in what felt like a few moments Torquatus and Manlia were outside the house, watching Becco and Pulex carry the bags of money to the litter. The Nubians could carry it home. Too many revelations, and too much time spent in Octavian's overheated rooms had left Torquatus with an aching head and a bad temper. He'd be better in the fresh air. Manlia chose to walk with him. The big slaves fell in behind as they began to descend the steps into the dark and empty Forum. The light thrown by the men's torches made their shadows leap and twist on the wet path. The whole place had a dank, underworld air.

'Nothing looks solid in this light,' Manlia agreed.

'A stony city, that's what Iucundus called it, so Felix

said.'

Manlia slipped her hand into his arm. 'But now you can plan ahead,' she reminded him. She laughed, a shocking sound in the damp darkness. 'Not so fast,' Torquatus said. 'There's a good deal I don't know. When you told me that our slaves had been following Demetrius - well, I never ordered that. Would you like to explain.'

'Of course. Felix told me everything that he told you. When I thought about those wretched tablets that seem to have bobbed around Rome like some sort of magician's prop, I could see that Iucundus really hadn't written that message to Stephanus. And if he hadn't, who had? Going through the household, looking at those who were here at the time and ruling out all the illiterate ones - which is most of them - Demetrius' was the most obvious name. I was going to talk to you, but you'd gone out. I was afraid Demetrius might have heard me with Felix last night: he was lurking about in the gallery when I left the room. So I spoke to Trofimus and we agreed that Demetrius would be kept under surveillance. When he went out soon afterwards he was followed.'

'I'm surprised he wasn't watching for spies.'

'Well, perhaps he was, but he had a very ardent young sleuth on his tail: Felix.'

'Felix! Well, perhaps that's for the best. Bringing Demetrius to justice might make him feel better about what's happened. Not that this is justice, of course.'

'And Felix told me something else, something that Iucundus had told him. Stephanus had taken something from Demetrius' room, according to Philip. He swore it was a gold ring, and thought Demetrius must have stolen it. Stephanus wasn't sure whether to tell you about it, because he thought, whatever Demetrius had got up to must have been at your instigation.'

They walked in silence for a few moments. Then Torquatus exclaimed, 'And there was I was thinking of going to Neapolis to find out what had happened there last summer! He shook his head sadly.

Manlia said nothing, and Torquatus went on, 'I was wrong about Demetrius, completely wrong. If only I'd had him searched: I'd have found that nasty little leather pouch, I suppose. And Iucundus would still be alive.'

Manlia nodded. 'That's true. But who could have guessed that it was Octavian behind the forgery? Octavian suborning your slave. And when he realised we knew he didn't give a shit - as Gnaeus would say,' she added as Torquatus turned to her in mild outrage.

He laughed. 'He didn't, did he?' By common consent they had chosen, not the darkness of the Ringmakers' Stairs but the more open Palatine Way and were now coming to the level ground at the bottom of it. Torquatus drew a breath. 'I still can't quite believe it. That it should have been Octavian - my friend - setting my slaves to search my papers, to commit crimes under my very nose - I mean, what if I'd found Demetrius out and made a stink? Would I still be alive, do you think?'

'I don't know.' Manlia's voice was very quiet.

Again they fell silent, just the sound of their feet on the paving breaking the darkness. Manlia sighed. 'And tomorrow, Lepidus triumphs, and we all have to smile and cheer, remember.'

'Oh, so we do. Could I eat something that disagrees with me, do you think, and be – unfortunately – simply too sick to attend?'

'Oh no. The whole Senate has been told – er, asked, I mean – to parade behind him. Your absence would be noted: you'd better go. But I of course, being only a woman, can stay comfortably at home in the warm.'

'Well, don't sound so smug about it.'

She laughed. They had reached the Argentarius, and felt its slope under their feet. 'I wonder which of these banks,' Torquatus said idly, 'enjoys Demetrius' custom. If he really does have a bank account.'

Manlia thought about this for a moment. 'I bet

Demetrius ends up richer than either of us, don't you?'

'Manlia, you terrify me sometimes.' They walked on in silence. 'What do you think our revered father would have made of my becoming a senator at twenty one?'

'He'd have made a speech denouncing the degeneracy of the age, and then he'd have thrown a huge party to celebrate,' she said at once.

'You think so? I don't believe he'd have approved of a single thing I've done.'

'I can't say. But we need to see things straight, don't we? We can't afford to live in a fantasy world: and the fact is that towards the end of his life he did.'

'Manlia!'

'Well, you know it's true. He died longing for a political system that's dead. For whatever reason – I don't know; does anyone? – it's dead. And Father never would see that, and nor did Lucius.'

'Admirable, though, don't you think? To believe so strongly in something that you'll die for it.'

'Oh, I'm just a woman.' Manlia pulled her arm away crossly, and began to walk faster. They hadn't mentioned her husband but surely he too was likely to die for his faith in the republican system. 'I have to be pragmatic,' she said at last. 'I have to think of my brother, trying to save his family from shipwreck, and, oh Aulus, I'd like my husband back.' She slowed down and put her hand back through his arm.

'And in the meantime, I have some other news for you.'

'Really? Good news, I do hope?'

'I'm afraid it will make more work for you.'

'What kind of work? Come on, Aulus, stop teasing.'

'Well, planning a wedding then.'

'Aulus! Oh! But how - ?'

'It's all Octavian's doing. He wants me to marry Balbus' daughter, and he says Balbus has agreed.'

'Cornelia! Goodness, how grand. Well. And I thought finding you a wife would take me, oh, months, perhaps, and I certainly wouldn't have found you anyone as - as superb as that.'

'I just wish I knew anything about her. I mean, she may be rich, but if she's awful - oh, I can't explain. Do you know her?'

Manlia clearly wasn't quite pleased: it was a moment before she shook her head. Then she seemed to come to herself. 'It's mother you're thinking of, isn't it?'

Torquatus nodded. He hadn't realised himself until Manlia said the words, but the thought of creating a household like the one he'd grown up in filled him with horror.

'There's no reason to think it will be like that,' Manlia told him. 'For a start, you aren't a bit like father. He married her for her money and to have another son, and I don't believe he took the least trouble to make her comfortable in Rome, just left her to sink or swim. I think that was one reason why she was always so sharp and critical. Balbus' daughter will be very different. Not a provincial like our mother, worried about her status and always trying to get a toehold in society. Everyone will want to know her. And if she's anything like her father, she'll be pretty intelligent, wouldn't you think? At the very worst she'll make a life for herself, and let you get on with yours. At the best, you'll have a real marriage, warm and loving.'

'You're cheering me up already.'

'Good. And you know - ,' Manlia stopped and Torquatus stopped with her. Behind them the slaves too shuffled to a halt. Manlia seemed to clear her throat. 'It takes two to make a marriage, so if you are willing to try, I think you can make it work.'

He put his arm round her and gave her a hug. 'Well, I will.'

Up ahead, Torquatus could see two lights where his house must be. Trofimus must have had them put there, to light them home. Torquatus laughed, his mood suddenly buoyant. 'Trofimus really thinks of everything.'

Chapter 20

Lepidus' triumph was as dull as Octavian and Antonius could have wished: no cascades of gold and jewels from exotic regions, no pearls or crocodiles, just a parade of cold and fearful-looking slaves. People turned out, cheered a bit, and went away again as soon as they decently could. If it had been a party, you'd have called it a flop. After it, Torquatus had himself wrapped in his best toga and carried over to Balbus' house in response to the (not wildly enthusiastic) letter he'd received the day before.

Once again, he was shown into the master's study. This time he didn't have to wait: Balbus bustled in at once, and shook hands in a businesslike way. Then he sat down, behind the desk this time, and looked at his visitor consideringly. 'I'm glad to see you so soon,' he began.

Torquatus pulled himself together. 'I was astonished and delighted when Octavian told me what he'd asked of you,' he said. 'I am extremely honoured, of course, by your agreement to give me your daughter.'

'I am naturally delighted that she is going to such an old and distinguished house as yours,' Balbus answered. Then, obviously feeling that enough had been said in the way of polite platitudes, he went on, 'The luckiest wedding dates are in June, of course, but I don't want to wait so long. If it must be, then - the fourth day before the Nones of January will be an auspicious day: let's do it then.'

Torquatus took a deep breath. 'Wonderful.'

'Now, as to the business side of things. Cornelia's dowry will consist of all my property in Spain: or rather, she will receive half of it as dowry, and will inherit the rest when I die. At that point she will become the chief patron of Gades, among other cities, and the owner of silver mines, large estates, vineyards, and oil production interests.'

Torquatus felt winded. 'You need to remember your nephew, presumably?'

'No. He can look after himself,' Balbus said curtly,

299

and Torquatus felt unable to pursue the question.

'I think you are well aware of my position?' Torquatus knew very well that Octavian would have made that clear to Balbus already.

Balbus smiled. 'I am indeed. So now to details. The first meeting of the Senate will be held on the Kalends, so the wedding will take place the day after.'

'Very well.' Still feeling somewhat breathless, Torquatus said: 'Is Cornelia in Rome? I've never met her, you know, and I'd like to.'

'She's in Neapolis,' Balbus told him. He sighed and pushed back his chair. 'Don't misunderstand me, Torquatus, when I say that this marriage isn't just what I'd have chosen for her.'

Torquatus looked a question.

'She was engaged to marry a merchant, a man I trust, in Neapolis. But he died before the marriage could take place, and since then I haven't pursued the matter. She's seventeen, so of course she needs a husband.'

'A merchant in Neapolis?'

'Ah! You sound dismissive. There speaks the Roman aristocrat. But look at it from my perspective: she's all I have. I loved her mother dearly, and when she died Cornelia was all I had left. I swore then I'd guard her with my life. While she was a little girl I knew she was safe in Spain with my wife's parents. Then her grandfather died, and a few years later her grandmother too.' He paused for a moment, thinking. 'By that time she was almost old enough to be married, and I brought her to Neapolis. I didn't want her in Rome where she'd be the target of every greedy young man. And I was right. Consider the position the wives and daughters of your great men have been left in after these dreadful wars and proscriptions: impoverished, ruined, even the greatest of them. Even Servilia, great lady that she was, Caesar's mistress, Brutus' mother, still had to apply to Atticus for protection. Your own sister, too. How could I want that for my daughter?'

Torquatus looked at him seriously. 'Most of the men who've been proscribed have been of the equestrian class, like yourself, ' he pointed out.

'True. But - well, anyway, there's no point in talking about it. I have agreed to do as Octavian wishes.' Balbus seemed uncharacteristically unwilling to come to the point. He sighed, sat up straighter, and said, 'What I want you to understand is this: I won't have my girl neglected or ill-used. If I think she isn't happy with you, I'll see that she's divorced. That sounds harsh, but I mean it. She is all the family I have. Except that nephew of mine, of course.'

Torquatus nodded. 'I can reassure you, I think: I was saying to Manlia yesterday that I couldn't bear to recreate my father's family. He only wanted my mother for her children. I see the family as more than that.'

Balbus seemed satisfied. He sat back in his chair and nodded. 'Good.'

'You must be very close,' Torquatus suggested. 'Manlia tells me Cornelia has run your household for some time.'

'Yes, that's true. It's been as if a part of my wife still stayed with me, while Cornelia was in the house. I shall miss her dreadfully. But of course she must marry.'

Torquatus had never seen this human side of Balbus before. 'We shall all be in Rome, and no doubt Cornelia will still see you very often: you will always be a welcome guest.'

He left Balbus apparently feeling far more cheerful: but he did wish he could have seen Cornelia before the wedding day.

Chapter 21

Octavian appeared at Torquatus' house early the next day, with his usual large escort of slaves and soldiers. He himself was riding in a big, comfortable litter, which he invited Torquatus to share with him. No sooner was he inside and comfortably settled on the cushions next to Octavian than the bearers - eight of them - picked up the poles and trotted off. This was a class outfit: the men had been trained to move so smoothly it felt like floating. What Torquatus couldn't do, since he'd been shown into the seat next to Octavian, was see his face. Even if he'd been opposite, though, he wouldn't have seen much. The curtains weren't of leather, but of linen, which let through a light which was soft and pleasing, but too dim to make out the subtle changes in what was always a wonderfully inexpressive face.

Torquatus tried to resign himself to not knowing what it was they were looking for. Not very successfully, however: he'd spent most of the night lying awake picking at the question over and over again, to no avail. The idea that anything of Caesar's could have ended up with Lucius, of all people, was strange enough. And surely, if Caesar had lost some document at Oricum, wouldn't he simply have cancelled it, replaced it? Or if for some reason he hadn't missed it, how had Octavian come to know of it? Most importantly, whatever could it have been that would drive Octavian himself out to the Via Salaria on a raw morning, rather than send one of his many underlings? Torquatus' mind was filled with these questions, but he knew better than to ask them.

Without being able to see where they were going, he had to rely on his ears. He heard the soldiers at the Quirinal gate call out to them to stop, then almost in the same breath order them through, seeing, no doubt, who they were dealing with. It wasn't far to the Manlius Torquatus tomb. The bearers ran smoothly past the temple of Flora, then

Torquatus felt the gentle turn onto a slight gradient as they moved down towards the main road. Like all Rome's roads, the Salaria is lined with tombs of all different shapes and sizes where it leaves the city. The Torquatus tomb was one of the handsomest: a small Greek temple, perfect in every detail, surrounded by gardens. They climbed out of the litter and Torquatus shivered as the bitter breeze blew round his legs. The smoke of a small fire, lit by gardeners tending to the neighbouring tomb, was as fragrant as incense. Torquatus, wrapping his cloak tightly round him, went quickly down the stone steps to the solid oaken doors, protected by a bronze grille. There are people so poor they will take up residence in any tomb they can get into, and no-one wants their ancestors dishonoured. The grille creaked open; the doors swung inward on well-oiled hinges.

Inside, the tomb smelt of earth and stone, but it wasn't only the mouldering scent that made Torquatus shudder. Generations of his forefathers lay here: it was a sacred place. His father's ashes had been placed in a handsome sarcophagus, the full details of his career spelt out across the front. For Lucius, Torquatus had thought a wall-plaque with an inscription more appropriate. It was brief, stating the facts of his life and death, his magistracies - moneyer, quaestor, praetor - and no more. Torquatus' eyes stung as he thought of his brother's bones, lying on the seabed, far away. Octavian was so close behind him Torquatus could almost feel the warmth of his breath on his neck. He beckoned forward the stone-mason with his bag of tools, and while the man carefully chiselled out the mortar around the tablet they stood back in silence. It was horribly quiet except for the scraping of the mason's tools and the faint rustle of falling mortar. The man seemed to take for ever. But at last he called Becco and Pulex over, and together they lifted the stone away in a shower of mortar fragments. And immediately behind the plaque, just where Torquatus had placed it, where the jar of ashes ought to have been, lay a small, battered leather satchel, rather dusty, its flap secured with thin cords, and sealed with a blob of sealing-wax. Octavian reached past Torquatus, picked up the bag, and carried it outside without a word. Torquatus followed him.

He could see as Octavian opened it that there were several different documents inside, of varying size. Octavian was clearly looking for something specific: rather than pulling everything out, his fingers teased the stiff documents apart. He gave a little grunt as if he had found what he was looking for, and pulled out a scroll, sealed with a blob of wax. Then his fingers were back in the bag again. He pulled out another document, checked it, and let it fall back with the others. The next one was a small scroll, which he pulled right out of the bag, reading the label. 'Your brother's last letter to you,' he told Torquatus. 'You said yesterday that you'd never read it, and I can see that it's never been opened. Do you know, I think that was a very wise decision. Letters from the dead: there's something in the very idea that makes me uneasy. But yours must be the decision, of course.' And he handed the little scroll over, apparently indifferent.

Torquatus weighed it in his hand. If he took the letter home now and read it, Octavian would always fear that his secret might become known, if only to Torquatus himself. And very probably the letter would contain, as Torquatus had always supposed, nothing more than empty accusations. And yet. And yet. It might also explain just what Octavian had so badly wanted. With a mental shrug Torquatus walked over to the gardeners' little fire, where a pile of dry leaves had been left to burn while the slaves busied themselves round the back of the tomb, and threw the letter onto it. It really wasn't worth risking his life for.

Satisfied, Octavian turned away and climbed back into his litter. Everything was now complete. Torquatus' position in Octavian's regard was secure. His problems were solved. It just didn't feel like that. Back at home, he couldn't settle on his reading-couch, but dropped the scroll and wandered about the room looking for something more exciting to read. Once again he decided that perhaps philosophy wasn't what he needed just now. History, maybe, something with a good exciting narrative and not too much moralising. He drifted into the library. The documents that Demetrius had been so conscientiously archiving were still all spread about the big table, and he picked one up at random: he wasn't surprised that it was yet another letter from his brother, written almost at the start of the hideous civil wars, telling their father how Pompey was amassing a superb army, much larger than Caesar's. All the great ones of the east were flocking to support him with troops, money, gifts. What chance had Caesar now? Sourly, he dropped the thing back onto the table and turned to find that Trofimus had padded into the room.

'I'm sorry to have left everything so untidy, lord,' he said. 'But since Demetrius had done such a lot of work, it seemed a shame to waste it. No doubt a new secretary will arrive soon. Perhaps you would like me to make enquiries among the slave-dealers?'

'Yes. I shall need a new man. And I think I shall set Felix to learn from him.' The idea had only that minute come into his mind, but it felt right. 'He's a bright boy; and he is my father's son, after all. He needs an appropriate position. Oh, and I suppose I'll need a new body-servant too,' he added awkwardly, but Trofimus only nodded, and Torquatus drifted back into his study, still without the history book. Manlia had come in, and was occupying his reading-couch.

'Oh, do sit down, Aulus,' she said, after he'd wandered around the room for a moment or two, picking things up and putting them down again. She lowered her book-scroll and gave him a firm, older-sister look. 'Tell me what happened at the tomb.'

So Torquatus explained how he had thrown the letter away, and was regretting it. Manlia was brisk. 'Just be glad everything's worked out so well.'

'I know, I know. But I can't help wondering, all the

same.'

'No point. You aren't going to find out. Your decision to throw the letter in the fire was absolutely right. And it probably didn't even say anything about Caesar's papers.' She put a marker in her scroll and rolled it up. 'And now I'm going to see Postumia.' She had almost reached the door when the curtain was pulled back rather tentatively, and Becco put his head in through the gap.

'Excuse me, master.' He stepped in carefully, looking awkward, and far too large for that small room. 'One of the gardeners on the Via Salaria asked me to give you this. He didn't think anyone else had been up there this morning who might have dropped it.' In his huge paw, held carefully away from him as if it might bite him, or explode without warning, was a little scroll, slightly singed. 'They found it at the edge of their fire.'

'Thank you. Just put it on there.' Torquatus nodded towards the side-table by the couch. Manlia was smiling. Once she was sure Becco was out of earshot, she said, 'It seems the gods want you to read that letter, doesn't it?'

'It seems like it.' Without really making a conscious decision, he had picked it up and his fingers had begun to explore the edge of the scroll, and he now tore suddenly at the cords, so that the wax split. 'I thought you were going to see Postumia?'

'Oh, you're not the only curious person around here.'

Torquatus grunted, and spread open the scroll, carefully, not sure how far the damage went. But only the top edge of the papyrus was burnt: the letter, in Lucius' neat, well-formed writing, was perfectly legible. 'I'll read it aloud. It's in his own writing, so he must have reckoned it was confidential, I suppose.'

Manlia nodded and sat up attentively.

'*To my brother, if he still lives.* When was this written? Oh, he says: *the sixth day before the Ides of April, Gaius Julius*

Caesar having declared himself consul for the third time, with Marcus Aemilius Lepidus. Not long before he died, in other words, four years ago. Oh, well, he was still speaking to me, then.'

'Yes, but do get on, Aulus.' Manlia was looking as excited as Torquatus felt.

'Very well. *I have no hope left. You can be happy in the knowledge that you've won. Our armies are shattered, dispersed. Caesar's men have been encouraged, it seems, to kill any of us they find. Metellus Scipio and I are making our way to Mytilene, from where we hope - or rather he hopes - to regroup, to raise more troops, supplies, arms. In the meantime, Pompey's sons Gnaeus and Sextus are in Spain, keeping the cause of the republic alive there, so even if - when - we fail all will not be lost. And, perhaps, even if we all go down the very idea of the republic will live on - and who can say if it might not be revived, maybe at some time in the distant future?*

If I am ever fortunate enough to return to Rome, you and I will no doubt be enemies for the rest of our lives. But why speculate about what can never come to pass? On a more practical note, then, I enclose with this letter a number of papers. Those that concern my own affairs can be kept for me. If we win, I will no doubt return to Rome in due course, to take up my interrupted life. If we lose, they will be of no interest to you or anyone.

But I am also sending you some papers of Caesar's. Yes. That's made you sit up, hasn't it? How, I hear you ask, could I, Lucius Manlius Torquatus, sworn enemy of Caesar and all his works, have come by any such things? I don't know, is the short answer, but I can guess, and my belief is that they were picked up by my secretary, Philo, when we left Caesar's custody. You'll remember how I was taken prisoner by Caesar after Oricum fell. I was an honoured guest, but not one who was free to leave the camp. My soldiers, damn them, quickly went over to Caesar's side. In March of that year, Antonius finally managed to bring his troops across to Macedonia, and in all the chaos and confusion of the break-up of Caesar's camp I found my opportunity to escape. With my two slaves I packed what little I had and rode quietly away. I was lucky, and fell in with Pompey's army without difficulty, where I was welcomed with open arms, and restored to a command.

I needn't tell you all that has happened since, but the other day my secretary Philo, a thoroughly unsatisfactory man, ran off and left me, together with my cash-box. His reason for this appalling act was, I think, that I'd found him out in a piece of dishonesty, and taxed him with it. Philo must have been aware that two documents in Caesar's own handwriting were in among my papers, but he had said nothing. No doubt he feared being blamed. Had he told me earlier, I could have done the honest thing and sent the papers straight back to their owner. But at this point I can hardly do so without looking thoroughly underhand, so I decided to send them instead to you. I am only glad I never freed the wretched man, something I had considered at one time.

So what are these valuable papers, I hear you say? The first, the most interesting, is a list, a list of senators. Details of each man's worth, or rather monetary value I should say, are noted beside his name. This looks remarkably like a proscription list to me: so much for your friend Caesar's repeated claims that he never dreamt of any such thing. Maybe a day will come when you'll regret the choice you made. Who knows? The second document is far less valuable, being merely a will. I presume that Caesar, having discovered its loss, will have replaced it. It's addressed on the outside to the Vestal Virgins in Rome, as you'd expect. It's quite entertaining, in its way: I read it, of course. The scandalous thing is just how much money that villain must have squeezed out of Gaul. He leaves huge bequests, and all of this money gained by the most dishonest means! Well, I'll say no more, since there's no point. The will itself is as you might suppose: Antonius the main heir, his cousin Pedius, Decimus Brutus and the boy Octavian each to receive a small legacy. Nothing there to surprise anyone, though Caesar does add that he had previously intended to make Octavian his heir, but was concerned by the boy's poor health, and had changed his mind.

Torquatus put the letter down and looked at Manlia. Her face was as white as his. She started to speak, then had to stop to clear her throat. 'Caesar's will was read in Rome after his death, and gave almost everything to Octavian, didn't it?'

'It did.'

'I thought - I'm sure I heard from somewhere, that

308

Caesar wrote his will much later than that: at Labici, the autumn before he died.'

Torquatus shook his head. 'I don't know that. He said at that time he was thinking about his will. Whether he changed it I don't know.'

'Surely Octavian wouldn't be so concerned to get this one back - urgently, secretly - if it weren't valid?' Manlia pointed out She was sitting upright, her face taut with anxiety.

'I don't know, Manlia. Anyway, I'll finish reading. *I am writing this letter amid chaos. But I want to state clearly, once and for all, that I don't regret any of the choices I made. The republic was worth fighting for, and it's worth dying for. I am conscious that the man I'm writing to was once my brother. What can I say to you? Nothing, I suppose, except that I always dreaded our meeting on the battlefield, and I give you credit for feeling the same. No doubt you are with Caesar. For years I hated you for joining him, but now? Well, now I feel that the gods hold the threads of our lives in their hands. No doubt it was ordained somewhere that you and I should oppose each other. I know that you chose honestly, as I did. If these documents of Caesar's fall into your hands, no doubt you will return them to him. Please do so with my apologies: they were not taken intentionally. There has been nothing underhand. And now I have nothing to say but farewell, to any of my family who have survived this firestorm. I pray that there will be some. May the gods favour you always.*

Torquatus put the letter down with tears in his eyes. 'That's the epitaph I should have put on his memorial tablet: he never intentionally did anything underhand.'

'Perhaps one day you will be able to put up a monument to him, somewhere public, not hidden away in our tomb.'

Torquatus gave her a sceptical look. 'And in the meantime, I must decide what to do with this.'

'Destroy it. That's all you can do, isn't it? Destroy it at once, Aulus.' She was still sitting up, tense and frightened.

'Oh yes, believe me. But I want to be sure I do so in the right way.' Torquatus sat for a moment, thinking, twisting the little roll over and over in his hand. Then he got up and turned over the writing things on the side table till he found a box with some fine cord, designed for just this purpose. He wrapped it round the letter, then warmed a stick of wax over the lamp-flame and dropped a blob onto the cords where they crossed. His own signet ring was on his finger: he took it off and stamped the wax.

'That's not Lucius' seal,' Manlia pointed out.

'Doesn't matter. It's only got to work from a distance.' Torquatus called for a slave, and when one stuck his head through the curtain he told the man he wanted a toga, and the household assembled in the reception hall. Victor hurried in with the toga, and they heard the slaves come pattering past the door, buzzing with questions. Then Torquatus went out, with Manlia behind him. Good: the hearth before the household shrine had a healthy fire blazing. What a great addition to the household Trofimus had proved to be: he would free the man before too long, he decided. Torquatus walked over to the shrine, and positioned himself next to the altar, under the light, skipping figures of the house's guardian spirits, the letter in his hand. He stood very straight, feeling the weight and bulk of the toga almost like some protective, holy thing, guarding him - no, his whole family - against the malice of the dead. He pulled up the fold of the toga so that it lay over his head. Every head of household is the priest for his house, and this was a priestly task.

Waiting patiently for all sound to die away, looking round to catch every eye, he couldn't help but be aware of the gaps: Stephanus, Philip, Iucundus, Demetrius. 'I have called you together to tell you that the problems in this household are over. I know there has been dissension here, and unhappiness. We had a killer in our midst: Demetrius.' There was a murmur of surprise, and he waited for it to die down. 'That is behind us now. I intend the house of Manlius Torquatus to take its rightful place once more among the patriciate of Rome. And I want you all to witness two things. The first is that I burn this letter, sealed, as an offering to my household gods. It is a letter from my dead brother; that is to say, a letter from the underworld, one that no longer belongs among the living but is best given back to the gods who direct all things.'

The slaves murmured to each other, then watched wide-eyed as Torquatus put the rolled edge of the scroll into the flame on the hearth. He had wrapped it as loosely as possible, and as it caught slowly and began to be consumed he moved it about, holding it over the fire, making sure that the whole thing burned; then when there was nothing left but the little rod at the heart of it he used that to stir the embers and make sure that not so much as a word would be left legible. The slaves watched with interest. Torquatus looked up, held their attention with his eyes, then laid his hand solemnly on the altar. 'The other day I swore that I would rebuild the temple of Hope. Now, in front of all of you, I renew that vow, and promise too that the precinct of Hope near my farm will also be rebuilt, and a priest appointed to care for it. This I swear in the presence of the gods of this house and its hearth.' He was just feeling that perhaps something more was required to complete the occasion when Trofimus appeared at his side with a dish of honey-cakes and a jug of wine. Torquatus laid the cakes on the altar, then took the jug and poured some wine over them. He stepped back, uncovering his head, and walked away, leaving the household to disperse.

'Impressive paterfamilias act, I must say.' Manlia said, once they were back in the study. 'You been practising or something?'

'Glad you thought so. I wanted to make sure that none of them forgot what they'd seen.'

'What they'd seen?'

'Yes. What did they see, since you don't seem to get it?'

'They saw you burn a letter, and they saw you promise to rebuild a temple.'

311

'They saw more than that. Yes, if anyone asks - one of Octavian's agents, for instance - they saw the letter burned.'

'How would Octavian even know it was brought away from the tomb?' Manlia sounded sceptical.

'I don't know. But it's amazing what that man does find out about. Now, Becco and Pulex can't read, and the letter wasn't opened when they gave it to me, so there's no-one to tell what it said. And if anyone did just happen to ask about a letter that had been given to me after being rescued from a gardener's bonfire they can say quite truthfully that they saw me burn it without opening it, still sealed and fastened. The occasion was as impressive as I could make it, so I think they'll all remember.'

Manlia sank back onto the reading-couch with a little shiver. 'You're right, of course. Isn't it extraordinary that Lucius should have had in his possession, all unknowing, a document that could have changed everything. Suppose Octavian, hearing about his great-uncle's death, had been told simply that he had inherited a small amount of cash, he wouldn't have come back to Italy to raise troops and collect money and start campaigning as he did, would he? He'd simply have been a sickly boy who had some sort of connection with Caesar. Antonius would have come to an agreement with Caesar's murderers, as he started to do in any case. And I suppose the republic would have lurched on until it hit its next crisis.'

'Which wouldn't have been long in coming. But you see, I don't think Octavian was expecting to be Caesar's heir. I was there with him in Apollonia, remember, and he was very surprised when he got the letter. I think Caesar had warned him not to expect to inherit: he must have been wondering ever since Caesar's death where that will had got to. And I suppose Caesar must never have questioned whether the will arrived in Rome. No wonder Octavian looked so satisfied when he got it back. I wonder how many other households have had his spies among their slaves, looking for it? I suppose, though, there couldn't have been too many of Caesar's enemies who would have had the chance to take a paper of his? Octavian will have had a list of them, you may be sure, and worked through it thoroughly.' He shivered. 'And now, my dear, we are going to close this subject, and never, never refer to it again. Not even to each other. We didn't read the letter, and we have no knowledge of any of Caesar's affairs.'

'What letter?' Manlia's eyes were all limpid innocence.

Chapter 22

It was mid-morning before the procession set out from the quietly luxurious house on the Carinae, and the day was as light as it would get. The house had been astir since dawn: a steady stream of visitors had been admitted, some to stay, some simply to bring good wishes and gifts, but now there was a sudden quiet from within. A stone altar had been set up in front of the house, scrubbed clean and adorned with bunches of herbs and flowers, and all morning a burly shepherd had been minding a sheep, walking it around the street, brushing tangles from its wool, tweaking into place the petals of the flower-garland which would go round its neck. Every now and then a military-looking young man would appear in the doorway to look frowning into the street. Each time he did so, the shepherd would nod, half-contemptuously, as if to say, yes, of course I'm here. And now the householder himself came fussing out, his toga immaculate, marshalling all the wedding party outside to see the sacrifice. Balbus had no family of his own in Rome, so the frowning young man was in fact a close friend of the bridegroom's, but no matter: he was Agrippa, Octavian's closest associate. Everyone would know that, and be impressed.

Agrippa knew what he had to do: he spoke the words, and the sacrificer brought down the axe on the sheep's neck. It fell neatly, toppling onto its knees, then onto its side, and the blood ran freely down into the gutters where the water from the fountain would carry it away. A haruspex, nodding his approval of the ceremony, came striding forward, the end of his staff clicking on the ground. His own assistant cut into the sheep's body below the ribs with a long and very sharp knife, and the haruspex leaned forward with a frown. He tutted, and pointed, and the assistant cut deeper. Now the haruspex nodded, and said loudly and clearly: 'The sacrifice is accepted, and the marriage will be auspicious.' There were whoops and cheers

314

at this, and Balbus, relaxing, invited everyone to join him in the procession to the bridegroom's house.

The crowd grew in strength as the moments passed. From inside came the sounds of preparation: voices called people into line: someone asked where those baskets had gone, and a girl's voice , high and agitated, told off a person who was about to stand on the end of her ribbons. At last the procession emerged. Strong young men led the way with torches of pinewood which sputtered and crackled in the damp air, pushing their way through the cheering crowd. After them, a troupe of dancers and singers came out, the dancers swooping gracefully here and there, coming together in flowing lines, then parting again, the chorus singing the wedding-songs everyone knew. The whole neighbourhood had gathered to see the procession; women laughingly prophesying disillusionment for the bride, but wanting to give her their blessings anyway, men speculating about the size of the dowry. A wedding is always a spectacle worth waiting for.

After the singers and dancers came a large group of boys, laughing and joking. Some had baskets of nuts; the others scooped up handfuls and threw them into the crowd, teasing the girls who were scrambling to catch them, hoping it would be their turn to be the bride next. The older women ignored the fun and games, craning their heads to see the bride. Everyone knew Balbus, as always splendidly dressed, but on this occasion he was overlooked. At his side was his daughter, known to almost no-one in Rome, a woman as tall as her father and much slimmer, covered from head to foot in a veil of shining silk. Its golden surface shimmered and trembled in the dull air. She was walking as brides are supposed to do, her face cast down in modest confusion and almost obscured by that golden veil, which was draped around her head, falling forward at the sides of her face, then drawn across at the base of her throat to tumble in glorious floating folds over the paler silk of her under-dress to her feet. Women fell silent, admiring the shimmering cloth, wondering at its cost. The bride had golden slippers too, which just appeared under the edge of her hem at every step.

Three little boys walked with the bride, their faces glowing with cleanliness and pride. One led her by the left hand, one by her right, while the eldest, in front of her, carried another torch, flaming almost invisibly in the daylight, a torch made of whitethorn. Behind the bride a neat little blonde lady in a matron's stola carried Cornelia's distaff and spindle, and the women murmured at Cornelia's good fortune in having Octavia as her matron of honour. Behind Octavia came a group of Balbus' grand friends, senators and wealthy equestrians and their ladies, all dressed in their best, and after them the procession tailed off into a great mass of freedmen and merchants and clients of all sorts, streaming endlessly down the hill and into the heart of the city.

There was no need for the party to process along the Forum and walk its length, but Balbus had refused Atticus' kindly offer of accommodation for the night before the wedding. Torquatus' house was only a few minutes walk from Atticus', and January was hardly the month for processions; but Atticus had been courteously turned down. Balbus, conscious that he could not muster a distinguished family party of his own, wanted the world to see that today his daughter was marrying into one of Rome's oldest clans. And so the procession wound raucously through the heart of Rome, women in the crowd calling out blessings on the bride and everyone joining in when the singers reached their regular chorus and called on the god of marriage. 'Talassio! Talassio!' rang through the cold air. And in between their songs the singers called on the boys behind them to throw their nuts and give the girls good luck.

As the party passed on, it became clear that wine had flowed fairly freely at Balbus' house: some of the clients stumbled a little, and others cheered, red-faced, at the crowd. Turning up the Argentarius, and beginning to ascend the

Alta Semita towards Torquatus' house, many of the Forum crowd followed on behind the official group of clients and friends of Balbus. So long did this train become that when Balbus and his daughter came to a halt in front of the tall black doors standing open in welcome the last of the revellers was only just leaving the Forum. The singing seemed to reach a climax as more voices joined in from inside the house. Large torches, held by huge slaves one on each side of the great doorway, sent up flames as bright gold as the bride's veil, and coils of smoke twisted themselves against the low clouds before blending into them.

It was the bridegroom himself who came out to greet the wedding party, at the head of his household. His eyes were on the bride, but she still stood impassive, her body almost concealed by the golden silk, her face demurely lowered. He watched as Cornelia smeared a little pig-fat from a pot Octavia offered her onto each door-post, then hung a loop of wool over a nail on each one. He greeted Balbus with a ceremonial kiss and led him in, followed by Octavia, carefully leading the bride, lest she stumble unluckily on the threshold of her new home. Torquatus watched them, wishing he could see Cornelia's face, wondering if she could hear the thundering of his heart. The bride was led to her place at the head of the reception hall's pool, and Torquatus joined her there, where everyone could see them.

A solemn, curious silence fell as Torquatus' sister Manlia came forward to help Octavia lift that shimmering veil off the bride's face without disturbing the crown of flowers beneath it. Torquatus could feel his breathing light and short. And then, at the crucial moment, Manlia stepped forward to make some minor adjustment and blocked his line of sight. It was only when his sister moved back, her work completed, that the couple's eyes first met. Torquatus gasped. His first thought was that surely this young goddess couldn't be Balbus' daughter? But no: this was no ethereal goddess but a most attractive woman: stern critics might find her chin a little too big for beauty, her mouth not the fashionable rosebud. But her eyes were the warm strong blue of the sky, her skin seemed to bring a touch of summer to the cold winter house, and her hair, the colour of ripe corn, was so thick and shining that even the traditional bridal hairstyle of six braids woven with bands of wool looked magnificent rather than silly.

For her part, Cornelia was looking at Torquatus with equally candid curiosity. She knew that he was a friend of Octavian's, and had had military experience. She knew that he was a patrician, the last of an old house. But from her father's description she had imagined him older, not this tall, energetic-looking young man, a typical Roman with clear brown skin, beautifully arched brows almost meeting over a large nose, thoughtful dark eyes, and a firm mouth just now widening into a smile. Manlia and Octavia were smiling at them, moving them together. Octavia in a low voice told them to join hands, and Cornelia made her vow, in the simplest words: where you are Gaius, I am Gaia. Then there was more ritual. Torquatus gave his new wife a small crystal jug of water: she placed it on the family shrine, after pouring a little onto the altar in front of it. He handed her a bowl with some flaming splinters of wood in it: she shook these out onto the altar, and returned the bowl to him. She took from the hands of one of her own slaves a small coin, an as, and gave it to her new husband. She took from another slave a little cone of incense, lit it and placed it on the altar too, just below the skipping figures of the gods of hearth and pantry who protected Torquatus' home from evil. He gave her a bunch of keys. They kissed for the first time.

All this was done in silence, everyone craning to see, but as the new couple kissed there was a cheer, and cries of Talassio, and feliciter, wishing the pair good luck. The singers began their song again, a song whose words couldn't now be heard in the hubbub of congratulations and exclamations, but Torquatus at least knew what they were: the poet Catullus had written them for his brother's marriage

318

to Iunia Aurunculeia. He himself had been nine years old, and had been furious that he had not been allowed to walk with Iunia, leading her to her new home. The three boys all had to be part of the bride's family, his mother had explained, so three little cousins from Picenum had walked with Iunia. He had stood beside his brother, here in this house, Lucius looking as calm as always, but had he too been shaking with anxiety? And now it was he who was the bridegroom, and three serious little Spanish boys stood beside Octavia, the youngest holding her hand, watching as he had watched.

Torquatus relaxed and looked around, his wife's hand still in his. There was Octavia, smiling at him maternally, and Manlia, giving him a wink. Behind them, Trofimus waited to lead them to the wedding-feast.

The past was just that, over and done. The future was all to come.

The second book in the Roma Capta Series is *Unquiet Spirits*. This is how it begins:

It was going to be another blindingly hot day. Annoyingly, the shrines of the Argei that were nearest to the priest's own house on the Quirinal had been on yesterday's route. Either of those would have been an easy walk for the priest's tired feet this morning. One of the tiny, ancient places was actually in the courtyard of the temple of Quirinus. The temple itself had been burned down in one of Rome's spasms of civil war two years ago and never rebuilt, so that the shrine sat among tall weeds; another was placed in a dusty little garden behind the statue of the ancient deity known as Semo Sancus.

In the middle of March he had walked this same route, as twenty seven man-shaped figures made of reeds had been placed in the little shrines. What the function of these figures was no-one could now say with certainty, but whatever it was they had now fulfilled it.

Yesterday sacrifices had been made and prayers said at twenty one of the shrines, leaving a little group dotted around the Caelian hill and the centre of the city for this morning. Behind the priest, a long tail of local worthies straggled, chatting quietly, or breaking off from time to time to encourage the strong young men whose task was to carry the lumpy reed figures in procession around Rome, and finally to throw them into the river.

Dawn had broken some time before, and the last few streaks of pink in the sky were fading away. There was still a slight freshness in the air, but that wouldn't last. Although it was only May it felt more like August, the heat fraying tempers and creating a feeling of exhaustion which hung like a fog over the stinking city. The priest straightened his back and put out of his mind the hot slipperiness of his feet in their patrician boots. The procession was slowing as it began the ascent of the Caelian: only three more shrines to visit, three more repetitions of the incomprehensible ancient prayers, three more sacrifices to make. What would it be this time, he wondered? A piglet, a lamb? In poor districts it was sometimes only a chicken.

The shrine was visible now in the growing light. But there was something wrong, he could see. Instead of the quiet, respectful gathering he'd been expecting, figures were hurrying here and there as if they hadn't noticed his arrival. And for a moment his nostrils caught for a moment a scent that always had the power to frighten. Smoke. The fire must be out, however. Nothing but the occasional lazy wisp of white showed where it had been.

As the priest noticed this someone up ahead caught sight of his party and came running down the hill, shouting. His face red and sweating in the warming air, his clean toga streaked with soot, he stood for a moment gasping for breath. It was clear that he was the man in charge. The priest waited patiently for him to speak.

'I am the magistrate here,' the man gasped out at last. 'What ought we to do, lord? This is such terrible bad luck.' He looked as if he were on the point of tears.

'Why? What's happened?'

'The shrine, lord. Someone's set it on fire. They've burned the reed man. What shall we do?'

The priest shivered. Nothing could be more inauspicious. The men behind him exclaimed in dismay.

'This happened when?' he demanded.

'In the night, lord. I checked that everything was in order yesterday evening. This morning, when I arrived just after dawn, I could see smoke coming out of the doorway.' As he spoke the two men walked up the last few yards to the little building. It was one of the most ancient he'd seen, the priest thought: not much more than a stone hut built against the back of the great temple of Minerva Capta.

'Doesn't seem to have harmed the building,' the priest pointed out.

'No, lord. That's because - you'll see - ,' and he snapped his fingers at a slave for a small clay lamp, its tiny flame invisible in the sunlight. 'Shall I lead the way, lord?'

The priest nodded and the magistrate hurried inside. The priest, much taller, ducked his head under the crooked old stone of the lintel and followed him. There was barely room for two inside the little hut, and the magistrate politely pressed himself back against the door-wall to make space for the visitor. In here the air was even hotter and heavy with the acrid smell of burning. The walls were black and running with water. Along the bottom of the wall opposite the door a heavy shadow lay: the reed man. Almost overwhelmed by the heat and smell, the priest nodded, said curtly, 'Get someone to bring that out,' and ducked back out of the doorway again.

The reed man, when exposed to the light of day, was a sorry-looking object. One side of it had been partially burned away, and what was left around the burnt edges was loose and blackened. Flakes of sooty material blew off it and tumbled about the street in the warm breeze.

'I'd have thought it would have burned like a torch, but it's gone out,' the priest observed. 'I suppose when it fell over it went out, and after that it just smouldered. You were lucky you came along, though. It would have broken out again eventually.'

The magistrate nodded. 'I think it helped that it was made by a different man this year,' the magistrate explained. 'This one's bound very tight, which would slow the fire too.'

The priest nodded. The figures were all roughly the same size and made in the same way: a bundle of reeds as tall as a man was made to look human by being tied around the waist with a cord. Some localities took a lot of trouble with their man, shaping a neck and a neat waist. Some hardly bothered with the details. All, however, tied their bundle just above the bottom, so that reed men appeared to have their feet tied at the ankles. This figure had been carefully made, the waist drawn in hard with tough cord and the neck and ankles formed the same way. It was unpleasantly realistic. The magistrate suggested, from the position of the burnt section, that a flame must have been held to the bundle quite close to the waist.

'You're right, I think. There wasn't enough air for the thing to catch light properly. You're lucky.'

'But what should we do, lord? We can't offer this man, can we?'

'No. I'm sure you can't.' The priest glanced over to where a group of his own slaves stood. 'Felix! Run down to the Forum, will you, to the Regia. Tell the chief priest I need advice, urgently.'

The boy nodded, and was about to run off when his master called him back, because two more slaves from his own household were hurrying up the hill towards them. The first man reached them, beginning speaking even before he'd come to a stop. 'The shrine on the Palatine, lord: it's been burned down.' He turned to the second man. 'Davus here had only just left, lord, when more news came in: the shrine on the Velia has been burned too '

The priest turned to the murmuring crowd. Raising his voice so everyone could hear, he said: 'Someone has attacked our city and its gods. I will go the Velia and will take advice from the chief priest there. Your magistrate can come with me. In the meantime I suggest that you clean the shrine and have it ready to fulfil the ritual.' He turned away. 'Felix,' he said in a softer voice, 'ask the chief priest to come to the Velia, will you? It'll be a lot easier for him.' The boy nodded and shot away.

The men in the procession crowded around him asking what should be done next.

'Take your reed men back to your own shrines, and tomorrow bring them here again. Whatever is decided we can do nothing more until a new reed man has been made to replace each of the burned ones. We will then be able to complete the ritual and so placate the gods.'

He hoped that was true. Rounding up his men with his eyes, the priest turned away and headed back down into Rome. He beckoned the slaves who had brought the news, and as they walked together he asked for more details.

'We heard about the shrine on the Palatine first,' the slave told him. 'They said it was gutted, the whole building gone. No-one had seen anything. The building wasn't guarded, and it wasn't until well after dawn that anyone went there, I gather.'

'The shrine there is just a thatched hut, like Romulus' hut,' the priest said. 'In a little grove of trees. It would be easy to attack, and would burn well. But they can't have started the fire by burning the reed man, because we took it away yesterday.' The priest frowned. 'So I wonder - '

Another man was hurrying up. 'Not more arson?' the priest asked.

'No, lord. I'm from the shrine on the Velia. I've been sent to say that we've found a body.'

'A body?'

'Yes, lord. Inside the shrine. Must have been the arsonist.'

'I suppose so. He went in there, set the reed man on fire, got trapped and died himself.'

'Yes, lord.'

The Velia was almost in the heart of the city, but although the street was crowded, everyone was keeping well clear of the ruined shrine. It was a sorry sight, its door opening onto nothing. It sat in the middle of a puddle of water tainted with soot, now rapidly drying in the hot air, in which pieces of tile and blackened timbers were scattered here and there. A few lazy twirls of smoke still rose through what had been the roof, but some building workers had already begun to pull some of the collapsed roof-beams through the doorway. To one side, a well-dressed crowd, balked of its chance to celebrate, was enjoying the catastrophe. The Velia was a wealthy area, and its households must have raised a good sum of money even in these hard times, because the chosen sacrifice was a large lamb, washed quite clean. It was bounding about among a group of laughing children, and trying to eat the garland of flowers which had been placed around its neck.

The local magistrate came over with a self-important frown and introduced himself as Marcus Claudius Erotes. He was a prosperous-looking man with a belly suggesting that whoever went hungry in hungry Rome, he did not. He wore the cap of a freed slave, and a green tunic with a woven border, stretched rather too tightly across his belly. At the moment his expression was one of extreme distress. The toga he would have worn for the ceremony had been thrown over a small statue, extinguishing it.

'I see you managed to put the fire out anyway,' the priest observed.

'Yes, lord. I was just about to come down to make the final arrangements for the day when a message came that the shrine was on fire.'

They walked across to the remains of the shrine together. A large man was inside, his feet protected by heavy boots, tugging the free end of one of the fallen beams, while another man tossed over the walls the tiles that had cascaded down when the roof fell in.

'Who discovered the fire?'

'Well, that's the strangest thing of all. My assistants were actually there in the street when the fire started. They saw a girl go in, but no-one else. The arsonist must have been inside already, I suppose. They were busy talking to the butcher, because he had the lamb that was to be sacrificed in the back of his shop. Then smoke began pouring from the doorway, and while they were still trying to work out what to do the roof went up. The reed man must have been dry and warm, I suppose, and went up as soon as the flame touched it. The roof had fallen right in by the time I arrived. The only thing I could do was to make sure it didn't set the Porticus ablaze. I got a bucket chain organised from the nearest fountain.' The priest could see how easily the Porticus Margaritaria, where vendors of every kind of luxury goods had their shops, could have gone up: the shrine was almost under its overhanging eaves. Perhaps the Palatine fire had been set first: it had burned out, after all. Then the man must have run up to the shrine on the Caelian and set that alight before coming down here. It must have taken some time.

As he turned to Erotes to tell him so, the man who'd been working inside turned and scrambled out over the jumble of beams.

'There's only one body in there,' he told them.

'Where can the girl have gone?' Erotes asked.

'No. It's the girl that's in there.'

The priest stared at him. Whatever he'd imagined, he certainly wouldn't have supposed a woman would have done this. Drunken young men, perhaps, for a prank, or some man who felt Rome had ill-used him.

'A woman did this?'

The incredulity in his voice prompted a sympathetic nod from the magistrate.

'I know, lord. It's not what you'd expect.' He turned to the sweating workman. 'Get her out as soon as you can.'

'We will, but we've got to move some stuff off her first.'

'So she was still inside when the roof fell in,' the priest said. 'I wonder why? The reed man was at the back of the shrine?' The magistrate nodded and the priest walked over to look in through the doorway. He stepped carefully into the shrine, climbing over a fallen timber onto a clear patch of the neatly paved floor, feeling the heat of it strike up through the soles of his boots. The little building was nothing but a stone box. On one wall a blackened inscription listed the streets responsible for the upkeep of the shrine. Facing it another named the local freedmen who had served as its priests. He noted the plain paving of the floor, and then stood very still, staring down. There was nothing intrinsically shocking, of course, in the sight of a woman's foot in a well-made sandal. But here, protruding from under a pile of timbers, streaked with blood and sooty water, it brought him up short. He climbed a little further, and stopped again, so suddenly he almost fell over. The men had cleared some rubbish away from around the woman's head. Golden hair: rich golden hair such as he had seen on his own pillow this morning. Corn-coloured hair like this was rare in Rome. It was streaked with dirt and water and lay over the face. He bent over, gently putting the veil of hair aside. No, of course this was not Cornelia: how could it be? He straightened up and stood still, waiting for the pounding in his heart to slow, conscious of the sounds of Rome going about its business. He noted the girl's dress, of which a shoulder was visible: torn and dirty it might be but it was of the finest cloth. This was no vagrant or prostitute, as he had assumed. He turned to go, and stumbled over a stone or something: looking down he saw it was a small clay lamp, the kind in use in all Roman houses. It had a single spout, no handle and the dished top had been filled with a charming little scene: a lively goat stretching up to steal grapes from a vine. No doubt this was what had lit the fire. He scrambled back out, the lamp still in his hand.

'She's just a girl,' he said to the magistrate, puzzled.

'Well, no-one cares what she was,' the magistrate told him. 'They want her out.'

The priest looked around and saw a group of men waiting with hooks like the ones used in the amphitheatre for dragging dead gladiators from the arena. He shuddered. 'No,' he said. 'No.'

327

24491363R00184

Printed in Poland
by Amazon Fulfillment
Poland Sp. z o.o., Wrocław